Nichole Severn writes expl[...] strong heroines, heroes wh[...] hell of a lot of guns. She resides with her very supportive and patient husband, as well as her demon spawn, in Utah. When she's not writing, she's constantly injuring herself running, rock climbing, practicing yoga and snowboarding. She loves hearing from readers through her website, nicholesevern.com, and on Facebook at nicholesevern.

Danica Winters is a multiple-award-winning, bestselling author who writes books that grip readers with their ability to drive emotion through suspense and occasionally a touch of magic. When she's not working, she can be found in the wilds of Montana, testing her patience while she tries to hone her skills at various crafts—quilting, pottery and painting are not her areas of expertise. She believes the cup is neither half-full nor half-empty, but it better be filled with wine. Visit her website at authordanicawinters.com

MURDER AT LAVA POINT

NICHOLE SEVERN

STALKED IN THE MOUNTAINS

DANICA WINTERS

MILLS & BOON

First Published in Great Britain 2025
by Mills & Boon, an imprint of HarperCollins*Publishers* Ltd
1 London Bridge Street, London, SE1 9GF

www.harpercollins.co.uk

HarperCollins*Publishers*
Macken House, 39/40 Mayor Street Upper,
Dublin 1, D01 C9W8, Ireland

Murder at Lava Point © 2026 Natascha Jaffa
Stalked in the Mountains © 2026 Danica Winters

ISBN: 978-0-263-42016-6

0126

MIX
Paper | Supporting
responsible forestry
FSC™ C007454

This book contains FSC™ certified paper and other controlled sources to ensure responsible forest management.

For more information visit: www.harpercollins.co.uk/green

Printed and Bound in the UK using 100% Renewable Electricity at CPI Group (UK) Ltd, Croydon, CR0 4YY

MURDER AT LAVA POINT

NICHOLE SEVERN

To Allex! Our walks saved my sanity.

Chapter One

She was going to die.

Not from the blazing wall of heat ahead of her but from the amount of sweat weighing her down despite her lighter protective gear. Aslen Woods gripped the fire hose hard as it bucked in her hand. Every muscle in her body ached after clinging to this thing for two hours.

She'd tried everything she could think of to get the blaze under control. Including clearing a perimeter of brush to ensure the fire didn't jump on this wind, but it didn't help. She and the rest of her team had been fighting a losing battle since around four this morning.

The other firefighters employed by the park scrambled to beat back the spread of the flames with shouts, orders and a whole lot of controlled chaos. This was what they did. This was what they were good at, but dousing fires in the wildland wasn't anything like trying to save a structure. With a structure, most of the fire was contained, and fighters wore more protective gear. Out here in the middle of Zion National Park? It took an army. The rip of a chainsaw reached her ears from the right as two of her fellow team members took precautionary measures to keep the flames from launching past the perimeter.

Once-green trees crackled with blackened bark. Embers seemed to breathe in the cracks, keeping up with her ragged pulls of oxygen. This was the third fire of the summer, though this one had started far north of the most tourist-saturated area in the main attraction of the park. There wasn't much out here at the far northern border of the park in Lava Point, apart from a man-made reservoir, Lava Point Overlook—a nearly eight thousand–foot cliff that looked down on miles of greenery and rolling mountains—the West Rim trailhead and the campground less than a mile west near the town of Virgin. Thousands of acres had already been consumed by human mistakes and lightning strikes, and there was no sign of slowing down anytime soon. The summer months brought on droughts, more tourists and charged thunderstorms: the perfect combination to keep her employed and on alert.

Zion National Park spanned over 232 miles of wilderness her fire management training hadn't prepared her to protect that first time she'd been thrust into the field. It was all learned experience and on-the-job training that came with a heavy purpose—to protect the people from the park and the park from the people. But this… This felt intentional.

Aslen swiped a gloved hand over her brow, surely smearing her face with the ash collecting on her gear. Heat seared into her lungs with every breath as the wind kicked back into her face, changing the direction of the spread of flames. And bringing a bitter scent with it. Something with a chemical signature that burned the back of her throat.

A wave of shouts punctured through the steady thud of her heart behind her ears as the fire changed direction. They were about to lose control if the conditions kept up, but she wouldn't let her nerves get the better of her. She'd never lost her calm in the field, and she wasn't about to start now. They'd barely managed to keep the flames from consuming a nearby campground. Now the flames seemed to take on a life of their own as she aimed pressurized water at the base of a patch of brush that'd caught. "Where do you think you're going?"

"There she goes again. Talking to the fire as if it's going to behave." Danny Kennex—the only other woman employed full-time in her unit—flashed a wild smile that showed a little too many teeth. Blond hair had escaped her team member's ponytail and whipped into Danny's face as she muscled the chainsaw in one hand. "Isn't that what they call delusional?"

Aslen couldn't help but take advantage of the distraction. "Isn't minding your own business good for your health?"

"Aw, come on. Minding your business is overrated." Danny threw a wink before surveying the wall of flames eating up the distance to Aslen's position. "Besides, I seem to recall my nosiness helping you out a couple times with a certain law enforcement ranger who shall not be named."

"Will you keep your voice down?" Aslen searched the surrounding woods as though Danny had summoned the man himself, but Murray Simpson, like most of the rangers in other departments, tended to keep his distance from her unit. Fire management rangers were only called when needed. They weren't invited to the yearly Christmas party or to chat in the break room at headquarters. They weren't considered full-time, despite Aslen's full-time status, and they most definitely were not on the radar of any handsome—although aggravating beyond belief—law enforcement rangers. She caught the bitter chemical taint to the air a second time and thanked heaven for a change in subject that wouldn't leave her skin feeling as though she'd been stabbed with a thousand needles, nodding toward the fire ahead. "You smell that?"

"Gasoline." Danny's shoulders rose on a deep inhale, perfectly arched and maintained brows pulling toward each other at the bridge of her nose.

The woman was a goddess, with long lashes, a full pouty mouth and a personality Danny's parents had once deemed perfect for serial killing or running a Fortune 500 company. With curves to make anyone's mouth water, she had no business hiding underneath fire-resistant protection in the middle of the wilderness and certainly not in the middle of nowhere Utah. And yet, despite their obvious differences in appearance, confidence and history—Danny coming from the world's greatest family and Aslen growing up in foster care—they were closer than any of their other teammates. It'd only made sense to room together after they'd been hired on a year ago. Though Aslen was beginning to regret that decision every time Murray's name came up.

She didn't want to think about him. And she didn't want anyone else thinking about him either. Murray Simpson was possibly the most frustrating man Aslen had ever met, and that was saying something, considering the ego it took to become a firefighter, but she'd managed to put up with him since she'd been a teenager living off of nothing but chocolate pudding cups in public school back home. The fact that he couldn't see her as anything more than a friend grated on her nerves more than Danny's nightly snoring that outdid the chainsaw in her hand. Honestly, what Aslen wouldn't give for him to look at her as anything more than an obligation. It was that stupid promise he'd made to protect her in middle school, after she'd been beaten to a pulp by another girl in her class, that'd had him following her to Zion. It didn't matter he'd chosen the law enforcement route or that they hardly saw each other on shift. Her awareness of him had been so thoroughly ingrained into her bones it overpowered separate departments and miles.

"Aslen." Danny penetrated her peripheral vision. A knowing smile crested her friend's face. "I know that look. You're thinking about him, aren't you?"

"Utter another word, and I will turn this hose on you." It wouldn't be the first time either. A flame jumped, and Aslen's instincts kicked in. She directed the hose to the base of the flame as an eruption of sound overpowered the crackle and pops of the fire consuming the park acre by acre. Collapsing wood and a renewed sense of panic filtered through the trees. "The fire must've reached the campground."

Her heart shoved higher in her chest. They'd evacuated the campground as soon as they'd arrived on site, but the idea of anyone getting caught in the flames had her taking a few more steps forward to beat the fire into submission.

"I got this. You check it out." Danny motioned over her shoulder before offering to take the hose. Sweat built along the blond hairline, revealing her perfect friend really was human after all. "It sounds like they're going to need someone trained in structural."

"Don't take your eyes off it." She couldn't stand the thought of losing Danny's bright light in a world repeatedly determined to drag her into the darkness.

"Yes, Mom." Danny gave a half-hearted salute.

"Don't think I won't call her." Aslen tossed the comment over her shoulder as she jogged for the burst of embers thirty yards north. The flames had found something fresh to chew on, growing in height and intensity. The heat licked up the front of her body and pooled beneath her hard hat as she closed in on the group of four other rangers armed with axes, shovels and hoses. She collected an axe along the way, the weight solid and counterbalancing as her emergency pack threatened to throw her off.

The outline of a structure took shape. What was left of the roof had collapsed inward, highlighting the crossbeams. The construction itself wasn't large. More like a maintenance shed. The thick wood door hung off the hinges and swung outward with a protest a split second before hitting the ground. There were a dozen or so of these sheds all over the park, but they'd lost this one in a matter of minutes. The trees surrounding the shed had already caught fire, and she maneuvered in front of the team, strategically trying to contain the fingers of flame stretching from one branch to the other.

"We need the extinguishers!" Her voice barely rose over the roar of the fire, but two of the rangers at her back scrambled to follow through. That bitter chemical scent hit her harder here, and her stomach rolled with the assault. Danny had been right. Whoever had set the fire had used gasoline as the accelerant. It would take them hours and cause a whole lot of damage to douse the flames. A glimpse of red at the base of the collapsing structure sucker punched her. A gasoline canister had melted into the floor. If it still contained any gas, her team was at risk. Aslen rounded on the rangers behind her, arms out as though she could protect her fellow rangers with her body alone. "Everyone get—"

The explosion licked up her spine and thrust her forward.

The ground rushed up to meet her. Her hard hat collided with a nearby rock, the impact echoing through her head, but she was alive. Debris rained down on around her as groans punctured through the high-pitched ringing in her ears. A chunk of wood collided with her boot as she assessed any bodily damage. No burning sensations. Nothing broken as far as she could tell.

The four rangers who'd been positioned behind her climbed to their feet, extinguishers back in their hands. The hose they'd been using to control the burn was out of control. Cold water umbrellaed overhead and gave the impression of one of her favorite summer storms as Aslen got to her feet. A wave of dizziness had her reaching out for something to hold onto.

"Aslen!" Danny's voice warbled from the left. Strong hands clamped down on Aslen's arms, holding her steady, right before her friend's face took shape in front of her. "Are you okay? What happened?"

"Gas can." The words scraped up the back of her throat as if she'd inhaled great lungfuls of smoke. "I'm okay. Just dazed."

"Your hard hat is cracked." Danny prodded along the ridge then reached back for her radio while leveling her gaze with Aslen's. "I think you hit your head. I'm radioing the EMTs to check you out."

"Danny, I'm fine." Stumbling forward, Aslen forced herself to release the grip she'd had on her friend's identical bright yellow fire jacket.

"What are you doing? You might have a concussion." Danny followed close on her heels, and in any other circumstance, Aslen would've been grateful for the concern, but she couldn't shake the feeling they'd missed something important. "You need to take it easy until the EMTs get here."

"I saw something. By the gas can right before the explosion. Clear me a path! Right here." The image had burned into her brain deeper than the details of Murray's face over the years. The four-man team slapping her on the back for the heads-up had control of the hose once again, carving a path straight to the heart of the collapsed structure. Water ricocheted off blackened plywood and siding as Aslen grabbed for the largest piece and hauled it out of her way. Her head hurt more than she wanted to admit, but she wasn't going to stop. Not until she proved she wasn't seeing things.

"What did you see?" Danny was right there, throwing smaller beams out of the way as the rest of the team continued the heated battle.

Aslen dragged another section of plywood free and tossed it to the side, revealing the human remains underneath. She straightened, all the strength leaving her at once. "A body."

Chapter Two

Murray Simpson didn't recognize the ranger acting as the first line of defense onto the scene, and he didn't care. Only one thing mattered the second he'd heard about the explosion over the radio: getting to Aslen.

"Whoa, buddy." Ash and sweat combined into a paste along the man's dark skin as he held up his hands. "This is an active fire. You can't go in there."

"Law enforcement division." Smoke twisted and curled over the blackened wasteland in front of him almost as far as the eye could see. It collected at the back of his throat, burning its way through him and raising his temper a notch higher as the reality of the situation set in. It didn't take much to imagine how close any one of these firefighters could've lost the battle they'd taken on. Flames had died down, but teams were still working the embers, ensuring hot spots were doused to prevent another breakout. A chemical odor churned acid in his gut. Gasoline. He'd recognize it anywhere.

Lava Point—though far north of the dense areas of the park—consisted of miles of woodlands and brush. It was any wonder this section of the park hadn't gone up in flames before today, but Aslen shouldn't have been anywhere near here. Her supervisor had given Murray his word she wouldn't be called to big events like this.

Something primal and aggravated worked through him as he set sights on the woman who'd somehow managed to undermine every single rule he'd set for himself when it came to keeping his distance. A vibration that seemed to tune directly to her shook him down to the bone, and without conscious effort, Murray was maneuvering around the man acting as nothing but an obstacle between him and Aslen. "Get out of my way."

"Hey! I'm going to have to report you to the chief." The firefighter scrambled to get someone's attention. Wouldn't do any good.

Murray didn't bother looking back. "Go ahead. See where it gets you."

At six foot four and 230 pounds, there weren't a whole lot of people who could stop him from getting onto the scene. He didn't like to use his size to intimidate, but in this case, he wouldn't hesitate. That hum, honed specifically to Aslen, threatened to pull him apart cell by cell if he didn't get to her. Now.

The woman who commanded his every thought and action sank down onto a bare patch of ground in the middle of the scene, staring out at the damage, unaware of him closing in on her. Ash darkened her hair from its normal brown to nearly black, and clumped random strands together. Taking a swig from the stickered green metal water bottle she'd carried around as long as he could remember, she tipped her head up to the sky and closed her eyes.

Murray pulled back on his pace. Some part of him wanted to tear into her for putting her life in danger while the other couldn't get enough of the look of peace in her expression. When was the last time she'd looked so…content? He couldn't remember. Though, if he was being honest with himself, he'd taken great pains to avoid coming into contact with her at all over the years. Distancing himself a little more. Setting up invisible walls to keep her from getting through. Didn't matter. The know-it-all he'd saved back in middle school got under his skin no matter how hard he fought her off.

Sun broke through the black swirls of smoke and highlighted the rough scrape across Aslen's face, igniting his protective streak all over again. It wasn't enough she'd charged into a dangerous situation, but she'd managed to get herself hurt in the process. His shadow cast ahead of him and fell over her closed eyes.

One eyelid cracked open, then the other, as she took him in. Shock interrupted that smooth look of contentment as she scanned the scene. In an instant, she was on her feet. "What are you doing here? This is an active scene."

"What the hell were you thinking taking on this assignment?" Murray didn't bother hiding the rage coiling in his gut. He'd promised to protect her since she'd been that skinny little thing he'd found crying behind a dumpster twenty years ago, and he wasn't about to stop now. Even if he had to protect her from herself. "You could've been killed."

"I was thinking I was doing my job." The muscles in her jaw jumped under the tension of her back teeth as she tried to control the volume of her voice. It was the same every time she got riled, and the fact he could get such a reaction out of her brought him the slightest hint of joy. Apart from being in the same room as her, hearing her laugh, oh, and having all of her attention. But she didn't know any of that, and he would do whatever it took to make sure she never would. "Putting out fires is kind of in the title."

"Not anymore. I'm submitting the paperwork to have you transferred." Because apparently, he couldn't trust her supervisor to follow orders. "Monday morning, you'll be with the information rangers in the visitor's center."

No way she could get herself hurt providing visitors directions, restarting the park video in the cinema and answering the same question a hundred times in a single shift. At least, that was what he would tell himself. When it came to Aslen, he'd learned nothing was a sure bet.

"First of all, you are not my department head. Second, you can't keep coming up with schemes to protect me like I'm made of glass. This is my job. This is what I'm good at, whether you approve or not." Shoving her palms against his chest, Aslen attempted to push him off balance. In vain. It would take a miracle for her five-foot-three frame to have any kind of physical influence on him, but stranger things had happened.

"It's already done." It wasn't, but she didn't need to know that. And if she ended up hating him more than she already did, he'd done his job. He'd keep his distance, he'd make her think he didn't care, he'd do whatever it took to protect her. Especially from the way he cared for her—because nothing could ever come from that. "Grab your gear. I'm taking you back to your place."

The tick in her jaw was back. Her knuckles whitened as she clamped down on the handle of her water bottle. He could practically see the gears turning in her head as she strategized where to hit him with the metal. It would hurt, but the pain would be nothing compared to the vise constricting his chest at the thought of losing the last person he cared about. "My shift isn't over, and you don't get to tell me what to do."

No amount of training could have prepared him for the

storm brewing in her green gaze. It was that same look that'd preceded her telling him she'd taken a job as a national park ranger here in Zion after graduation. Against his advice. She was supposed to take a safe job, meet a nice guy—one Murray would've vetted ahead of time with his connections to the Salt Lake Police Department—get married, have a couple of kids and live a boring life behind a white picket fence. But Aslen Woods had never been that woman.

Numbness prickled in his fingertips as he gauged his chances of surviving the oncoming explosion. Battle-ready tension tightened through her shoulders as she took a single step toward him. He caught hints of gasoline and smoke coming off her clothes.

"Aslen!" Another fire ranger—a blonde bombshell who had no problem carrying the forty-plus pounds of gear strapped to her back—jogged to close the distance between them with a wide smile. "Look who's up and about. How's the head?"

Aslen's wide gaze aimed at her friend broke the contained anger simmering beneath her skin. "I have no idea what you're talking about."

She was a terrible liar. He narrowed his attention on the woman he couldn't pry from beneath his skin if he was armed with a crowbar, scanning her from scalp to chin. "What's wrong with your head?"

"Oh, is this the law enforcement ranger you've been talking about?" Something along the lines of fascination hiked a wave of pink into the blonde's face. Clear interest transformed her expression from concerned into something brighter and more put together. "He's much more handsome than you described."

It took everything he had not to roll his eyes. He was well aware of his influence on the opposite sex, but he was losing patience, which was already thin to begin with when it came to being around the one woman he couldn't have. Murray framed Aslen's chin with his index finger and thumb, forcing her attention back on him, and she came willingly. Despite his history of overstepping, he wouldn't ever hurt her, and some part of her knew that. Allowed him to touch her, get close even. He softened his tone. "What happened to your head?"

"Nothing." Aslen shook her head as if that would rewind time.

"The force of the explosion knocked her on her ass and cracked her hard hat." Her friend nodded at the back of Aslen's skull. "I told her to get assessed by the EMTs, but she refuses."

Panic crested Aslen's expression, and she wrenched free of his hold, adding a good bit of physical distance between them, as if his touch burned. Problem was, he was a man of his word, and the promise he'd made years ago to protect her would die with him. She gave him a clear view of the back of her head. And the crust of blood drying in her hair. "Traitor."

Dread coiled at the base of his spine. She'd stood here acting as if nothing was wrong when she might've sustained a brain bleed? This woman would be the death of him. Curling his fingers around hers, he hauled Aslen into his side. "Your shift is over. You're getting checked out."

She tried—and failed—to overcome his hold. "I can walk, Murray."

"And yet you chose to sit down knowing you'd hit your head." This wasn't up for negotiation. He didn't care how much she hated him. She wasn't getting out of this. "You think I'm going to trust you to take care of yourself now?"

Aslen kept up with him despite their size differences. "It's not your job to look after me."

"Someone has to do it." He walked her over to an ambulance outside the perimeter, sitting her down harder on the back bay than he intended. "She hit her head. Run a full workup and make sure she's okay."

The EMTs scrambled into action, closing in on either side of her.

"This is ridiculous. I have a job to do." She waved off the EMT shining a light into her left eye while the other bandaged the scrape on her face. "You know as well as I do embers can resuscitate a fire. Not to mention destroy any evidence the arsonist might've left behind."

"Arson?" He'd almost forgotten the bite of chemical odor coming off her clothes. She'd gotten close to the source. Too close. Damn it. Aslen was lucky to be alive. Did she really not understand how close she'd come to being ripped away from him? "You're sure?"

Crime of any kind fell under the purview of him and his division. If someone had started this particular fire, he would find them—plain and simple—but more, someone had put Aslen in danger to begin with, and he couldn't let that go.

"Hard to miss the signs." Aslen nodded toward what looked like a collapsed shed a dozen or so feet into the tree line, completely at ease with the two EMTs poking and prodding at her scalp. "Or the body they tried to get rid of in the process."

Murray's insides went cold. "Show me."

Chapter Three

She was going to kill him.

She'd already worked out how. It wasn't a new fantasy, but it got the job done in bringing her heart rate back to normal. Though, what could she really consider normal any time she was around him? Pain shuddered through her jaw. Her dentist had warned her about grinding her teeth, but all this frustration had to go somewhere, and she couldn't take it out on him in front of all these people.

What right did Murray Simpson have coming onto her scene and demanding she transfer to a different department? The second any one of her teammates lost confidence in her, there would be mistakes. Lives lost. She couldn't afford that. The male rangers in her department weren't the most accepting of her and Danny in the field, but they trusted her to get the job done. Except now Murray had called her out in front of everyone, implying she was incapable of doing her job and keeping her fellow rangers safe.

The man was out of his mind and clearly in need of a punch to the groin after the way he'd acted. Overprotective, unemotional, overbearing, berserk. Had she expected anything less? From the moment Murray had found her beaten to a pulp as a scrawny thirteen-year-old kid, through the nights she'd climbed in his bedroom window to escape her foster mother's tirades, and following her into this job, he'd made himself clear. He knew what was best for her. It didn't matter what she wanted, that she wasn't that punching bag anymore or that she was capable of taking care of herself now. For him to keep his promise to never let anything bad happen to her again, he would always impose his will over hers, but the pressure of being his perfect little project had started to break her in every regard. He hadn't made that promise out of anything but pity and a sense of obligation, and now all she got out of him was resentment.

She saw it in the way he'd watched her—disapprovingly—as the EMTs poked and prodded her skull, how he held himself with his arms crossed over his chest, intimidation on display. The laceration at the back of her head was just that. A cut from the crack in her hard hat after impact. Nothing to suggest she would drop dead right here in the middle of the field, but with Murray scaring off anyone who got too close—even Danny kept her distance—she wished she could just shrivel up and die.

She didn't have proof, but Aslen was fairly certain he'd driven off any guy who'd even dreamed of asking her out over the years, which left her isolated in that crappy house with a crappy excuse for a guardian during prom, homecomings and regular Friday nights.

"You're making a scene." Aslen took the lead as she headed for the now-cold remnants of the maintenance shed a few yards past the tree line. She didn't look back at Murray to see if he'd followed. She could feel it. This ridiculous hyperawareness of his every move. "Try to take some of the serial killer out of your expression. You're scaring my coworkers."

"Soon the information rangers will be your coworkers." His voice cut through the headache spiraling into the base of her skull, low and soothing as always. Jerk. "I doubt these rangers will come visit you."

Aslen turned on him, which was laughable in and of itself. The top of her head barely brushed his collarbone, and it took every muscle in her neck to meet his blue gaze, but she wasn't scared of him. Murray Simpson could intimidate anyone in a five-mile radius with one of his looks, but he'd never once raised his voice to her, moved to physically harm her or so much as gotten inappropriate. For all intents and purposes, he was the big brother she'd never had. And, considering his history, she didn't blame him for his overprotective nature. She pressed her index finger into his chest, trying not to appreciate the unyielding muscle underneath the thin cotton of his shirt. "Listen to me, you barbarian. This is my job. This is what I've been trained to do. I'm good at it, and no one—not even you—is going to tell me I can't fight fires like the rest of these rangers because I have the wrong set of reproductive organs."

"Your biology has nothing to do with it, Aslen, and you know it." If she hadn't spent the past twenty-plus years studying his each and every mood based off the slight changes in his face, she might've missed the softening around his mouth. His ridiculously full mouth surrounded by a thin layer of facial hair she'd thought about way too many times. Nature had made its permanent impression in the few sunspots down his arms and lightened the dark brown hair at his temples at thirty-nine. He wasn't old in any sense of the word, but experience had injected a certain wisdom in the blue depths of his eyes. Looking at him straight on—if anyone dared, that was—one would assume he'd come straight out of the military. Same no-nonsense haircut since high school, no tattoos or jewelry. He took better care of his fingernails and cuticles than she did and never went anywhere without the same worn pair of leather boots he'd picked up after college graduation. The man kept to himself better than a monk but valued the people he let close. Though she'd stopped being one of them around the time she'd graduated high school a few years after him, and she couldn't remember the last time he'd dated anyone. Did he have anyone left?

Murray didn't bother to give in against her finger digging into his chest, taking one step into her. The big ape probably couldn't even feel it, which only made her angrier. Couldn't he, for once, stop trying to bend everyone to his will, and listen? "You're putting yourself in unnecessary danger chasing after these fires, and now you're telling me someone left behind a body and used accelerant to cover up the crime. I can't have you putting yourself anywhere near someone capable of this kind of evil."

"That's not really your choice though, is it, Ranger Simpson?" The use of his title was a reminder of where they were, who was watching. He'd charged onto a scene uninvited and demanded a ranger not under his supervision to leave an active investigation. He'd outright used his authority against her, and she wasn't sure she'd ever forgive him for that. For embarrassing her. For overriding her own authority in this unit.

He had a point. No part of her wanted to be anywhere near a suspect capable of disposing of a body without any consideration for the damage that had followed or the lives that had been put at risk due to the fire's spread, but she sure as hell wasn't going to admit it to him.

This job was important. Couldn't he see that? Choosing to be a ranger here in Zion had given her something of her very own. Something the state or guardians or social services couldn't take away as they had so many times before. It was hers. She'd worked hard for it all through college with her degree in emergency management, and she wasn't letting it go. Aslen wasn't sure where this newfound confidence had come from, but she'd hold on with everything she had.

She'd spent far too many years bowing to his every word, worshipping the ground he walked on and never standing up for herself in a stupid hope he'd notice her. Not the obligation of a promise. Not the weak kid he'd pulled into the closet or back to his bedroom night after night when her foster mother drank too much. Her. But that wasn't ever going to happen. They had too much history. Too much pain they couldn't acknowledge and couldn't overcome on their own. "The body is over here."

Her breath shook through her chest as she breached the tree line. The hairs on the back of her neck stood on end as she considered the fallout of what she'd just done, calling Murray out like that. She'd never done it before, but there was also a strange current of power coursing through her veins at the thought of finally standing up to him. Despite his distorted perception of her and their years of history together, she wasn't some wallflower who needed a big, strong man to get her through life. She'd come to Zion for independence and to show herself she wasn't a victim. That she could be something more. And, yeah, she wanted to maybe find someone to share it with. But Murray had gone and ruined that, too.

Her boots sank deep into mud created by the hoses and ash. Hints of gasoline caught at the back of her throat as she passed the surrounding trees. She could smell it even twenty feet from the destroyed shed, clinging to the blackened, flaking bark. Two firefighters sprayed another round of water across the shed to make it safe for investigators to come through. Again, Aslen felt more than confirmed

Murray's presence at her back. It was the subtle shift of her teammates' body language, a predator coming into their territory. It took everything she had not to roll her eyes. What did they think he was going to do? Go for their throats for looking at her? "The gas can was most likely full before the fire got to it. We can't be sure if the canister was already in the maintenance shed or if the perpetrator brought it in to aid in getting rid of the body, but we can confirm the fire started here with a good helping of accelerant. We found traces of it in the brush surrounding the shed."

She motioned to the perimeter, the grass here a slightly different color in a weblike pattern. "It looks like whoever set the fire was throwing lines of gas, probably in a panic, up and over the shed compared to strategically dousing the wood."

The weight of Murray's attention pressurized along the side of her face, and she couldn't shut down the need to meet his gaze. He stared at her as though he'd never seen her before.

"What?" She scraped the back of her hand over her mouth, drawing his attention lower. "Do I have spinach in my teeth?"

"No." He seemed to shake himself out of whatever thought had held him paralyzed. "Show me the body."

Aslen rounded the still-standing corner of the structure. The gasoline explosion had blasted outward into the opposite corner of the small building—toward her and the four other firefighters—leaving only a few beams still standing. Crouching, she held her breath against the stench of gasoline and seared flesh and hair. "She's female based off the shape of her pelvis and the diamond stuck in her ring finger. The gold melted underneath her hand. Your medical examiner will need to confirm, but my guess is she's older, considering how quickly her bones burned. The gasoline could also have something to do with that."

"You got all that just from looking at her for a few minutes?" Murray arrowed his attention on the remains. Well, what was left of them. There were a few good limbs still missing due to the explosion, but her team would navigate the scene to help investigators recover as many as possible. It was part of the job.

"To be fair, I think there are pieces of her stuck in my hair I got a good look at." Ugh. She'd never get the smell off her, but she'd survived worse smells—and fires—than this. "But yeah. We've all been trained in death estimation for burn victims. I'm sure any one of them can help during your investigation."

"I don't want anyone else on this investigation." Murray stood, turning that unreadable gaze on her. "I want you."

Chapter Four

The gasoline had started rotting his brain.

There was no other explanation for why he'd drag Aslen into the middle of a homicide investigation. It certainly wasn't because the moment he'd seen the laceration at the back of her skull that he'd succumbed to the incessant need to keep her close.

Murray didn't give into distractions. Once he set his mind on a goal, that was all, plowing through projects, casework, even personal achievements. He focused on what was important and refused to back down until he had it in sight. Finding this arsonist. Stopping anyone else from getting hurt. That was what mattered, but the second the words *I want you* had left his mouth, a certain rightness had settled in his chest. Aslen wasn't trained in law enforcement. While her expertise butted up against his during investigations like this, she wasn't qualified to carry a weapon, direct interrogations or hunt a potential killer. But the idea of leaving her here to work this scene, to be here if the arsonist returned to the scene of the crime, broke the dam he'd fought to build for the past twenty years.

She was the one for this job.

And once he made a decision, there was no backing down.

Aslen was his complete opposite. Where she analyzed

every angle, pulled apart different scenarios and gathered as much information as possible, Murray bounded into action. It'd frustrated him to no end the older they'd gotten. Sometimes there was a right choice and a wrong choice. Didn't need to psychoanalyze it to within an inch of its life, but no matter how many times he'd tried driving that point, she stood her ground and took her time. No diving head-first into the unknown. Even if he didn't go about things the same way, he admired her pigheadedness.

But, right now, he was only asking for trouble. Going against everything he'd worked for to protect her from danger, sometimes even from herself, by ordering the collaboration of their two departments. And he was pretty sure it was going to blow up in his face. For years, he'd kept his distance. Emotionally. Mentally. Mostly physically. Now, he was basically tying himself to her at the hip in the name of keeping her safe.

Nothing could go wrong.

Firefighters had allowed the scene to settle over the past few minutes. The ground under his boots had turned mushy, mud filling the gaps in his soles. The added weight didn't faze him, but he noted Aslen's struggle to navigate what was left of the woodlands with the unstable landscape. He knew her past, understood how difficult it must be to face her fears on a daily basis after losing her parents to a household fire at only eight years old. But she was strong—stronger than most if he was being honest with himself—but the admission did nothing to curtail the feeling of being watched.

Murray grappled with his ingrained nature to keep an eye on her and scan the trees for potential threats. She and her friend—Danny, was it?—had joined the rest of her unit in scouring the brush for potential hot spots and signaling the hose jockeys for extra assistance. What had once been a shed housing maintenance resources for rangers on patrol had been cordoned off with tape to protect the decimated remains inside at Murray's insistence. Onlookers from the nearby campground had been evacuated, but it looked as though a few found their way to the perimeter tape on the other side of the clearing where firefighters had set up their command center. The hook lodged in his chest from the moment he'd set eyes on Aslen all those years ago dug deeper as he put distance between them to check in with the supervisor in charge.

"We had an agreement." Murray didn't bother with the small talk.

"Figured you'd have something to say about that." Deep lines sprawled across Chief Higgins's forehead as he scrawled notes over the map spread out in front of him on the folding table. Bleached, ear-length hair hung into his eyes and blocked Murray's view of the man's face. Lean muscle flexed in Higgins's hands as he braced his weight every now and then. The chief couldn't have been anywhere near retirement, yet signs of age added to the sallowness in his sharp cheekbones and around his chin. His gear hung off him like an ill-fitting suit, worn in some places more than others. "There's only so much I can do before my guys start asking why I'm sidelining a female ranger. Because I can tell you right now they'll make her life a living hell if they think she's getting preferential treatment. Besides, this got close to getting out of control. I needed everyone I had."

Murray couldn't argue against any of that. Okay. So maybe he'd overstepped in making his deal with the chief in the first place—his inclination to jump into action without looking could've blown back on Aslen in more ways than one—but he wouldn't apologize for putting her safety first. Even if it made her hate him more than she already did. Acid burned up his throat at the thought. "You got a photographer on site?"

Higgins nodded across the clearing to the male ranger staring down at the camera slung around his neck. "Just got here."

"Have him take pictures of the crowd gathering behind you." Arsonists had a tendency to return to the scenes of their crimes. They liked to watch law enforcement scramble to control the blaze or relive the sexual effects the fire had on them during the initial start. Arson was considered a gateway crime in his book. Dangerous offenders started their criminal careers setting fires in an attempt to gain control and power, and attain a feeling of success in their lives. It provided manipulation in its purest form through any victims caught in the fire, firefighters, law enforcement officials and other figures of authority, the media and the community in general. Arson, for all intents and purposes, was a crime committed by cowards. Hands off, simple, selfish. While Zion had become its own closed off community from the world, news of the fire—and the body recovered—would spread. It was only a matter of time before the arsonist got the attention he wanted, bolstering his ego and doubling that craving for fame. Arsonists primarily worked in groupings, usually three fires at a time, with an ultimate goal in mind. If Murray could identify that goal and avoid the media feeding into the suspect's ego, he might be able to stop this before the killer escalated. "Then have him send me all photos of the scene when he's finished."

Higgins set worn blue-gray eyes on him. "You think we're dealing with a professional? That this might happen again?"

Murray looked at Higgins and shrugged. He didn't have an answer for that, but his gut was telling him he had to be careful with this one. Years of studying for his criminal justice degree in college then transferring from the Salt Lake City Police Department to what he would absolutely consider small-town rural USA to keep up with Aslen had manipulated him into thinking he'd see less homicides. Clearly, he couldn't have been more wrong. The use of accelerant to destroy the body might've been a crime of convenience or it could've been a premeditated strategy.

Either way, he wasn't leaving Aslen unprotected while an arsonist roamed the park.

Tendrils of smoke curled into the air and thinned out above him. The wind had kicked most of the smoke west toward the reservoir and would take a few more days to clear out of these canyons, but the stench of smoke and decay clung to his shirt.

He'd already lost his brother to an unknown hiking accident that remained an open missing persons case years ago, then his parents soon afterward when they'd given up hope on finding Jackson. He wasn't going to lose her too. No matter how much she fought him.

Murray scanned the faces of the bystanders trying to get a better look at the scene from behind the perimeter tape. A couple rangers had taken up the responsibility of acting as scene security, but he'd need to get his own rangers out here. People trained to navigate and investigate and ask the right questions. For now, he studied the onlookers' faces. Watched what they did with their hands. There was a sexual component to arson most authorities didn't want to put too much stock in, but the spread of campers didn't give him any indication the arsonist had returned to the scene. Yet.

"You're scaring everyone with your resting bitch face." Aslen barely cast him a glance as she maneuvered to his side. Her voice soothed the jagged edges of doubt cutting through him. Years of investigation hadn't affected him nearly as much as finding the body in that shed an hour ago, and there was only one reason he could pin it on: The woman standing next to him. He'd spent the better part of his life protecting her from the violence he saw every day, never once sharing stories about his day-to-day or recalling investigations with her around.

But he couldn't shield her from this.

Today was the first day she'd witnessed the harsh reality of this life.

A line of soot carved a sharpness into her jaw, as though she'd swiped at her face without realizing. All that dark hair he'd imagined wrapping around his hand while she gazed up at him from between his sheets escaped her ponytail, but Aslen had never been one for perfection. More…functional, and he wanted nothing more than to smooth the frizzed pieces back behind her ear. Exhaustion lined her eyes. It was deep—soul crushing.

Murray forced the tension out of his upper body, dropping his arms to his sides. Always on alert, he'd never let himself be blindsided by a threat, but when she got this close—as close as he allowed her—all that diligence drained. Leaving him boneless and relaxed. "How else am I supposed to exert my dominance?"

"What I wouldn't give to watch someone knock that ego right out of you." Her mouth curved at one corner. It wasn't the gut-punch of a smile she'd slowly lost over the years, but it wrenched his insides into a knot all the same.

A smile he'd helped diminish. Murray didn't let himself think too hard about that. He could breathe easier with her here, no longer hyperaware of the odor coming from the shed. Instead, sunshine and something floral replaced the bitter, and he breathed in a bit deeper. The tightness in his chest eased until there was nothing but a straight line to her. "Care for a crack at it?"

She jabbed her knuckles into his gut. Faster than he expected. The impact wouldn't knock him off-balance, but it sure as hell surprised him. Seemed Aslen was good at that. Somehow, over the course of the past few years, she'd left behind that scrawny little kid he'd stood up for in middle school. Now, there was a full-fledged woman standing up for herself. "Come on. The medical examiner just arrived. He's going to want to get a better look at the body."

Murray followed on her heels, winding through the areas firefighters had deemed safe toward the maintenance shed. How much longer would she tolerate his overprotective ass before she realized she didn't need him anymore? What would he do then? He didn't want to know the answer to that, lowering his attention to the flex of muscles along the backs of her hamstrings as she maneuvered through the brush. Her gear was too big, overwhelming her frame, but warmth seeped into his gut then burrowed lower as images of those thighs draped over his legs every morning filled his head. He instantly forced his attention higher, hands curled into fists to keep himself from reaching out for her. Not happening. Ever.

She wasn't some badge bunny he could take the edge off with. This was Aslen. His best friend. The girl he'd fought tooth and nail to save from a failing system and a guardian who hadn't given a crap about her. She was more than temporary. She was his reason for every decision he'd made, every step forward, and he wasn't going to mess with that.

Aslen rounded alongside the exposed wall of the shed, staring down at the charred, flaking remains of the body as the medical examiner ran through his initial assessment. So out of place in the middle of a crime scene.

"The fire did a good job of destroying fingerprints and DNA." The medical examiner used the end of his pen to pry the victim's jaw open. Exposing an empty black cavern. "But whoever left her here removed her teeth."

"What does that mean?" Aslen's gaze flicked to his. So brief, he might've missed it had he not been waiting for her to succumb to the shock of the day.

Murray tried to keep the frustration from his voice. And failed. "It means we're not going to be able to get an ID."

Chapter Five

I want you.

She'd heard those words, right? She hadn't made them up?

One minute she'd been standing there accepting—once again—that Murray Simpson would never see her as anything more than a friend, and the next she'd gotten everything she'd ever wanted. Pathetic. It took everything she had not to read into that single sentence, but she couldn't stop the rush of blood into her face at a fantasy come to life.

He wanted her.

Aslen couldn't stop herself from sneaking glances in his direction as Murray coordinated with Chief Higgins under the temporary command tent. The medical examiner had taken custody of the remains a little more than ten minutes ago, and with the hot spots managed and the rest of the firefighters clearing out, she wasn't exactly sure what those three little words she'd craved to hear her entire adult life meant.

Danny waved from the passenger seat of one of the rigs brought in to manage the flames as it pulled away. Bringing her outstretched thumb and pinky finger to her ear, she mouthed, *Call me* a split second before the driver maneuvered back toward Lava Point Road.

Aslen's nerves tripped as Murray broke off from the chief.

She didn't miss the apologetic look carved into her supervisor's face despite Murray's size working to get in the way. In an instant, she knew. The head of the law enforcement division had gotten his way. Again.

Murray didn't bother looking at her as he pulled his keys from his pocket and headed for his truck parked behind the perimeter tape. The small crowd that'd gathered to watch the firefighters' attempts to control the blaze—hadn't her team issued an evacuation order?—had thinned, but for some reason, she felt as though every appraising eye in the state was on him. That shouldn't make her nauseous, should it? "Let's go."

Every cell in her body fought against the compulsion to follow, to earn just a little bit of that affection so many other women had taken for granted over the years by giving in. She wasn't under any delusions. Murray had always been out of reach. Out of her league. Whatever people called it these days. He wasn't hers. He'd made that clear too many times to count. This whole day was just another reminder. He outranked her in the hierarchy of the National Park Service, and he had every intention of using it against her. From what she could assume from the chief hightailing it off the scene as fast as his oversized gear allowed, he'd approved her being put on loan to the law enforcement division. She would be expected to follow Murray's every command. "I'm not a dog to be called, and I'm not law enforcement."

Okay. That sounded childish. She would always be grateful for what he'd done. If Murray hadn't interrupted Brittany Olsen's determined attempt to reorganize Aslen's face—and every other body part she owned—she wasn't sure where she'd be. She owed him more than her thanks. But rescuing her from potentially permanent scars didn't give him the right to control the rest of her life. She wanted to travel, learn about other cultures, battle fires, make a difference in people's lives. She couldn't do that with a 230-pound jackass keeping her on a leash. No matter how handsome he was.

Murray pulled up short, sensing she hadn't followed. Then again, he always seemed to know where she was at all times. Like he'd cast some invisible thread between them the day he'd rescued her. Sometimes, after her shower, she'd inspect her body for that invisible anchor that seemed to take root in her the moment they'd met in middle school, like a tether between them. It would explain so many things. Like how he'd managed to find her that night she'd left her phone at home and snuck off to the bar in Springdale with Danny, where she'd had one too many drinks. The guy who'd grabbed her backside had managed to only walk away with a swollen face after Murray had finished with him.

The muscles along Murray's spine rippled as he twisted to face her. His size never intimidated her, but the hard edge to his expression hardly failed to make his displeasure clear. It was the same look he'd given her when she'd told him she'd accepted a job in Zion National Park and was moving to southern Utah without so much as warning him beforehand. She'd hoped to use the opportunity to give him an opening. Beg her to stay with him. Tell her he'd shared her feelings all these years and that he couldn't live without her.

She hadn't gotten any of that.

Instead, he'd packed his bag in minutes and shoved himself into her too-small sedan with nothing more than a grunt and an email tendering his resignation from SLCPD. Of course, the law enforcement rangers had hired him immediately with his experience. He'd worked some of the city's biggest homicide investigations. He'd been a hero. To then give it all up. All because of that stupid promise. What kind of person hung their entire life on something they said when they were fifteen years old?

"Get one of your rangers to help you during this investigation." Crossing her arms across her chest, Aslen let every ounce of restrained frustration taint her voice as she faced off with him. "You don't need me."

He never had.

Murray closed the distance between them. His hand twitched at his side, as though he intended to reach out and touch her, but he curled his fingers into his palm. "That's where you're wrong."

A shift occurred beneath the stone-cold mask he usually kept in place. It only ever broke around her because she'd been there before he'd felt the need to construct it in the first place. It was all the cases he'd worked, the violence and grief he'd dealt with as a police officer. He'd never talked about any of his cases, especially the more gruesome ones. Some part of him trusted her enough to let the real him show through, though it was usually when they were alone. Not in the middle of the field, and sure as hell not around fellow rangers.

Something had shaken him.

The laceration at the back of her skull pulsed with renewed pain.

"What does that mean?" The words escaped her control as nothing more than a whisper. She couldn't. She couldn't let him affect her this way anymore. She'd wasted too many years hoping he got the message without her bashing him over the head with her feelings. There'd been too many nights crying herself to sleep, praying with everything that she had that he would just see her. Want her. Love her. But he'd never once responded or shown evidence of considering her anything but a burden.

"Out of every firefighter the National Park Service has, you're the one with the most training concerning arsonist motives and behavior." Lines deepened between his eyebrows as if his answer was the obvious conclusion. "I had Chief Higgins's photographer take pictures of the crowd because of something you said during one of your classes about arsonists frequently returning to the scene of their crimes."

"Oh." Right. It took a second for Aslen to pull herself out of the depths of misery she'd created to torture herself. Of course, he'd only recruit her into the investigation because of her training. That was their relationship now. Other than that night at the bar, Murray had ensured to keep his distance, not even bothering to sit next to her during mandatory ranger trainings throughout the year. No more movie nights or playing video games until sunrise like they used to as teens. All of that had come to an end when she'd graduated college. And, if she was being honest with herself, it hurt. More than she wanted to admit. She'd made a mistake letting him follow her to Zion. Maybe if she'd held her ground, he could've found a way to be happy. Met someone—nope, she was not jealous of the amalgam her brain supplied—stayed with SLCPD where he'd started climbing the ranks to captain and built the family she knew he wanted. Instead, he was going to let himself rot to protect her from invisible threats out of obligation. "I wasn't sure you were listening."

"I listen to everything you say." He cocked his head to one side like he'd told her this a thousand times before and was waiting for her to finally believe him.

She didn't know what to say to that. Goose bumps prickled underneath the heavy layer of her jacket despite the heat. The fire-resistant material worked great when confronted with a fire, but the loss of adrenaline, the pain in her skull and Murray's emotional whiplash dragged on her shoulders.

Aslen directed her attention to the endless acres that'd gone up in literal smoke this morning. She couldn't partner with him on this investigation. It was grating to be this close and have him look at her as nothing more than a resource. "You have training in motives and criminal behavior, Murray. Whoever set this fire is going to want to get out of the park as soon as possible to avoid suspicion. Just like any other suspect."

"I've already got my rangers posted at the main entrance to the park, out at Kolob Canyons and running campground visitor background checks." The muscles in his forearm flexed as he clenched his keys. He seemed to have everything handled. There was no reason to drag her into a homicide investigation or a manhunt. "But why this location?"

"What?" Her attention snapped back to him.

"Lava Point isn't anything special. The only reason people come out here is for the view from the overlook, and most hikers and visitors to the park don't know it exists." Murray closed in by another couple inches. Close enough she swore she could smell the spicy scent of his shampoo and conditioner, triggering her insides to melt through her detachment. Damn him. "So why would an arsonist intent on getting rid of a body choose this location? Why Zion at all?"

His gaze locked on hers. The scene, the last of her unit disassembling the command center, the mud clinging to her boots—everything disappeared until it was just the two of them. As it should be. Her mouth dried as the answer solidified and her brain caught up with reality. "Because this place means something to him. The victim… I didn't see any signs of a struggle or violence on her remains other than her teeth had been removed. No broken bones in the face or hands, which makes me think he might've cared about her."

Murray's expression didn't budge, but she was more than aware of what Zion could mean to someone. Especially someone who'd lost as much as he had.

She swallowed through the lump forming at one side of her throat. "It's possible he came here as a child. Maybe with his victim. He wanted her to die in a place he was comfortable in. I'm sure he knows the area and is familiar with the geography from multiple visits, which means you might be able to narrow down the suspect list to annual passholders."

The toes of his boots grazed hers as he stared down at her. Too close. Too reachable. "Then let's get started."

Chapter Six

He shouldn't be here.

Murray sank down onto the secondhand couch in Aslen's living room. The cushions barely supported his weight. It would take a crane to get him out of it.

The house she and Danny shared looked exactly like all the others in the neighborhood with its too-small, L-shaped, closed off layout, but the insides had been renovated in the past few years. Laminate-flooring stretched from one end of the house to the other in a beach sand color that added a lot of light despite the lack of windows. White cabinets in the galley kitchen, white appliances, cheap countertops and little storage. These government projects housed rangers from every department in Zion National Park. They were cheap and barely maintained but provided park employees affordable housing just outside the park's borders.

Aslen had gotten in his truck and immediately demanded he take her home for a shower and food. The scene was under control, and with the victim's remains currently stored in the medical examiner's freezer, there'd been nothing more for them to do in the field.

Didn't help with the pent-up anxiety crawling beneath his skin. His brain demanded action—to start looking into annual passholders, to get boots on the ground in a search for the arsonist, to question campers near the epicenter of the fire, to do *something*—but it'd taken him years to recognize Aslen required more rest than he did. More alone time, an empty schedule, more sleep, comforting foods. If he wanted her on this case, then he had to go at her pace. After all, she'd spent the morning in the throes of combating one of the most quick-burning, dangerous fires the park had seen. Which meant he would sit here until she'd had her shower and lunch.

The high-pitched tick of water hitting tile filled the house from down the hall. These houses were meant to be shared, which meant the single bathroom had been situated between both bedrooms, mere feet from the living room. He could hear Aslen stripping free of her boots and uniform, knowing the exact moment she stepped beneath the shower's spray. A moan escaped from underneath the door, and Murray curled his fingers into his palms. All too easily, he imagined what waited on the other side of that thin wood, how her skin would be flushed from the heat, how she'd feel beneath his hands.

What the hell was he doing?

Aslen Woods was not his. Far from it. The way he saw things, she was his to protect, to befriend, to care about, just as she was to any other ranger in her unit. But she wasn't *his*, no matter how many times he liked to think otherwise. If anything, she was more of a little sister. Nothing more.

Frustration built the longer he was forced to listen to the crash of water coming from the shower. Aslen's roommate must've gone back to headquarters because they'd had the place to themselves since Aslen had shoved through the door and told him to back the hell off.

The entire place was neat and well taken care of, with small mementos of a combination of Aslen's and Danny's lives sprinkled throughout. It took every ounce of strained intention to focus on those instead of the images his brain conjured. The blanket she'd crocheted in home economics in high school. The single photo of her family she'd managed to save from the fire that'd killed her parents. The mug he'd gifted her for her sixteenth birthday sitting upside down to dry on the counter that read I Will Probably Spill This. Small moments that made Aslen... Aslen. She'd kept them all. Built a life for herself despite every avalanche of crap thrown her way.

She deserved better than the scraps she'd collected over the years. She deserved the world. To be happy. Free. She couldn't do any of that tied to him, but the thought of her attaining it with someone else... Fire exploded in his gut. Damn it. He had to get out of here.

Murray shoved to his feet, running one hand through his hair as he practically lunged for the front door. The vise around his ribcage tightened with every step. He'd never thought that promise he'd made back in middle school would need to include him following her here, but he couldn't hold her hostage to his own emotional needs anymore.

The bathroom door clicked, and there she was, standing in nothing but a towel with all that dark hair plastered to tanned skin he had no business noticing. Air crushed from his lungs at the sight. Hell, she was beautiful. As many times as he'd tried to douse his attraction by losing himself in countless badge bunnies and rangers—though never in the law enforcement division—Murray understood right then it'd all been for nothing. Every cell in his body had somehow tuned into every cell in hers, as though she'd been made specifically for him with that birthmark above her lip, the clearest shade of green in her eyes and the sweet curve of her mouth he imagined fit perfectly against his. What would she sound like when he kissed her? Would it match the moan she'd let escape when she'd gotten in the shower?

Aslen scrunched a second towel into her hair to sop up some of the water dripping over her shoulders. "Give me ten minutes, and I'll be ready to go."

He'd seen her like this plenty of times. Early in the mornings after he'd dragged her out of her foster mother's house to stay with him and his family, at the pool every summer where they spent the entire time trying to knock other people over in games of chicken—reigning champions, right here—and that time he'd dumped an entire cooler of Gatorade on her after he'd scored the winning touchdown during homecoming. But the years had changed her. She'd added a few pounds of muscle since college, lost that orphan look that gutted him every time and gained an insurmountable dose of confidence sometime over the past few years. It looked good on her, added a glow he wasn't sure any cosmetic could achieve, and left a full-blown woman capable of leading any man with a pulse off a cliff with her siren smile in her place.

Aslen straightened. "Are you okay?"

Clearing his throat, Murray mentally kicked himself. This. This was why he'd kept his distance, burying himself in his cases, limiting their interactions as much as possible since she was able to move out of that house. That first time he'd fantasized about her had scared him enough he'd disappeared for two weeks after her college graduation. Since then, he'd kept himself in check through every birthday, holiday and promotion, but her need to celebrate—and be celebrated for—their major life milestones had brought his resistance down brick by brick. They were all they had now, and he would keep showing up for her. Even if it drove him mad. "You need to eat."

"I'll just grab one of Danny's protein shakes before we head to headquarters." Furrows deepened between her eyebrows a split second before she turned toward her bedroom. In an instant, the invisible thread that connected them pulled taut.

Murray rubbed at his chest where he thought that connection might live, right over his sternum. He called through the door, ensuring he didn't get anywhere close to the handle. "I'll make you something."

"I can feed myself, Murray." Her voice grazed his senses as though it'd taken on a physical presence. Soothed his climbing heart rate, calmed the animal that wanted nothing more than to tear through that door and claim her as his. "I've managed this long."

"Protein shakes aren't food, Aslen." He didn't wait for a response, rounding into the kitchen. Spotless. Everything in its place with a clear purpose. Nothing extravagant. Purely functional. It was a side effect of her upbringing, having lost her childhood home in an accidental fire that broke out in the middle of the night. Then moving from foster home to foster home before she'd landed in the house next to his at twelve. Actually, he was pretty sure Aslen would have a meltdown if he misplaced a single item, so he'd memorized where everything went the first few times he'd visited.

And replicated her preferred brands and favorite snacks in his own house to make her more comfortable visiting.

She hadn't visited. In fact, ever since she'd accidentally walked in on him with one of the women from the bar he and his fellow SLPD cops frequented years ago, Aslen had stopped making an effort with him. And within a couple of days after that incident, she'd announced she'd taken a job here in Zion.

It hadn't made sense at the time, but since then, he'd had nothing but quiet and opportunity to think over the devastated look he'd caught on her face before she'd muttered an apology and fled his house as fast as her legs could carry her.

He'd broken her heart. And she'd tried to escape to the one place she was sure he wouldn't follow: Zion National Park. Little had she known his need to protect her would far outweigh his own survival instincts. And losing someone else he cared about to this damn park hadn't been an option.

Her confronting the impossibility of the two of them together had been for the best. Though he was having a hell of a time reminding himself of that as he'd literally just sat on her couch a couple minutes ago and imagined what her skin might feel like under the shower spray.

But Aslen was off-limits.

Murray made quick work of the last few eggs in the refrigerator, throwing in a handful of mushrooms, spinach and some shavings of shredded cheese he found. He set the omelet on a plate a split second before the sound of her bedroom door opening reached him in the kitchen.

"You didn't have to cook for me." She secured her hair into a high ponytail that accentuated her cheekbones and slender shoulders. And highlighted the contorted skin along the right side of her neck. Scars from the fire that'd killed her parents. She'd changed into a clean uniform, the scent of her bodywash driving into his lungs. Vanilla and coconut. Same fragrance he'd caught himself memorizing as a teen when she'd curled into his side on the nights she needed someplace else other than that drunk woman's house to sleep. He'd never been able to convince Aslen she could take his bed and he'd be fine on the couch. She'd slept like crap the few times he'd tried to give her space. Tossing and turning all night. It wasn't until he'd slipped beneath the covers beside her she would settle down. "A protein shake would've held me over."

"Sit down and eat." He added a fork beside her plate on the table and backed away as if she'd turn on him any second. Which had happened on occasion.

Dragging her chair back, Aslen took a seat and dove into the omelet, triggering that ridiculous primal need he had to provide for her. "I can't imagine why you're still single."

Could've been that any woman he'd been with over the past twenty years hadn't come close to the one sitting in front of him. He'd keep that truth to himself until he died. Extracting his phone, he unlocked the screen and handed it over. "One of my rangers sent over a list of all annual pass-holders and narrowed down our suspect list to those who have used their passes over the last few days."

"All right. I'll help you find your arsonist. I'll let you boss me around and throw around your authority during this investigation like you've been trying to do for years." Aslen's gaze raked over the screen. Then lifted to him. "But I want something in return."

Chapter Seven

Something had changed.

Aslen couldn't put her finger on it. Murray had always been intense, protective and…well, occasionally aggressive, but him bursting onto the scene and bulldozing her fellow rangers this morning had reached a whole new level of absurd. If she didn't know any better, she would've said Murray had gotten scared. Except the man had never been scared a day in his life.

Even though she'd showered, she still caught whiffs of smoke and decomposition clinging to her skin. It would take a miracle and a whole lot of tomato juice to get rid of it. Exhaustion weighed on every muscle in her body. She'd trained for this job and kept up on her physical fitness but couldn't shrug off the weight pulling at her shoulders.

Her phone vibrated from her pocket for the hundredth time with an incoming message. First Danny, then a couple of the other firefighters in her unit. She didn't know how to respond to any of them. They all wanted to know the same thing: What did the lead ranger of Zion's law enforcement division want with her?

"You want to make a deal. To do your job." The lack of tone in Murray's voice, one that he'd used many times when showing all that disapproval over the years, squeezed her insides. It was an automatic reaction that left her empty and full of shame, though she had nothing to be ashamed about.

He wanted her involved in this investigation. He could tell her it was for her knowledge of arsonist behavior and motivation, but she knew the truth. His experience in law enforcement gave him all the information he needed to track down this suspect, and she was sure there was someone far more qualified he could reach out to—hell, even in her own department—to get the job done. No. He didn't need her help. He wanted to keep an eye on her.

To be fair, there'd been more than enough times he'd done just that. Not just that first time a classmate had tried to cave Aslen's face in for showing up to school wearing the sweatshirt she'd left in their shared locker, but countless other nights. The ones she'd tried to forget when she closed her eyes. Murray had been there through almost all of them. Defending her. Comforting her. Giving her a safe place to hide. Fighting the battles she couldn't win.

But she was never going to be able to make it through this life on her own with him standing in her shadow. No matter how much she appreciated his efforts.

"I want to get something out of this arrangement." It took everything she had to keep her face expressionless and face off with him from across the two-person round dining room table that'd come with the house. Deep regret carved through her at even the thought of what she was about to demand, but they'd done this dance long enough, hadn't they? Her wanting more. Him rejecting her over and over. There was only so much she could take, and after facing off with that fire this morning and witnessing the power he held over the rangers in this park, Aslen had reached a breaking point.

Murray waited with that legendary patience he'd never been able to teach her.

"I'll lend my expertise for your investigation to find the arsonist." She sucked in a deep breath, her hands shaking on either side of the plate of food he'd made her. "And after you've made the arrest, you'll let me go."

As much as he fought to keep his own expression clear, she couldn't help but note the slight tightening around his eyes. Murray leaned forward in his chair, anything but relaxed, as he interlaced his hands on the table's surface. "Go where?"

"Anywhere." That single word hurt more than she wanted to admit. He'd sacrificed everything to keep his promise—to protect her—but now it was time for him to let her go. She'd wanted nothing more than for him to look at her the same way she looked at him since she'd been thirteen years old, but that wasn't ever going to happen. No matter how many times she tried to convince herself otherwise, Murray Simpson wasn't capable of that kind of love. And she deserved to find it for herself. "I want a choice, Murray. I want to make my own decisions and make mistakes, even if they get me into trouble. And I want you to trust that I know what's best for me."

He didn't have an answer for that, didn't even seem to breathe as that dark gaze pinned her frozen in her chair. Muscles flexed in his forearm, and he tore his gaze from hers.

Aslen couldn't hold back the compulsion to touch him. Sliding her hand across the table, she slipped her fingers over his scarred knuckles. Knuckles that had given a beating when her first boyfriend had gotten too handsy at the back of the movie theater despite her protests. Or when her foster mother had come at her with a broken wine bottle one night, and he'd stepped in front of her with his hand raised to take the hit. "I know you feel the need to watch my back until the day I die, but you've been teaching me how to take care of myself for years. Remember all those times I managed to use your momentum and weight against you and had you pinned? Or when I accidentally sliced open your hand by using the knife skills you drilled into me for days on end?"

She traced her thumb over the jagged scar tissue, back and forth, trying to bring his attention back to her, but wasn't that what she'd been doing for the past twenty years? It didn't matter how hard she'd pushed herself, how many times she'd aced her classes or that she'd gotten the job of her dreams—it wasn't enough to impress him. And she never would. But she couldn't stay in this limbo, waiting for something that would never happen.

His body heat threaded up into her fingers and down her arm, working its way into her chest. The physical weight grounded her, giving her all the more courage to see this through. She loved him. Always had, but he wasn't ready for that kind of commitment after everyone he'd lost. The moment his brother had vanished, Murray had closed himself off to anything but casual one-night stands and whatever he considered her. And she was afraid that wouldn't ever change.

"Knowing how to defend yourself and being able to do it in a real-world situation are two different things." Murray shifted his thumb over hers, the rough calluses dragging against her skin. He redirected his attention to their hands, hers reaching across the table, his close to the edge, and wasn't that just the perfect representation of their relationship? Her always reaching for him. Him tolerating her effort. What she wouldn't give for him to ask her to stay, to tell her all the things she'd wanted to hear from him so badly, but it hadn't worked when she'd told him about her taking this job, and it wouldn't work now.

"But it's a start." She could feel his resolve cracking. "How am I supposed to prove all that time you spent training me is worth anything if you keep coming to my defense?"

He hadn't pulled away as he had so many times before, as if he needed the physical connection as much as she did in the face of what this deal would mean for both of them. Still, her brain rushed to fill the silence with outlandish and impossible scenarios to counter the pressure in her chest. He could turn his hand over, drag her into his lap, thread his fingers into her hair at the base of her neck just before he kissed her senseless. She'd imagined what that moment would be like so many times, she could practically feel the sweep of his lips against hers from the other side of the table, taste the mint of his preferred toothpaste on her tongue.

Murray retracted his hand, taking his body heat with him. "All right. You have a deal."

That…that was it? A sense of acceptance echoed through her head, throwing her back to the day she'd threatened to take the firefighting position in Zion. She'd known exactly how he'd feel about her coming here, to the same national park rangers and police believed to be the last whereabouts for his brother Jackson, but she hadn't felt like she'd had any other choice to get him to do *something* at the time.

The weight of his statement nearly crushed her, but she couldn't back out. Murray Simpson had always been this presence in her life—almost as far back as she could re-member—but right then, she saw the pain of losing one more person in his expression. Summoning the last of her reserves, Aslen pulled her own hand back, tucking it be-neath the table out of sight with a false brightness in her voice. Her stomach clenched, but the thought of eating only made it worse. She pushed the plate a few inches off to the right. "Guess that means you're off the hook. Promise fulfilled. What are you going to do with all the free time you're going to have?"

The joke was meant to lighten another round of heartache threatening to crush her from the inside, but Murray simply shoved away from the table.

"You done?" He unpocketed his keys, fisting them tight as he stared down at her, bringing her attention to the familiar switchblade he kept within hand's reach since she'd gifted it to him when he'd made the cut as an officer for the Salt Lake Police department. "We've got work to do."

Aslen could only nod. She'd thought this time would be different, but her optimism was running out when it came to Murray Simpson. As much as it would hurt to lunge into a world she knew nothing about with no backup or support, it was the right thing to do. For both of them. "Okay."

She made quick work of discarding the omelet he'd made—the couple bites she'd taken sitting in her stomach like a rock—and loaded the dishes into the dishwasher. Her phone vibrated again, but she didn't have the energy to answer Danny right now. This was happening. She would consult Murray and his law enforcement rangers throughout the investigation and then…she would be on her own.

A tremor of excitement skittered through her as Murray held the front door open for her exit. She'd always wanted to travel. In a few days—maybe a couple weeks—she'd have her pick of location. The Grand Canyon, the Pacific Ocean. Oh, maybe she'd head straight to Scotland. She had the funds. She'd taken a job the minute she'd turned sixteen, gotten scholarships for school and packed a brown-bag lunch every day of her life other than when she and

Murray had something to celebrate. Losing everything in the fire and then having nothing to her name in that foster home had taught her to be frugal and save everything she made outside of monthly expenses.

She could do this. No. She *was going* to do this.

Taking her keys, Aslen locked up once they were outside, then headed for her crappy four-door sedan that had more miles on it than she wanted to admit and a glowing engine light she hadn't told Murray about for months. "I'll meet you at headquarters."

A large, familiar hand slid between her rib cage and arm, directing her toward his truck. Her heart skipped a couple beats at the contact, but she wouldn't let it show. "We ride together."

"You can't be serious." Aslen dragged her weight, just as she had at the scene. The man was impossible. "I'm perfectly capable of driving myself there, Murray."

He opened the passenger door for her, guiding her inside with a practiced gracefulness. He gestured for her to fasten her seat belt, then pinned her with an intense gaze that sucked the air from her chest. His hand reached out and framed her jaw, those eyes dipping to her mouth and back, and she was frozen. Completely and utterly frozen as she let his touch linger. This was new. This was…everything. "You said there's a chance the arsonist will begin to escalate. And since I have your full cooperation until this investigation is closed, I'm not letting you out of my sight."

Chapter Eight

She was leaving him.

Murray swallowed past the acid lodged in his throat.

She'd tried once before when she'd come to Zion, and he'd followed. But this time… This time felt different.

Aslen crossed park headquarters' open floor plan toward her roommate, leaving Murray at the two-story entrance. Tinted windows fought to keep out the summer sun, but he couldn't avoid the slap of heat against his face. Exposed beams added a cabin-like feel to the open structure designed to compliment the park's visitor's center with raw wood, beige rock accents, tan walls and yellow signage directing rangers to department offices. Headquarters wasn't anywhere near the size of Zion's visitor's center, tucked just north of the museum along North Fork River. It looked just as any other building in the park but managed to provide a bit of peace from the onslaught of hikers. The people in this building kept the park running, including him.

Murray couldn't help but watch Aslen as she settled into comfortable conversation with Danny, the only other female firefighter in the unit. A few more rangers had gathered nearby, but it was obvious both Aslen and Danny were kept at arm's length until absolutely necessary. Something he'd never allowed in his own department. Each of his rangers, no matter their experience, gender, sexual preference or race were integral to the team, and if he got so much as a word differently, he addressed and neutralized it. As law enforcement rangers, his department had to work together to protect this park and the people in it. There was no preferential treatment, and he sure as hell didn't encourage an every-man-for-himself mentality. They were all working for the same cause. Period.

Higgins obviously had a different management style, allowing division between rangers. It was one of the reasons Murray wanted Aslen out of the fire unit. If her fellow rangers didn't go out of their way to include her and Danny in a meeting, what kept them from turning their backs on both women in the field?

Aslen's flash of a smile lit up her entire face as she laughed at something her friend had said. Every sense he owned locked onto it, memorizing the sound, the way his gut tightened in response and etching the sight into his memory. She didn't laugh like that around him.

Then again, he hadn't given her a whole lot of reasons to.

Let her go. Out of all the requests he'd expected her to make, that possibility hadn't ever crossed his mind. They were a team. Had been since she was thirteen years old. They'd survived the worst life had thrown at them by sticking together, and now she wanted to go out into the world alone to prove something? Not happening.

Word about the fire had gotten out. Each department had called their rangers to headquarters to exchange information and build a plan. Everyone from information to resources had been invited. With any luck, the National Park Service would get a leg up on whoever had set that fire and discover what'd happened to the body found in the maintenance shed. He caught whispers and glances in his direction. He'd gotten used to them over the years. His size alone tended to get people to talk, but he didn't have the patience or the desire to confront them now.

"Ranger Simpson, it's been a while." A voice as smooth as silk and just as deadly when used with intention slithered to his position a split second before rich brown eyes locked on him. Eleanor Richie broke into his personal space, sliding a soft hand across his forearm. She'd pulled her hair back in some half-up twist, accentuating too-dark eyebrows that didn't match her coloring and the few dozen layers of makeup cracking around her eyes and mouth. "I was hoping I'd see you here. You never called me back after our date."

Probably because going out with the information ranger had been a mistake. It wasn't her attempt to turn every word out of her mouth into a sexual innuendo or that she wore earrings twice the size of her ears that had kept him from taking her back to his bed. It'd been the flare of victory in her eyes when he'd asked her out—then subsequent anger when he'd ended their date early. It certainly had nothing to do with the confounding brunette who'd been a fixture in his life for nearly two decades.

Murray's gaze snapped to Aslen. To see her monitoring his conversation with Eleanor. A sickening churn swept through his stomach. He had nothing against office relationships. Hell, he'd dabbled in a few during his time with SLCPD with women far more into themselves than Eleanor, and he sure as hell wasn't celibate. But Aslen hadn't been working with him at the time, nor with the women he took home then, and he couldn't help but catch the slight fall of her expression before she turned back to Danny. Something like…disappointment?

What did she care who he slept with? Or hadn't slept with, as was the case with Eleanor. And why did he want to punch himself in the face for giving her the impression he'd gotten any closer than a casual date with Eleanor? "Ranger Richie. I wasn't aware you'd be here."

"I'm an information ranger." Eleanor's lips curled into a smile that would give the Cheshire cat a run for its money. Manicured nails scraped against the skin of his forearm, forcing goose bumps to pimple up his arm. "It's my job to ensure every department is up-to-date on the situation and visitors are informed of the state of the park."

Right. Wouldn't have anything to do with the fact the superintendent had brought him in to update the rest of the departments on the investigation. Murray pulled back out of her reach, ignoring the downturn of her mouth into something resembling a pout. "Excuse me."

It was the same with every woman he'd set his sights on. Hope the next one would be different, disappointment when he found himself feeling emptier than when he'd started. No amount of pleasure could fill the hollow hole carved into his chest. It'd been gaping for too long, getting a little worse every day. The only times he could think past it were when he got Aslen within view. He didn't have to explain himself to her or go through the motions. He didn't have to answer a thousand questions from a stranger hoping to get to know him better or to be the one to heal his trauma. There was no healing. And there hadn't been for a long time.

With Aslen, he could just…be. But if she wasn't here to keep him from falling apart? Hell, he didn't want to think about that. Ever. At the same time, using her for his own selfish survival would only push her farther away. And she deserved better than that. She deserved a man who could love her as much—if not more—than she loved him, and Murray wouldn't ever be that guy. All the love he'd had— for his parents, his brother—had been taken from him.

He didn't have anything left for her.

Murray headed for the front of the lobby, the weight of Eleanor's gaze locked between his shoulder blades. It was like a shard of glass digging into his spine. "Everyone, if I could have your attention." Instant quiet filtered through the room as he crossed his hands in front of him. "For those of you who don't know me, I'm Murray Simpson. I head the law enforcement rangers."

A high-pitched "Woot" sounded from the back with the pump of a small fist.

"Thank you, Ranger Jordan." He couldn't keep his restrained laugh to himself as he surveyed the thirty or so rangers gathered. "As most of you have heard, there was an incident out at Lava Point around four this morning. A fire broke out and has since destroyed approximately two thousand acres of land. As of now, the fire department has the blaze under control and hasn't needed to call in additional help from the state, but there is the potential for hot spots to reignite. The campground and the trails have been evacuated, and we want to keep it that way until Chief Higgins gives the all clear. Kolob Canyons has sent us a handful of rangers to look out for and turn back hikers out on the trails, but we're going to need to dispatch another half dozen to take over night shifts and patrol the backcountry routes around Lava Point."

Hands popped up from mass of volunteers, and Murray issued their orders to head out. Silence fell over the group as the rangers extracted themselves from the herd, but his heart rate ticked higher as he noted Aslen's attention fully on him.

Her mouth curled at the corners in a half-assed attempt to erase the flash of disappointment from earlier.

If he was being honest with himself, not one of these

rangers held his attention as much as she did. Like she possessed her own gravitational pull specifically designed to trap him. It'd been that way since the moment they'd met. He'd recognized her as the girl who was always getting yelled at next door, who'd sat at the front of the class pushing her broken glasses farther up her nose, the one who raised her hand for every answer and outsmarted every single kid in the class despite being two years younger. He didn't realize it then, but it'd been that moment he'd taken her back to his house to clean and bandage her face that had forged this invisible connection between them. Something had snapped into place and only seemed to get stronger every day. There'd been something deeper about Aslen Woods's near compulsion to spew random facts when she got nervous, and he'd been caught up in her since.

Someone cleared their throat, drawing his attention back into the moment. Eleanor tossed him another one of those wide smiles, and his stomach lurched.

It took a moment for Murray to realize he'd been staring. At Aslen. Hell. He'd broken one of his own damn rules he'd put in place for himself when he'd landed in Zion by unnecessarily drawing attention to her. No one needed to know about their relationship—however that word applied to them. "Chief Higgins and his unit have concluded the blaze was started and fed by an accelerant, most likely gasoline, which means we're looking for an arsonist."

The whispers were back, spreading through the collection of serious faces. A voice raised above the others. "Is it true a body was recovered from the scene?"

"Yes." There was no point in denying it. He needed as many eyes and ears as he could get to cover the 232 square miles Zion offered. "The Springdale ME won't have any information for us until the autopsy has been done, but we are running on the assumption the fire was started to destroy evidence of homicide. Thanks to the fire department's insight, we've learned the suspect we are looking for is potentially as familiar with the area as we are."

He nodded at Aslen, and that nervousness Murray had been able to spot a mile away flooded through her. Her unit cast glances in her direction, and right then, he knew what had to be done. What would get her to stay in Zion. With him. "Ranger Woods, what more can you tell us about the arsonist we're looking for?"

"All right." Aslen took that step forward, keeping her chin level and her shoulders back as she faced off with her fellow rangers. Danny clapped and shouted her approval while the rest of their unit stared in open shock. As if they couldn't see anything special about the woman standing next to him. Idiots. "Every arsonist I've encountered has one thing in common—they've practiced their skill set for years. Mostly during their teens and early adulthood. This arsonist has set fires before today." She turned that bright gaze onto Murray with an inhuman amount of determination. "That's how we're going to find him."

Chapter Nine

She knew what Murray was doing.

He wasn't going to convince her to change her mind. She'd stuck with him for the past twenty years, all for the slightest chance of taking their relationship to the next level. But the way he stormed onto that scene this morning had shown her exactly how far Murray Simpson would go to keep her at his side. That just wasn't where she wanted to be anymore.

The weight of the unit's attention stalled the air in her chest. She could do this. She was good at this. Out of everyone in fire management, she'd gone the extra mile to study arsonists and the patterns they created with their fires. Nobody else had the qualifications for this investigation. Which was Murray's point in bringing her in, wasn't it? To show her she had a reason to stay here in Zion?

"In the past six months, fire management has extinguished and neutralized three fires, including the one started this morning in Lava Point." Aslen backed up toward the oversize map pinned to the wall behind her. "The first was here." She pressed her finger into the map, highlighting the location. "Near the West Rim Trail leading to Lava Point. The second farther south, near Orderville Canyon." She allowed her arm to drop to her side. "During these summer months, lightning is our biggest threat for starting fires, which is the case for the blaze at Orderville Canyon. However, the fire along the West Rim Trail was investigated and labeled arson due to the chemical odor and burn patterns left behind."

"So the arsonist used an accelerant." Murray crossed his arms over his chest, eyes on the map behind her, and damn it, she couldn't help but admire the view. His expression fought to remain unemotional, almost bored, as he considered the map at their back, but Aslen had studied that face a thousand times over the years. Worry. That was what hounded him in the tightness of his jawline.

"Yes. Started with gasoline, same as this morning's fire." She couldn't help but shift her weight as reality set in. The fire this morning could have very easily gotten out of hand and reached the campground if her team hadn't been on the ball. What if there was a next time? What if the arsonist used more accelerant or her team couldn't reach the blaze in time? What if someone else got hurt? Her throat threatened to close as she evened her voice out. "At this point, we can't discount there's a possibility the two fires are connected by the same arsonist."

A hand went up in the back, but she couldn't get a good look at the ranger several rows behind. "Were there any remains found in that initial fire?"

"Not that we uncovered." A wave of nerves ratcheted up her spine, and Aslen sought Danny's gaze for the invisible slap she needed. Her friend gave her a personal thumbs-up with that cock of a smile she'd come to rely on after every shift, but nervousness refused to back down.

"But why that location for both accelerated fires?" Another voice from a few rows over raised above the rest. "Why set fires in a national park? Lava Point isn't as popular as the main vein of Zion. Why not choose a more populated area if the intent is to cause as much damage as possible?"

Murray shifted his attention to her—as though she was the most important person in this entire room, the one he'd look to when times got hard and options were limited—and her mouth dried.

Why couldn't he look at her like that all the time? What was so wrong about her that he'd never even considered seeing her as more than a little sister or obligation? Why didn't she deserve the secret smiles he'd thrown the women he brought back to his house? And why the hell couldn't she move on?

A throat cleared from the front row. Danny cut her gaze to Murray and back with a sharp nod.

Aslen risked a glance at the man standing sentinel at her side then forced her head back in the game. "Arsonists initially like to keep to a set boundary for their first fires, especially in terms of an escape route if interrupted. Sometimes, the boundary is around their base of operations like their home, which tends to narrow down potential suspects quite easily, but in this case, I believe whoever started this morning's fire—and possibly the first accelerated fire six months ago—is as familiar and comfortable with the Lava Point area as his own home."

Another hand shot up, this one from the front row, but Aslen noted her own team had yet to add to the conversation. Her fellow rangers—all but Danny—were talking amongst themselves. "You said *his* home. You believe we're looking for a male suspect?"

"Statistically, men commit more external crimes such as arson and homicide whereas women commit internal crimes against themselves, but there is always an exception." She fought the urge to cross her arms over her chest, to protect herself from the onslaught of prodding and questions. Murray had no right to put her in this position. She could've given him all of this information before the meeting, but he'd wanted to make a point. Show her what she was capable of. Only it wasn't his place. She was supposed to make her own choices, but this little stunt would only backfire in his face. She'd make sure everyone in this damn room looked to her for this investigation rather than him. Maybe that would knock his arrogance down a peg. "At this point, we cannot definitively say our suspect is a man, but eighty-two percent of arsonists are young white males with below-average intelligence, academic struggles, poor home environments and difficulty building social relationships. There is also the potential of a sexual component when it comes to starting fires. Many arsonists use it as a substitute for physical connection, but we do not have any further information on who might be behind these fires as of right now."

One of the male firefighters raised his hand, and Aslen sucked in a sharp breath. Her chest shook as she tried to control the tremors working up the backs of her legs. Holy hell, her ass was going to be sore tomorrow from clenching so hard to stop shaking. "What do you suggest we start looking for?"

She…hadn't expected that. Tension bled from her shoulders as she put together a plan of action. Aslen hadn't realized how much tightness had restricted her chest—how much she'd needed her team's approval—until she didn't have a reason to hold on to it. "The law enforcement division will be taking the lead on investigating the remains recovered at this morning's blaze, but we can all contribute to preventing the suspect from starting another fire. As our arsonist may be focusing on the area in and around Lava Point, I'd like to first focus our attention there. We need to collect statements from campground visitors to find out if they've noticed any unusual behavior. If we are dealing with a serial arsonist, he or she will most likely have a criminal record. We will want to run background checks on annual passholders and campground registrants who have visited the park more than once in the past six months. If neither of those strategies produce a suspect, it's a matter of monitoring this morning's scene for return bystanders then attempting to predict where the arsonist might strike next, which will most likely be within a two-mile walking distance from their base of operations."

"What do you mean, monitoring the scene?" Danny leaned forward in her chair, no hint of the lightness or encouragement from a moment ago. This was the firefighter who'd put her life on the line right next to Aslen for the past two years. And Danny had never once let her down.

"Over half of arsonists return to the scene of their crime to relive the feeling they experienced while setting the fire, whether that is sexual in nature or another dose of dopamine they're after." It'd been far too long since she'd been able to use the information etched into her head since college. "There's also a chance our arsonist will try to reignite the fire he started this morning, though we have not had that outcome at the first incident six months ago, which tells me our suspect is more intelligent than most arsonists. He is not following a compulsion. Rather, he is being very deliberate in his choice of locations."

"Bringing us back to Lava Point." Silence encapsulated headquarters as Murray edged closer, his boot grazing hers. It was the connection she needed, settling the fire simmering under her skin. The tremors lessened the longer he held that grounding connection, and Aslen eased a calmer breath. "All right. We have a plan. Fire management, I need you back at this morning's scene. Take note of any repeat faces, unusual behavior or evidence our arsonist might've left behind and report to Ranger Woods. Law enforcement, you're on scouring through campground registrations and annual passholder information for felony and misdemeanor convictions. Any leads, you send them directly to me. As for the rest of you, including information and resources, I want you to stay in touch with any news that would affect this investigation. Tips, smoke sightings—anything. Ranger Woods and I will be interviewing Lava Point campground visitors about this morning's events."

And there went her plans for that roll of cookie dough.

Exhaustion stiffened her joints as rangers were dismissed with orders.

A callused hand threaded between her elbow and rib cage, turning her into the mountain of muscle she'd fantasized about climbing like a tree too many times to count. He grazed her side with warmth and another dose of that grounding element Murray constantly gave off. "You did good for your first consultation."

"You sound surprised." She couldn't hide her internal battle against the desire to sag onto one of these chairs or pass out from her voice. She caught Danny's wave goodbye as her team filed out headquarters' front door. Everyone had their assignments, and now Aslen would be stuck collecting statements with Murray for the day, and she was just so…tired. From battling that fire, from feeling stuck, from the emotional whiplash Murray gave her.

Heat tunneled through her uniform. He hadn't removed his hand from her arm, and she was tired enough to lean into him if she wasn't careful. To hope. Aslen added a few inches of space between them. To prove she could. He didn't get to avoid her with little to no word from him for two years then suddenly act as though he couldn't breathe without touching her. Her stupid heart couldn't take it. "Please continue to bulldoze my participation in this investigation rather than ask for my cooperation, Ranger Simpson. I'm sure it won't blow up in your face next time."

His brows nearly met over the bridge of his nose as he studied her. "You're angry."

"You're trying to manipulate me into changing my mind about leaving. You want me to feel needed and useful while we look for the arsonist so I'll consider staying here with you in Zion instead of just telling me how you feel about our deal." Her body ached but worse, she just didn't have it in her to go through all this again. She couldn't keep doing this to herself. Waiting for him to come around, for him to tell her how he felt, for him to fall in love with her. "Why would you agree to it in the first place if you weren't going to hold up your end?"

He didn't answer. But that was his number one defense mechanism, wasn't it? Stonewalling was his most efficient weapon against her when things got uncomfortable.

When would this game between them end? When would she accept he wasn't ever going to be the Murray she'd desperately imagined all these years? He was all she had left. Everyone else was gone. No one left to want her. Why couldn't he see it? The strength left her all at once. "I'm tired. I'm taking your truck back to my house. I'll be back in an hour to pick you up and head to Lava Point. Until then, try not to make any other decisions for me."

Murray handed her the keys. And let her walk away.

Chapter Ten

She'd seen right through him.

He shouldn't have been so surprised. If he was being honest with himself, Murray was angrier with himself rather than with the deal they'd made this morning. It was why he'd given her the break she'd asked for without argument, despite every cell in his body screaming at him to keep her by his side.

Aslen had always been the outgoing one in class. There were only a couple times he could think of where she hadn't immediately shot her hand into the air when the teacher asked a question, but after the incident in middle school, he found she'd more often than not lean into observing, even collecting information to use to her advantage. Or maybe she just knew him too well at this point.

Back in the day, there hadn't been anything he'd been able to get past her once she'd finally agreed to move in with him and his family. Her foster mother had only been interested in collecting a paycheck that rarely funded enough meals to keep Aslen healthy or pay for the clothes she needed in below-freezing Salt Lake City winters. His parents had been willing and capable of watching out for her and offered a room right next to his with the intention of making the change official after a trial period. And she'd caught him sneaking out most nights, knew the names of the girls and the places he went under his parents' noses. Hell, he breathed wrong in his sleep, and she was right there hovering over him to make sure he wasn't dying. Which he'd woken up to. Multiple times.

Even now, Aslen had directed her attention out the passenger side window as they made their return back to Lava Point two hours north, but his instincts told him she was cataloguing every move he made. And every word he didn't say. The two feet of space between them across the pickup's bench felt like a hundred miles. Since hearing about the explosion this morning and realizing Chief Higgins had assigned her onto that scene, his nerves couldn't handle her so far away, but Murray had become an expert in keeping his distance. He'd survive not touching her, even if his brain told him otherwise.

"Are you doing anything for their anniversary this year?" Her question nearly got lost in the full force of the air conditioner. Summer in Zion wasn't for the faint of heart, and he caught a glimmer of sweat at the back of Aslen's neck as she turned her attention to him. "It's next week."

"No." He never did. His parents had died a long time ago. Mom had accidentally fallen in the canal chasing after his brother's Scottish terrier in the dead of winter. She'd ignored the symptoms for close to a week before the pneumonia did her in, but Murray's father had never recovered from the loss. Aslen believed he'd died of a broken heart, leaving Murray to look after her and his younger brother at nineteen. Though he hadn't done a very good job of that either. Why bring all that up once a year and remind himself of the aching tears in his chest? He'd moved on. Mostly.

"I took the time off to visit their graves." She kept her face turned from him, but he didn't need to see her expression to know every thought swirling in that brilliant brain. The time they'd spent together over the past twenty years had honed almost an entirely new language, one they'd designed based off body language and tone of voice. Aslen rubbed her hands down her slacks, gearing up to push him further. "You're welcome to join."

His knuckles protested the grip he had around the steering wheel. As much as he wanted to argue she didn't have any right to invite him to his own parents' graves, Murray couldn't deny they'd loved her as their own. His mom had always wanted a daughter. She just hadn't expected to find it in the scrawny teenager from next door. And she hadn't expected not to be around to watch Aslen become the beautiful, dependable, smart woman she was.

Her gaze landed on him at the edge of his peripheral vision. "What about Jackson?"

Heat burned up his neck despite the onslaught of the air conditioner.

"What about him?" Murray didn't like talking about his brother, and he sure as hell didn't need Aslen to remind him about his failure to protect his brother.

"His anniversary is coming up, too." She tried to keep her voice light, but he picked up on the strain. Aslen couldn't hide anything from him. She'd felt Jackson's loss as much as he had, maybe even more so considering he'd had a teenage girl to stay strong and provide for. So he'd distracted himself by applying to the police academy, made becoming a cop his entire personality, but it hadn't stopped there. There'd been the promotions, the high-profile cases, the task forces. All to be who she needed. Someone she could rely on when he'd failed so many others. "I thought this year we could hike out to the arch together. Maybe bring a photo to leave on the trail."

His blood ran cold.

"You're not going out there. Ever." The mere thought was enough to send him into a spiral he wasn't sure he could escape again. Murray hadn't meant his answer to sound as harsh as it did, but there was no way in hell he'd let her ever step foot on the Kolob Arch Trail again. He'd said as much in the years following his brother's disappearance off that trail and made her swear she wouldn't go anywhere near Kolob Canyons when she'd made the brash decision to become a ranger in Zion. She knew that, and yet she still tried to get him to wallow in that dark misery he couldn't face every year.

Her laugh lacked humor as she pressed her spine harder into the seat back. "Murray, you can't just forbid me from—"

"I said no." It took everything he had not to pull the truck over and jettison himself from the vehicle to get away from the sinking feeling in his chest, but it would just follow. It always did. "End of conversation."

"And I'm telling you, you don't get to make my decisions for me." The tension in her shoulders drained, and Aslen sank back against the seat. "You can't protect me from everything. It's not possible. And the more you try, the more you suffocate me. The more I'll resent you for it. Don't you see that?"

"You can resent me all you want. At least you'll still be alive to do it." He wouldn't budge. Not on this. He'd lost everyone he'd ever cared about. He couldn't lose her, too. He wouldn't survive it.

"Is that what you want?" Her voice broke. The question left her mouth as little more than a whisper over the roar of the air conditioner, but he'd heard every word. Etched it deep into his memory. "For me to resent you?"

He didn't have an answer for her. Not one that she would

like. Because the truth was as much as he needed to ensure she was happy and healthy and safe, he would deserve
the guilt and pain that came with losing her. He deserved
to be reminded of his failure to keep his family safe. And
whether she liked it or not, he considered her family. It was
why despite every dream, every fantasy, every time they'd
gotten too close, he hadn't let himself cross that line. He
was older by three years. He was supposed to be the more
mature one, the logical one, but nothing stopped him from
thinking about taking their relationship over that line time
and time again over the years.

She was freaking beautiful. Compelling, confident. She
seemed to know everything about every subject, but he'd
never seen anyone as passionate about fire management as
she was. To Aslen, knowledge was a defense mechanism, a
way for her to protect herself by knowing everything about
everything. It was one of the reasons he could count on her
to give insight into their arsonist. She'd taken her basic edu-
cation and pushed herself to dive deeper, to have an answer
for every incident, and he loved that about her. Loved the
way her brain worked and how she never accepted the bare
minimum. Never settled.

And she'd be settling for him. She might not see it that
way, but Murray didn't have a damn thing going for him. No
family left to make up for the one she lost, no roof of his own
to put over her head, no amount of space left for her in his
chest. Whatever love he'd been capable of giving had died
little by little with his mother's death, then his father's and
finally, the day Jackson had gone missing. He had nothing
left to give her but scraps, and while she was good at clinging to those small efforts he'd made over the years, they'd
never make her happy. He would never make her happy.

Murray leaned into the center console, grabbed for his

phone and tossed the device in her lap. "I asked Chief Higgins to send me the photos taken of the scene this morning as soon as they were ready. Tell me what you see."

She thumbed in his passcode and swiped through his inbox from memory out of the corner of his eye. Secrets weren't something he'd allowed once he'd been made to be her and Jackson's guardian. They'd shared everything, including passwords, pin numbers, and drug, alcohol and sexual history. They trusted one another, built their own little family after his parents had passed. Right up until Aslen had surprised him by accepting a fire management position in Zion without talking to him first. That ember of resentment he'd tried to bury had flared little more than three hours ago when she'd told him she was resigning after this investigation. Now it felt like it was rising to a full-on flame. "Most of these are of the body we recovered in the shed. Wait. Here we go. The photographer got some shots of the crowd from this morning, and it looks like he went back a couple hours later to photograph the onlookers again."

Seemed the chief had been as influenced by Aslen's intuition as Murray was.

"Any repeat customers?" It'd be difficult to spot patterns without laying physical photos side by side to analyze, but according to Aslen, the arsonist was suspected of starting two fires already. The second had included a body. There was no telling when or how intense a third might start.

"Give me a minute." Narrowing her eyes on the phone, she pinched the screen before swiping to the next photo as Murray fought to keep his attention on the rocky dirt road and not how she pursed her lips anytime she tried to concentrate. It was a habit she'd picked up well before he'd met her, but he couldn't help but smile at the ridiculous way it contorted her face. "I've got something."

"Already?" He chanced a glance at the screen but couldn't see anything from here. Ripping the steering wheel to the right, Murray eased the truck to a stop.

Aslen handed him the phone, pointing out a man dressed in a tan jacket and jeans. The guy's baseball hat hid most of his face. "Him. He was at the scene this morning." She flicked her finger to the next set of images. "Then again or still a couple hours later. Same jacket and baseball cap."

Murray tried to find a better angle, something that would give them a lead. Caucasian, maybe mid-thirties, though it was hard to tell at a distance. Scraggy blond hair stuck out from beneath the baseball cap, but every photo failed to provide more detail. "The photographer didn't get a shot of his face."

"Look at the rest of the photos." She swiped through, each more focused on the crowd than the last. But not on the man she'd singled out. "He knew where the photographer was at all times."

Understanding hit, and Murray raised his gaze to Aslen's, absolutely awestruck by her brilliance. "Because he was avoiding the camera."

Chapter Eleven

Only one bystander had gone out of their way to avoid the photographer.

The arsonist. It had to be him.

And the most logical place to start searching for him was Lava Point campground. Positioned a mere two miles from the epicenter of this morning's fire, the campground really wasn't anything special with only six available sites, but this area had obviously held importance to their suspect.

Aslen shouldered out of the pickup, surrounded by flat red dirt, towering trees and multiple campground sites containing picnic benches, firepits, vehicles and RVs. Crisp air cut through the trees and eased the heavy scent of smoke and ash, but there was no getting rid of that smell permanently. It would permeate everything in the area for months until summer storms and wind currents cleared it from the valley. "Registration reported all six campsites are currently occupied, but the evacuation order cleared everyone out this morning. Some may have returned since we lifted the order a few hours ago, but the odds of questioning campers isn't great."

Murray climbed out of the vehicle after her, the entire truck rocking with the slam of his door.

Rounding to the head of the pickup, she was nearly

knocked on her ass by the sight of Murray shrugging on his official uniform jacket complete with vest, badge and the pistol at his hip. She'd always appreciated the way he'd filled out his police uniform back in Salt Lake City, but now… He was every woman's fantasy all wrapped up in a tight, uniformed package. There was something about seeing him like this in the middle of the wilderness—on official business and not just to stick his nose where it didn't belong—that had her heart thudding hard against her ribs. Her face heated as Murray's gaze cut to hers. Because he'd caught her staring.

Crap on a cracker. Sliding slick palms down her slacks, Aslen cleared her throat and put everything she had into focusing on the layout of the campground and not the feeling of his attention dropping from her face, down the front of her body and back.

Did he just…check her out?

No. Not possible. At the very least, not plausible. That fantasy remained purely in her head. Not reality. And she definitely wasn't under any illusion Murray Simpson was saving himself for the right woman to break through the ice around his heart, but he didn't go out of his way to find company either. He was just cocky and good-looking enough he didn't have to. He had no reason to turn all that smoldering intensity on her. She must have something in her teeth.

"N-nothing." Aslen swiped her index finger across her teeth to make sure none of the omelet he'd made her caught, then nodded toward a blue SUV angled into one of the camping spots. Movement on the driver's side settled her nerves. Great. Something new to focus on. "It looks like a couple of the campers have returned."

Aslen took the lead, unwilling to turn back and see if Murray had followed. Nope. She didn't care. And she wasn't clenching her backside because of nerves either. Her breath shuddered free of her chest as she approached the first campsite ahead. Red dirt clung to her boots as she came around the back of the vehicle. She had to get it together. This wasn't some fellow ranger she thought was cute and might ask out. Murray didn't give a damn about what she looked like, what she wore or if she showered. He was practically her ornery best friend who got on her last nerve at least once a week. She had no reason to be nervous.

Except they'd never had to work together before.

Warmth that had nothing to do with the midday heat charged up her neck then exploded downward. Right between her legs. Uh oh.

Brother. Big brother. Nothing more.

Ha. Right. Normal people didn't think about what all those muscles might feel like against her hand as she unbuttoned his ranger uniform.

Aslen pasted a smile on her face as she approached the woman hauling two bright backpacks into the back seat of the SUV. "Hi, there. I'm Ranger Woods, and this is Ranger Simpson. We'd like to ask you a few questions if you have the time."

Exhaustion darkened the circles under the woman's eyes. Echoes of children from inside the canvas tent—arguing about something Aslen didn't catch—bunched the woman's shoulders closer to her ears as she faced off with the rangers. Dull blond hair fell from a rushed ponytail as the woman—obviously a mother, a very tired mother—shoved the packs into place. Sweat collected under her arms and around her T-shirt neckline. "I'm sorry. We really just need to get packed and get out of here."

"I understand, and believe me, we don't want to keep you any longer than we have to. This will just take a couple minutes." Aslen tried to keep her voice even, calm. The woman looked as if she might bolt and take her chances with the desert instead of trying to break up another sibling argument. Aslen didn't even blame her. "If you're worried about the evacuation order or the fire—"

"Rebecca, where are the damn car keys? I told you not to touch them, and now they've up and disappeared." The man's voice preceded him only a couple seconds before he came into view. Glasses reflected the afternoon sun and accentuated a long, thin—almost gaunt—face. His frame was swallowed by a long-sleeve shirt complete with hiking vest and jeans as he approached. Tall, taller than his wife and Aslen. "Oh, I didn't realize we had visitors. Is there a problem, rangers?"

Two small faces peeked through the opening at the front of the tent, then quickly disappeared. Aslen only caught a glimpse of the kids before their argument picked back up behind the canvas.

A wall of muscle pressed into Aslen's back, almost unconsciously, but she couldn't deny the added comfort of having Murray so close. "No problem. I was just speaking with your wife. We'd like to ask you a few questions about this morning before the evacuation order went out."

The woman—Rebecca—handed off the car keys to her husband then folded her arms across her chest. Making herself look smaller than a moment ago. "I told them we were in a hurry."

"That's right." The man slid his arm around his wife's shoulders, triggering a flinch in Rebecca's frame. Like she'd been physically repelled by the touch. Sweat built on the man's receding hairline. His gaze flickered past Aslen and Murray, somewhere off to his right. "The fire got a little too close for comfort. I'm sure you can understand. We'd really like to get out of here as soon as possible."

Aslen leaned back into Murray's chest in silent warning, and his hand settled at the small of her back in response. They'd been around each other enough over the years to develop their own nonverbal communication. Just as she'd learned how to read past the stony blankness of his expressions, he'd come to interpret the way she touched others and needed to be touched. "Of course, and as I explained to your wife, we don't want to keep you any longer than necessary. We'd just like to know if you or your family saw or heard anything out of the ordinary this morning around four. Before the fire started."

"I'm sorry. We were passed out from hiking all day yesterday. Even the kids went straight to bed." Another cut of the husband's gaze past her shoulder. Only this time Aslen dared a glimpse in that direction. Toward the RV parked across from this campground site. "Don't."

His plea froze Aslen to the core.

Strong fingers pressed into her lower back, grounding her better than any meditation, yoga practice or good book.

"Please. Don't give us away." The man—she didn't know his name—shook his head. His tongue darted across his peeling bottom lip, and it was then Aslen noted the split on one side. "He'll know we talked."

"You were threatened." Murray's voice vibrated along Aslen's spine, full of justice and violence and all the things he'd promised to do to those who'd hurt her. "By the camper across from you?"

Rebecca buried her face in her husband's neck. "Please. We don't want any trouble. Just let us go."

"Did he hurt you?" Aslen fought the urge to take that step forward, to offer any kind of comfort she could. Memories, ones that could only be chased back by climbing through Murray's bedroom window for years, threatened to super-impose into this moment, but she wouldn't let them free. Of pain, betrayal. Of bruises, broken bones and screams from someone who was supposed to care about her. They had no place in her life now. Not as long as Murray was here. The thought physically jolted her, and the pressure at her lower back intensified. How was she supposed to travel the world on her own if she couldn't even battle those demons alone?

The woman nodded, careful to keep her mouth turned into her husband's shoulder. "He came into our tent this morning. Took our driver's licenses and told us he knew where we lived. He said he'd hurt the kids if we told anyone what we saw. Please. We just want to go home."

"I can't help you unless you tell us what you saw." Murray's body heat countered the ice coursing through Aslen's veins.

"Rebecca got up to visit the bathroom a little before four this morning." The man ensured to keep his voice even, free of emotion for fear of alerting their campground neighbor. "She wasn't gone long, but..."

"I saw him. He was carrying a gas can." The exhaustion Aslen assumed had come from mothering two small chil-dren and surviving a controlling husband etched deeper into her face. This woman wasn't tired. She was terrified. "He must've seen me, too, because just before I got back in the tent, someone grabbed me and shoved me through the opening. I landed on my shoulder. He...he could've killed us, but my son was awake. He was crying."

Sobs cracked through the woman's strained composure.

A gas can. Aslen craned her gaze to meet Murray's. Un-derstanding filtered into his expression. "Did you see any-thing else? A lighter or matches? Did he tell you what he was planning on doing with the gasoline?"

"No, but when we heard about the evacuation order due to the fire, we decided to end our vacation early. He still has our driver's licenses. He knows where we live. When you arrest him, please, leave my family out of it." The man pulled his wife closer, as though he could protect her with his touch alone. "Well, if that's all, rangers, I'd like to finish packing and get my family home. I don't want to take any chances with this fire."

"Thank you for your time. You all have a safe trip home. If you remember anything unusual from this morning, please call into the visitor's center and ask for Ranger Simpson." Aslen raised her voice with a nod of appreciation. Walking away to create some distance between them and the family, she angled her back to the RV across from the campsite to give Murray the best vantage point. She'd agreed to consult about the arsonist's behaviors and motives. She wasn't trained to make an arrest or pursue a suspect, but she couldn't leave Murray to do this alone either. "What now?"

A door slammed behind her.

Aslen twisted in time to catch a glimpse of a tan coat disappearing around the RV.

"Call it in. He's on the run." Murray tossed her out of his way and bolted after the suspect.

There one moment.

And gone the next.

Chapter Twelve

The flash of tan vanished from right in front of his eyes.

Murray barreled past the tree line, instantly surrounded by thick walls of forest, dead pine needles under his feet and silence.

His heart threatened to beat straight out of his chest. Despite Aslen's attempt to ensure that family's safety, the suspect had caught on and run. Murray had caught little more than a few facial features before he'd had taken off toward the wilderness, but the jacket matched the one captured in the photos from the scene of the fire this morning. Murray couldn't fail to locate him. Not with the information the son of a bitch had on those kids.

Murray wouldn't be able to live with himself if he failed another family.

The trees seemed to breathe around him. Sooner or later, he'd give himself away. Murray just had to be patient.

A snap of a twig had him reaching for his weapon.

Unholstering his weapon, he spun on his heels, taking aim at the figure running straight at him. And froze. "What the hell are you doing here?"

Aslen struggled to catch her breath, nearly doubling over as she slowed her pace. Her hands met her knees just before she held up a finger to ask for a minute. "Hang on. You run faster than I do."

No, no, no, no. Murray closed the distance between them, holstering his weapon a split second before gripping her arm in one hand to turn her right back around and march her out of here. Lean muscle almost cost him his grip. She wasn't one of those women who worked out seven days a week on the treadmill in hopes of staying skinny. Aslen liked to throw around heavy weights, just like he'd taught her, and right now, she was prepared to argue. He lowered his voice. "You can't be here. This guy is dangerous. There's no telling what he might do to get away with what he's done. Get back to the truck and wait for me."

"I know exactly how dangerous he is, and there's no way I'm letting you chase after him in the forest alone." Ripping her arm free of his touch, she faced off with him with every ounce of determination she owned.

"I have a gun." Did he really have to explain this? "I'm trained to pursue and confront a suspect, who, might I add, is getting farther away while I explain how bad an idea it is for you to be here."

She puffed her chest, hands on her hips as she surveyed their surroundings. It would be cute if he wasn't close to losing himself in all the ways having her here could go wrong. "I have… Okay. I have nothing, but I'm still not letting you do this alone. I radioed into headquarters. Backup is on the way, but it's going to be at least an hour before they can get here. You promised to protect me. That includes making sure you come back alive, Murray Simpson. So I'm not going to sit in that truck and worry about something happening to you. I'm your backup until your rangers can get here."

A growl resonated through his chest. There was no winning when she used that damn promise against him, and they were losing precious seconds arguing. The more time he wasted trying to get her to turn back, the more danger that family would be in. "Fine." Murray crouched, pulling his backup weapon from the ankle holster beneath his jeans and handed it to her. "Don't accidentally shoot me in the back."

"If I shoot you, it won't be an accident." Aslen went through the routine he'd had her develop since that first time he'd taken her to the gun range. She dropped the magazine free and mentally counted the bullets inside before clearing the chamber and shoving the magazine back into place. Then loaded it again. "It's just a matter of making it look like one, and believe me, I've read enough about making it realistic."

He tried not to smile at that. And failed. Hell, he loved her back talk.

Footsteps registered about two hundred yards off to his right. From what he'd noted in the few seconds he'd eyed the suspect, the arsonist wouldn't get far in those heavy hiking boots at a run. It was only a matter of staying on his trail and catching up. "Anything happens, you get behind me. Use me as a shield. Understand?"

Aslen nodded, her eyes set in the direction from where the shuffling had come. Color drained from her face. She didn't like that plan. "Yes."

"Promise me, Aslen." He wouldn't budge on this. He'd barely survived losing his parent, then his brother to this damn park. He wouldn't survive losing the last person on this earth he'd given a sliver of himself to. "You don't put yourself in unnecessary danger. You don't risk your life to save mine. Something happens to me, you run for the truck, and you get the hell out and wait for my team. Are we clear?"

"Yes." Her voice had a bit more strength behind it that time.

"Stay close." Scanning the disturbed pine needles at their feet, Murray started jogging to stick with the trail the arsonist had carelessly left behind. He wasn't a tracker, but it didn't take a hunter to figure out where their suspect was headed. "He's going for the reservoir."

"Murray, the evacuation order was revoked, and today is supposed to reach around 105 degrees." Her breaths came short and fast in keeping up with him, but Aslen moved exactly as he'd taught her. Weapon framed in both hands, pointed down. Moving fast but staying low and alert. Ready for anything. How had he thought for one moment she wouldn't be able to take care of herself? He'd trained her to rely on her skills over anyone else. To trust herself. Maybe the real problem was him. That, after everything she'd been through and the losses they sustained, he wanted her to need him. "There will be hikers there."

Murray picked up the pace. He couldn't let the arsonist get anywhere near innocent bystanders. Damn it. It would be an hour before the other rangers made it this far out. They didn't have that kind of time. Aslen seemed to understand the urgency, keeping pace with him.

Sunlight pierced through the canopy overhead and exposed a clearing a hundred yards in front of them. Throwing his arm out, Murray stopped her from charging into it without hesitation, forcing them to pull back. It was the perfect ambush point, one he wasn't willing to let Aslen walk into. "Get behind me."

She did as he instructed. "Where did he go?"

"I don't know." But Murray had to consider every possibility. If a man was willing to start two fires to inflict as much damage and manipulate anyone involved in the blaze as possible, he wouldn't have escaped without a plan. Or a way to defend himself. "Keep your eyes open."

He took a step. Then another. His weight gave away their position, and Murray swallowed back the urge to glue Aslen to his side every step of the way. Raising his arm, he silently ordered her to peel off to the right, behind one of the thicker trees a few yards away. To add some distance between them. He was the greatest threat to the arsonist's escape. Hopefully, it was enough to draw the bastard's focus and leave Aslen out of it.

Unless… No. Murray couldn't think about her becoming a game piece in the son of a bitch's plan to slip arrest. He ordered her to stay with a flat palm as she took up position behind the tree he'd indicated. And stepped into the clearing.

Insect drones quieted. Bird calls silenced. As though a predator lurked nearby. Murray scanned what he could of the clearing, trees swaying on an invisible current and throwing off his senses. He caught a brief whiff of something chemical and biting, and every cell in his body honed on the odor.

Gasoline.

Understanding hit. The wind shifted, and he sensed Aslen had pulled up short behind him.

Murray turned back the way he'd come. He met her wide gaze as he confirmed she'd caught the scent of an accelerant and lunged with one hand out to reach her. "Aslen—"

In the blink of an eye, the clearing burst into flames.

A wall of fire climbed between him and Aslen until he lost sight of her completely. Heat seared the exposed skin along his face and neck, nothing more than his cotton uniform protecting the rest of him from the blaze.

"Murray!" Her scream raised the hairs on the back of his neck, and his mind instantly went to the worst-case scenario. Just as it had the thousand times he'd imagined what'd happened to his brother in his final moments. That scream would stay with him until the day he died. If he made it out of this alive.

"Get back to the truck!" Dead leaves and pine needles fed into the flames, just as the arsonist had planned. Within seconds, the clearing ringed with fire, caging him in the shrinking center. Murray covered his face in the crook of his elbow to keep his lungs clear of smoke, but it was no use. The debris burned fast. Black smoke closed in on him faster. Murray waved his free hand at her, unsure if she could even see him. "Go!"

"I'm not leaving you!" A tendril of flame parted enough to give him a clear view of where she stood on the other side, locked out of the clearing. Of getting to him. She'd dumped her gear back at her house. There was no breaking through without it. Silver glinted in her eyes as she stared on helplessly. No amount of books and research articles were going to help them out of this. She had a chance to escape. She needed to take it.

Damn it. She'd promised. She'd promised to leave him if anything happened. The fire seemed to roar as it ate up the debris at his feet. Temperatures climbed, beading sweat along his throat and in his hairline. The clearing was closing in on him. The fire was spreading up the trunks of the trees around him, closing off any potential of escape. There was nothing they could do. No way for him to outrun this.

"Get out of here!" Smoke caught in his airway. Burned. He gasped for breath, the sound blocking out any response Aslen might've had. Coughing up what felt like his lungs, he forced one foot in front of the other. To put space between them. She didn't need to see him die. He wouldn't let her last memories of him tarnish her love for her job. Murray tried to suck in clean air, but there was nowhere in the tightening circle for him to go.

This was it.

This was how he'd lose her forever. Not through any deal he'd made to let her go or by suffocating her with his overprotectiveness, but by his own stupidity in assuming the arsonist hadn't taken the time to set a trap for anyone who might pursue him on foot. The bastard had rigged this clearing to catch fire before Murray and Aslen had showed up at the campground. He'd been waiting. For them.

And now Aslen would pay the price he'd tried to protect her from for the past twenty years.

His energy seemed to bleed from every pore as the heat intensified and the smoke worked its way into his lungs, stealing precious oxygen. Pain spiked through his knees as he hit the ground. "Aslen…"

Just as an explosion rocked through the park.

Chapter Thirteen

The blast reverberated through the trees, shoving Aslen onto all fours.

Debris and rock pierced the soft tissues of her palms. Blood drained from her face and neck, holding her hostage in place. Her instincts honed in on the direction the explosion had come from as the fire in front of her climbed higher, walling her off from the man stuck on the other side. The campground. Her heart rate kicked into double time. The arsonist… He must've rigged his RV to explode as a fail-safe. Black smoke shot into the sky through the tree line, and it took everything Aslen had not to collapse completely. "No."

Rebecca and her family… They could've gotten caught in the aftermath. Every cell in her body screamed for her to move—to do something—as her body temperature skyrocketed. The accelerant the arsonist had used added to the fire's heat. Cooking her blood in her veins. Backup was already on the way, but would they reach the campground in time? Would there be anyone left to save?

"Aslen, get out of here!" Murray's voice choked off in a coughing fit.

One objective. That was all she could focus on. Save Murray or help that family. Her stomach rolled for fear of failing them both, but her gut supplied the deep-rooted answer she'd never be able to live with if she made the wrong choice. Murray. She couldn't lose the one thread tying her to this life, the one who'd kept her going despite the rejections, the loneliness and hurt. He was trapped. Losing oxygen as the fire closed in around him. She caught a glimpse of him through the flames, his hand protecting his face as much as possible. But it wouldn't be enough.

"Aslen!"

The walls were on fire. Too hot. Gravity clawed against her stomach and chest. The fire licked at the edges of her bed frame. It was so close, but terror had frozen her in place. Kept her from shouting out as her dad stormed into her bedroom. That same terror contorted his face as he circled her room, going for her closet first then ripping back her sheets on her bed. He was looking for her.

But she couldn't tell him she was here. Under the bed. She couldn't tell him what she'd done. He'd be so mad at her. He'd stop loving her.

Her mom had told her matches were dangerous, but Aslen was so careful. She'd blown them out before the flame had gotten all the way down to her fingers, but the last one had burned faster than she'd expected. The fire had bit at her fingers, and she'd dropped the match on the carpet. Right over the nail polish stain she'd tried to hide from a few weeks ago. The entire carpet had gone up in flames in an instant. So fast. She'd tried to stop it with her pillow, but that'd only made it worse. Within seconds, her entire room had caught fire, and there was nowhere for her to go.

"Aslen, where are you!" Her dad dropped her bedding in the middle of the floor. "Aslen!"

Her whimper was lost to the crackle of flames as Daddy raced from the room. No. He couldn't just leave her here.

Sobs tightened her chest and throat. The tears dried almost instantly when met with the suffocating heat trapped beneath the bed frame and mattress with her.

She dug her fingers into Felicia's soft body, her red-headed Cabbage Patch Kid's face too pliable against her cheek. The fire was getting closer, nipping at her bare feet pressed against the back wall. A sob broke free. "Daddy."

She couldn't breathe. Aslen tossed Felicia from under the bed, her nails biting into the untouched section of carpet ahead of her to crawl out of her hiding spot. "Come back!"

He didn't have to love her. He could hate her forever as long as he didn't leave her here alone. Crackles and pops sounded from her right. The single window in her room shattered into a million pieces, and she ducked her face between her arms. Her scream barely reached over the roar of fire pillowing along the ceiling. Black smoke raced toward the broken window. "Daddy, I'm sorry! I'm sorry! Please don't leave me."

She shoved her princess comforter out of her way, sacrificing it to the flames charging along the wall. Tears blinded her as she grabbed for Felicia's soft arm and lunged for the bedroom door. Flames licked out from the doorframe and bit her arm. Her scream was short-lived as the pain flared faster and spread to her shoulder.

Her shirt was on fire.

The whole house was on fire.

And Daddy was gone.

She lost her hold on Felicia as she slapped at the sleeve of her shirt, but it was no use. Her shoulder bumped into the opposite wall, and she fell to the floor. Her hair caught, curling in on itself in black threads. The smell curdled her stomach and burned her nostrils. Someone was screaming, and it took a few seconds to realize it was her.

"Aslen!" Her dad lunged from his bedroom into the hall-way. His hands were all over her, shoving her down onto the floor and forcing her body to roll back and forth until the fire was gone. "I've got you. I've got you."

But the pain stayed. More than getting shots at the doctor's office or breaking her wrist last summer trying to skateboard for the first time like that boy down the street.

Daddy scooped her up into his arms, and suddenly they were moving. But the flames were everywhere. Following them. "It's going to be okay." Her body bounced in his arms as they jogged down the stairs, and she believed him.

Right until the world ripped out from underneath them.

"Aslen, go!" Murray backed away from the wall of flames spreading and bearing down on them both, and Aslen couldn't help but add a few feet of distance between her and a very painful death.

The flames had stripped the needles off the trees ahead of her. Climbing higher and cutting her off from Murray. She hadn't been able to save her father that day their house had burned to the ground, not knowing that her mother had already suffocated from the smoke. But she was going to save Murray.

Training pulled her from the past and slapped her into action. She'd dropped her gear back at her house, but the lack wouldn't stop her from managing this fire as she had every other she'd faced. Scanning the downed trees, dead leaves and boulders around them, she mentally discarded all of it. Whatever accelerant the arsonist had used would ensure the fire burned beyond natural timing and temperatures. She had to create a barrier between Murray and the fire. Something strong enough to withstand those temperatures for just a few seconds. The boulder to her right. It was large enough to add a break in the fire wall closing in on him. It could work.

Aslen darted for a felled branch of dead leaves nearly as wide and tall as she was. The bark had so far been left untouched despite the proximity to the fire, and didn't smell of accelerant. It would work. It had to work. Dragging the tree carcass toward the ring of fire she laid it perpendicular to the boulder. The leaves caught immediately. She might not be able to contain the fire, but she could manipulate it into going where she needed it to. "Murray! The boulder!"

His frame shadowed through the flames as he followed her voice. Arms protecting his face, he seemed to read her thoughts. "It won't work! The fire. It's blocking me from the rock!"

Acid charged up her throat. The past threatened to consume her as he backed off from wall of flames. No. This wasn't the end. He couldn't give up yet. Her eyes burned with tears and smoke. "You have to try! Please!"

She couldn't lose him. He could ignore her for the rest of her life. He could hate her for leaving. He could never love her the way she'd wanted since she was thirteen years old. He just had to live to do it. He had to fight.

Murray seemed to still behind that wall that gave her mere glimpses of his handsome face, the crack and pop of the fire consuming the debris along the forest floor louder than the buzz in her head. "You have to leave, Aslen."

"Don't you dare." The warped scars of melted skin running up her right bicep and over her shoulder seemed to burn all over again with remembered pain. The muscles in her jaw ached under pressure as tears burned her nose and eyes. "Don't you dare leave me here alone. You promised to protect me. So fight!"

His outline was lost as the fire surged another foot in her

direction. Panic clawed up her throat. She was running out of time, and they'd already lost the one resource they had to get him out. Wait. No. The reservoir. They were close enough—within a quarter mile. Aslen stripped free of her jacket and T-shirt, clenching them both in her fist, leaving her in her sports bra. If she could soak her clothing enough, she might be able to use it as a defense against the smoke and flames over their exposed skin. "You better be alive when I get back."

"Aslen, no!" Murray's voice bellowed over the roar of the fire. "You don't know if he's still out there."

She ignored the pained plea in his voice and raced north, toward the reservoir. The chances of coming back with enough water in her clothing to help were slim at best, but it was worth the risk. Her life was worth the risk, no matter how many times he tried to tell her otherwise.

Her lungs ached with effort as she dodged a labyrinth of downed trees, sandpits and sharp rocks working to throw her off. The muscles in the backs of her thighs protested every step, but she wouldn't stop. Not until she'd done everything she could. Murray had saved her life. Not just physically. Mentally, emotionally. He'd given her a home, a family. A second chance when no one else would. He'd always sacrificed everything to keep his promise to her. This was how she repaid him.

Branches scraped at her exposed skin and drew blood, but Aslen only pushed herself harder. Firefighters were required to run three miles through woods just like this, weighed down with fifty pounds of gear. She could sprint the quarter mile to the reservoir and back without breaking a sweat.

Sunlight brightened ahead, and she glimpsed the shore and the surface of the reservoir. Azure blue and untouched by the fire set this morning. She could see it. Feel the cool breeze coming off the top countering the summer heat for the dozen families enjoying their vacation. She was almost there. She could reach out and touch it. Taste the fresh water from the edge of the tree line.

Pain seared across her scalp. Aslen wrenched backward, her feet coming out from underneath her. Her jacket and shirt fell from her hand as she reached back to ease the tension pulling her hair into a fist. Agony reverberated up through her knees as she landed on a jagged rock trying to escape the floor of red sand. Her scream was cut short by a hand over her mouth.

"Now where do you think you're going?" A low voice pressed close to her ear. "I wouldn't want you to miss all the fun."

Chapter Fourteen

He was going to kill her.

Murray didn't know how or when, but the second she came back from whatever harebrained scheme to get him out of this mess, he was going to let her have it. He knew Aslen. He knew the guilt she carried from the fire that'd cost her parents' lives. He knew the truth—that she'd been the one to start it by playing with matches under her bed. And he knew how far she would go to make up for that mistake. Even if it meant putting her precious life in danger. "Aslen!"

Damn it. Sweat cascaded down his face and into his eyes. Murray swiped at it, but it was no use. Salt slicked his skin, the deposits overheating, crusting his hair and face. His body couldn't stave off this heat forever, but the fire wouldn't relent. It'd gained another few feet, corralling him into a circle no more than five feet in every direction. And closing fast. She was out there. Fighting for him when it should've been the other way around. How could he have let this happen? What the hell had he been thinking in dragging her into this investigation?

He should've known better. She'd had no intention of keeping that promise to leave him behind from the start, but if he lost her… That tightness that'd nearly strangled him at her small dining room table after negotiating her deal returned ten times stronger. It curdled the acid in his gut and shoved deep into the recesses of his nerves. Grief hit hard and fast. There was no stopping it. No shutting it down as he had so many times in the past. When he'd lost his mom, his dad. Jackson. He hadn't let himself feel any of it for Aslen's sake. He was all she had left, and he'd done whatever it took to be there for her. Only to die at the hands of the very element that'd ripped her life apart.

Murray tried to breathe through the physical ache threatening to crush him from the inside. The tips of his fingers burrowed into calloused palms. She'd disappeared right in front of his eyes, put herself at risk to save him because that was what she did for the people she cared about, and that anxiety he had whenever he lost sight of her surged. Choked him.

It was the not knowing. Of where she'd gone, if she was safe. After everything they'd been through together since middle school, Aslen had become part of him. A vital organ he couldn't live without. He needed her in his sights, craved her presence as much—if not more—than those pointless facts she used to distract herself.

She'd stripped free of her jacket and T-shirt and run in the direction of the reservoir. While fire management wasn't his area of expertise, he had to trust she knew exactly what she was doing. That they would get out of this. Because the other option was losing her, and Murray wouldn't accept that. Ever. Focus on what he could control. That was what Aslen had taught him when news of Jackson's disappearance had arrived, when she'd crawled beneath his covers that night and held him as if he would break apart into a million pieces if she didn't. He growled to himself. "Control. What can you control, damn it?"

Had she made it? Was she already on her way back?

The thoughts seemed to attack from every direction, but he couldn't give them any energy right now. Couldn't waste what little he had left. Survival. That was all he could focus on. Murray spun in a circle, searching for that weak spot in the wall closing in on him with every breath. Pops and crackles sparked dangerously at his feet as debris caught fire, closer and closer. The arsonist could still be out there. Could have gone after Aslen. Stopped her from coming back for him.

His blood burning in his veins, Murray ripped off his own jacket to stop himself from cooking to death in his clothing. In his rush to search for the arsonist, he hadn't brought any water out here with them. Right. So what could he use?

The low hanging branches of the trees circling the clearing wouldn't do him a damn bit of good. They were already lost to the flames, but the thicker ones, the older ones that had maybe dried out over the years and might not hold his weight, were his best bet. His heart thundered hard in his chest. He put any remaining energy he had into following the uneven rhythm to hone his focus to the here and now. Not into the idea that he was about to become a rotisserie chicken. The now-blackened boulder Aslen had tried to convince him would hold against the encroaching flames provided a break in the deadly wall heading straight for him.

He'd only have one shot at this. One chance to escape. With Aslen out there, alone, potentially in danger, he would take it. For her. He'd done everything he could to uphold his promise to protect her all these years, but maybe he needed to admit to himself there was a part of him that wanted more than what they had now. Was scared of watching her walk away, finding happiness somewhere else. With someone else. Maybe the thought of losing her hit so much harder than losing his family because he didn't just want to protect her anymore. He wanted her.

More than he wanted anyone and anything else.

Not as his investigative consultant.

Not as his friend.

As just…his.

A different kind of fire took hold inside of him then, and he shoved his arms back into his jacket for extra protection. A breeze cut through the clearing, riling the fire past a frenzy. The flames licking at the boulder parted for a brief second, and Murray charged for it and the branch hanging directly above without another thought. His heart rate climbed with every stride. He slammed one boot against the boulder face and thrust himself upward. Except the angle of the rock was much steeper than he'd expected. His balance was thrown off, but he managed to secure his hands around the curve of the tree branch overhead. He dangled over the boulder, losing his momentum. Hands made of flame stretched and reached for the bottoms of his boots and cuffs of his jeans. He was losing his grip as bark peeled free of the tree beneath his fingers.

Seconds. He had only seconds before it'd fail altogether.

Wood cracked and groaned under his weight. Throwing his feet behind him, he tried to gain back the momentum he'd lost, only to rip the branch clean from the tree. Wood rained down as Murray flung his hands for the top of the boulder and curled his fingers into unforgiving stone.

The *hiss* of searing skin reached his ears a split second before the pain registered. It radiated through his fingers and across his palms. His scream filled the woods around him, but he couldn't stop. He couldn't back down. Throwing himself over the top of the boulder, Murray lost all sense of logic as the world spun. He slammed into the ground, his shoulder nearly buckling beneath his weight. His chest evacuated every molecule of oxygen, lungs pulsing for the sweet release from paralysis.

Move. He had to move. Now.

Smoke-laden air charged down his throat within a few seconds. The fire wouldn't give him a reprieve and neither would the arsonist if given the chance to escape arrest. Knowing he only had moments to escape certain death, Murray planted blistered and warped palms onto the forest floor, barely holding in a second scream as the pain flared. Rolling onto his side, he thrust himself to his feet and added a good twenty feet of space between him and the spreading wildfire. Infection would set in quickly if he didn't get the burns treated soon. The first aid kit in the truck came stocked with burn ointment and bandages. He carried a fire extinguisher, too, but that invisible thread in his chest that connected him to Aslen pulled taut. Struggling to catch a clean breath, Murray took one step in the direction he'd watched her disappear. He tucked his injured palms to his chest, careful not to aggravate the red skin peeling up in curls. It wouldn't take much to cause permanent damage, and he couldn't afford to slow himself down. Not when it came to Aslen's safety.

"Aslen!" Her name escaped as little more than a croak.

No answer.

It felt wrong to turn his back on the raging flames, to leave the fire for the incoming rangers to deal with, but time hadn't been on their side since he and Aslen had stepped into the Lava Point campground.

Hell. The campground. The explosion. He could make out the tendrils of black smoke over the tops of the still-standing trees from here. The arsonist must've set something in his RV to explode in case rangers had closed in, endangering all those people—the children—who'd returned to the campground after the evacuation order had been lifted. He had to help them, to make sure no one else was hurt. And seeing as how he was the only ranger on the scene with backup more than thirty minutes out at this point, Murray had to ignore that pull toward the reservoir. Had to leave Aslen.

Every cell in his body screamed to turn back as he stumbled toward the campground. Soon his legs remembered how to hold him up, the pain in his shoulder lightened and his head cleared. Faster. He had to move faster. The smoke thickened, seeping into the surrounding trees. Then he saw the flames.

The RV he'd noted when they'd first arrived at the campground was gone. Only twisted metal and glass remained, jagged and threatening. Four tires had somehow survived, which told him the arsonist had angled the blast to shoot out and upward to cause as much damage as possible. Shouts reached his ears as campers rushed to fill anything they could with water from the communal bathroom and water pump to help, but putting anyone else in danger wasn't an option. Murray swatted one arm out to catch their attention as he charged past the perimeter of the campground. He couldn't risk this fire spreading. Not as another burned a mere quarter mile into the woods, heading this way with the winds. "Get back!"

He ran for the truck and tucked blistered fingers under the passenger door handle. A hiss escaped up his throat as the pain surged, but he couldn't let it stop him from doing his job. He ripped the fire extinguisher out from underneath the passenger seat and raced to get the RV fire under control. In minutes, he'd managed to hit the valve with his damaged fingers and release the suppressing foam, suffocating the flames into something more manageable. It'd take more than one fire extinguisher to put out a fire this size, especially fed by an accelerant, but Murray would control it until his backup arrived. "Is anybody hurt?"

Low murmurs from other campgoers confirmed no one had been caught in the explosion. A miracle.

The van he and Aslen had approached earlier, belonging to the family who'd been targeted by the arsonist, was gone, the campsite empty. They'd gotten away before the explosion. Something in his chest released at the realization. Except every second he fought this fire, another raged. And left Aslen unprotected in those woods. He mentally catalogued the families looking on in horror, mothers holding their children to their sides, fathers racing to continue to help throw water on the flames. Murray didn't have the energy to tell them water wouldn't do a damn bit of good against a fire fed by gasoline or some other compound.

Sirens echoed up the single-lane dirt road just before three ranger SUVs shot into the campground, and Murray peeled his burned hands from the fire extinguisher. Rangers spilled free of the vehicles with their own supplies as a fire truck rolled up on their tail. Handing off his now-empty fire extinguisher, he targeted the woman climbing down the fire truck's raised platform with several other teammates. Danny. Aslen's friend. Hoses were in hand, orders shouted as the team raced to meet the latest threat. "You're in charge of the scene. There's another fire about a quarter mile past the tree line and spreading fast in this wind. I have to go."

"What? Where?" She scanned the campground, her face losing color. "Where is Aslen?"

Murray forced one foot in front of the other. Allowing himself to be consumed by the wilderness all over again. "That's what I'm going to find out."

Chapter Fifteen

Well, that didn't feel right.

Aslen's chest burned as if she'd inhaled a lungful of pure fire. Something hard pressed between her shoulder blades then dragged up toward her neck. Her legs felt as though she'd run three miles with fifty pounds of gear straight uphill, tingling in her toes and down her calves. Pain flared along her right side, and she tried to force herself to sit up.

A piercing brightness singed her corneas, and she twisted her head to relieve the onslaught, like those times Murray had barged into her room and opened her blackout curtains without warning before school most days. No matter how many times she'd begged for five—even ten—more minutes, he'd never let her go back to sleep, insisting she get up and get dressed so she wouldn't be late for her college classes.

But some part of her brain recognized that this wasn't one of those mornings. That Murray wasn't the one holding onto her ankles. That the pain along her back and scalp wasn't where he'd accidentally landed on her trying to get her up for the day. Aslen raised her hand in front of her face to dim some of that bright sunlight. The jerking sensation triggered a rush of acid and nausea. Oh, hell. She was going to lose the calories Murray had practically forced down her throat earlier that day. "Stop that."

"Look who's awake." Despite her hand blocking the sun's assault, her brain refused to note a single feature of the man's face. Tall. She could tell that much. Not as built as Murray, but close. Enough to intimidate a five-foot-three firefighter. But that voice... Something about it tugged at her soggy memory. "Don't worry. We're almost there."

"Almost where?" Bile pulsed into her mouth as another tug shot her stomach upward. It took everything she had to swallow it back down, which only intensified the headache thudding along to her heart rate. Another line of pain struck along her spine, and she heaved her back off whatever was pressing between her shoulder blades. "Where's Murray?"

Panic squeezed around her heart as the last dregs of unconsciousness bled away. She'd almost made it to the shore when... When something had hit her from behind. No. They were going the wrong way. He was pulling her toward the reservoir, but Murray needed her. He was still caught in the fire. She had to get him out. Adrenaline spiked in her blood, and she tried twisting out of the man's grip. "Take me back. I have to go back."

Strong hands locked down on her ankles, punishing. Enough to leave marks. Rough wood dropped out from underneath her backside, and her lower back hit the edge of a stair. "You can't save him."

Dragging. He was dragging her down a dock, loose sand and boards skinning her upper body raw. The realization sent another surge of pain down her back. Her whimper at the impact failed to get his attention, and Aslen fought harder. She'd planned to soak her jacket and T-shirt in reservoir water in hopes of giving Murray something to soak his clothing and stave off the chance of burns. At the very least keep the smoke from slowly suffocating him, but he was still out there—struggling for his life—while this stranger dragged her farther away from the man she needed to save. Her fingernails caught on the dried, swollen wood and ripped free. She tugged at her feet, trying to dislodge his hold, but exhaustion from this morning's fire and the hit to the head had done more damage than she'd estimated.

How *had* she hit her head? She couldn't remember. It didn't matter. Aslen managed to turn onto her stomach and clawed for the stairs. "I have to try. Please. Let me go. I can't leave him."

"You're not going anywhere, Ranger Woods." He jerked her entire body to the edge of the dock.

She hit the wood harder than expected and lost the last remnants of air in her lungs. A slip of shade provided by the rocking boat swaying a few feet away offered a sliver of relief, and for a brief moment, Aslen wanted nothing more than to fall back into unconsciousness as her body temperature ate up the coolness coming off Blue Springs Reservoir.

Her head protested every move against the rotting wood, but a warning rang loud and clear. How did he know her name?

Oh. The tag pinned to her uniform. Except…she wasn't wearing her uniform shirt, and she'd left her ID in Murray's truck. Her tongue felt two sizes too big for her mouth. What was happening to her? Why couldn't she focus? Fight back? Run? "How do you… How do you know my name?"

"Did you really think I would go through all this trouble and not get what I came for?" His knees popped as he crouched beside her, unwinding the rope holding the mid-size boat to the dock. Blond hair cut across deep forehead lines. Four of them to be exact, with little branches striking out on their own toward his temples. Natural, with some darker lowlights. Kind of like Danny's, if Aslen didn't know her best friend relied on her hairdresser every six weeks. A neat beard cut close to his mouth while a hardness she wasn't sure she'd ever encountered entered those glacial-blue eyes. The blue plaid of his shirt only added to the washed-out emotional shield locked across his expression. Callused hands collected her wrists, grabbing for the section of rope he'd unbound from the boat. "From what I hear, you've been sticking your nose where it doesn't belong. Telling your law enforcement division all about me. I was warned you might come sniffing around the campground, so I put a couple safety measures in place. One of which is keeping your partner busy as we speak. The other should keep whatever backup you called for busy for a while."

The RV. The explosion. Those families would've been in the blast radius. The other campground visitors wouldn't have stood a chance. Had they gotten clear? How many more people had been killed for one man's escape?

"Why are you doing this? Why kill that woman?" Emotion clogged her throat. Was this… Was this what Murray had to deal with on a daily basis as a police officer in Salt Lake City? Was this why it'd been so easy for him to leave that life behind and follow her to Zion? How? How did he make it through a single day without the nightmares of his work haunting him every time he closed his eyes? Aslen pulled at her wrists, but her captor had already tightened the strands to the point numbness pricked at her fingertips. It was him. The man they'd been looking for, the arsonist who'd started the fire that'd literally blown up in her face. The unconscious haze was clearing. Slower than she needed, but her survival instincts finally kicked into place.

"Let's just say I learned who she really was." A breath eased out of him as if he hadn't spent the past few minutes dragging her across the park. "You know, we really need to be better at taking people at face value. We give them chance after chance with their apologies and promises to change, and yet they still find the best ways to hurt those closest to them, but I couldn't stand by and watch her get hurt anymore."

Her? He moved to secure her ankles, and understanding hit as hard as whatever she'd taken to the back of the head.

"Wait. No." Aslen tried to pull her wrists apart, to add some kind of give to the rope grating through the first layer of skin, but the fibers refused to budge. She kicked her feet, but he was so much stronger than her. Holding her without a mere hint of effort. He dodged her attack, letting loose a warning growl, before planting her calves against the dock. Hard. "Please, you don't have to do this."

"That's where you're wrong, and as much as I wish you hadn't been dragged into this, I can't have you coming after us when this is finished. Problem is, I can't just toss you in the fire like I did with dear old Mom this morning. Otherwise, your law enforcement friend might start connecting the pieces before we have a chance to get the hell out of this place." He stood to his full height then, a god of violence among mere mortals trying to keep everyone and everything in this park safe. "So, I'm going to leave you in the middle of the lake. Should give me enough of a head start to help her disappear while they try to find you, don't you think?"

Blood drained from her face and neck as the world tipped on its axis. He'd lifted her as though she weighed nothing and hauled her legs over the lip of the boat.

No. No, no, no, no. She wasn't going to die like this. Her heel connected with the boat's windshield as she scrambled to free herself from his hold.

It wasn't enough. She wasn't enough. Her abductor manhandled her onto the narrow slip of space between the galley and driver's seat, the rough texture of the nonslip coating along the boat's floor biting into her bare skin as effectively as a cheese grater.

"Help!" Her plea went unanswered as she tried to stand. Where were the other boat owners? Where were the smiling families seeking relief from the summer heat? Where was Murray? Smoke tendriled higher where the fire burned the hottest over the few trees she spotted from her prone position. He was in there. Battling to survive, and she'd just left him in a pointless attempt to pay back everything he'd done for her. But the truth was, she couldn't ever pay him back.

The boat's engine rumbled through her frame, and the first jerk set them into motion across the reservoir.

Her heart shattered at the thought of what she'd said to him this morning. How she'd negotiated to leave him behind. But the truth was, she needed him. More than her next breath. She needed him to keep showing up, to keep scowling at her, to keep protecting her.

The roar of the boat's engine failed to drown out the screaming in her head. The bow arched up out of the water as her abductor increased their speed, the cool wind doing nothing to calm her racing nerves. She was going to die out here. Never getting the chance to tell Murray how she truly felt.

Aslen pressed her heels into the floor, angling her head up over her shoulder in search of something—anything—she might use as a weapon, but the boat had been cleared of fishing gear and tools. Probably stored in the seats ringing the back of the boat. Fear welled up inside her chest, threatened to overwhelm her.

No. She thought of everything Murray had taught her, had tried to drill into her over the years. About protecting herself for those times he wasn't there for her. She would fight. Until her final breath. Keeping her eyes on the driver, she inched back toward those seats.

The boat jerked to a stop, rocking her forward, and she lost every inch of distance. The engine died. Then those callused hands she hated so much were on her again, hauling her upright, maneuvering her to the back of the boat. "I really wish it didn't have to be this way, Ranger Woods, but I'll do whatever it takes to protect my family."

The water blurred in her vision as the arsonist threw her overboard.

Chapter Sixteen

Her scream pulverized through the last of his adrenaline. Leaving him defeated and outright terrified.

Murray's legs ached with every step as he raced down the small dock shooting into the reservoir. His lungs threatened to burst as he gulped down humidity-laden bouts of air. The midsize boat peeling away from the aged wood shot spurs of water behind it.

He was too late. She was gone. The arsonist had taken her.

Sweat dripped into his eyes, siphoning off the last of his energy reserves. His pulse thudded hard and added to the headache splitting his head in two. *Think.* He had to think. The evacuation order that'd gone out an hour ago thanks to his call for backup had cleared innocent bystanders from around the reservoir. But they hadn't taken their boats.

Murray lunged for the nearest boat. Every second of searching for a forgotten engine key would cost him. The first boat didn't produce anything but a couple spools of fishing line and a cooler of beers despite the park's guidelines against alcohol. He dropped into the second boat, his blood pumping too hard for his heart to keep up with.

Nothing.

Damn it. He was running out of time. He couldn't think

about any of the reasons Aslen might have been taken. Fire management had already contained the aftermath of the RV explosion and were working to douse the wildfire in the woods at his back. But Aslen was out there, alone, fighting for her life against a threat neither of them understood. He'd promised to protect her, and he was on the verge of failing her as equally as he'd failed his family.

And Aslen… She was getting farther out of reach. That invisible thread that'd tied them together since the first time he'd set eyes on her was close to breaking. He wouldn't survive it. Losing her. It would be like ripping his heart straight from his chest with no hopes of recovery. The mere thought threatened to send him into a spiral he'd never surface from.

Murray dropped into an undersized fishing boat that looked as though it'd tip over with his weight, but the electric outboard didn't require a key. The muscles along his rib cage and deep into his shoulder socket shrieked from where he'd hit the forest floor escaping the fire as he quickly unwound the ropes holding the boat to the dock. He started the engine, angling the boat straight ahead, but with so little power, there was no chance of catching up to the powerful speedboat. "I'm coming, Aslen. Just hold on."

He could just make out the shape of the white outline ahead, two trails of water guiding him better than any radar on a clear day like this. The sun assaulted the back of his neck as he chased the speedboat north across the smooth surface of the reservoir. He could do this. He'd get her back. Because the alternative was too dark to deal with, a stain on his heart that would never wash out. Oily and thick and life-ending. Because if he didn't have Aslen, he would be left with nothing.

Without any potential of…them. And that was what maybe scared him the most. That he'd cut himself off from feeling anything more for her out of fear of losing the last bright light in his life, and only ended up hurting and depriving himself of something that could've made him happy. "Come on, Aslen. Keep fighting. Just a little while longer."

The twin shoots of water disappeared in the distance, and Murray found himself straightening to get a better view over the water. The speedboat had pulled to a stop more than a half mile ahead. He didn't dare let up on the small fishing boat's speed as his brain sped through all the possibilities of the arsonist's next move. This was Aslen's arena. As much as he'd hated the idea of dragging her into this investigation, he'd relied on her insights into the arsonist's motives to get them this far. Never once doubting herself or second-guessing their next move. That confidence was one of the few things that'd gotten him through the worst of his grief, her unwavering knowledge that no matter what happened, they would be there for each other.

Despite crossing several hundred more feet of calm blue water, Murray had no better understanding of why the boat ahead had stopped dead. Had Aslen somehow managed to fight back? That thread inside of him was still alive, pulsing for him to go faster, faster, faster. Alive. She was alive. He had to believe that, but even knowing she'd do whatever it took to survive didn't release the phantom pain in his chest that came from potentially losing her. "What the hell are you doing?"

Then he knew. Ice punctured through his veins, and Murray gripped the outboard steering handle with everything he had. The plastic screeched in protest as he tried pushing the motor beyond its capabilities. He wasn't going to make it in time—

A splash shot up from the port side of the speedboat. Then those two shoots of water were spraying out behind once again. Murray forced himself to keep his seat when every cell in his body screamed for him to get to her as fast as possible. The son of a bitch had thrown her overboard. Terror unlike anything he'd felt gripped him in a vise he couldn't escape. "No!"

His roar bellowed over the reservoir's surface, and he could've sworn the arsonist looked back to find the source. But his fishing boat couldn't go any faster. Seconds ticked off. Maybe a minute. The speedboat was getting even farther away from that spot where she'd gone under, the surface of the lake smoothing over once again. How long until he lost sight of where she'd gone under altogether? How long could she hold her breath? How much longer to reach her? He tried keeping his gaze centered on where he believed she'd disappeared beneath the surface, but the ripping wind and the burn of afternoon sun blurred his vision.

"Swim, damn it! Fight!" Why couldn't she break the surface? Had she been knocked unconscious? Was she drowning this very second? His mind tunneled deeper and deeper into panic with every gut-wrenching second the surface of the water remained unbroken. He was getting closer. He was almost there. She just had to hold on a bit longer. He'd get her out of this. Just like he'd gotten her out of everything else. A beating from Brittany Olsen behind a rusted, old dumpster. That reeking, alcohol-soaked foster home she'd lived in next door. Bouts of depression around her parents' death anniversaries. He'd been there for her for twenty years, taught her how to defend herself, to shoot a gun, to hold her own in any confrontation, helped her with her homework and taught her her first swear words. He'd witnessed her transforming from a shy, barely-there girl into the woman who could knock him on his ass with one look. She was a survivor, through and through. No matter how many times she'd fallen, she'd always gotten back up. She could hold out for anything. She just had to do it again. "Come on!"

The distance between his boat and that unbothered spot where he calculated she'd been thrown closed. Murray was up and out of his seat in a split second after cutting the outboard motor. He couldn't see past the first few inches of water, but he didn't care. Stripping off his boots and T-shirt, he tossed them to the bottom of the fishing boat and dove in.

Lukewarm water swallowed him whole, easing the pain in his blistered palms only a fraction before resurging with a vengeance. He stroked downward, putting everything he had—sore muscles, burned skin, unstable emotions—on hold as he dove deeper. Sunlight pierced through the surface but didn't light his way the deeper he swam.

No sign of her.

Nothing to suggest he'd gotten the location right, but that thread—the one he'd tried to cut too many times to count—kept pulling at his chest. Pressure built in his lungs, bubbles escaping his nose and tickling at his sensitive skin. The temperature of the water gave him a false sense of security. Not too cold, not too hot. But still dangerous enough to drown. He didn't know how deep he'd swam. Layers of disturbed sediment clouded the water in front of him along with sickly waves of plant life that reminded him of car-lot dancing tube men. One tangled around his foot, trying to pull him deeper. To keep him forever. But nothing would stop him from finding her.

Warning shot through his chest as the precious reserves of oxygen depleted with every stroke. The faster he swam, the faster he burned through his air supply. But he couldn't leave her down here. Couldn't let her die alone.

His eyes burned as he cut through a wall of disturbed sediment. Thicker here than anywhere else he'd seen. Aslen.

She had to be here. The water cleared for the briefest of seconds, and if he hadn't already been searching to his left, he might've missed her altogether.

There. A dark outline that had no business being here other than if it'd been dumped. He couldn't make her out completely, but his gut was already urging him to get to whatever had sunk this deep. Murray kicked as hard as he could, denying the pressure screaming in his chest. His jeans tangled between his ankles, but he only pushed himself harder. Draining the last minute of air. Water, dirt and other debris clouded his eyesight, but a single brush of his hand against the shape confirmed everything he'd feared.

Aslen.

Fisting one hand around what he thought was her silky-smooth upper arm, Murray tried to drag her toward him. Except she wouldn't budge. She was stuck. Darkness penetrated the edges of his vision as he tugged again. Still, her small frame refused to follow. She wasn't struggling, didn't even seem to know he was there, and a flood of true terror squeezed the last dregs of air from his chest.

He ran both hands down the length of her body, catching on the rope binding her wrists. She could've kept herself afloat with bound wrists, which meant the son of a bitch who'd abducted her hand most likely bound her ankles. Forcing himself deeper, he felt more than saw the rope tangled around what he assumed to be debris from a crashed boat that'd sunk in the reservoir. There was no current here, no way to use the motion to get her free as Murray pulled against the ropes at her feet with everything he had.

Grabbing for his jeans pocket, he drew the pocketknife Aslen had gifted him upon his entry into the police academy, and flipped the blade free. His forearms burned as he cut into the thick ropes, the water having made the strands swell almost double their size. Hold on, he wanted to tell her. He was here. He wasn't going to leave her. The rope broke under the blade, and Murray unwound it as quickly as possible.

He secured his hand around her arm again and yanked her upward. The darkness drew to a circle in his vision, a tunnel he could barely identify which way was up. The outline of that too-small boat came into view, but he didn't bother changing direction. She needed air. As soon as possible.

Murray broke through the surface first, gasping hard enough to make his lungs spasm, and dragged her up beside him. No response. Tipping her head back against his shoulder, he swam one-armed toward the boat swaying five feet from their location. "I've got you, Aslen. Don't give up. I'm here."

In less than a minute, he'd hauled her into the boat then followed after and pressed his mouth to hers. Pushing as much air into her lungs as she could afford, he fisted both hands over her sternum and started counting off compressions.

One. Two. Three. Four. He forced another round of air into her chest and started compressions all over again.

Water leaked from the corners of her mouth. Just before she coughed and took a lifesaving breath.

Chapter Seventeen

She was dead. Right?

That was the only explanation for how heavy her body felt. Pain speared down her throat at her attempt to swallow. Like her esophagus had undergone torture while she'd been unconscious.

Wait. Why was she unconscious? A puff of air shot up her nose, and Aslen grabbed for her face, coming into contact with some kind of tube. A groan escaped, aggravating the grated skin along her airway. That wasn't normal, was it?

"You're awake." Footsteps shuffled closer. Warm skin connected with her hand as someone held onto her. Hints of clean soap and the perfume she caught in the face almost every day clamored for her attention. "You scared the crap out of me, As. You've been out of it for two days."

Two days? No. This wasn't heaven. This was definitely hell, but at least she knew that voice. And there was that incessant beeping telling everyone in a five-mile radius she was still alive. Ugh. She'd always hated that sound. Hated that her machine kept going while her parents' had been unplugged before she'd woken after the fire that'd taken them from her.

Aslen forced the lethargy clinging to her eyes—okay, her entire body—back to get a look at her best friend. Danny lowered her face level with hers, scratchy white sheets washing out whatever color her friend might've earned this summer in the park. Usually perfect hair clustered in greasy strands as if Danny hadn't washed it in days, which couldn't be right. The lines around her best friend's eyes seemed deeper than the last time they'd been together, too. When was that? Where was she?

"You look like crap." Aslen tried to sit up, but her body had other ideas. While the IV in her arm told her some kind of painkiller was mixed in with fluids, a bone-deep ache refused to die. Nope. Not happening. Sinking back down into the pillows stacked at her back, she stared up at the ceiling to get her breath back. Oh, hell. Why did it feel like an elephant had sat on her chest?

"Speak for yourself." Danny squeezed her hand. Bits of hot-pink polish were chipped at the ends. "You're still just as pale as when Murray pulled you out of that damn reservoir."

Murray. The reservoir. He'd…saved her? She attempted another swallow to ease the dryness in her throat but only found more parched flesh. Dang. She was thirsty. And hungry. And tired. And confused. "Where is he?"

Danny flashed a splinter of a smile. Nothing compared to the usual full display that'd gotten Aslen through the worst nights when she'd learned Murray had gone home with another ranger or found someone else to warm his bed. Or pissed her off in general. Her heart hiccupped at the realization that he wasn't here. He'd pulled her out of that reservoir—saved her life—but he couldn't be here when she woke up? "One of the doctors wanted to check his hands for infection. The burns… They're pretty severe. He's been here since you got to the hospital, but I told him he couldn't take care of you unless he took care of himself first. Guess I convinced him."

"What burns?" How was he still alive? The fire. The accelerant. She'd been knocked unconscious by the arsonist. How did Murray survive? Aslen pushed her upper body forward. "I need to see him."

"You will." Danny set one hand over Aslen's chest and pressed down, pinning her to the bed. "But I promised him I would get you to drink some water and eat something while he was gone." Twisting, her friend aimed for the stackable drawers acting as a bedside table and grabbed for the over-size plastic mug with bendy straw. She handed it off, waiting until Aslen took a few good pulls.

And, oh, hell, that felt good. "Thank you."

"As for the burns, I don't know how they happened, and Murray isn't really the talking type when it comes to anyone but you." A softness Aslen never wanted to see on Danny's face soothed those rough edges around her mouth and voice. "He's been trying to track down that boat and the man who abducted you. Got the whole law enforcement division working overtime. Running himself thin in the process. Do you remember what happened? Anything that might help us catch this guy?"

Too many memories to sift through assaulted her from every direction. Bits and pieces of what she thought might be the last few minutes of her life. Flashes of Murray, of realizing she wouldn't see him again, of Danny and the two years they'd had each other's backs. More than friends. Sisters. The kind Aslen had never imagined having after losing her family. Then of all the things she hadn't been able to do and would never get to try. "I didn't know him. The man who took me, but..." His voice echoed in her head, sharp and acidic. Her stomach threatened to roll, but whether it came from two days of being in this hospital bed or something deeper, she didn't know. "But I think I've met him before. His voice. It sounded so familiar."

"You mean in the park? Like a hiker?" Danny's blue eyes widened. "You think he knew who you were?"

"No. Well, yes. He…knew me. He knew my name even though I wasn't wearing a tag." The back of her skull pulsed with her heartbeat. Some painkillers. Couldn't even do their damn job. Aslen scrubbed at her face, ignoring the slight sting of the IV pulling at the back of her hand. "I don't remember much, but I know I would recognize his voice if I heard it again."

Danny smoothed her hand over the back of Aslen's. "You don't have to worry about any of that right now. I'm just glad you're okay."

"Me too. Thank you for being here with me." It took everything she had not to let the tears burning in her eyes fall. It was too much. Too much like waking up in a room just like this all those years ago. Of learning that her mom and dad hadn't made it out of the house. That she'd killed them. And Murray… She'd almost lost him. Her last line of defense in a crappy world that insisted on taking everything and everyone she cared about.

The door swung inward, putting the man himself in the frame. His shoulders curved inward as his gaze met hers. Relief. She felt it, too, as if the elephant dancing on her chest finally gave her a chance to breathe.

"I'm going to give you guys some time." Danny patted Aslen's hand before she shoved herself up to stand. Grabbing for her backpack, her friend rounded the end of the bed. "I've got to wash two days of smoke and ash out of my hair, but call me if you need anything. All right? Anything at all."

"Thank you." Aslen's voice broke on the crap lining her throat.

Murray stepped aside to allow Danny her exit but didn't seem interested in coming any closer with the drink in his hand. He'd showered, changed his clothes. Looked as though he hadn't nearly died in that fire. The traitor. Why did he have to look so good when she was sure she looked like something that'd crawled out of an evil well? "She was supposed to call me if you woke up."

"It's only been a few minutes. You didn't miss much." She attempted another valiant effort of sitting up, which Murray seemed to take offense at.

He closed the distance between them, setting his drink on the bedside table beside her mug. Hands hovering over her shoulders, he shifted his weight to help take some of hers but didn't seem to know where to touch her. If he could touch her. "Be careful. You're still recovering."

Ah. Yes. There was the alpha-hole she'd missed so much. "I'm okay, Murray. I promise. Just a little sore."

The muscle along the left side of his jaw jumped. He grabbed for the drink, and it was then she noticed the bandages. Thick and winding over both hands. She couldn't seem to look away from them. "I brought you a Diet Coke. Thought you could use the pick-me-up. I know you're not a fan of hospitals."

Now she really was going to cry. She grabbed for the Styrofoam and slugged a few gulps. Aslen almost melted into a soggy puddle as the combination of caffeine and carbonation did its job. She met his gaze. "You had them add fresh lime."

"Isn't that the way you like it?" His eyebrows cut across the bridge of his nose, mere centimeters from meeting. "I can take it back and get you something else."

"No. It's perfect. Thank you." She pinched the straw between her index finger and thumb and took another pull. Ah, sweet relief. "I just don't remember telling you what I get at the soda shop."

"You didn't." Taking the seat Danny had vacated, Murray didn't explain, but her best friend had been right. He was a man of few words. He merely watched her until she'd drank every drop.

She kept the cup as a distraction. Something to look at to keep herself from staring at him. It really was unfair how put together and handsome he was right now. Despite almost dying, she was positive she resembled drain hair compared to him. "How are your hands?"

"Medium well." The humor failed to reach his eyes. He turned his palms up toward the ceiling, glancing between them. "Second-degree burns. Nothing that won't heal in a few weeks as long as there's no infection."

"I'm sorry." Those two words felt heavier than anything else she'd said since coming around. She couldn't imagine what he'd gone through in trying to escape that fire, but if he walked away with solely his hands injured, she'd thank whatever god had watched over him. "I should've predicted the traps he set. Arsonists will do whatever it takes to escape, even hurt civilians if they have to."

Oh, no. That family the arsonist had threatened—

"Look at me, Aslen." The intensity in his expression held her hostage, but he didn't need it. A mere glimpse from him in her direction had always set her nervous system into overdrive. "You have nothing to apologize for. Do you understand me? This wasn't your fault. I'm not disappointed in you or whatever emotion you've concocted in your head. You were a victim just as much as anyone caught in those fires."

Didn't he understand? He'd spent the past twenty years trying to protect her, and she'd failed him. Wasted his time. His life. But worse, she didn't know what to do with the hole in her chest knowing he'd been hurt. Because of her. "You could've died out there."

Murray leaned forward in his seat, his blistering gaze re-igniting that tightness behind her sternum. "So could have you. But we didn't. We fought back. We survived. Together."

Because he'd saved her. Somehow, he'd known she'd been taken and pulled her from that reservoir. Her wrists and ankles burned then, the scratches from the swollen ropes she hadn't been able to escape shooting into awareness through the pain meds. She'd come so close to losing her life. Losing everything.

"Wait." His words registered slower than she'd expected. "What do you mean I'm as much a victim as anyone caught in those fires? Did someone else get hurt?"

"Danny and the rest of your unit got the explosion from the RV and the wildfire under control within a couple of hours." Sorrow etched across his features. So quick she might've missed or imagined it. "But we found another body."

Chapter Eighteen

He'd meant to give her more time.

To ease her back into the investigation when she was ready, but once again, time hadn't chosen their side. With two victims in the Springdale morgue and an arsonist still on the loose with little to no leads since Murray had pulled Aslen out of the reservoir, he had to move fast. He'd had her physician check her over twice before Murray let her sign the discharge papers, wanting her to stay hidden under layers of added security and watchful eyes within the hospital walls. Away from him and this manhunt. But the arsonist had targeted her, would come back for her. And Murray wasn't going to make it as easy as the first time.

Holding the door for her, Murray surveyed her two-bedroom rambler as she passed in front of him. Her movements weren't necessarily slow but hesitant. As though she expected her abductor to jump out from the hallway and take her all over again. The house hadn't changed any since he'd last been here that morning after the fire, but her entire world had, for a second time in her life. The nightmares would be the worst part. The feeling of helplessness he'd spent years helping her navigate when they got to be too much after losing her parents. He'd almost convinced himself she'd overcome them in the past few years, but after what happened in those woods, on that boat, in that reservoir—it would be like starting over. "Danny is staying with a couple other rangers in your unit. She thought you might want some space."

Aslen didn't answer. Hadn't spoken a damn word since they'd left the hospital. Studying her living room, she seemed to accept the bogeyman hadn't been squatting in her house these past few days and shuffled to the kitchen. Dejected. Almost…detached. She pried the refrigerator door open and bent to inspect its contents. The scrubs she'd been offered from the hospital were far too big for her, gracing him with a glance straight down the front of the V-shaped neckline.

Murray swung his duffel bag onto the nearest section of her worn couch that sure as hell wouldn't fit him, even if he curled up into a fetal position. But he wasn't leaving her to go through all this alone. He wasn't going to give the arsonist another crack at taking her from him, and he certainly wasn't going to ogle her as she tried to come to terms with her kidnapping and near drowning.

What the hell? He wasn't going to ogle her at all. Murray forced himself to breathe through his nose as he closed the front door behind them and twisted the dead bolt. Next time he stopped by the hardware store, he'd upgrade the locks on her doors. The windows, too. Maybe get her an alarm system and a few cameras. Who was he kidding? No amount of security would satisfy that part of him that'd wanted to save her from pain since he'd been sixteen. "I'll take the couch. Keep watch. You just get some rest."

"I don't want to rest, and I don't want to be coddled." Throwing the refrigerator door closed, she pressed her lower back into the opposite countertop and bit into what looked like a piece of cherry pie straight from the store-bought tin. She closed her eyes a split second before a moan escaped, and hell, that sound would stay with him through the night if not into the next month whenever he had a quiet minute to himself.

No. This wasn't happening. He wasn't attracted to Aslen. He would not let the events of the past three days change anything because the closer he allowed people, the greater chance he had of losing them. And he couldn't lose anyone else. He wouldn't survive it, which meant keeping his damn hands—and his damn thoughts—to himself.

Though he couldn't deny that small part of him that had always wondered what it would be like between them. How she'd grace him with that wide smile in the mornings from the other side of his bed. The way she fit against him perfectly on the couch during movie nights, like a puzzle piece he'd been missing his entire life. The places they would travel, the nights he'd replicate that moan she'd just given up for a piece of cherry pie. How he'd help her battle every nightmare, every night if that was what she required to feel safe again. He would do it all. For her.

"Murray." Aslen had lost the metallic tin of pie. Staring at him in expectation.

He tried to recover, to recall something—anything—she'd said in the past few minutes while he'd been fantasizing about a future he'd never have. How long had she been trying to get his attention? Murray cleared his throat, shaking himself back into the moment. "Sorry. What did you say?"

"I said I want to know where you are in the investigation and what you know about the man who abducted me." Those green eyes assessed him straight down to his soul. No. Deeper. To his very being. Concern, anxiety, a little bit of bravery—it all combined in her expression and raised the hairs on the back of his neck.

"The medical examiner doesn't have a lot to go off of with DNA, fingerprints or dental records for the victim you recovered in the shed. Basically, all we have is what you'd surmised on the scene. Older woman, possibly in her fifties or sixties, but the ME was able to identify the object in the victim's hand. A photo. Seems her body protected it from completely becoming ash." Rounding fully into her living room, he sank onto the couch. Yeah. There was no way in hell he was going to be able to sleep on this ratty thing. Not with the threat to Aslen's life and not with her scent clinging to the fabric. "The heat of the fire did a lot of damage to the image, but we're working with Springdale PD to bring in a forensic photographer. They might be able to tell us who the subjects are."

"It must've been important to her. To hold on to it even in her final moments." Her voice had lowered to whisper softly, grazing his senses in more of a caress than he cared to admit. Hand pressed against her neck, Aslen moved into the living room and took a seat on the opposite couch. As far from him as she could get without making a point. Still shaken from the abduction. Still trying to come to terms with letting anyone close. Including him. "And the second victim?"

His heart strained at the thought, that she could ever think he would hurt her. That he wouldn't give his own life in order to protect her, but trauma didn't have to make sense, and he wouldn't push her. "Your team found him in the RV."

"Him?" The breath seemed to suck straight out of her, and it took every ounce of Murray's training to not think about those moments he'd had her on the boat, willing her to breathe with every cell in his body. He shut it down—that raw helplessness—and focused on the fact she was sitting here. Alive. Alive. Alive. She was alive, and that was good enough for him. "The second victim was male?"

"The medical examiner puts him in the same age range as our female vic." Murray had been going through every avenue while she'd lain unconscious in the hospital hooked up to all those tubes and IVs. Late nights, early mornings, scouring the evidence, revisiting both scenes, calling in every favor he might have to find that boat—none of it had done a damn bit of good. No one had reported the boat missing from the dock, but owners were still trickling in after the evacuation order had been lifted. "Considering the arsonist is responsible for both deaths—"

"They're connected." A shiver tremored across her shoulders. "Possibly a couple."

"I came to the same conclusion." Murray sat forward, which put his knees practically against his chest from his position on the couch.

"I told you everything I remember." Silver lined her eyes, and right then, Murray saw through the detachment and the bravery and the slight attempts to keep her distracted. "I thought I was going to die. I thought I'd never get to see you again."

He was moving before she'd even finished that last sentence, hauling her small frame against him. Right against his chest. Where she belonged. And he stopped caring about whether or not their relationship would survive her leaving him behind to discover the world. Murray curled both arms around her, ignoring the flare of pain in his hands and shoulder. He'd do it all over again. The fire. The explosion. The burns. He'd subject himself to a lifetime of pain for this moment. To be here for her when she needed him the most. "I saw him toss you in that lake, and my heart stopped."

He couldn't admit to the fear that still burned under his skin, but he could give her this. "I couldn't get there soon enough. I was afraid I would be too late, that I wouldn't be able to find you."

Aslen tipped her head back, her scalp setting against his sore arm, but he refused to move an inch. Her body heat bled through his shirt, a hint of the soap he'd had Danny bring from her shower—lemon verbena—soaking into him. He never wanted to wash it off, to lose that small piece of her. Her fingers grazed over the couple days of bristle along his jaw, eliciting his own shiver across his shoulders. "I fought as long as I could. I didn't want you to blame yourself if something happened to me."

Whispered words he would never forget. That, even faced with her own death, she'd put him first. Murray didn't know what to do with that. Didn't understand. How? How could this beautiful, ridiculously intelligent woman care so little about her own life when she'd become the center of his entire universe? "You have very little self-preservation. Always have. But if you ever break your promise to me again, I will void our deal and follow you to the ends of the earth out of spite."

"Shut up." She swatted his chest but didn't make a move to leave his lap. Her laugh cut through the darkness that'd taken up residence since he'd realized she'd been abducted and filled him with a light he'd only ever found in her. No. Maybe for a long time before that.

"I'm not kidding." Murray tightened his hold around her, as if he could weld her to him. Though she'd probably resent him for that. "You think I'm a pain in the ass now. You haven't seen how overprotective I can get."

Her laugh pummeled that dark space in his chest to ashes, removing a weight he hadn't even realized had been there.

When was the last time he'd heard her laugh? Had he ever been the one to give her reason to? Murray didn't like the answers to either of those questions and would leave them to sit at the back of his mind in the mental box he'd shoved all his feelings for her.

Her smile slipped as she locked her gaze on his. Aslen tightened her fingers at his collar. Not to keep herself on his lap, but to drag him closer. "Kiss me."

He hadn't heard her right. "What?"

"Kiss me." She crushed her mouth to his.

Chapter Nineteen

His mouth closed over hers as though he'd been surviving in a desert with no water, and she'd become his oasis.

Aslen had always imagined what it would be like to kiss her childhood friend, but this…feast. An all-consuming sense of rightness with the only man she'd ever wanted. Her fingers ached from the tight hold she had on his T-shirt, and she forced her hands to release. To press against his chest where she could feel the rapid pace of his pulse. Equally out of control as hers. A heat that had nothing to do with the summer temperatures outside exploded in her low belly and spread outward.

Yes. This. This was all she'd ever wanted, what she'd fantasized about so many times between them. His fingers pressed around her spine as though she was something precious he was afraid of letting slip free.

She'd never allowed herself to touch him like this, to hope, and now that she had it, Aslen never wanted to give it up. Every swipe of his tongue against hers, every hint of mint gum, every pound of her pulse—it all intensified to the point she felt surrounded by him. Protected. Electrical jolts sizzled along her nerve endings that pulsed through every muscle in her body. She'd never had an awareness like this. Of him, of her body. An ache stretched deep in her core, to the point she might explode if he didn't do something—any-thing—to relieve the building pressure. But Murray only kept his hands still as he tasted her.

She wanted this. Him. All of him. She'd survived fires and drowning, leaving her raw and a little desperate to feel something more than fear, and he was here in her house. Standing guard against the next threat, touching her, hold-ing her. He always had been, whether she appreciated the effort or not. Always sacrificing himself to protect her, even from himself, she knew, but she didn't need his protection anymore. And she didn't need him holding himself back.

Being in his arms, his skin touching hers, she felt like she'd come home for the first time since her parents had died. Was it possible to see stars from a kiss alone? The thin fabric of the scrubs she'd been offered at the hospital failed to suppress the heat coming off his body and soaking into her skin. He was light and strength and her constant shadow in the best way, and Aslen would kill to keep this feeling as long as possible. In his grasp, under his kiss, she felt small and feminine when she'd never really been given the chance as a survivor. A fighter. But he made her feel beautiful. Wanted.

"More." Spreading her hand over his heart, she reached for the hem of his shirt and moved to drag it up over his head. To have him relieve the ache she'd never be able to ease herself. Him. She needed him. "Please. More."

Except Murray slammed his hand over hers. "Stop."

One word. That was all it took to break the spell. Her hand shook as she released her hold. "What?"

She was nothing to all that considerable strength moving her off his lap and onto the couch opposite him.

"We're not doing this, Aslen." The muscles along his neck and shoulders strained with some internal battle she couldn't see. Scrubbing a hand down his face, Murray shoved himself to stand, unable to hide the desire he'd felt for her during the past few minutes. "You're not thinking clearly."

No. Her stomach knotted. No. She wanted to keep that feeling, wanted to keep him, but it was all slipping through her fingers. Too fast. She couldn't stop the burn of tears as he added as much distance between them as her too-small house allowed. Knowing the only reason he didn't walk right out the front door was because of his promise not to leave her alone tonight. "Shouldn't I be the one to decide my mental state?"

"You've been through a lot this week. You don't know what you want." Murray wouldn't look at her, as though just a glimpse might remind him of the line they'd crossed. "You should go to bed. Get some rest. We can come up with a plan to have you back on the investigation after you've gotten some sleep and cleared your head."

It was getting harder to breathe. Harder to think. She swiped her damp palms along the tops of her thighs. It wasn't supposed to be like this. She'd finally gotten what she'd wanted after all these years, and now he was just going to rip it away? No. He'd kissed her back. He'd wanted her as much as she'd wanted him. She'd felt it, and damn him for trying to convince her otherwise.

She couldn't let herself throw up. She had to live through this moment, remind herself of all the times he'd used his power over her, made decisions for her so his rejection didn't hurt so bad. Whether they'd been in her best interest or not. Coming to Zion was meant to test his feelings for her, and he'd given her his answer then. Why hadn't she taken it seriously? How could she let herself get this far down the road with blinders? "My head is clear."

Maybe for the first time in years.

Murray's mouth pressed into an unforgiving line, and she couldn't help but hold her breath for the next words out of his mouth as dread crawled up her spine. "I don't want this. Not with you."

The words slammed into her like a cannonball to the chest, would've rocked her off balance if she hadn't already been sitting. He waited, as if expecting her to answer, but there was nothing Aslen could say. Of course, she was the last person he would want any romantic entanglement with, but that didn't change how she felt. How far she'd fallen for him over and over. Every time he went out of his way to check in to make sure she'd done her homework in high school. Every time he brought her food when she got sick in college and after she'd graduated. When he'd shown up the night a date had ghosted her with chocolate, flowers and a movie. Even the Diet Coke he'd brought to the hospital. He knew her better than anyone else—anyone she'd let close—and she loved him. More than anyone else. Why couldn't he see it?

Or maybe he did. Maybe the distance he'd been trying to add between them these past few years had been a clue to his true feelings. Maybe the women he'd dated and the rangers he'd never bothered to hide and taken back to his house were meant to be a point. For her. So she would realize that there wasn't ever going to be anything between them. That she wasn't ever going to be more than the obligation he'd taken on in a brash decision as a teen.

The blood drained from her face, and too soon, that dread turned into something far more acidic and hopeless. In an instant, she was right back at the bottom of that reservoir. Drowning. Unable to set herself free. Lungs screaming for air. Her heart splintered right there in her chest, ready to shut down altogether, and it just felt wrong. So wrong compared to that kiss, but the stupid thing kept thudding in her chest. As if her world wasn't crashing down around her.

Aslen had always known him to be loyal, committed to those he cared about, but what if those characteristics were keeping him tied to her when all he wanted was his own sense of freedom? What if his promise was actually doing more harm than the good he'd intended? Her throat ached all over again, like she'd swallowed a gallon of salt water. "Is it the scars?"

He looked at her then. His expression more closed off than he'd ever shown her. Not a hint of the man who'd stood by her side and even ahead of her to take the brunt of what life had to throw her way. This man? She didn't know this man. "Go to bed, Aslen."

Not an answer. Most likely to save her from the truth, and she was never more aware of the differences between them as she was right then. That he would always see her as someone needing to be saved. That she wasn't strong enough or capable enough to take care of herself in his eyes. "You really are a bastard, you know that?"

Her legs moved without conscious decision. Every cell in her body screamed for her to run the short distance between the living room and her bedroom, to lock the door and never resurface, but she had a job. She had a life. Friends. Responsibilities. Things that didn't rely on the brooding a-hole standing in her front room. The tightness in her chest didn't release as she closed her bedroom door behind her. It didn't lighten as she changed into her favorite pair of pajamas or got ready for bed, and it only seemed to get stronger as she slipped into bed.

Minutes—hours, she wasn't sure—stretched as she stared up at the ceiling. Movement registered from the other side of that thin piece of wood between her and the man in the living room. Whether he intended to sleep on her uncomfortable couch or stand vigilant all night, she didn't care. She didn't care. At last, that was what she kept telling herself.

Had he even slept since pulling her from that reservoir? Had he eaten? Nope. She wasn't going there. She wasn't going to give him an ounce of consideration after he'd brought her body to arousing heights she'd never known with another man in no time flat then ripped her heart straight from her chest and stomped it into nothing. But that ache wouldn't go away. Aslen turned onto her side, forced her eyes closed.

She could still taste him. Feel his hands pressed into her back. Remember the rhythm of his pulse and the way he'd claimed her mouth as though he'd been conquering a nation. She flipped on to her other side. Restless and more than ready for another round of arguing to distract her from this need she couldn't relieve.

A knock sounded at the door. So light, she wasn't sure she'd heard it until he spoke. "Aslen."

"Go away." Her sheets were too hot. Then too cold. Then came the memories that had given her a reprieve as Murray had plundered her mouth and soul. Of her abductor. Of the fire closing in on Murray and the resignation in his expression through the flames. Of the pressure in her chest when she couldn't get enough air.

Seconds turned into a full minute. Was he still out there?

Aslen threw off the covers and bounded for the door, not bothering with the robe at the end of her bed. She nearly ripped the door off its hinges, her blood boiling in her veins, coming face-to-face with her childhood protector. Well, face-to-chest. He was so much bigger than her. "What?"

He stared down at her, every emotion he'd tried to hide behind that defensive wall on display, and her heart almost stopped.

She didn't know what had changed. Didn't know how long it would last, but he'd given her this: a raw look at his fears, the pressures he faced and the desperation to keep her as much as she wanted to keep him. She would have to be out of her mind to forgive him, but Aslen found herself extending her hand in offering. "Come on."

He intertwined his fingers with hers.

And she pulled him over the threshold.

Chapter Twenty

The bed was empty.

Murray smoothed his hands over where she should've been, the sheets cold but slightly rumpled. Morning light blurred around the edges of her blackout curtains. His watch said it was still early—earlier than when she normally woke up on days she didn't have to work—but no signs of movement reached his ears from the rest of the house.

She'd pulled him into her bedroom last night, but that was where her offer had ended. Leaving him standing at the end of her bed, Aslen had taken one side of the mattress and left him to decide what to do next. Exhaustion biting every muscle, Murray had chosen the other side of the queen-size bed, keeping as much space between them as possible.

It hadn't lasted long. Sometime during the night, he'd sought her out after hours of tossing and turning. He'd pulled her back against his chest, letting go of the tension in his upper body as her heart echoed the rhythm of his own. Only then had he been able to really fall asleep. And, hell, the zombie apocalypse wouldn't have been able to wake him, he'd slept so deep. Deeper than he had in years.

She hadn't even woken, her breathing smooth and even, as he'd held her. To make up for crossing that line. For hurting her with his implication of using her scars against her.

He didn't give a damn about the whorls of scar tissues along her neck and shoulder, and had spent a good majority of last night visually tracing what he could see of them over and over. She was beautiful, in every way. But he couldn't give Aslen what she needed, what she deserved. No matter how many times he'd replayed that kiss. The way she'd melted under his touch, the small whimper that'd escaped when he penetrated the seam of her lips, how she'd gripped his shirt harder.

He'd never had such a visceral reaction to a woman in his life. Like that invisible thread that'd formed between them all those years ago had somehow guided him on how to touch her, where she needed him the most, how to make her feel what he was feeling. In return, he hadn't been able to breathe from the force of Aslen Woods. Her taste lingered in his mouth and triggered a craving he'd never had before, even now urging him to find her and soothe the itch to find out if a second kiss would be as good as the first. She'd always been the center of his universe, even more so than his parents and brother, but now? It was as though his entire being had honed itself on her. Breathed for her. Lived for her.

Murray swiped one hand down his face and shoved himself upright. She was right. He really was a bastard for taking advantage of her after what she'd been through, and he hated himself for allowing it to get that far. He'd broken his promise to always protect her. Turned out, he couldn't even protect her from himself.

He swung free of the bed, sweet hints of lemon verbena clinging to his skin and clothes, and crossed into the hallway outside her bedroom. Danny's room off to the left remained empty, the roommate keeping her word to give Aslen space after coming home from the hospital. The rangers' lease agreements didn't allow for painting, but Aslen's friend sure as hell had made her room her own. Danny hadn't bothered making the bed—another queen-size—and obviously didn't believe in a laundry hamper with how many clothes she'd tossed across the floor and over the dresser. Photos in silver and crystalized picture frames faced the bed from the single nightstand, but he caught a blurry sight of a group of four people. Most likely her parents and siblings.

Aslen didn't have that. While she kept a partially burned photo recovered from the scene of the house fire, the faces behind the frame had worn and aged. He doubted she could even picture their faces clearly anymore. She'd lost everything the night her parents had died, and he'd somehow convinced himself he could be enough to make up for that by giving her a new family. Him.

But all he'd done was give her a false sense of hope.

A mistake he wouldn't make again.

Moving into the main living space, he froze at the sight of her at the small, round dining table. She'd dressed in her ranger uniform for the day without so much as waking him, and he didn't want to think about the reason why his brain had found her a safe place to let go and rest. "Good morning."

Aslen set down her coffee mug at the sight of him. Waiting. "Morning."

He internally cringed at the cold distance in that one word. And he didn't blame her one bit. "You're up early. Figured you might want another day to recover before diving back into the case."

Was this how it would be between them from now on? Years of late nights, of inside jokes, of showing up for promotions and celebrations and holidays, of breakups and illnesses—gone? Had he so thoroughly rejected the idea of them becoming more than friends that he'd broken everything he'd worked for since he was sixteen years old? Murray couldn't get enough air, choosing to distract himself with a mug of his own from the kitchen.

"I'm fine." Shifting in her seat in his peripheral vision, Aslen took another sip of her coffee.

Hell. Those two words screamed of anything but her being fine, but he wouldn't push her. Not after what he'd said to her last night. It was anything but fine between them, and he had no idea where to go from here. How to repair the damage he'd done. "I thought we might visit the scene of the RV explosion at Lava Point campground. From what my rangers can tell, it was a rental under a false name, but I'd like to see if you can pick up on anything about the arsonist from the belongings left behind."

"Okay." Nothing more. No nervous recounting of facts. No argument about how to spend her time on the investigation. No telling him to go to hell and never come back. It was as though she'd become a shell, and his heart jerked hard enough at the thought of losing that brilliant light it physically hurt.

Murray closed his eyes against the pain ricocheting through his chest as he set the pot back into its holder and turned toward the table where she sat. "Aslen, I'm going to need more than one-word answers from you."

A burst of fire lit up her eyes. There. Not wholly a shell then. But she was trying to emotionally detach from him. "I think you made it more than clear last night that you don't need or want anything from me. Why start now?"

"Aslen." He didn't know what else to say. That he was sorry he'd hurt her feelings? Sorry he couldn't give her everything she needed in a partner?

"You don't have to explain. I'm used to you pushing me away when things get uncomfortable for you." She shoved herself to stand, carrying her half-full mug of coffee to the sink, and poured it down the sink with a little too much force. Black liquid charged up the sides of the sink and soaked the front of her uniform. She hissed a split second before the mug fell from her hand and shattered at the bottom of the sink. "Hot! Hot! Hot!"

Murray pulled her away from the sink, turning her into him to assess any damage. He'd spent a lifetime worth of adrenaline trying to save her from the man who'd abducted her. He wasn't sure if his heart could take much more. "Where does it hurt?"

"Don't, Murray." She backed out of his reach. Pain reflected in her expression, but all he could do was wait for the shoe he'd been avoiding to drop. "Just…don't. You can't pretend that you didn't kiss me last night or that there's nothing wrong between us and try to take care of me when I burn myself."

Peeling her uniform top away from her stomach, Aslen allowed her expression to fall, which made him sick all over again. "This isn't like the time you forgot we had a dinner date after work because you decided to go out drinking with your department or when you made a point to bring Ranger Richie home a few months ago, claiming you forgot we had plans to go to the movies."

The air thinned, making it that much harder to get a full breath.

"You've been trying to put distance between us for years, and I think it's because you knew." Tears lined her eyes as she seemingly forgot about the coffee dripping down her slacks and onto the floor. "You knew I had feelings for you."

His blood ran cold.

"I think you realized it early on. You were waiting for them to go away the older I got, but I think you also figured out they haven't. And that scares you." Her shoulders rose on a strong inhale, and Murray wasn't sure he could take much more of the dread pooling at the base of his spine. "You can deny it all you want. You can pretend it never happened, but you kissed me back last night, Murray. You were just as affected by what we shared as I was. No matter what you do or what you say, you can't take that from me, and you can't convince me you didn't feel something."

His throat worked to swallow but all he found was emptiness. "Aslen—"

"You know the worst part? It's not you telling me that kiss was a mistake or that nothing will ever happen between us. I'm used to your constant attempts to push me away. I've gotten used to the wall you keep trying to build between us since Jackson disappeared." A weak smile crested her mouth. A mouth he'd tasted and hadn't been able to stop thinking about since last night. She was right, damn it. She was right. He'd felt something, and it scared the crap out of him. Because the possibility of them? He couldn't risk it. He was all out of love, every ounce stolen from him in illness, heartbreak and a disappearance. Her tears breached, skimming down her perfect face. "The worst part was you climbing into my bed to hold me all night and letting me hope all over again. Only to realize you did it for you."

Murray didn't know what to say to that, to this woman who was the same Aslen he'd known all his life and yet not. He'd known about her crush on him from the beginning. She hadn't made an effort to hide it with her side glances when she thought he wasn't paying attention or her attempts to get them alone and spend time together. And, yeah, he'd gone out of his way to prove he wasn't interested by forgetting dinner dates and getting involved with the vainest information ranger he could find, but not to hurt her. Never to hurt her.

It'd all been to stop himself from ruining the very last relationship he cared about. Because that was the only ending for them. No matter how many times he'd tried to convince himself otherwise, in the end, he'd fail her just as he'd failed his family. He was a ghost of a man with no heart left to give, and she deserved so much better. "Aslen, you don't understand. I can't give you—"

A shrill ping escaped from his pocket. Murray unpocketed the device, reading over the ME's message. Confusion warred across his face—he could feel it.

Aslen swiped at her face. "What is it?"

"The ME is finished with the external examination of the second body we found in the RV." Murray forced himself to meet her gaze. "He recovered something in the victim's hand. He believes it's a copy of the same photo left with the first."

Chapter Twenty-One

Was it always going to hurt like this?

Aslen couldn't stand the ache in her stomach, the fact no matter how many times she begged Murray to want her, it just wasn't going to happen. She'd spent every day since she was thirteen years old hanging on to the scraps of his attention, clinging to the idea one day he would realize she'd been the woman he was looking for all along. Standing right there in front of him all this time.

He'd made fun of her so many times for her obsession with romance novels, telling her how unrealistic the heroes were and the expectations that real men could never live up to. And now she couldn't even argue with him. This wasn't a love story. This heavy feeling in her body was hell. How had she let herself get so far down this path? Why couldn't she just let go?

Murray swung his pickup into the funeral home parking lot, throwing off her balance. The bandages around his palms slipped along the worn leather, and the steering wheel jerked to straighten itself.

Metland Mortuary was the closest funeral home equipped to handle the remains of both of their victims. Twenty-two miles outside of Zion National Park, the town of Hurricane—pronounced "Hur-i-cun"—wasn't much better off than the tourist town she'd come to love right outside of the park. Without more than an emergency clinic—of which she was all too familiar with at this point—Springdale didn't offer much in the way of a morgue. The Office of the Medical Examiner needed to rely on the closest funeral home to store and examine the bodies of the two victims recovered during this investigation. Beautiful green grass and flower-filled beds that had somehow survived the summer heat stretched across the property and highlighted white pillars and Jefferson-style architecture of the property. The stone sign spelling out the mortuary's name welcomed the grieving and visiting in a combination of cursive and sans serif fonts so similar to the one where her parents' service had been set. Must be some kind of funeral home template.

Her body rocked forward as Murray pulled into an available parking spot, and she moved to open her door before he could come around to do it for her. Summer heat blistered along her exposed skin, the cotton of her uniform doing nothing to allow the sweat dripping down her spine to dry. She'd had to change her uniform after spilling fresh hot coffee all down her front, but the burns lingered. She'd cleaned herself up and applied ointment on the worst spots. It was nothing compared to the pain assaulting her insides, but she wasn't going to think about that. About how the dream she'd built up in her head since Murray had saved her at thirteen years old had shattered into a million pieces she'd never be able to put back together.

The investigation. Identifying the two victims they'd recovered. Finding the arsonist and predicting what he might do next. That was all she could think about. First step, force herself into that building and pretend her heart wasn't on its last legs. She could do that. She was good at pretending.

Before she had a chance to head toward the double glass

doors leading into the last place on earth she ever wanted to be, Murray blocked her escape. "How long are you going to punish me for what happened last night, Aslen?"

"I'm not punishing you." She wasn't. Right?

"You haven't said a single word to me since we left your house." Murray hiked his hands to his hips, accentuating the strong bulge of muscle in both arms and that terribly flat stomach she'd been pressed against last night as he'd held her.

She could still smell the hints of his soap clinging to her skin—clean and earthy. Feel his body heat through her pajamas. If she hadn't already inspected her stomach after dousing herself in hot coffee, she would've sworn she would've found the exact location where his fingers had rested against her hip all night. As though he'd been afraid she would slip away in the night.

"Did you maybe stop to think it had nothing to do with you and everything to do with the fact we are visiting a funeral home?" Okay. That wasn't entirely true, but she couldn't do this anymore. She couldn't keep hoping for him to come around, for another kiss, another night of him holding her, for him to stop trying to get out of being alone with her. This… It was tearing her apart being this close to him and not *being* with him. Like that kiss had stripped away every ounce of armor she'd donned to protect herself all these years. Her nerve endings felt raw, a throwback to the first days after waking in that damn hospital in Salt Lake City and being told her parents hadn't survived the fire she'd accidentally started. So, yeah, maybe she was punishing him by hanging on to this hurt, but she didn't have the will or the energy to put the mask she'd carefully crafted for him in place.

Murray seemed to grow taller. Revitalized pain flashed

in his gaze, and she hated the sour taste at the back of her throat that came with it. "I'm sorry. I didn't... I know you miss them. That you still have nightmares about the fire and that you didn't want to stay in the hospital after your abduction."

Of course she missed them. Her parents... They'd been everything to her at eight years old, even if she didn't really know them like most kids didn't know their parents. But they'd been hers. There'd been family game nights where she sneezed soda through her nose from laughing so hard, surprise Christmas vacations, visits to the aquarium on the weekends and cuddles on the couch every night after dinner. Cooking lessons, even though she'd always made a giant mess or her mom didn't trust her with a knife yet. Helping her dad clear out the garage and change the oil on Mom's car so she didn't have to take it in. Days where they'd taken advantage of early out hours from school to go to a movie or a hike or out to lunch. They'd been...happy. She'd been happy. And she'd burned it all down with one mistake. "It was a long time ago."

The words didn't feel as though she'd spoken them, and that old familiar sense of disconnect settled in. Hollowness. She'd felt herself slip into it so many times living with her foster mother, pretending her life belonged to someone else just to get through the day. When was the last time she'd felt like that? When she'd been truly happy? Aslen took in Murray's unlimited patience as he waited for her to make the decision and had her answer. The times she'd laughed the hardest, smiled the most, allowed herself to be free of the grief—they'd all been with him.

But that kiss and his rejection had changed something in her last night—changed everything—and maybe for the first time, she was seeing Murray Simpson clearly. Not through the eyes of a thirteen-year-old girl crushing on the boy who'd saved her from being beaten to death, or the one who'd taken her into his family when her own foster mother neglected her. Or as a woman who'd let that crush transform into something else entirely and imagined them starting a life and a family together, one built to heal the loss they'd suffered.

But as a man who let fear rule his every decision.

That was why he'd made that promise twenty years ago. That was why he'd given up his career as a decorated Salt Lake City police officer and followed her to Zion to head the law enforcement rangers. That was why he went out of his way to ensure the boundaries he set between them never shifted. That was why he'd tried to have her removed from fire management and stationed in the visitor's center and why he'd knocked on her door last night. All of it done out of fear.

And Aslen didn't know what to do with that, know how to fix it, and she didn't have the mental capacity to deal with it anyhow. They had an investigation to focus on, an arsonist to find and potentially two families to inform. "We should get in there. The ME is waiting for us."

He studied her as though he could see straight into that space where she locked the emotions and pieces of herself she didn't dare let anyone witness. But then stepped out of her path.

She took the lead through the double doors, following the front desk receptionist's directions down the stairs and into the cold room in the basement. The space was nothing like she'd seen on the crime dramas Danny forced on her every night. The single room had been painted in a dark gray with two oversize panels of florescent lights installed equal distance over a stainless steel examination table. Epoxy floor made to look like concrete—in the same shade as the walls—glittered with flecks of reflective material while builder-grade cabinets lined with linoleum configured a large L-shape around the room. Nothing like the sterility of a hospital room, though Aslen was certain everything in this space had been equally sanitized and cleaned. The temperature. That was what surprised her the most. Over-all, the space was warm. Warmer than she'd expected as the medical examiner looked up at them from the opposite side of the exam table.

"You made it." The medical examiner rolled his gloves free and rounded the table. Covered in a white long-sleeve gown and a mask complete with goggles, the man she'd met at the scene of the first fire where she'd found the victim in the maintenance shed extended his hand in welcome. "Ranger Woods, nice to see you again." He offered his hand to Murray. "Ranger Simpson. I have some updates for you concerning our new guest."

Guest. It was then she noticed the charred bare feet exposed from beneath a white sheet behind the medical examiner, and a cold that had nothing to do with the environment she found herself in crested beneath her skin.

The ME collected another set of bright blue latex gloves from a box on the countertop and lowered the sheet to expose the blackened remains of the victim. Images of the first victim—the woman they had yet to identify—assaulted her along with the stench of burned flesh and hair, but this victim hadn't remained in one solid piece. A wrist had detached as had the man's leg below one knee. The arsonist had done a thorough job in ensuring his latest victim couldn't be recovered. Just as he'd tried to do with Aslen. "As you can see, we had a bit of a puzzle to put together before I could do a complete examination, but I would say our current assessment is that these two victims were killed by the same offender."

Aslen moved closer. While she wasn't nearly as qualified with identifying victims as the medical examiner or a forensic anthropologist, she noted several differences between this victim and their first. "The arsonist doesn't seem to have a type, which makes me think he's targeting these victims for a specific reason. You told Ranger Simpson you recovered a photo with this body, like you did with the first?"

"I did." The ME raised one finger as though he expected a light bulb to light up above his head before shifting toward the back counter for an evidence bag. "Considering the fire this victim was recovered from also included an accelerant, I can confirm DNA is not an option to identify the remains. Fingerprints are unreliable, and his teeth have been stripped, just like our female victim. However, while this photo suffered far more damage than the one found with the first victim, I'm confident in saying they are, in fact, the same photo found at both scenes."

"He's sending a message." Aslen was afraid of that. That it would be too late before someone recognized what that message was and who it was intended to reach.

"Can I see that?" Murray grabbed for the evidence bag then handed it off to her. "Look familiar?"

Confusion warred with an innate compulsion to see what he was seeing, to live up to every hope he had in her to help solve this case before someone else got hurt. Aslen shook her head. "I don't think so."

"Really? Because I've seen this photo before." He nodded toward the bag in her hand. "In your house."

Chapter Twenty-Two

He could see the smoke from the freeway.

The closer they approached Aslen's house, the harder his stomach clenched.

"Oh, no." Aslen leaned forward in her seat as they turned on to her street. The anxiety pouring off her soaked down into his bones as what used to be her house had become engulfed in flames. Throwing off her seat belt, she was out of the truck before Murray had a chance to shove it into Park. "Danny!"

"Aslen, wait!" He shouldered free from the pickup and tried to catch up with her as she gained on the perimeter tape set up to block the public from getting any closer.

Flames cracked and groan as they consumed everything Aslen had to her name. Everything. Everything was gone. Fire trucks and rangers swarmed the too-narrow street complete with cookie-cutter housing. Every single one of these homes had been leased to a ranger working for the National Park Service, and now they were all at risk of catching fire. Hoses did their best to douse the fire, but the winds in this damn state worked against them at every turn.

He didn't recognize the firefighters calling out orders and taking control of the scene. These were structural fighters. Not the wilderness fire management team he'd come to know the past few days.

Aslen covered her face with both hands as she watched on. "That's my house! Please. You have to find my roommate. Her name is Danny Kennex. She's a ranger with the national park. She was staying at a friend's house last night, but I haven't seen her since yesterday afternoon."

The ranger holding the perimeter of the scene took notes, asking for Aslen's name and a description and contact information for Danny.

Murray pressed his chest against her back, knowing full well how much it was taking for her to stay on her own two feet. She'd already lost everyone she'd loved to a fire just like this one. He wasn't sure he was enough to pull her out of the devastation that might follow this one if Danny was caught in the destruction. Or if she'd let him after they'd laid their feelings on the table last night and this morning.

The firefighters were doing their jobs the best they could, but there was a chance the entire neighborhood would have to be evacuated, including his home one street over. Murray set his hands on her shoulders, keeping her close, willing an ounce of his strength into her.

She turned into him, burying her face against his chest, and he couldn't help but close his arms around her. To protect her from the heat and the emotion that came with it. "I need my phone. I need to call her."

"Yeah. Okay. You can call her from the truck." He freed his keys, guiding her back to the pickup down the street with a hand at her lower back. She was holding it together, struggling against the memories she still carried from losing her parents and worried for her best friend. Murray would do whatever it took to make this easier on her. "Fire and Rescue has your number. They can call you with updates. Until then, you can stay with me. All right? We'll make it work."

"How could this happen?" She swiped at her face to clear the tears tracking down the sharp angles of her cheekbones. "Oh, my gosh. What if she came home? What if they haven't found her yet?"

"We don't have any information yet." Murray swung the passenger side door open and helped her in, buckling her in as she scrambled for her phone. "Come on."

He secured her in the truck, trying to expel the burn of smoke from his throat and lungs. Seemed that odor was determined more than ever to haunt him, but he wouldn't let the dangers of this investigation touch Aslen anymore.

The arsonist had found her. That much was clear. Fires didn't just start themselves, and neither Aslen nor Danny would've taken risks with their home as fire management rangers. The son of a bitch had failed to kill her in that reservoir and had hunted her down. Tried to get rid of her the same way he'd disposed of his last two victims. Only now Danny might've been the one caught in the back draft. Murray didn't know how, and he sure as hell didn't know why the bastard wanted Aslen, but he intended to find out. Her statement about her abduction had been thin, but trauma did that. Forced the brain to focus on survival while something else was happening in the background. All he could do now was keep her safe. Live up to his promise.

But the proof he'd needed to connect the victims to Aslen's roommate was gone. He'd seen that photo this morning as he'd passed Danny's room right on her nightstand. The same photo found with both victims, he was sure of it. He hadn't been able to see the subjects' faces, but the same poses and groupings of people were clear enough he had no doubt. But how did Danny factor into this case? What connection had Murray missed?

He climbed up into the driver's seat as Aslen lowered the phone from her ear. Color had leached from her face. Not a good sign.

"It just keeps going to voicemail." Throwing her attention out the passenger side window, Aslen stared at the remnants of her house. There wasn't much left. The house itself had burned hot and fast, destroying everything in a matter of minutes, which potentially meant another accelerant. It was a miracle no one had been hurt so far, but the firefighters were having trouble getting control of the blaze. Everything Aslen owned had been in that house. Everything she'd kept from before her life had gone up in flames. And now it was gone. "She's not picking up or answering my text messages."

Despite their disagreement last night and this morning, Murray couldn't deny the need to touch her. To remind himself that she was here. That she was safe. He slid his hand over her thigh, reveling in the warmth through her uniform slacks as he put as much calm into his voice as he could manage under the circumstances. "We'll find her. I'll check in with Chief Higgins. Maybe she's on shift and not able to answer her phone."

"Yeah. Okay." She nodded, staring down at his hand before she summoned the courage to wrap her fingers between his. She closed her eyes, and he watched as days' worth of stress and exhaustion claimed her. It was any wonder she was still standing after what she'd been through this week, and Murray could do nothing but admire her resiliency and hate the reasons she needed it in the first place. "Thank you."

"Slide over. Lean on me." Extracting his hand, he started the truck but immediately hugged her frame against his side as she shifted into the middle of the bench. Close but not close enough. He was instantly reminded of the position they'd found themselves in last night, her pressed against him, her mouth surrounding to his. He hadn't let himself think about those few minutes when the world hadn't existed, and it'd just been the two of them. When the chaotic storm of responsibility, duty and loss had finally quieted. Because of her. Even now, Murray was more focused on the feel of her tucked under his arm, how he'd never noticed the freckle on the back side of her left ear.

He thought he'd known everything there was to know about Aslen Woods, but last night had only proven he hadn't even scratched the surface. Murray navigated through the neighborhood, avoiding curious bystanders flocking toward the fire but noting details in case the arsonist returned to the scene of the crime. He'd message the chief for updates and photos of the house once he took care of Aslen. Rangers faced danger every day on the job, but this attack had hit close to home. He couldn't fault them for rushing to provide aid, but all he wanted to do was get Aslen as far from the blaze as possible. To protect her from the past and her guilt as much as he could. Though he knew that wasn't entirely possible. There was only so much he could do to keep her here in the present, and he'd already felt her disconnecting.

Pulling into his driveway, he cut the engine and dragged her across the seat to exit the driver's side door. Someone had started a fire in her house. He wasn't letting her out of arm's reach. She went along willingly, barely protesting as he scooped her up into his arms. And that told him everything he needed to know about her mental state. Until she heard from Danny herself or someone got eyes on her roommate, Aslen would blame herself for what'd happened. "I've got you."

He carried her into the house, kicking the door closed behind him, and set her on the couch. His house wasn't much different from hers. All the houses in the neighborhood were built with the same layout, but different owners over the years had upgraded some elements while leaving the rest in the nineties. His carpet had been replaced just before he moved in, the paint grayer than beige like Aslen's and Danny's place. The cabinets in the kitchen didn't sport the giant knots he could practically see through and had been painted white to make the place more marketable. He hadn't bothered decorating, knowing, sooner or later, Aslen would get sick of living in the desert, and he'd follow her wherever she set her sights on next, but this house was his. One of the perks of heading the law enforcement division was choosing not to have a roommate, and he was never more thankful for that than right now. That she could feel safe here. Well, that, and the fact he didn't own enough to make an actual mess. "I'll get you some water then check in with the chief. There's a blanket behind you. You should lie down until we hear something."

"I'll never forgive myself if anything happened to her." She clutched her phone as though unable to bear the thought of missing Danny's reply.

Murray's knees popped as he crouched in front of her, centering himself between her knees. "Look at me." He waited until her watery eyes raised to his. "Whatever happens, Aslen, this is not your fault. You are not responsible for the actions of a madman. Understand? We don't have any information about how the fire at your house started or if Danny was home when it started. I need you to focus on helping me figure out how the arsonist is connected to Danny. You've got to give me something I can use to find him."

"I smelled the gasoline." Gravel coated her voice, so

unlike Aslen in every way. She'd always been strong, but that mask she'd built to keep him from knowing how much pain she was truly in over the years cracked, and he nearly flinched from the onslaught of raw emotion. "From the perimeter. I could smell it. The arsonist… He figured out I survived. He knew where I lived, and now Danny is in danger. Because of me."

"No." He didn't know how many times he would have to say it for her to believe it, but Murray willed her understanding with his entire body. Pressing closer, he framed both sides of her face with bandaged palms, drawing her closer. "You did everything right. You survived. I don't know what I would've done if you hadn't, Aslen. You have no idea how much just the thought of losing you guts me to the point I can't breathe. I've lost too many people. I'll be damned if I lose you, too. You're here, and I'm grateful for that every single day I get to have you in my life. I need you to believe that."

She didn't move, didn't even seem to breathe as she studied him. One heartbeat. Two. "But are you ever going to love me, Murray?"

Air crushed from his chest. His grip on her jawline faltered, and he sat back on his heels. Silence pressed in on him as he could do nothing but tell her the truth. "No."

Chapter Twenty-Three

"Okay." She wasn't entirely sure that she was the one who'd said that or some disconnected part of her that'd taken control. A crack physically split down the center of her heart as she moved to stand. The pain tried to rip her to shreds, but she wouldn't let it. Not yet. And not for him. Not ever again. Tears burned hot and thick down the back of her throat, almost choking her as thoroughly as that damn reservoir water. "Don't follow me this time."

Murray rocked back on his heels, keeping the distance between them as he got to his feet. She couldn't read his expression—this one was new—but he'd always gone out of his way to keep her at a distance, hadn't he? "Where are you going?"

She wasn't sure, not entirely sure if she was making the decision or if that eight-year-old girl who'd killed her parents and survived her first fire had. Aslen clutched her phone with everything she had. Danny. She had to find Danny. She had to make sure her best friend was okay, that the arsonist hadn't used her roommate in his sick game to get to her. "It doesn't matter. You don't have to protect me anymore. Consider your promise fulfilled. You're free, Murray."

Away. She needed to get away. Out of this house that smelled like him, away from the memories of that kiss, of the feel of him holding her last night. Away from him. Because if she didn't, she would spend the rest of her life waiting for him to change his mind. Holding on to those scraps of affection he granted her at the oddest moments. And she couldn't wait anymore. Every time he reached out, she held on with everything she had, but when he pulled away, she was left a little bit more broken. Empty. Sooner or later, there would be nothing left for him to love.

So she had to save herself. Before it was too late.

Murray broke into her peripheral vision but thankfully kept his hands to himself. "Aslen, I can't."

The metal of the doorknob warmed under her palm. It wasn't an attempt to stop her from leaving. It was the truth. He'd lost so much in his life—his parents, his brother— he didn't have the strength or the courage to risk his heart again. Not for her. Maybe someday with a woman he didn't have any obligation to or a history filled with so much loss. But not for her. "I know."

There was nothing left to say, was there? No combination of magical words that could fix years of wanting to be loved and accepted by the wrong person. She wasn't mad. She wasn't going to scream at him for wasting precious years of her life leading her to believe they could've been something more. Because he hadn't. She'd been the one to believe the fantasy she'd built up in her head, to see bits of love where there were none.

Crossing the threshold, she closed his front door behind her. Cutting off the possibility for either of them to go back. She could only see the plumes of smoke rising from her house this far back into the neighborhood, and the heartsickness hit all over again. She'd lost everything. And not for the first time. Except there wasn't going to be a foster mother or a handsome teenage neighbor to take her in. She was going to have to do this on her own.

Aslen forced one foot in front of the other. Find Danny, submit her resignation to Chief Higgins, get the hell out of Zion.

Her phone pinged with an incoming call, and a sob clawed up her throat as she read Danny's name. Swiping her thumb across the screen, Aslen threaded her free hand through her hair as another fire truck turned into the neighborhood. "Danny? Thank heavens. Where are you?"

"Hey, I'm out at Lava Point. The reception isn't great, and I missed your many calls. The chief has me going through the RV scene to identify the explosive that was used." Static popped over the line, taking Danny's voice with it for a moment. "Do I hear sirens? Aslen, what's going on?"

Alive. Danny was alive. The relief alone hit her hard enough she couldn't stop the tears from escaping then. Plugging her opposite ear, Aslen tried to get an idea of where firefighters might've moved her car. It'd been parked in front of her house, but they would've moved it to get better access to the scene. "Danny, it's gone. The house. Everything. It's all gone."

"What are you talking about?" Shuffling broke through the line. Danny was on the move, probably trying to get better reception or privacy. "What happened?"

"Our house is on fire. We lost everything." Aslen caught sight of her crappy four-door sedan that'd somehow managed to last since her college days—smelled like it, too—and patted her slacks for her keys. Fire and rescue had towed it down the block, out of the path of the fire. At least one thing had gone right because this was where she would be sleeping for the foreseeable future. Her heart urged her to turn around, to go back to the safety of Murray's house and his protection, but the traitor had done enough damage. Aslen wasn't sure she could ever trust it again. "It's my fault, Danny. The arsonist… He found out where I live."

"But you're okay, right? You're not hurt?" The words were rushed, like Danny was now in a run. "If you are, I will personally castrate Ranger Simpson for you, and I have two years' worth of grudges against him to suffer for."

Her laugh breached through the hollowness. It would've been so much easier if she'd wanted anyone other than Murray, but she'd always wanted him. Long enough she wasn't exactly sure where to go from here, but whatever future she'd imagined hadn't really existed. Not for him. And she was so tired of not having what she wanted.

Wiping at her face, Aslen shoved her keys into the driver's side door and collapsed into the seat. "No. I'm all right. Murray and I were checking in with the medical examiner."

Danny seemed to absorb that for a moment. Her voice evened out. "Did the ME have anything new to add about the victims or figure out who they are?"

"No. DNA, fingerprints and dental were inconclusive considering how much damage the bodies had sustained." Which had most likely been strategy on the arsonist's end. This killer, whoever he was, wasn't following the rules she'd studied over the years. This wasn't a show of power or an effort to get attention from the media, police or the rangers. This felt like...punishment. "But he thinks the photos found with both victims might be the same."

"Whoa." Danny's favorite word in the English dictionary. "Higgins isn't giving us much information to go off of here. Were they able to recover the photos?"

"A little. That's something else I wanted to talk to you about. I don't think the arsonist chose the victims at random." Movement registered at the perimeter tape. He was impossible to miss, standing at over a foot above everyone else on the scene. Murray scanned the street, the scene of the fire, grabbed for one of the firefighters. Looking for her. He was looking for her. Aslen sank a bit lower behind the steering wheel. Didn't he understand? She didn't want an apology. She didn't want to hear his reasoning why she wasn't enough for him or how much he needed her in his life. Not out of love. But out of purpose. To give him something to focus on other than the life-altering losses he'd sustained. Because then she would be right back where she'd started. Waiting for a life that would only ever be one-sided, and she couldn't do it anymore. She deserved more than protection. She deserved to be with a man who loved her as much as she loved him. And through his own admission, Murray Simpson couldn't be that man.

"What do you mean?" Danny had always given her the grace to work out whatever thoughts Aslen needed to get straight in her head, but there was no perfect way to explain this…connection between her roommate and the man who'd tried to kill her.

"Murray is convinced he's seen the photo recovered with both our victims before." She surveyed the street, failing to pick Murray out of the crowd this time. He was gone, but she'd been losing him for a while, hadn't she? And this time was her choice. A new kind of hollowness—deeper, more significant—threatened to break into the moment, but Aslen didn't have time to think about what came next. Just the present. Neither of them had asked for the loss and grief they'd survived, but they could make better choices. He could choose her if he had the courage to let go of his fear. "On your nightstand. The one of your family."

"I don't… I don't understand." Danny's voice wavered. "The arsonist has a picture of my family?"

"Yes. Both victims were in their fifties or sixties. We found evidence their wedding rings had melted due to the high temperatures of the fire, but the medical examiner be-

lieves the deaths were connected, that they were a couple."
The pieces were adding up if Murray had been right about
that photo, but who in their right mind would want to hurt
Danny? And why try to kill Aslen? "Have you heard from
your parents recently?"

"We aren't… We aren't really on speaking terms. Haven't
been for a while. Not to say I haven't tried." Danny hadn't
ever really gotten into why, only that her brother was the
only one still talking to her. "I don't remember the last time
I talked to either of them. Years, maybe. They didn't like
that I left the church I grew up in. Told me I wasn't their
daughter if I wasn't God's. My mom, she was more open,
but I think my dad kept her from reaching out."

Her heart hurt all over again as Aslen considered the possibility of being cast out by the very people who were supposed to love you the most. "Danny, I need you to think. Is
there anyone who might want to hurt you or your parents?"

Her roommate didn't answer.

Aslen checked her screen to make sure the call hadn't
been disconnected, but the clock was still ticking off seconds. "Danny?"

"Yes. There's someone who's wanted to punish my parents for what they did for a long time, but… Could you meet
me?" Danny lowered her voice. "Out here at Lava Point,
please? I just… I can't talk about this over the phone in the
middle of a scene."

"Of course. Ping me the location to meet when you get the
chance. I'm on my way." Aslen started the car and shoved it
into Reverse to avoid the scene of her and Danny's house in
flames. "It'll be okay. Well figure this out when I get there."

"Thank you, Aslen." Danny ended the call.

In less than an hour, she pulled over along West Rim
Road, putting Lava Point Overlook to her south. The pic-

nic area Danny had pinpointed was a little less than a ten-minute walk, complete with devastatingly beautiful views. But no sign of Danny. She checked her phone for the GPS ping her best friend had sent then brought up Danny's contact info and tapped to call.

A phone rang behind her.

Aslen turned, expecting her friend.

"Hello, Ranger Woods." The arsonist who'd tried to drown her smiled with a phone pinched between his index finger and thumb. Every detail she'd catalogued during those frightening seconds of not knowing whether she was going to live or die stared back at her with a too-wide smile. "I've been waiting for you."

Chapter Twenty-Four

He'd lost her.

Physically, emotionally. Murray had searched the entire neighborhood for her, noticing too late her vehicle was no longer parked on the street. She must've gotten access during the chaos of the scene.

Firefighters still worked to put out the blaze consuming Aslen's and Danny's lives. He'd watched her walk out of his life without so much as an argument. Damn it. The arsonist was still out there. He had some connection to Danny—Murray was sure of it—and he'd just let Aslen leave.

He shoved through the front door of his house, slamming it behind him. He had to get to her. Had to make this right. But no matter how many scenarios he played out, he couldn't for the life of him pull himself together enough to figure out where she'd gone.

Are you ever going to love me, Murray?

Her voice wound tighter and tighter in his head. Cutting him apart with every round. Sooner or later, there wouldn't be anything of him left, but he didn't know how to fix this between them.

Because he'd lied to her.

No matter how many times he'd tried to convince himself otherwise—to convince her—he already loved her.

He'd been in love with her the moment he set eyes on that know-it-all who sat at the front of the class and refused to let anyone else answer the teacher's questions. Those feelings had only grown in the weeks leading up to finding her bleeding on the pavement, had driven him to save her. He'd reached down to take her hand, giving her the choice to accept his offer. And then the invisible thread connecting his soul to hers had solidified.

He'd wanted to preserve that connection as long as possible, hiding her in his bedroom when her foster mother went off the rails, introducing her to his family and inviting her to dinners a few times a week. His parents had loved Aslen, especially her ability to bring his ego down a notch with a cutting remark or joke. In their eyes, she'd kept him on the straight and narrow and within a few months, they'd accepted her into the family as one of their own. As though she was always meant to be in his life.

He couldn't feel that connection between them now though.

In its place, something hollow and empty spread. Something dark. Murray absently rubbed at his chest as though he could dislodge it with a few deep breaths, but this wasn't acid reflux. A part of his soul had been severed and walked out the door with a request not to follow.

And now Aslen was gone.

As quick and as easily as his brother had disappeared, as his father had given up, as his mother had withered away. Everyone he'd ever loved had left him here to pick up the pieces alone, only this time he couldn't blame illness or heartbreak. He couldn't blame anyone but himself. His instinct to avoid any kind of relationship short of physical had failed him. Aslen had practically begged him to face his loss over the years, to lean on her for support and allow her to help him through it. Visits to his parents' gravestones, treks to Kolob Canyons where Jackson had last been seen on the anniversary of his disappearance, but the idea of facing a pain that had compounded over years threatened to shut him down entirely. And he couldn't do that to Aslen. He couldn't just disappear from her life to wallow in his self-pity and loss. He'd had to be strong for her. To protect her. The promise he'd made her as a teen had given him purpose, but now he saw it'd only been a distraction.

And the grief of losing his family—of not knowing how his brother had died or being able to provide Jackson a proper burial—had done nothing but eat at him until he wasn't sure he could feel anything anymore. Least of all love. While he'd resented Aslen for trying to make him confront his own grief while she held on to the loss of her parents, he'd known as long as he kept his emotions close to the vest, the numbness couldn't infect her.

Scrubbing a hand down his face, Murray grabbed for his phone and tapped Aslen's number. She couldn't be out there alone. The arsonist had already ambushed her once and most likely had been the one to burn her house down. The line rang. Over and over. Each time ratcheting his blood pressure higher. Until the call went to voicemail. "Damn it."

He disconnected the call and tried again. No answer. "Aslen, I know you're mad at me, but I need you to call me back. Tell me where you are."

He sent a text message, and an immediate response came through. Driving with focus on. Navigating to her contact information, he tried using the GPS app that friends used to keep tabs on each other, but the data refused to load. She'd either turned her app off or she'd changed the setting so he couldn't track her. Murray was betting on the latter, and he couldn't blame her. Hell, he couldn't blame her for never wanting to speak to him again, but this wasn't about them. This was about a killer solely focused on ensuring Aslen didn't survive this investigation.

His phone vibrated with an incoming call, the caller unknown.

Hope exploded behind his sternum as he answered. "Aslen?"

"Ranger Simpson, this is the ME's office. I'm calling with a new update on your investigation of the two burn victims recovered in the park." The distinct tapping of a keyboard echoed through the line. "I've finished the examination of both bodies, and we've got an ID on your second victim."

This was what they'd been waiting for. Murray lunged for the kitchen junk drawer and scrambled to find a pen and paper. "The victim found in the RV? I thought all DNA, fingerprints and dental were inconclusive."

"They were." The earsplitting squeak of a chair in need of repair screeched in the background. "However, after an X-ray, I discovered this victim had knee surgery about ten years ago and had surgical pins implanted to keep the knee stable. From what I've found in the victim's history, the damage after the physical assault was substantial. Without the pins, the victim never would've recovered use of the leg."

An assault? Murray pinched the phone between his shoulder and jaw, pen at the ready. This was it. Their first real lead into finding out who'd come after Aslen. "Do the pins have traceable serial numbers?"

"They do. All registered." He could practically hear the smile in the ME's voice. "Your victim is Randy Kennex, age sixty-eight from Provo, Utah. Married to Elizabeth Kennex, presumably the female victim you recovered from the first fire, but I'll need more time to establish her identity considering the damage done to the remains."

He knew that name. Understanding hit. Followed quickly by a flood of adrenaline as Murray raced for the door. He didn't bother locking it behind him. If anyone broke in, they could have what little he'd brought with him from Salt Lake City. None of it mattered compared to Aslen's life. "Thank you. I'll call you back."

Disconnecting the call, he extracted his keys and shoved himself behind the wheel of his pickup. He tapped Chief Higgins's information. The line connected almost instantly. "Higgins, where is Danny Kennex stationed today?"

"Danny Kennex? Thought you liked to keep tabs on the other one. Woods." Higgins's voice grated on his every nerve.

Murray threw the truck into Reverse and rocketed out of the driveway, his heart thudding ten times its normal speed. "Where is Danny assigned today, damn it?"

"All right. All right. Keep your shirt on." Rustling told him the chief was likely stationed at his desk like the good administrator he'd become in the past decade. "Kennex. Kennex. Here we go. She's out at Lava Point campground today. I had her working with one of your rangers to identify the accelerant your arsonist used to blow the place up. Haven't heard from her in a while though."

Lava Point.

"Get a hold of her." Murray broke a few dozen traffic laws as he barreled through Springdale, heading straight for Zion's main entrance. The sticker on his windshield would get him past the main gate, but visitor vehicles were already backing up. Twenty to thirty cars in each lane as the temperatures dropped with the onset of evening. Aslen was thrown off enough by the fire that'd brought down her and Danny's house that she would want to get eyes on her friend as soon as possible. That was where she'd gone. "Now. I need to know if Aslen's with her."

"Listen here, Simpson." The chief's voice hardened a touch, which was still impressive for a man with so many years out of the field. "I went along with your request when it came to your little girlfriend because I was doing you a favor I intended to call in when I needed something from law enforcement, but I have been running this department longer than you've been alive, and I'm sure as hell not going to let some hotshot order me around. You want Kennex? Go find her yourself."

The call ended.

Panic contorted and writhed until it became nothing but unfiltered rage. Murray threw his phone against the dashboard, not bothering to dodge exploding glass. The device hit the passenger side floor as his bellow filled the cabin of the truck. He slammed his hands against the steering wheel. Every emotion he'd swallowed over the years escaped, tearing up the skin in his throat. All the pain, the loneliness, the loss. His parents had been his pillars right up until their deaths. Examples of true love and soulmates wrapped into one. They'd loved each other so much his father hadn't been able to live more than a few months without his wife, and Murray had wanted nothing more than to have what they did when he grew up. He thought Aslen had been that woman for him, his other half who understood the darkest parts of him and loved him anyway. His parents had thought so, too.

Right up until Jackson had disappeared on that hike. When he'd realized that love hurt more than it healed. That it had the power to destroy him, but he couldn't bury those feelings anymore. He couldn't lose Aslen. He loved her. Had been in love with her for over twenty years. Her random facts, her bravery for facing her fear of fire every day on the job, her affinity for sentimental anniversaries and eating entire rolls of uncooked cookie dough as comfort food.

He loved her. Because the sad truth was protecting this wound in his chest had started protecting him from feeling anything for anyone again, and so he'd shielded the wound even harder. But he never would've met Aslen—the greatest light in his life—if it hadn't been for their circumstances. Their lives had crashed and burned in so many ways, but they remained.

She'd never given up on him. Not like he'd given up on her.

Shouts reached through the windows as he forced his way through the onslaught of visitors at the main gate. She'd been gone for twenty minutes. Getting farther and farther away from him. Out of reach. This. This was what he'd feared all these years. That Aslen would reach her limit and finally accept that he wasn't good enough for her. That he wouldn't ever be good enough for her.

But Murray wasn't finished with her. Not even close.

Chapter Twenty-Five

"You weren't supposed to hurt her."

Aslen mentally struggled through the haze that'd taken over. The ground bit into her shoulder, tingling pinpricks dancing in her fingers. She rolled her head to one side. Pain threatened to splinter her brain in half. It took more effort than it should have to open her eyes. Her attention went straight to the swaying pine tree overhead. The sky had turned a bruising purple, bluer to the right and lighter to the left.

"She'll lead the police right to us." Familiarity bled into Aslen's awareness. That voice had haunted her straight down to the bottom of the reservoir. The arsonist. He'd found her. He'd ambushed her. "We talked about this. She's a threat. She will lead them straight to you. We have to do this."

Tension hardened the muscles down her spine as she rolled onto her side. That was all she could do with her hands bound at her lower back. Only this time, zip ties secured her ankles too.

"It wasn't supposed to be this way." Movement filtered through that unconscious haze. Blond hair swept down the woman's back, straighter than Aslen's, frizzed from over playing with the strands and nervous pulling. But it was her voice that seized Aslen from head to toe. Danny. "You burned down the house."

The arsonist—she didn't know his name—stepped into her best friend's personal space. Raising his hands to Danny's arms, he brought her in for a hug. "I'm doing this for you. Remember? They deserved every second of pain they suffered from what they did to you. To us."

Aslen pulled at the zip ties, trying to ease onto her stomach without drawing the duo's attention. She didn't understand.

"I know. I just… She's my friend. She doesn't deserve any of this." Danny craned her chin over her shoulder, locking Aslen in her blue gaze. Her roommate swiped at her face then closed the distance between them. Crouching, Danny reached out, her boots level with Aslen's face. "Aslen, please. I can explain—"

She jerked out of reach, driving dirt and rock deeper into her pinned arms and hip. A picnic bench sat positioned near a chain-link fence roping off the peak of Lava Point Overlook. She'd come here to find Danny, to make sure her friend hadn't been hurt, only to find the arsonist himself. With Danny's phone. They'd lured her here. Were working together. "You know him?"

Danny threw her attention over her shoulder. To the man standing between Aslen and the only shot of escape down the overlook. "Jaylan's my brother."

His voice. That was why she'd recognized it on the dock. She'd heard it before, from the few times Danny and her brother had video called each other. Her roommate hadn't given much information about her family, but Aslen knew she hadn't been close to her family in a long time. Her brother had been her only point of contact over the years, and now he was here. He'd killed two people. He'd tried to kill her. She could see the resemblance now. The same blond hair, the blue of their eyes, but that was where the similarities ended. Jaylan Kennex was a mountain of muscle that might come close to Murray, where his sister was soft. Danny had the strength of a firefighter but not the bulk.

"I never wanted this, Aslen." Danny shook her head. "I tried to keep you out of it, but then Murray drafted you into the investigation, and you were making all these connections... Jaylan didn't have a choice—"

"You knew." Betrayal scorched up her throat and triggered a wave of nausea. How many times had she trusted Danny to have her back? How many nights had she cried in Danny's arms when Murray had failed to live up to her expectations? Two years. They'd been roommates. They'd been friends. And it'd all been a lie. "You knew what he was doing, that he was killing people—that he tried to kill me—and you never said anything. How is that trying to keep me out of it?"

A line of silver glistened in Danny's eyes as she maneuvered herself back onto the park bench. "I didn't know. Not at first. Please, you have to believe me. I didn't know he'd set the first two fires. I didn't even know he was in Zion until I was assigned to respond to the campground explosion."

Stinging pain bit into her palms as she tried to break the leverage of the zip ties, but even if she managed to free herself, it was two against one, and Aslen wasn't sure she could hurt her friend. Or that she'd survive the encounter with the arsonist. The weight of his attention pressed on her chest as Aslen cut her gaze to Jaylan Kennex. "Who were they? The people you killed."

"Our parents." Two words had never held so much weight to them. The arsonist—the murderer—slid both hands into his front jeans pockets, legs spread as though he expected her to tackle him at a moment's notice. Which she hadn't de-cided against. She owed him for throwing her overboard into the reservoir. A red gas can at his feet claimed her focus.

"You killed your parents." Bile slithered up her esophagus, and Aslen tried to pull one boot from the zip tie at her ankles. "Why?"

Danny leaned forward on the bench, her elbows against her knees. She picked at the calluses she and Aslen had both developed over the years of wrangling hoses, hauling equipment and having to get their hands dirty in every fire they'd been dispatched. Sisters. She'd thought they were sisters, but now? Aslen didn't know the woman sitting in front of her. "I told you my mom and dad were angry when I left their church, which was an understatement, but that's not the whole reason."

It took a few breaths and a glance toward her brother for Danny to corral an explanation. "Growing up, our family would come here to Zion, specifically to Lava Point. There weren't as many rangers patrolling this area as the more popular areas of the park. My parents knew that, and they took advantage of that to…educate me and my brother"

"I don't understand." And why on earth did she want to? Why was she looking for ways to be less angry at Danny than she was? Her best friend had let this happen. She and her brother had abducted her. Again. They'd bound her wrists and ankles and intended to ensure she couldn't tell Murray and his rangers the identity of the arsonist.

"Our parents believed the entire world was about to collapse to make way for their God's second coming." Jaylan Kennex moved in, his boots scuffing on the packed dirt of the overlook where thousands of visitors had come before him. The events of the past few days—a wildfire, the explosion, news of an arsonist on the loose—had kept hikers clear of the area. No one was coming to save her.

Least of all the man who'd outright rejected the love she had to offer since she'd been thirteen years old.

"My entire life, Jaylan's too, we prepared for that day. As a family. We were told it would be us against the whole world, and we needed to know how to survive the evil coming for us. We moved to a compound in the middle of nowhere with people who thought just like my parents. Cut off from everything we knew, everyone we loved." Danny wiped her palms down her uniform slacks. "We grew our own food, stocking up on guns and ammunition. We had Bible study morning, noon and night then survival training."

Danny looked to her brother then, her face losing color.

"They left us in the middle of these woods for days to see if we would survive. Same with the other children from our compound." Jaylan's attention locked on his sister, and Aslen could see the hurt there. The difference in their ages was obvious as they stood together, Danny a few years younger. "No tents, no food, no water. No supplies. We were instructed to meet at a location within three days, and if we didn't make it, we weren't coming home. Our parents couldn't afford weak children in times of chaos. I had a few more years of experience. I spent a good amount of time learning the skills I needed, but Danny... Our parents dropped us off, blindfolded, at two separate starting points. She was only four the first time."

Aslen's heart hurt. For the treatment they'd suffered, for the pain of being hardened so early in life, for the understanding the siblings shared in this moment. The same look she and Murray had shared so many times. But none of it justified the murder of two innocent people and the attempted murder of a ranger.

"It took me two days to find her. I didn't even care about meeting our parents' timeline. I couldn't leave her out there to die." Jaylan slid his hand over Danny's shoulder, and his sister covered his hand with hers. "She was soaking wet, suffering from hypothermia after falling in one of the streams. She was so blue, I didn't think I'd ever be able to get her warm. I swore then I would never let anything happen to her again, that I would protect her. It wasn't our family against the world. It was me and Danny against our parents. So I taught her what she needed to know every time we were dumped in these damn woods, just enough to keep her alive until I could get to her. And I took the lashings our parents doled out when they found out I was helping her survive."

Aslen's heart shot into her throat. That same promise Murray had made to her all those years ago. She couldn't breathe, couldn't think. That promise was responsible for transforming Murray from the popular, fun, outgoing boy who'd brought her into his home into an arrogant guardian, and she'd hated it. Murray's commitment to her protection had made her feel as nothing more than an obligation he couldn't rid himself of, but seeing how far Jaylan Kennex had gone to ensure his sister's survival ripped the world right out from under Aslen.

Murray had told her he couldn't love her. But the truth was, he already did. In the way he'd followed her to Zion, in riding her to study harder than anyone else through high school and college, to have her reassigned to the visitor's center after the explosion, confronting her foster mother every night, vetting those boyfriends before allowing her on a date, keeping her from drinking at restaurants, training her to defend herself from some invisible threat she never understood. She'd hated it all, but now she understood. It'd been his way of not just keeping that promise but showing her how much he cared. That he loved her.

And, damn it, she would go to war for him. For them.

"So you killed them." Aslen swallowed against the rush of relief as the zip tie at her back broke. Using the lessons Murray had taught her to escape, she'd angled her wrists against a rock, and the pressure had snapped the plastic, but she kept her hands hidden. She couldn't go anywhere with the ties still secure around her ankles.

"They were a threat to my sister." A hardness Aslen had glimpsed in the second leading up to her going over that boat railing filtered into Jaylan Kennex's expression. "And so are you. You've seen our faces. You know our names. I can't let you turn us in. Danny deserves better."

"So do I." Aslen snapped her knees apart. The tension severed the zip tie around her ankles, and she pushed to stand.

Jaylan didn't have the chance to defend himself as she rammed her shoulder into his soft organs and shoved him off balance. He tripped over the gas can at his feet and hit the ground.

And she ran.

Chapter Twenty-Six

His headlights cut across the landscape, but he was losing daylight every mile he raced to get to Lava Point. He'd cut the drive that normally took two hours down by pushing his pickup as fast as it could take the dirt road leading him north.

Murray couldn't neutralize the terrifying need to get to Aslen as soon as possible. Sweat built between his bandages and his burned palms, aggravating the healing skin, but he didn't care. He'd face a thousand more fires and third-degree burns if it gave him the chance to find her.

Because he loved her. He was in love with her.

And he'd already wasted too much time trying to convince himself otherwise. She'd withstood years of his rejection, fighting for them over and over, supporting him the best way she knew how, while he'd practically paraded an endless line of women in front of her. She'd campaigned for him to hold on to his family with memorials and celebrations while he'd tried to brush the people he'd lost from his mind. Aslen had given him purpose through the promise he'd made her all those years ago, but she'd stopped him from losing his humanity. And he'd let her walk away.

Murray would never forgive himself for that. He'd spend

the rest of his life making it up to her if that was what she needed from him, but he had to find her first.

His tires skidded across packed dirt as he cut onto West Rim Road. The one-lane road took him past the West Rim Trailhead toward the campground. Chief Higgins had said that was where he'd find Danny Kennex, but Murray's rangers finished at sunset. While Springdale PD and other departments were equipped to continue investigations late into the night with manpower and spotlights, Zion law enforcement had limited resources they didn't dare waste. Which meant Danny had most likely ended her shift, maybe even had gone to meet Aslen, considering neither of them had a home to go back to at this point. He hadn't spotted any other vehicles heading back to headquarters on his way north, and right then, he wished he hadn't destroyed his phone.

Murray pulled the pickup to the side of the road and hit the brakes, palming the handheld radio Velcroed to his dash. He hit the power button and adjusted the channel settings. Static crackled through the speaker. "Ranger Kennex, come in."

His heart thundered behind his rib cage as he surveyed the darkening sky. Lava Point Overlook stood tall to his left at almost eight thousand feet of sheer cliff. No response on the radio. Damn it. Aslen hadn't answered any of his calls or responded to his texts. Danny Kennex was the only lead he had to finding her. "Ranger Kennex, come in."

No answer.

"Any law enforcement rangers in and around Lava Point, respond." Night was steadily falling now, tightening the vise in his chest. He'd taught Aslen to gruelingly defend herself and escape. She could take care of herself, but that didn't mean she should have to fight this alone.

A couple of his rangers checked in with no sightings of

Danny Kennex or Aslen Woods, and Murray pressed the radio into the dash with a little too much force.

A flash of light pierced through the night from his left. Then disappeared. The air remained dry, no evidence of a storm moving in. He could clearly pick out a number of stars and the moon rising in the east. Air stalled in his lungs as the light reappeared, steadily moving down the path leading to the overlook. He took a step into the middle of the road, trying to force his senses to adapt faster. "What the hell?"

Shouts echoed down the cliffside, and every cell in his body honed in on the slash of movement ahead of the light. A person. Running. His instincts filled in the gaps his senses couldn't account for, and Murray ran for the truck, pulling a flashlight from the glove compartment, before checking his sidearm at his hip. He shot down the narrow trail that would take him straight up the Overlook. "Aslen."

He tried keeping that lone light in his sights as he navigated over rolling elevations and through the trees that'd survived the initial fire, but he lost sight of the runner within seconds. It didn't matter. There was only one way down the overlook unless hikers deviated from the path, and he was on it. He could intercept her. "Aslen!"

The overlook almost towered straight overhead. He was getting closer, gaining on her, though he could barely see a few feet in front of him as his flashlight bobbed with his movements.

Then a burst of fire lit up at the top of the Overlook. And dropped. Murray visually followed the flaming mass. Right until it disappeared into the trees. The explosion threw redhot licks of fire several feet away from the impact zone, and the trees caught fire. Holy hell. Had that been a gas can set on fire? In this summer heat, it took less than a few seconds for the wildfire to gain intensity. He'd lost track of that lone flashlight up against the threat of a third fire. Lost track of Aslen.

He hit the incline of the trail that would take him up to the overlook, but she'd been running in the opposite direction. He hadn't intercepted her on the way back. She'd had to have gone off the path. Damn it. "Aslen!"

The crackle of flame drowned any attempt to get her attention. She was here. She had to be here. Scanning the trail ahead, Murray tried to make out the threat she'd been running from but only met darkness. Whatever light had been chasing her was gone now. That left him with one choice: To follow her into the trees currently being eaten alive by the flames. Sweat slithered down the back of his neck. The sensitive skin beneath his bandages screamed warnings before he dove past the first lick of flames.

He'd made her a promise, and he had no intention of breaking it ever again. He'd wasted years of his life living in his misery while she helplessly watched on, but he wasn't going to be that person anymore. He was going to choose her. Over the comfort of being on his own, over ever having to feel again, over his fear of losing her. He'd follow her into the depths of hell if that was what she required of him, and he had to admit, this was pretty damn close.

But despite what he'd told her back at the house, they had a future. With the mornings in bed and the nights tangled in each other. The movie nights and surprise lunch dates, the weekends shooting off to wherever she wanted to go. Hell, he'd saved enough money over the years with the life insurance money from his parents' and brother's deaths they could both quit their jobs and travel the world if she wanted. They could do it. Together. He'd spend the rest of his life trying to make up for the pain and rejection she'd suffered, proving his love to her every day. He wanted it all. And he wanted it with her.

They just had to survive first.

Smoke burned down his throat as he raced across the epicenter of the fire. Chief Higgins's crews were already stationed out here. They would see the flames and respond as quickly as possible without him needing to call it in. Until then, Murray had to focus on Aslen. On getting her the hell out of here. His chest constricted from the lack of oxygen, and he coughed to clear his lungs. In vain.

He followed the pattern of the widest openings between trees. Adrenaline did funny things to the brain, shutting down some functions while pouring everything the body had into others. Escape under the influence depended on the easiest way out of any given situation, and Aslen would be no different. But the wildfire seemed to be jumping ahead of him, catching up to her faster than he could keep up. Murray raised his hand to block the exposed skin of his face, but it wasn't enough.

Within seconds, he'd be surrounded and completely useless to her as he had been at the reservoir. He wasn't going to take the chance of getting trapped this time, and the son of a bitch responsible wasn't getting his hands on her either. Not again.

The arsonist. Where had the bastard gone? How did Danny play into all of this? Had she known the killer? Had she helped in luring Aslen out here or had she been a target all along? Murray shook his head as though he could dislodge all the little distractions vying for his attention and put everything he had into his senses. Into finding Aslen. Because he wasn't leaving Lava Point without her. He wasn't going to leave her to fight this on her own. "Where are you, woman?"

The smoke grew thicker, getting trapped within the trees and barreling down on top of him. It burned his eyes and drilled into his pores. There was no escaping it. Whatever the arsonist wanted, Aslen was part of it. But Murray wasn't giving her up so easily this time. Never again.

A tendril of fire lashed out across his arm. He swallowed the scream ripping up his throat as the flames started closing in on him ahead. "To hell and back."

Charging the flames head on, Murray leapt through the thin layer of fire gaining strength and landed on the other side. His shoulder ached under the pressure of hitting the ground with his entire weight, but he wasn't going to let anything come between him and getting to the woman he loved. He'd always told himself she deserved better than a man who didn't know how to love anymore, that he'd never be good enough. But she was worth the pain. And he would do whatever it took to become the partner she needed.

A scream tore through the trees.

His nerves shot into overdrive. He couldn't tell the direction it'd come from, but he knew that scream, understood the pain in it. He'd heard it in the middle of the night from the bedroom next to his for years. Desperate and horrifying and filled with the kind of loss he'd never been able to vocalize.

It was the scream of Aslen's demons catching up to her.

The fire. Panic seized his limbs and paralyzed him at the realization she wasn't in these woods as a firefighter as she had been for the past two years. She was caught in the flames. Just as she had been at eight years old. Now. He needed to find her now. Murray took that initial step in the direction he believed she'd gone, the thread connecting them tugging hard in his chest. Like he'd unblocked some kind of invisible barricade between him and Aslen in the past couple of hours. His entire system seemed to restart and clear out all the fear that'd held him back from just reaching out for her. North. She'd gone north toward the campground where she might get help. It made the most sense and would register even in an adrenaline-induced panic. He could still make it. He wasn't too late.

Pain exploded along the back of his head.

His knees hit the ground, and Murray fell forward. Dirt and rock cut into his face as his vision wavered. Footsteps registered through the darkness closing in around him. Then a pair of boots. A thick branch dropped beside his body.

"I'm sorry." The voice was female. Recognizable. Danny Kennex crouched beside him, unholstering his weapon and tucking it straight into the back of her uniform waistband. "I know how much she means to you, but I can't let you do this. I can't let you save her."

Chapter Twenty-Seven

The world fell out from underneath her.

Her dad's arms squeezed the life out of her rib cage as they plummeted down, down, down. A scream exploded from her chest a split second before they hit the floor. She landed on top of her father, and his hands released their hold on her. Fire consumed everything around her. It hurt to breathe. They had to get up. The stairs were just...gone. Disappearing right out from beneath them. "Daddy."

Pressing against his chest, Aslen forced herself to sit up. Her neck and shoulder burned. It felt like the skin was melting off. Fat tears choked her as she swatted at the flame attacking her shirt, and she jumped off her dad. Stop. Drop. Roll. That was what they'd taught her in school during an emergency, but her teacher didn't say anything about the pain. She'd put out her shirt, but the burning wouldn't stop. Why wouldn't it stop? Why wasn't Daddy helping?

The entire house groaned. A big chunk of wood fell from the ceiling. She couldn't stop that scream either. So loud it hurt her ears. Aslen pressed her hand against her neck, and another burst of pain stole the strength in her legs. Her knees bit into the hardwood. She could see the door. They just had to get to it. She peeled her hand from her shoulder and neck, coming away with blood. Her stomach clenched hard enough she thought she might throw up.

Then she saw her dad.

He wasn't moving. The fire roared loud enough she thought it might be screaming at her to run, but she couldn't leave him. He needed to get them out of here. "Daddy, get up!"

She smeared blood across his shirt, shaking him like she did every Saturday morning when her stomach couldn't take another minute without breakfast, and she'd watched all her cartoons. Sweat slicked under the new shirt her mom had bought her after school today. Mom was going to be so mad she'd ruined it. Another round of tears spilled down her face. She'd ruined everything. Her shirt. The house. They were going to take her to the zoo and leave her there for real this time.

But Daddy still wasn't moving. Aslen shoved at him again. His body shifted, but he wouldn't open his eyes. She grabbed her dad's oversize hand and pulled as hard as she could. Pain bolted across her neck, and she fell forward. "Daddy, come on! Wake up. We have to go!"

Her sobs were out of control now. She could barely get a full breath. She managed to pull his shoulders a few inches, but that was all. She wasn't strong enough. "I'm sorry! I'm so sorry. I'll never play with the matches again. I promise. Please, you have to get up."

Shouts reached over the sound of the flames. A hard thud attacked the front door across the living room. Aslen ducked against her dad, making herself as small as possible as the door hit the wall behind it. Flashlights blinded her a split second before someone's hands wrapped around her arms.

"It's okay. You're going to be okay." She didn't like that voice. It sounded too deep and far away. A hiss broke

through the too-loud pounding of her heartbeat behind her ears a split second before the man pressed something against her face.

A burst of air shot up her nose, and Aslen twisted away.

"Let me go! Daddy!" She kicked with everything she had but couldn't force the man to let her go as he pressed her against his chest. The pain in her shoulder didn't hurt anymore. She caught sight of two other people crouching next to her dad. One shook his head. Firefighters. They were here to help. They were going to help Daddy. Energy left her as they reached the front door.

She reached over the man's shoulder for her dad. "Bring my daddy."

Aslen clutched her head between both hands as she stared at the flames gaining inches with her every breath. She was trapped. The fire had grown out of control. A sense of raw nakedness brushed over her skin as she ached to have her gear. Her uniform wouldn't be enough to protect her. Nothing would stop the fire from claiming her as it should have all those years ago. Her spine bumped the tree at her back, her knees begging for relief as she crouched up against the bark. She'd tried to do what her dad had taught her when in danger. "Hide. Make yourself as small as possible. Small as possible."

Her whispers barely rose over the crack of the wildfire, but the mantra was the only thing keeping her from losing it altogether. She'd killed her parents. Mom had suffocated from smoke inhalation in her bedroom and Dad had died on impact when the stairs had given out. He'd been trying to save her, and instead, she'd killed him. Pressing her fingertips into her scalp, Aslen watched every shift of the flames as they gained ground. There was no stopping it. No escape this time. "Small as possible."

Maybe it wouldn't hurt so bad. Maybe it wasn't as painful as she remembered. Her scars warmed with awareness, as though warning her to put as much distance between her and this place as possible. But there was nowhere to go. No random fact that could get her out of this. And Murray... He didn't want her. Didn't know she was out here.

She was alone. She deserved to be alone for what she'd done. She'd had love right in front of her with two supportive and kind parents, and she'd killed it. She'd set herself on this course, and she couldn't help but wonder if the violence of her foster mother, losing Murray's parents and brother, losing him had been some kind of long-awaited punishment she'd been trying to outrun her entire life.

Aslen rocked forward and backward on her toes. "Small as possible."

Movement registered in front of her.

Jaylan Kennex met her at eye level as he crouched a few inches away, and her gaze automatically sought his. Something along the lines of understanding—and sadness—softened his expression. "I'll make it quick. You won't feel a thing."

He nodded as though asking permission then extended his hand toward her. He pried one hand away from her head, tugging on her arm for her to stand, but it...didn't feel right. Him touching her. This wasn't what she wanted.

Her opposite hand fell away as he tugged her away from the protection of the tree she'd chosen. This was...wrong. Something was wrong, but she couldn't pull herself together enough to voice the words. She parted her lips to speak. Only burning heat drove into her lungs.

"Turn around, Aslen." Jaylan Kennex had his hands on her again. His touch softer than she'd expected. Gentle, even. So why did it feel so wrong? What were they doing here? "Look at the park you've worked so hard to save. Remember it how it was."

The past superimposed over the present. *Turn around, sweetheart. You don't need to see this.* The firefighter had been assigned to stay with her as the EMTs had treated the burn on her neck, but she did need to see it. She needed to see them get her parents out of the house. To remind herself of what she'd done. To never forget that she deserved to be alone and unwanted.

Aslen looked out at the bright trees being consumed right in front of her, just as her childhood home had fallen apart that night. The nightmares still haunted her, that last look her dad had given her—relief when he'd found her in her bedroom—still as fresh as ever. He'd tried to save her and paid the ultimate price in the end.

But he'd given her a second chance. He'd inspired her to face off with the very thing that'd taken her parents from her and do the same for other little girls who might make the mistake of playing with matches under their beds. Her dad had sacrificed his life for hers, taken the brunt of the impact so she wouldn't have to. He'd protected her in his last moments, just as Murray had protected her all these years later. Even from herself at times. Decades apart, two men brought together by one common goal: To keep her safe.

And Aslen wasn't going to let their efforts go to waste.

Pain licked up her pant leg. The haze that'd overtaken her body cleared, throwing her into the present and the fire raging ever closer. Its bellow tried to raise her defenses, but she wouldn't let it have control this time. She wasn't scared anymore. She'd already survived the worst life could throw at her.

Strong hands framed her jawline. Jaylan Kennex set his

mouth against her ear, his breath caressing the sensitive skin over her scars. "It'll all be over soon."

"No." She wasn't going to die here. Not in a place she loved, and not at the hands of a man who'd hurt so many. Aslen allowed gravity to consume every muscle in her legs. She dropped out of Jaylan's hold and hit the ground, spinning before he had a chance to get her under control. She thrust her boot heel into his shin.

The arsonist rocketed forward, falling into the tree that'd protected her. The softness she'd found in his expression drained. "Son of a bitch!" Jaylan grabbed for her, missing the collar of her uniform by mere centimeters.

Aslen did what Murray had taught her. She swung her fist straight into Jaylan's ear, the impact jarring his eardrum and throwing him even more off-balance. She got her bearings, but the fire had cut off any escape. Sooner or later, it'd eat them both alive. Putting a larger tree between them, she struggled to regain her breath.

"You're going to pay for that, Ranger Woods." The arsonist's voice wavered, louder then softer, closer then farther away. He was toying with her. "I was going to do you a favor. Finish this with as little pain as possible, but now? Now I'm going to make it hurt. I'm going to draw it out. I'm going to make that law enforcement ranger hear your screams and know there's nothing he can do to save you."

Murray? No. He wouldn't survive it.

"Looking for this?" Murray's voice tunneled past the too-hard beat of her pulse in her head and drilled straight through her. Her heart threatened to stop altogether as her partner came into view, all six foot four and 230 pounds of intimidation. With Danny positioned in front of him and his sidearm in one hand.

"Danny." Her name left his mouth as more of a prayer

than anything else. Jaylan's entire frame straightened as he focused on his sister's position. Every ounce of violence in those blue eyes was solely focused on Murray, but Aslen couldn't let it get that far. She couldn't lose him either. "Get your damn hands off my sister."

Aslen took advantage of the distraction. And lunged. She threw her whole weight into tackling the arsonist to the ground. Except he'd been ready for her. Turning at the last second, Jaylan twisted her around, slamming her back into the forest floor. His head connected with the bridge of her nose. Blood plunged down the back of her throat and cut off her air, all too similar to the feeling of drowning at the bottom of that reservoir. Her body arched off the ground to ease the threat, but it was no use.

"Let her go!" Jaylan straddled her hips and gripped her collar to keep her from escaping. Eyes on Murray, the arsonist threw his elbow back. "Do it!"

"Aslen!" Murray threw Danny out of his way and charged.

She didn't have time to avoid the next strike. Pain exploded across her face. Lightning struck behind her eyes then made room for tears. Aslen twisted onto her stomach, coughing up the blood stuck in her throat, and reached for Murray. Her partner. Her everything.

He collided with the arsonist. Aslen could do nothing but try to get out of the way as the brawl intensified and the fire raged closer. Sirens announced her unit had been deployed to manage the wildfire. Help was coming.

"Jaylan, stop!" Danny's sobs squeezed Aslen's heart until she was sure it would pop. Pure agony ripped her best friend's expression apart as she flung her hands out. "Stop!"

Jaylan Kennex froze under Murray's attack, his gaze centered on his sister as Murray prepared to strike.

"Just…stop." Danny took a single step forward. "It's over,

Jaylan. You did what you said you'd do. You saved me. Now we have to face the consequences."

Murray shoved away from the arsonist, turning Jaylan Kennex onto his stomach and snatching his hands behind his back. "Jaylan Kennex, you are under arrest for the murder of Randy and Elizabeth Kennex and for the attempted murder of a federal officer."

Aslen didn't have the strength to try to make sense of anything that happened after that and lost consciousness.

Chapter Twenty-Eight

He'd made it in time.

Dawn broke from the east, painting the sky in pastels and bright oranges as smoke from the fires of the past couple days mixed into the atmosphere. For the first time in nearly a week, Murray could breathe easier.

Crews—both fire management and law enforcement—had worked through the night to get the fire under control and neutralized the last few embers that refused to go out thanks to the canister of gasoline Jaylan Kennex had used to start the blaze. But the fire was under control.

He'd managed to contain Jaylan Kennex with ease once the bastard realized he'd lose his sister if he killed Aslen. Murray didn't know what to do with that information, the lengths the arsonist would have gone to protect his sister, to keep a promise he'd made to her. It was…all too familiar. And terrifying. Because Murray wasn't sure if there was anything that would stop him from doing the same for Aslen.

Law enforcement rangers had taken custody of the duo within seconds of arriving on the scene. His rangers did their jobs well, taking statements from both him and Aslen and collecting the evidence they needed to make the arrest—including the physical damage done to Aslen's face.

It was clear what had happened, and considering Aslen's and his eyewitness statements and the evidence collected during the investigation, Murray was sure Jaylan Kennex would spend the rest of his life getting visits from his sister from behind bars. Though Danny hadn't had a direct hand in killing her parents, she too was arrested on charges of obstructing the investigation and currently waited in the back of a separate SUV from her brother as they finished up at the scene. But Murray couldn't deny her hand in saving Aslen's life. Without her interference, Jaylan Kennex would've killed Aslen right in front of him, which he would be sure to mention to the judge come trial.

Murray scrubbed a dirty bandage down his face as one of the EMTs assessed his other palm. The blisters had broken open during his struggle with the arsonist, but it was nothing compared to the pain that'd nearly suffocated him in watching Aslen take those punches. He'd wanted nothing more than to destroy Jaylan Kennex for putting his hands on her, but he'd have to leave that to the justice system.

"Switch." The EMT grabbed for his opposite hand, unwinding the old bandage, cleaning the wound and applying more burn ointment, but Murray didn't notice the pain as Aslen finished up with the EMT across the clearing.

The blood had been cleaned away from her delicate features, but the swelling and bruises—along with the bandage across her nose—told a gut-wrenching story of survival. One she almost hadn't made it through. Staring out at what remained of the woods surrounding Lava Point Overlook, she closed her eyes and tilted her head back as if to absorb the morning's sunrise. And, damn, she was beautiful standing there. Though he was ready to drag Jaylan Kennex out of that SUV and beat the man into unconsciousness for breaking her nose.

"We're done here." Murray ignored the EMT's protests as he crossed the clearing to reach her. She opened her eyes and turned at his presence, like the invisible thread tying them together warned her of his approach. But she wasn't yelling at him to get the hell away from her after how he'd treated her the last time they'd had a conversation, so he'd take that as a win. He wished he could go back in time and keep her from having to go through any of this—his rejection, the fire, her abduction, the brutality spelled across her face. Except there was nothing he could do to fix this for her. Whatever happened, he could only promise to be at her side. If she allowed him. "What's the damage?"

"Broken nose, a few lacerations. Nothing I haven't survived before." She tried shrugging her shoulder but only managed to upset some unseen injury. "Your self-defense lessons came in handy. Jaylan Kennex is sporting a busted lip and a cracked cheekbone right about now."

"Let me see your hand." Murray reached for her, letting her meet him halfway. Relief charged through him as she slid her hand over his bandaged palm. He probed her knuckles and the tendons running down the back of her hand with both thumbs. "Nothing broken as far as I can tell."

Aslen retracted her hand in offense. "Excuse me, I know how to throw a punch."

"That's because you learned from the best." His smile came easily without the weight of a killer on the loose, but Murray realized he might have unintentionally done more damage than Jaylan Kennex ever could between them. "It was never about you, Aslen."

Her smile slipped. She seemed to stand a bit straighter but wasn't cutting him off entirely. "I know."

Where he expected hesitation and fear to strangle him, courage took the lead. He'd already faced the nightmare of losing her, watched her nearly be taken from him. There was nothing left to fear, and he was tired of letting the grief win. He loved his parents, he loved Jackson, but denying himself the ability to remember the moments he had with them had been nothing short of a disgrace to their memories. And he didn't want Aslen to become one of those memories he refused to acknowledge. "I lost everyone I've ever cared about. First Mom, then Dad right after her. I suddenly had these two teenagers to take care of and all the pressure that came with it. I was determined to give you and Jackson everything you deserved no matter what sacrifices needed to be made, but when he disappeared…" Murray cut his gaze to the rising sun still hiding behind the mountains to the east and let it cleanse the final remnants of grief from his system. "I let myself become numb."

She didn't interrupt, didn't give them a way out with shallow attempts at forgiveness or platitudes.

Murray ran a bandaged hand through his hair, igniting the pain in his palm. It kept him in the moment, allowed him to push through. "I didn't want to feel anything for anyone ever again, including you. I counted down the days until you graduated high school, and you would go off on your own and leave me for bigger and better things. I wanted the misery of being alone because it was easier than letting anyone else in, but you decided to stay in state for college and live at home. You kept insisting to be part of my life, to remember Mom and Dad and Jackson, and I kept trying to push you away because I was afraid of the pain I'd been ignoring."

Tears glinted in her eyes.

"When I made that promise to protect you all those years ago, I meant physically. I wasn't going to let anyone else hurt you that way, but over time, that promise transformed into something bigger. I found myself protecting you from me. You deserve better than me, Aslen. I've always known that. I've always wanted that for you." The muscles in his jaw ached under pressure of his back teeth as all the wrongs he'd committed in the past few years rushed to the forefront of his mind. "I was supposed to let you come to Zion alone. I told myself you were better off, but you were the last link I had to my family. You felt like home. You always have, and I couldn't let you go. You stayed strong for years, stronger than I could ever be, and now I know I don't want to let you go."

"What are you saying?" Her voice barely carried over the chaos of the scene as shouted orders, fire hoses and sizzling trees demanded attention.

Murray closed the distance between them, locking his gaze with hers. She could run, she could leave Zion like she'd planned and never give him a second thought, but Aslen only stood her ground against him. Just as she'd done from the beginning. "I'm saying I crave your scent on my clothes and the glances you steal when you think I'm not looking." He secured a strand of her hair behind her ear. "I've come to need you in the same room as I'm in and get anxiety in less than five minutes if you're not. I've never slept better than when you've been next to me, every single time."

Her inhalation hitched as she looked up at him, and a single tear slipped free down her face.

"I love the way you fit in my arms, even though I'm three times your size. I love the passion you have for your job and all those random facts you spew when you're nervous." He skimmed his thumb over the tear then across her split lip, careful of the injury but needing to make himself very clear when it came to the woman standing in front of him. "I respect the hell out of you, Aslen, for a lot of things, but especially for showing me how to face my fears. You became a firefighter after everything you've survived, and I've always admired that. And I need you to know you will always be safe with me. You will always belong. You're a gift I've been denying myself for twenty years. I care about you, and if at any time you didn't feel those things from me, I failed. Because I love you, and I will do whatever it takes to make sure you know that every day for the rest of our lives if you'll give me the chance."

"Took you long enough." Aslen shot onto her toes and threw her arms around his neck. Crushing her mouth against his, she pressed herself against his chest as if in attempt to make them one. But they'd always been two halves of the same soul. That familiar tug in the center of his chest where he could've sworn a thread of connection stirred was like a balm for the wounds that'd been bleeding for years.

His heart beat so hard he was sure everyone on the scene could hear it, and he didn't give a damn. Murray wound his arms around her waist, hauling her off her feet. The hollowness behind his sternum screamed to let it survive, to go back to thriving in loneliness and misery, but as long as he had Aslen, that darkness would never take hold again.

This was nothing like that kiss they'd shared on the couch a few nights ago. This was something more, something he'd never imagined.

A small moan escaped up her throat. She pulled back, her eyes brighter than he'd ever seen them before. Fisting her fingers in his shirt, she pressed her mouth to his with a smile that threatened to buckle his knees. That smile. He'd waited so long to see that smile, and now it was his. "Oh, I love you, too."

An animalistic growl resonated through him as he fought

the urge to simply claim her right here in the middle of the woods in front of their colleagues. He'd waited twenty years for Aslen Woods. He could wait a little longer. For her, he'd wait forever. Murray narrowed his gaze on her kiss-swollen mouth and thumbed the sensitive flesh again. "Your lip is bleeding."

"I don't care. I don't care that everyone can see us making out in the middle of the scene. I don't care I don't have any place to live. I don't care that I look like I lost a fight with a kangaroo." Aslen shook her head then dragged his mouth to hers. "You're finally mine, Murray Simpson, and I'm never letting you go."

He liked the sound of that, kissing her hard enough to leave another bruise. "Forever."

* * * * *

STALKED IN THE MOUNTAINS

DANICA WINTERS

To my readers,

Thank you for your ongoing support and love.
You are the reasons I write.

A huge shout-out to my team at Mills & Boon—without
them these books would not be possible. Their hard
work and dedication are truly second to none.
Thank you for all that you do.

Also, thank you to my team of reviewers. I appreciate
each and every review posted for my books. They make
a huge difference. Keep them coming.

Chapter One

Scarlett Leafletter never wanted a child. She didn't want the incessant wailings of a newborn, the sleepless nights, a toddler clawing on her legs, or the disgusting and messy battle of potty training.

She didn't begrudge any woman who wanted the life— no, far from it. In fact, those women deserved statues in their honor instead of simply one day a year when they were forced to choke down runny eggs with shells and half-cooked pancakes.

There had never even been a fleeting moment as a teen-ager when she'd envisioned herself setting the table for her husband and children after cooking the traditional dinner and conforming to the gender roles that usually came with rural Montana living. Especially as one got deeper into farming and ranching country.

Scarlett had grown up smack-dab in the center of no-where and grab-your-husband's-slippers, and she had got-ten out of there as soon as she'd tossed her graduation cap into the air—so fast, she wasn't sure she'd even seen the thing hit the ground.

Her parents hadn't understood her rush, but they also hadn't seen the girls in her high school. When she'd gradu-ated, there were thirty girls in her class. Five had already gotten pregnant and had their first kid—all with members of the football team. Ten others had decided to get married to their high school boyfriends, most of whom had dropped out a year or two before them and had gone to work on one of the many wheat ranches on the other side of the continental divide. Only three of the girls she'd graduated with, including herself, had plans to go to college.

One of the three had already screwed up and just found out she'd accidentally gotten pregnant—and that, right there, had been why Scarlett had never been one to drink to excess. The only other girl who had made it out of West Glacier High School and their tiny town had ended up married to a super sweet woman five years ago after she had become an orthopedic nurse in Missoula. She and Scarlett were still friends, but only in passing and on social media.

So the last thing she'd expected was to find herself facing a near-miss pregnancy, a mess of a personal life and thinking about running home with her hat figuratively in hand.

There was no way she could tell them she was coming—if she had they would have turned her and her assistant away at the airport. Heck, they would probably meet her with a mob complete with pitchforks and shotguns. Her sister, Jamie, and her brother Cameron were the only ones at the ranch now, and the last time she had seen Cameron they had been throwing hands.

Ever since their father had been killed and major drama had unfolded at the West Glacier Cattle Ranch, she had been following the news out of Kalispell that had been twisting tales about their infamous ranch. It had seemed in the last two years since Cameron, and now Jamie, had taken the reins that things had started to take a turn for the better financially.

The latest headline announced they were opening the

ranch up for guests and for a new foundation called JMac, an equine therapy program geared toward children. Both were booking out for this summer. It was that headline, and some fortuitous timing in her personal life, that had beckoned her home like she was some kind of goddamned lost lamb.

She just wasn't sure if she was ready to go there—if she went home, she had a feeling she was coming home for slaughter.

Her phone rang. She hit Ignore when she saw the screen, and then she blocked the caller. A minute later it happened again, but this time the number had changed. This repeated another ten times before she finally just turned off the device and tossed the damned thing into her purse. It made a loud *ting*—it must have hit the black bottle of YSL perfume she always kept inside next to her wallet.

Her cell phone company was going to get tired of seeing her face. This would be the fifth time she would have to go into the store to change her phone number.

"If you're not careful, you're going to bust that bottle one of these days—not to mention it may cost you a new phone…again." Her best friend and personal assistant, Kelcie Sherry, came sauntering out of the back bedroom of the hotel suite carrying a makeup bag and a handful of brushes. "You already used up your free insurance phone claims for the year, and mine. No more breaking them. It's going to start getting expensive."

She waved off her friend. This thing with her agent—well, her *ex-agent*—had already gotten expensive and obnoxious. She had been hoping he would get the hint that she really wasn't interested in taking things anywhere near the bedroom with his Harvey Weinstein ass, but clearly, he wasn't getting the picture.

Ever since she had rebuffed his advances at the wrap

party for this season of *Rogue Crafter*, things between them had gotten worse. What had been a call a day and maybe ten to twenty texts, which she had thought was already quite a bit for an agent, suddenly turned to twenty calls and hundreds of inane texts about nothing.

The night of the party six months ago, there had been an open bar and exposed secrets. He'd thought their conversation had been an invitation into her heart and pants when in reality it had been nothing more than a miscalculation of who she thought she could trust.

She would like to say she had learned her lesson, and she had moved on, but even though she had let him go as her film agent and put her career on hold to do so, his behavior hadn't stopped.

Right now, he was probably sending her a flurry of messages on one of the social media platforms because her voicemail was full. The thought of him scrolling through all her pictures, many of which he had taken as part of her "portfolio," made her stomach roil and a bit of acid move up into her throat. She could taste the bile.

What a fool she had been to let a predatory man like him into her life.

When she'd been signed by him and the Cucco Film Agency—he was the sole owner—she'd thought she'd finally broken into the big leagues in the world of acting. He had gotten her one of her first roles in television, a commercial for yogurt. She still had a copy of it somewhere downloaded on her laptop. If she couldn't find it, she was sure she could get it on YouTube.

It was funny how much time had not really passed, but with film years being like dog years, it seemed like a lifetime. Since then, her stock in the industry had exploded—and he had leveraged his role in her life to keep her not only as a client but as a supplicant. It had been a strange, codependent and well-groomed relationship. One that, until she'd been pulled out of and seen others' *normal* relationships with their agents, she hadn't understood for the toxicity that it had been.

Now she was in damage control.

"Kelcie, would you hand me my computer?" she asked, motioning toward the bag on the floor by the glass door that led out onto the balcony.

The hotel the studio had been putting them up at was beautiful in Santa Barbara, and from where she sat, she had a view of the ocean and a smattering of palm trees. They really had pulled out all the stops this time. Maybe they knew they had underpaid her by thirty thousand dollars. It was fine—when she got a new agent, she would make sure the next one was a pit bull when it came to negotiations.

She pulled up the website for her family's ranch. It drew up the sting of familiar memories as she saw the old barn, where she had spent more than a few nights hiding from her parents, and the beaverslides from her grandparents' farming days. If nothing else, she could dream about the foothills of the steep mountains and the smell of the pine pollen in the air. Though she wasn't a cowgirl by any stretch, there were things about that world she had always loved. Country living did have its charms.

On the front page of the website there was a link to adventure rides and something about the new equine therapy program. She clicked on the adventure rides link, and it led her straight to the picture of a man holding the reins of a beautiful gray mare. As stunning as the horse was, the man was a thousand times better. According to the little write-up beneath, the man was one of the guides for their trail rides and his name was Miles Miller. Even his name was cute.

The marketers behind the ranch had made a mistake not putting him on the landing page, because his face was one that could have launched a thousand ships—or at least a thousand women on planes, trains and automobiles into the backcountry.

Though she tried to avoid her email, it popped up. She was flooded with emails from Butch. So far, there were thirty-seven. The first were innocuous enough. Why didn't you answer? to Are you okay? But as she got to the most recent, they rapidly devolved into threats, and the last read, You stupid witch. You'd be nothing without me. I'm glad you lost your baby.

Another email popped up from him just as she exited out and opened a new browser. He could take his emails, his phone calls, voicemails and texts and stick them all where the sun didn't shine.

She needed to get out of California and as far away from him as possible.

She pulled up her Alaska Airlines account. Using some of her hundreds of thousands of miles, she booked them on the first flight to Montana.

Butch's Facebook profile pic popped up on the corner of her screen just as she was finishing up their reservations. There were the little dots indicating he was typing. It didn't take long for him to send his message: I'm going to kill you.

She had never thought she would run away from danger, but there was no safer place in her mind than the backcountry of Montana—and, if push came to shove, there was no better place to hide an enemy's body.

Chapter Two

Healing a broken heart was like attempting to train a shark while there was blood in the water. A person could try but they were probably going to only get really hurt—and wound others in the process.

Miles Miller wouldn't have considered himself the sensitive kind. In fact, he was about as far from emotional as a cow's tail was from its nose. Sure, once in a while he'd brush up against a feeling, but it left him wishing he'd never touched the damned thing as it had a way of leaving a whole lot of crap behind.

After this last relationship with Chloe Purvis, he wouldn't be dating for a long, long time. He looked down at the ring on the top of his dresser as he grabbed out a pair of fresh Wrangler jeans. She had made such a big, damned deal about wanting to get engaged and getting a ring and then he'd never even gotten a chance to ask. She had decided to kick him to the curb and start dating his former boss at the Joy Luck Ranch on the other side of Flathead Valley. In retaliation, he had taken the head guide position at their largest competitor, the West Glacier Ranch.

He smiled at the thought of how much it probably ticked off his old boss, Drake Rex.

Just today, he had what was left of the Sullivan family coming out. They normally visited the Joy Luck every summer, but after Catherine Sullivan had passed away last fall, her husband, Aiden, had jumped ship to follow Miles. Aiden wanted to get his son, Thomas, involved with the youth equine therapy program to help him through the grief of losing his mother.

Miles loved his new job and the possibilities of more that came with it. Cameron had been great, his wife, Deputy Emily Trapper, was always a kick, and Jamie had given him pretty much free rein when it came to helping her to run the equine therapy program. She was away on a retreat for the day and wouldn't be back until at least tomorrow or perhaps two more days, depending on how things went.

He pulled on his jeans and cinched his belt tight. His silver belt buckle had been a hand-me-down from his grandfather's rodeoing days, and it had a gold bull on its face with a nearly illegible engraving that read Cheyenne Frontier Days 1973. His grandfather Dickie Cox hadn't been the overall champion that year, but he'd taken home the championship buckle in bull riding and had worn the thing every day until he'd passed. It had been given to Miles with the caveat that he wear it as much as possible to keep his grandfather's memory alive.

He'd embraced the buckle, the task and the honor with both hands and an open heart. He'd worshiped the ground his grandfather's boots had touched. When he'd been young, everywhere they'd gone, his grandfather had gotten free coffee and lunch, and people had wanted to talk about "the old days." Jamie had loved it, thanks to her rodeoing past, and he held no doubts it was part of the reason he and his brother Jackson had gotten jobs at the ranch.

Even now, when Miles was out with the guests, he'd always end up telling them all about his grandfather and his days on the rodeo circuit. In some ways, it felt as though it was stolen valor. He'd never made it in the world of bull riding—his mother hadn't wanted him to go down that dangerous path.

Between relationships and bull riding, she'd been wrong about which would bring the most danger.

He took one last look at the diamond ring. The one saving grace about the damned thing was that it had never really been hers. If only he was a better bull rider, he would have sold it for an entrance fee in the Cheyenne Rodeo so he could have a run at winning his own buckle. At least that way, one way or another, he could have honored his grandfather's memory.

He slipped on his cowboy hat as he walked out of the bunkhouse. Today he was the last one out. There were only two other hands that lived in the bunkhouse, but if he had his way, soon his brother Brent, Andrew, Xander and Gus would all be working the place along with him.

It was a bit of a haul up to the barn in the pickup. When he arrived, there were two women lolling about by the green steel gates leading into the main pasture. The blonde lady was breaking handfuls off the tall, green grass outside the fence and feeding it to MacGyver, Jamie's horse. She was scratching the blaze marking on the gelding's forehead as the horse nibbled at the grass in her hand and she whispered sweet nothings into the big man's ear.

He seemed to be eating up the attention.

The woman's friend was tapping on her phone. She looked out of place in Montana, with her big brown purse with some guy's name written on it, gold hoop earrings and a fur-edged jacket that was so big, if she actually did need it to keep warm it wouldn't hold any warmth in—it fit her like a giant collapsible canvas wall tent.

But the woman did have a beautiful white felt hat. He could tell it had never touched the ground, but it did wonders for her brunette hair and olive-hued skin. She was out of his league, as she could have been a model for any one of the fashion websites his ex used to scroll through, but undeniably stunning.

He got out of the pickup and strolled over toward them. "Good morning, ladies," he said, touching the brim of his cowboy hat and giving them a tip of the head in greeting. "How y'all doing today?"

The one feeding MacGyver jerked like she hadn't heard his truck pull up or him making his way over to them. The other just looked annoyed. He glanced down at his watch. None of the guests on today's ride were supposed to have been there for another hour, so he wasn't exactly sure why they would be annoyed with *him*.

"*We're* cold." The one in the jacket pranced over to him in her too-tall heels, carefully picking through the dirt and muck in front of the barn.

For spring, it was unseasonably warm, but when it came to the ranch's guests, he'd learned not to point out the obvious—it didn't help him earn his tips. He was here only to make them happy and to serve them and let them have the experience of their lives, nothing less.

"If you're cold, I can take you back to your cabins to warm up—if you are staying on the ranch. I won't be ready for us to head out on the trail for another hour or so."

"We're not booked into a cabin yet. Let's see how the ride goes first." The sour but beautiful woman scowled. "We were told the horses would be ready at eight o'clock. It's eight now. Do things always run late on this ranch?"

And they were off to the races.

This was clearly not going to be one of his favorite outings.

He did a quick recalculation of the map route he'd intended on taking them on with the horses—if he stopped before last corner, they could cut three miles and at least an hour off their time together. *Perfect.*

In fact, if he could get Jackson or one of the Trappers to take this group…

He glanced toward the main ranch house, but there was no one outside and the trucks that were normally parked around it were already gone for the day. Jackson wouldn't be back to the barn from checking on the cattle up in the high pastures for at least a couple more hours.

Today would be all on him.

He checked his sigh before facing the firing squad that was Ms. Model. "We pride ourselves on working on time, efficiently and as safely as possible here at the West Glacier Ranch. I'm sorry to tell you, but it's actually only seven o'clock I'm afraid you have the wrong time."

The model waved him off, her fingernails catching the light and showing off the white tips. Everything about this woman had been coifed and buffed. She wouldn't last a minute on this ranch if she was left to her own devices. "That's impossible. Everything is digital and updates automatically."

He shrugged. "Well, ma'am, that may be true in most places around the world, but we often run into technological snafus here in the high country—sorry to tell ya." He tried to sound apologetic for something he actually kind of loved. He appreciated the fact that tech was still something that had to be sought out instead of instantly accessible every second of the day. "I will have everything ready in an hour."

She looked furious.

He needed to turn things around before he heard about it from Cameron. The last thing they needed was a bad review on their new guest services—and this woman looked like exactly the type who would go out of her way to sink a burgeoning business just because he'd annoyed her.

"By the way, my name is Miles Miller," he said, extending his hand.

She looked at his calloused hands and dirt-stained fingers for a long moment. "Miles." She clipped his name. "That's Kelcie Sherry. She's my personal assistant." She put her hand in his for a brief second and gave it a weak shake. "As for me, I'm Scarlett Leafletter."

The name was so strange, but he simply nodded. "Nice to meet you, Ms. Leafletter."

"You may call me Scarlett." She pushed her loose brunette hair back over the fur collar of her jacket with a twitch of the head like a headstrong mare.

"We are waiting for a father and son to join us for the ride today."

She huffed. "I was hoping to make it a private ride. Is there any way we can make it happen?"

He shook his head. If there was any way he could come up with to unload this woman on anyone else at the ranch, he would have done it. "Unfortunately, all our hands are out working today and assisting other guests. The Sullivan family booked their trip nearly six months in advance. According to my emails, you booked *yesterday*."

Again, he was met with that ridiculous flip of the hand to wave him off.

She would be riding at the back of the group.

"You're welcome to join me in the barn while I get things ready. If I don't get moving, we really won't get out on time," he said, trying to remind himself to be patient.

He saddled up six of his favorite horses. He made sure to pick a headstrong mare for the headstrong woman. It was strange, but often two like-minded beasts tended to work the best together. It was as if somewhere along the line in their push-and-pull they developed mutual respect and from there a good working relationship. If he didn't work it that way, one often had a way of running over the other and neither the horse nor the person had a good experience.

As he was tightening the straps on the last mare's saddle, Scarlett pranced over. "Are we going to have a chef with us for the day?" She looked around the ground expectantly, like Gordon Ramsey was going to pop up from behind one of the horses to join them.

"Yes, that would be *me*." He sent her a wide, sarcastic smile, though he was more than aware he was pressing his luck with this city woman.

She gave him a slow look up and down, sizing him up, and then she glanced back down at his hands where they rested on the saddle. "I guess you really are a jack-of-all-trades."

For the first time since he'd met her this morning, the words coming out of her mouth weren't entirely off-putting. She still looked at him with a bit of hostility. However, based on her tone, he would have almost thought it was something approaching a compliment. She had him confused.

"I'm the man those around me need me to be," he said, sending her a smile he hoped would melt away any ice that still rested between them.

She gave a slight nod. "I can tell. Your bosses must be happy to have you on staff."

There it was—a genuine compliment. What was happening?

Did she need something?

He was still going to make her ride in the back of the string.

"I don't know if I've been around long enough for them to go on and be thinking that." He gave an uncomfortable laugh. He wasn't used to being complimented by good-looking women. "I'm gonna step into the barn here and start gettin' the horses ready."

"Do you mind terribly if I tag along?" She looked over her shoulder, toward the main road.

Something about it struck him as odd, but he brushed it off. City girls were strange creatures, and he had never been one to understand them. They tended to see things that he wasn't used to looking for and vice versa.

"You're welcome to join me. Kelcie, too." He motioned toward the blonde who was petting Mac.

Kelcie turned toward him at the mention of her name. "I'm good. I'll just pet the horse, if that's okay."

He smiled. "That boy's name is MacGyver. He's a retired barrel racing horse and he'll eat up all the attention you want to put on him." He motioned for Scarlett to follow him as he slid open the heavy red doors. They squeaked as the casters moved on the steel rails overhead.

She took off her coat as they walked into the barn.

"Here, let me take that for you." He took it and her purse and hung them on the hook for the bridles just inside the barn door.

There was a clink of glass and keys. He could only guess what the woman was carrying in the bag that was nearly as large as the panniers he used on the pack mules.

There was the sound of a truck pulling up and doors slamming. The mare he was working with lifted her head and gave out a long exhale, then shook her head. Even she could tell it was going to be a long, exhausting day.

The princess beside him walked over to the mare he'd chosen for her, the buckskin quarter horse with mustang lineage, and started to scratch the area right above the mare's tail. The horse lifted her foot slightly and softened with Scarlett's touch.

"So, you know horses?" he asked.

She nodded. "Some. The last series I worked on, we worked out of Belarus. I had four different horses that I rode for the show. By the end of the shoot, I really wanted to bring my favorite girl home, but the owners of the horse wouldn't sell."

"You're a star?" He should have known. With a name like hers and a persona like that, she had pain in the ass written all over her.

She smiled, but the humble look he assumed she was going for didn't quite make it to her eyes. He could see pride in them, but he couldn't begrudge her—he had no doubt she had worked hard for her position in life. Yet, she was wrong if she had thought she was the only one who worked hard in this world.

"I've done three television series—I've even won an Emmy." She sent him a charming smile.

"You looked familiar," he lied. "Thought I knew the name, but I don't get a lot of downtime to watch TV, ya know?"

She seemed mollified by his answer as she scratched the horse. "I'm sure. I don't get a lot of time to come out here and do this kind of thing, either."

For a fleeting moment, Miles found himself surprised, for in this second, he'd found a common thread with the most uncommon of people—and, he could almost say he'd found the mustard seed of friendship.

Chapter Three

The cowboy who she'd thought looked so handsome on the internet was even more striking in person. It was just too bad he seemed to have taken an instant disliking to her. He wasn't the first.

In her world, it seemed like people took one look at her and decided to either love or hate her, and there was no bringing them back from the dark side once they decided. It was too bad. Having him along to flirt with for the horseback trip would have been a fun diversion—and she was pretty good at charming people, if she said so herself.

Sickeningly enough, she had a stalker to prove it.

That wasn't funny. It really wasn't. However, months ago she had resigned herself to a sick sense of humor to deal with the problems she had been facing in her job.

Though she hated to admit it, she had probably brought the agent's unwanted advances upon herself. If she hadn't played into the gender roles maybe she wouldn't have sent her career into a full tailspin complete with this fireball that was the cowboy at the end.

She had just wrapped up filming her last season for the new show on the Syfy network, *Rogue Crafter*. If the show didn't find a solid footing with viewers, her career would be as good as over. She didn't have an agent anymore. Which in her world meant she wouldn't get pitched for possible roles. Which meant she didn't get any other acting jobs.

Her emotions caught in her throat.

She had worked so hard and sacrificed so much to become an actress—she had even given up Montana. One jerk without boundaries and the ability to hear "no" had killed her dreams.

She was angry on so many levels, but firstly at herself for making it so easy for some guy to take her out at the knees. In her head, she was so much stronger than she had proven herself to be.

Her horse moved, exhaled hard and shook the nerves off as the group started forward. Of course the fireball cowboy, Miles, had put her at the back of the line. He mustn't want to be anywhere near her. He probably thought she was going to whine and complain and didn't want to hear any of it. Clearly, he didn't have a clue who she really was.

The saddlebags were making a loud squeaking noise as her mare, Seagrass, moved. It was a leathery sound, but as they moved, the *squeak, squeak, squeak* made her want to drive a nail into her eardrum.

She moved to pull her phone out of her jacket pocket, but then she remembered that she had taken off her adorable Gucci jacket after Miles had said it would spook the horses. Clearly, he didn't understand fashion, and he underestimated horses.

Instead of taking out her phone, she reached forward and gave her girl a nice scratch to the side of her bobbing neck. She did love horses. She always had, though she was nowhere near the rider her barrel racing sister had always been and would be. The thought made Scarlett miss her.

She touched the tip of her nose. If her sister, Jamie, had

seen her on the ranch, she was sure that she would have recognized her, but she had been careful in planning. According to the man she had spoken to when booking, her sister was out of town today, so if she was careful, they would never cross paths.

As for the rest of her family, they weren't actively running the guests' section of the ranch. All she had to do was keep out of the way and she could go unnoticed. It wasn't like she was there under her real name. Even if her brother did see her, she wasn't sure how he would react—he would probably kick her out. If he had wanted her back here, he would have reached out when their father had passed away.

The lack of care from her siblings and family stung. Regardless of the fights in their past, she would have thought that one of them would have reached out to let her know about their father's and brother's passing. She deserved to be informed and to have had the choice to come back for the services. That was, assuming they had services—she didn't really know what they had done, given the circumstances of their deaths.

The smell of horses permeated the air as one of the animals in front of her made itself lighter for their ride. Miles probably thought it was hilarious watching her deal with the realities that came with this kind of world. Well, he could laugh at her all he wanted. She wouldn't let him see she was bothered. Kelcie looked back at her over her shoulder, and she crinkled her nose in disgust. Scarlett laughed like it was nothing, and she caught Miles's gaze as she did. Put one on the board for the starlet.

As she relaxed, Seagrass picked up pace and tried to pass the gelding on the right to move to the front of the string. She seemed annoyed with being forced to be in the back of the pack. Scarlett pulled her back. The mare threw her a backward ear and pressed hard against the reins, checking her rider to see who was really in control.

The mare had another think coming if she thought she could take her for a ride. She wasn't the best rider on the ranch, but second only to the guide, she was the greatest in the group, and she wasn't about to let a horse best her.

The family of two in front of them was talking about horses and Glacier National Park and the bear they had seen one time that was *just huge*. So far, the kid hadn't stopped talking. The more she listened the more she was convinced it really wasn't that big and was probably nothing more than a black bear cub, but she didn't interrupt. It was cute listening to the five-year-old boy, Thomas, talk about the bear like it was the coolest thing he had ever seen in his entire life.

If only Scarlett could go back there, to those days and that level of innocence.

Instead, she was in the darkest moment of her life, passing through a cloud of stink while looking for answers and a means for escape.

When she'd left the ranch, she had thought life couldn't get harder, but now she knew that wasn't true. Life had one hell of a way of looking at a person at their lowest and saying, "I can beat that… Hold my beer and watch this."

The only saving grace, at least now, was that she had some financial freedom. When she'd left, she hadn't had two dimes to rub together.

Her mind wandered as she thought about her past and her days spent on the ranch. It was strange, but as they moved up the trail that led toward Glacier National Park, she couldn't remember ever having been on this pathway before. She was sure if they followed it for a full day, it would take them all the way into the park. But Miles had told them they were only going to be skirting the edges as it was just a day trip, and they would have to ride back to the ranch.

From inside the saddlebag where her coat and purse were stuffed, she could hear her phone ringing, and ringing, and ringing. A part of her felt a deep satisfaction that she couldn't pick up and that something else and *someone* else had stopped her from being at Butch's beck and call.

If he knew she'd left California and his immediate grasp, he would be so angry. And, if he found out she was in Montana…it would make him beyond rabid—he would go straight for her jugular.

In their many travels abroad together, she had talked about her childhood and her parents. He'd been her sounding board, and she'd revealed pains of her past that she couldn't remember sharing with anyone else. Now, if he knew she was here, he would use all those secrets against her and tell her what an idiot she was for coming here—how weak she had become in falling back into the safety net of Montana. In that, he wouldn't have been wrong. She did feel weak running home. Yet, he had left her with no other moves. He'd put her in check.

Her horse flicked its ear toward her like it could sense her unease, and it gave a long huff beneath her thighs. Then it shook, forcing out some of their shared anxiety.

The medley of thoughts about Butch, her family, the cowboy, Kelcie, her job, her love life, her living situations…all of it…could wait. For now, she needed to enjoy the pines around her, the clip-clop of the horses' shoed footfalls on the packed earthen trail, and the view of the cowboy's Wrangler-covered behind in the saddle in front of them.

As though he could sense her looking at him, Miles moved to the side and let the family take the lead. He pointed up the trail, probably telling the father to just keep going. He pulled his horse to a stop and waited for her as she and Kelcie moved up the trail toward him. As soon as she reached him, he started forward at her side. "How's it going? You've been pretty quiet back here."

"Just picking up the slack back here, no problems." She smiled, trying to hide the fact she hated being last at anything.

"Seagrass is normally a nipper. I'm surprised you're not having a bit of a rodeo back here."

She lifted a brow. "If you know my horse has a biting problem, why would you put her in the back?" She knew the answer before she even asked, but she had to see his reaction. She needed to know who this man really was—and what kind of ego she was dealing with.

He sent her a guilty smirk—it was dangerously sexy, and she was torn as to whether she wanted to slap or kiss the smile from his lips. For the time being, she settled on looking down to Seagrass and pretending not to be taken by the handsome cowboy.

He rode ahead and turned in the saddle to address everyone. "Let's stop here and have a little lunch," he said, motioning toward a small meadow.

She had been so wrapped up with the cowboy, staying straight in the saddle and going through all the things in her mind that she hadn't really paid attention to the ride. As the group came to a halt, there was a wooden hitching post grayed with age and weather. The ground around it had been trodden to bare dirt and mud thanks to what must have been a regular stream of horses and riders.

Though she was completely capable, she waited for a moment for Miles to help Aiden and Thomas to dismount and tie up. Then he made his way over to her. He held Seagrass steady, though the horse was like a rock and didn't budge as she swung her leg over and stepped down. She gave the horse a pet as he tied her up.

"How are you doing? Hips and back okay? I know riding can be hard on the body when you're not used to it," Miles asked, giving her a kind smile.

The smile was one that had probably melted the clothes off many a guest and even more buckle bunnies.

Thomas, the blond five-year-old, came bouncing over in a half run, half skip. "Heya, whatcha doing? Did you know there's a river thingy over there?" He pointed vaguely to the right. "And there looks like there's been all kinds of animals. From my tracking app, I think there's been at least three deer, an elk and a rabbit. Do you wanna see?" He talked so fast that it took a second to make sense of everything he was saying.

The kid was undeniably cute and could have probably been cast as the precocious but darling kid in some Hallmark movie, but she wasn't about to fall for his charms.

He slipped his hand into hers. "Come see the river, Ms. Scarlett." He tugged on her as she looked at Miles.

He chuckled as he waved her on. "Go ahead. I'll set up our picnic. You guys go. Lunch will be ready in a few." He turned toward Kelcie and started to help her down. "Why don't you go ahead with her, as well? I can tell she is chomping at the bit to play with that kid."

She hated that her discomfort must have been visible on her features.

It wasn't that she *disliked* kids, it was just that she had so much life that she wanted to live. As it stood, she'd only been to four of the seven continents. A kid would only slow her down.

"Kelcie?" She called for a lifeline.

"Come on!" Thomas urged.

Her assistant laughed as she pointed toward the scowling kid who was now tugging violently on her arm. "I don't think he wants anyone but you."

She sighed, resigning herself to the fact that for the next few minutes she would be a child's plaything, and she would just have to suck it up. "All right, Thomas."

His hand was sticky with sweat and something unnamable, and it took all her willpower not to extract her hand and wipe it on her jeans. She could only guess at the number and types of bacteria and germs on his hands.

Don't touch your face, she thought, cringing as she hurried along behind him.

There was a thicket of willows heavy with green leaves. The grass along the edges of the stream bank was knee-high, and mixed throughout were the purple flowers that came with June and the red sprigs of Indian paintbrush. There was a pang of childhood memories, as she recalled picking bunches of them and giving them to her mother.

There was a yellow flower—she didn't remember their exact name—but her mother had loved the soft leaves of the plant. Actually, if she recalled, her mom had called them mule's ears, but she doubted that was their scientific name.

"Thomas," she said, pulling the boy gently to a stop.

"Yeah?" he asked.

"You see that flower there?" she asked, pointing toward the gray-green plant with palmate leaves and the densely packed purple pea-shaped blooms.

"Uh-huh?"

"That's called a lupine. Soon, they get pea pods and then they dry out and they *explode*."

"No way!" He let go of her and dropped down to his knees next to the plant, picking one of the blooms.

She smiled. "It's not ready yet, but I promise it's super

cool. If you're really quiet, you can hear all these little things bursting in the late summer. It kinda sounds like popcorn popping, but it's the plant sending out its seeds for the next year."

"That's cool."

"Yeah. They're my favorite flower. You know…anything that *explodes*." She held out her hand and helped him to stand up.

He slipped his sticky hand back into hers. "It's my favorite, too."

She felt her Grinch heart grow three sizes, not that she would have admitted it to another living soul.

He looked up at her as he handed her the flower. "This is for you, Ms. Scarlett. I like you."

She took the stem and gently spun the spiked flower in her fingers. It was sad, but she couldn't remember the last time anyone but Butch had given her a gift. "Thank you, sweetheart. I like you, too." She awkwardly patted him on the head, the flower bopping his ear and making him squirm.

As they giggled, they weaved through the thicket of the willows toward the babbling sound of the moving water until they broke through and found what turned out to be nothing close to a river; instead it was a meandering high-mountain stream. The bottom was covered with smooth stones in a rainbow of colors, and as the sun shone through the clear, clean water, it looked like something from an art studio instead of real life.

"Wow," she said, not meaning to speak.

"Isn't it cool, Ms. Scarlett?" Thomas bounced excitedly from foot to foot as he looked up at her and then back down at the thicket and creek around them.

"Thomas, it's perfect. You are quite the explorer, buddy."

His smile faded. "That's what my mom used to say."

And just like that, she was reminded of the conversation she had overhead between the boy's father, Aiden, and Miles. Apparently, they had come here as part of Jamie's equine therapy program to help the boy recover from the loss of his mother.

She was so not equipped to help this boy deal with his loss—she could barely deal with the drama in her own life. If she was, she wouldn't have found herself standing in Montana.

She watched him play at the edge of the stream for a few minutes. She couldn't quite see what he was doing, but he seemed content and happy in his play, and given the reason he was here she felt righteous in allowing him the freedom to continue.

After a bit, there was a cattle call whistle from the distance. It made a shiver of unexpected excitement run down her spine. There was something about that sound that she had always loved. Perhaps it was just so commanding, but it was also sexy.

She couldn't help but smile, and it struck her that perhaps she was here for equine therapy of her own. "Hey, Thomas, why don't we go ahead and head back for lunch?" she asked.

He looked at the water as he shoved something into his pocket.

She cleared her throat. "I'll race you," she said, trying to convince him it was a good idea.

"Okay!" he said, taking off on the trail that they had followed in through the brush.

She made sure to watch him as they broke through the thicket and back into the meadow. He beat her by a landslide.

As she jogged toward the red-checkered blanket that was spread out beneath a large pine, Miles stood there and smiled. No matter how good-looking this white-hatted cowboy was, she couldn't fall for that man. In some ways, falling for him would be even more dangerous than the man who had made her go on the run.

Chapter Four

The way Scarlett's hair picked up the sunshine made it shine like brown satin. Though he would have expected her to be smiling, the expression on her face made it look like she had just left the dentist's office.

She must have really hated running, but damn did she look good while doing it.

He shouldn't have been checking out a guest, but there wasn't really any harm in window shopping. If anything, it would help him to forget all the reasons he could think of to never jump into a relationship again. From the way her body bounced as she ran, he could definitely think of all the reasons he could jump into bed. Sure, that wasn't the best way to start a relationship, but in the world of love, he'd recently learned there were no clear-cut rules.

She came to a skidding stop with Thomas. He wrapped himself around his father's legs and giggled as Scarlett turned away from him and bent over like she was catching her breath. Watching her bend was too much. He had to look away, in an effort not to look like some kind of pervert.

He made his way over to the horses.

There, across from where he'd tied them up, was a trail camera. He watched the shutter flicker open and closed as it took stills. Up here, the camera could have belonged to any number of people, including the Forest Service, who sometimes ran counts on the number of riders who moved through an area.

Trail cameras weren't that uncommon in the area. Hunters used them to watch game animals, hikers used them to check their trails, and even he had used them in the past to track animals so he could make sure to take guests to areas they would be sure to see specific animals on their "must-see" lists. They were a handy tool. However, something about this camera made him feel uncomfortable. He couldn't explain exactly why—perhaps it was merely the fact he had actually noticed the device. Often, the person who'd placed them made sure to do it in such a way that a person or animal never noticed, as it kept the camera from being stolen or vandalized.

He tried to ignore the way the hair on the back of his neck stood up as he thought about the invasion of privacy. It wasn't like the owner of the camera was taking pictures inside his bedroom. He was in public—they had every right to take any picture they wanted.

He ran his hand down his mare, taking a moment to scratch her favorite spot right above the base of her tail. She let out a long exhale and shook her head as she relaxed.

Miles's phone pinged as he put away the cooler of sandwiches into the saddlebag on his mare. She looked back at him with annoyance at the sound. "I know, lady, I don't want to hear that nonsense out here, either." He laughed, pulling the phone from the pocket of his plaid shirt. "And make sure to give the camera your good side," he said, giving her a little slap on the hind quarter.

The phone pinged with a second message. At the point in the day, the phone call could have been just about anyone, but he hoped it wasn't one of the Trappers. They were nice to work for and pretty good bosses, but if he was on the trail and they were texting it only meant one thing—he was in trouble.

Unlocking the screen his stomach sank. It was worse—it was the ex, Chloe.

He wasn't sure he really wanted to ruin his day by reading her messages, but sometimes the best thing to do with a splinter was to pull it out. If not, it had a way of festering.

He squeezed his eyes shut and then sucked in a breath as he summoned the strength to face the unknown as he tapped open the phone.

You're a thief now? The Sullivans are clients of the Joy Luck. How dare you steal our business!

Of course, Chloe would think the worst of him. She would never take responsibility for her role in their breakup or the fact that she had cheated on him. Now she had the audacity to act like she had any skin in the game when it came to the business of the ranches.

He scrolled to the next message.

How many other clients have u stolen? We're watching. This better be it.

He glanced up at the trail camera, wondering if the device was one of theirs. There was a deep urge to flip the thing the bird, but he reminded himself that Thomas may have been watching. Besides, he wasn't afraid of her empty threats. Chloe didn't have any teeth. If the ranch owner had texted, Drake, he would have been slightly more concerned—but even then, he had never known the guy for anything other than being full of hot air.

It wasn't Miles's fault the clientele had followed him to his new home. At least at the West Glacier, he was treated right.

He carried the cooler bag out to the picnic area where the guys and the two pretty women waited. Kelcie was tapping away on her phone, smiling in a way that made him wonder if she was texting with a man. Aiden was also on his phone, but he scowled and dialed.

"Jennifer, I don't care about what Roger said, you need to make the trade," he ordered, sounding irritated. Aiden looked up and, when he noticed Miles, pointed at Thomas then the basket and gave him a thumbs-up before turning away and moving off into the timber.

Not for the first time, he wished this picnic spot didn't have phone service. In the past, it had worked to their advantage. Today, however, was not one of those days.

After making sure Thomas got his favorite peanut butter and grape jelly sandwich with no crust, cut-up strawberries and Goldfish crackers, he gave everyone else their specialty Italian subs that he'd put together that morning while packing for the trip.

To her credit, Scarlett was the first to take a bite. She nodded in appreciation. Aiden looked at the ciabatta bread that Miles had picked up at the bakery before the sun had even risen with disdain.

"The sandwiches are freshly made and have a variety of meats including mortadella, capicola, *soppressata*, prosciutto and Genoa salami, provolone and a nice tapenade spread," he said, anxious that his guests enjoy the meal he had put effort into creating. "If the muffuletta sandwich isn't something you are interested in, I always keep a vegetarian charcuterie plate."

Scarlett leaned over to her friend and whispered behind

her hand, "And I was worried about not having a chef. All we need is wine and it's like we are back in Italy."

He hadn't packed wine, but he smiled widely as he reached into the bag and pulled out sparkling waters and handed them to each, with the exception of the chocolate milk he'd handed to his little buddy. It wasn't the first time someone had complimented his cooking, or sandwich making as it was, but it was the first time it came from someone as sexy as Scarlett Leafletter. Something like that should qualify for placement on his résumé.

Thomas happily munched away, but his father wrapped the sandwich in his napkin and walked off into the meadow. A few minutes later, he spotted him throwing the perfectly good food into the timber.

After everyone finished eating, and Aiden loudly argued with someone on the phone about what sounded like stocks, he packed up the picnic supplies. He carried the bag of garbage over to where the horses waited and undid the straps on his saddlebag. The stupid trail cameras were still where they had been, and he didn't know why he hoped for anything different—of course, they wouldn't have gone anywhere.

He tried not to think of Chloe and Drake as he lifted open the leather flap on the bag. As he did, Seagrass nuzzled his neck with her nose, and when he ignored her, she opened her mouth and moved to nip his shoulder. He pushed her away. "You know better. Don't you think you're going to get away with that, Seagrass."

She shook her head, her dark mane flying with attitude. It made him chuckle, but the horse really couldn't get away with that kind of behavior if they were going to keep her around the kids. The last thing he wanted was for a kid to get bitten. He'd have to reevaluate her for guests. For right now, she was being precocious, but that could have been rubbing off on her from her rider.

He tried not to stare as Scarlett bent over and said something to Thomas. He handed her a wilted lupine and she smiled as she put it behind her ear. She was still out of Miles's league, but the way she dealt with Thomas made her seem more approachable.

She smiled widely as she stood up and patted Thomas's head. The action seemed a little forced, but endearing as Thomas reached into his pocket. In the center of his starfish hand was a coiled little ball. From far away he wasn't quite sure what the black thing was until it started to writhe and slither up the boy's arm.

Scarlett squealed and jumped back, covering her mouth with her hands.

He tipped his head back in a laugh.

Thomas squatted down and let the snake go, and it slithered happily off into the grass. The boy turned to Scarlett and put his hands on her arms and pulled her hands down from her face. Miles could hear Thomas trying to comfort her.

The terror on the city girl's face was cute as all get-out.

He walked back to the group, picked up the red-checkered blanket and shook it out. Scarlett grabbed the bottom corners and brought them over to him, helping him fold as he silently chastised himself. "What is the plan? Am I still in the back of the group?"

He laughed. "Yeah. I wanted to keep the Sullivans at the front. We don't want any more surprise garter snakes," he said with a laugh.

Kelcie looked back at her friend and frowned, as if asking if she was okay. Scarlett gave her an almost imperceptible nod.

"You have a good friend there," he said, nudging his chin in Kelcie's direction. "How did you meet your girlfriend?"

"We've been friends for a long time, then I hired her as my assistant. I needed the help, and she needed a job. I knew we could travel well together—two birds, one stone kind of a thing."

"So, you two aren't a *thing*?" he asked.

"No." She shook her head as she looked up at him, seeming to laugh at the idea and how far off the mark he was. There was something in her eyes that he couldn't quite make sense of, but he begged it was that she was attracted to him.

To hope for something like that was silly. "How did you guys meet?"

She lifted the other edge of the blanket and their fingers grazed against each other's. Her skin was so soft, but she didn't seem to notice the touch at all. He told himself to ignore the sensation of disappointment that moved through him.

"We met when I moved to Hollywood. Her father worked in Burbank. We ended up becoming roommates while we both tried to break into acting," she said, smiling at the memory as they walked toward the horses. "I made it, and she decided it wasn't for her but liked the lifestyle. Now, she's trying to break into screenwriting. She is really talented. She just got done writing a Western, based on..." She paused, as she let him help her up into the saddle. "Well, something like this, but in the 1800s. It's super good. I have my fingers crossed."

He opened his mouth to speak then promptly closed it. There were so many things he wanted to say, but all he could think about was the firmness of her calf where he had touched her through the fabric of her jeans. Every part of this woman was perfect. "I'm not sure exactly what it takes for her to get picked up, but if you say she's talented, I believe you."

Her face fell. "It can be very dog-eat-dog."

"We live in very different worlds, but some parts of life are the same everywhere you go."

He moved to Kelcie and helped her up and then the Sullivans, making sure everyone had their helmets strapped tight. Aiden was still on his cell phone and Miles had to tap him on the arm and give him the cut-it-off signal. The guy rolled his eyes, so Miles tried to mime that they would be losing service around the next bend. He felt ridiculous with his hand signals, but Aiden seemed to have put it together and ended the call.

After getting everyone moving down the trail, Miles got into the saddle and moved after the group. His mind turned toward their conversation. She hadn't said she was exactly single, but he didn't get the impression she was in a relationship. As far as he was concerned, the playing field was wide open for a pass—if she hadn't been a guest.

As for her dog-eat-dog comment, there had been a darkness in her tone that made him sense there were things to unpack from within that sentiment. No one said something like that without having been hurt, and hurt badly. He didn't mind baggage, though—he certainly had enough of his own. His baggage had even texted him today.

He nudged his horse to a trot, not wanting to be left to his own thoughts. It didn't take long to catch up, and they rode in silence on the trail for the next mile. He was glad after the inane chatter of Aiden's phone call that had effectively ruined the tranquility of the picturesque meadow.

He wondered how often the man missed the moments of true living with his son by being on his phone and working. Though Miles could understand the needs of a job, he had a hard time watching workaholics fail to enjoy the adventures they worked so hard to afford and provide for their child. He could only imagine how hard it must have been when Aiden had lost his wife, Catherine, last fall to cancer. Miles had met the woman a couple of times and she had been so sweet and kind, and Thomas had taken after her. Perhaps that was what Aiden was really running away from.

Seagrass shuffled in front of him and tried to push past Kelcie and her horse, Oreo, while Scarlett was only half paying attention. Kelcie's horse slowed, and as it did, Seagrass lifted her head and took her chance, landing a bite squarely on the mare's gray haunch.

Kelcie's horse lurched forward with a painful squeal. It bucked. The paint's back rose like an arch and all four feet left the ground. Oreo's hooves hit hard, jarring Kelcie and forcing her sideways in the saddle.

Oreo bucked again.

Kelcie let go of the leather reins and reached for the pommel, but as she moved the horse spun and kicked, sending Kelcie right as the horse went left. For a moment, it looked as though Kelcie was flying, except her right foot was still holding strong in the stirrup.

"Whoa, buddy!" Miles called the mare, kicking his horse forward and moving toward the horse in an attempt to gain control over the situation.

Kelcie landed in the dirt with a *whump*, and the mare started to run, dragging her by her right foot. Her helmeted head bounced on the ground until Kelcie lifted it and curled her body upward.

"Dammit! Whoa!" Miles yelled, racing over to the mare and grabbing the reins. He pulled hard against them, jerking the horse and his to a full stop.

Blood poured from Kelcie's mouth and nose. Her eyes

were wide with fear as she struggled to breathe. Tears rolled down her cheeks as she looked at Scarlett.

"It's going to be okay, Kelcie. You just need to remain still." He tried to calm her as he reached for his phone.

Then he remembered they were out of contact right at the moment her life was on the line.

Chapter Five

"I am so sorry," Miles said, making sure Kelcie was safely seated in Oreo's saddle after the horse had calmed. Her arm was up in a makeshift sling made from his black bandana, and he hadn't dared to pull her right foot out of her boot. That could wait until they were in the emergency room.

In his days at the ranch, he'd seen that kind of injury a time or two and it never turned out pretty. At the very least, she'd sprained her ankle, but at least there wasn't any visible blood coming from her hip or leg. She'd not torn any muscles at least that he could tell. One of his rodeo buddies had gotten caught in a stirrup and torn his hamstring so badly that it took surgery and months of physical therapy before he was supposed to be back in the saddle again.

Of course, his friend had been back in the saddle in less than four weeks, but what the doctors hadn't known hadn't hurt them. The requirements of life were therapy for the working man—it was how cowboys were made.

He and Scarlett had been doing well together, but now she was scowling at him. Of course, she would be furious. He'd told her the horse was a biter, and she'd even questioned Seagrass being in the back—she was a horse that needed to be in the lead, and even Scarlett had known it.

Miles made a mistake, and he had been the one to cause

this disaster. Now, he was going to have to turn the entire group around and head back to the ranch. The Sullivans, well, Aiden to be exact, were the type who would ask for a refund because they hadn't reached the promised destination—regardless of the circumstances. Cameron Trapper was going to be upset. JMac Equine Therapy and guest rides were their new business endeavors, and the insurance costs had been through the roof. With this accident and the resulting claims, their premiums were going to skyrocket.

That was all without mentioning the fact he'd been hoping to bring on the rest of his family to the ranch as staff members to help wherever they were needed. His brother Jackson was already at the ranch, but the rest needed jobs, and with the economic situation in Montana being what it was—where even minimum-paying jobs were hard to find and housing costs running at a premium—the West Glacier Ranch was their best option.

This guide service had been his idea. He had a lot riding on this, and he'd already screwed up…royally. Not only were his other brothers not going to be hired, but he was going to be out on his butt.

Kelcie shifted in the saddle as she readjusted the bandana on her arm. She winced in pain as she moved. It was going to be one heck of a long ride out for her. "Are you sure you are up to riding?" he asked.

She nodded, her split lip puffy, and there was a crust of blood from her bloody nose. "What do they say? 'You have to get back on the horse'?" Her black helmet was gray with dirt and dust from her unexpected ride on the bucking bronc.

"I'm impressed that you're so willing, but if you're hurting, I can get a UTV up here or call in a helo to life flight you to the hospital. You don't have to tough it out. It's important to me, and my employers at the West Glacier Ranch, that you get out safely and—in this situation—avoid further injury." His voice wavered slightly as he said employers, unwillingly giving away some of his unspoken fears. He hated it, but there was no hiding his misstep, there was only hoping Scarlett hadn't heard his falter.

Kelcie waved him off as Scarlett rode up to her side.

"Look, Miles," Scarlett said, almost hissing his name. "Why don't you just run along with the Sullivans. Kelcie and I don't need you. I've seen this kind of injury before on set. There's no TBI and the pain is under control. I can get us back to the ranch and my car is there. I can take her to Logan Hospital in Kalispell to get checked out. And don't worry, we won't tell the Trappers a thing."

He glanced back at the family. The duo was standing at the edge of the trail. Aiden had his arms crossed over his chest and looked pissed off that his vacation had been interrupted. Thomas was shaking his head and tears were running down his cheeks. "Let me talk to them and see what they want to do."

"We'll just start heading back." Scarlett motioned toward the ranch. "You'll know where to find us." She turned Seagrass and nudged her forward, making sure to take the lead.

Kelcie gave him a stiff nod. "See ya."

"Again, sorry about what happened." He felt ridiculous apologizing repeatedly, but there was no other move in his cache. He could only repent. The beautiful woman he'd been making progress with was furious, and rightly so, he was quite possibly on the brink of losing his newly acquired role at the ranch, and he may have also cost his family their potential careers. No biggie—he'd just taken his whole family down in one fell swoop.

Nice job, jackass, he silently chastised himself.

He desperately wanted to jump on his horse and go back

with the two women, but he was torn. He didn't want to tell Jamie Trapper that he'd failed in his role with JMac and in helping Thomas deal with his past trauma—if anything, he had only worsened the boy's anxiety. He needed the family—and specifically Thomas—to continue.

Picking up his phone, he searched for service, but without going a mile back down the trail and risking coming out with the Sullivan family in the dark, he was stuck trusting that Scarlett and Kelcie could find their way safely back. As soon as he hit service again, he'd let Jackson know they were on the way and to keep a lookout.

As he watched Scarlett lead Kelcie away, he held no doubts that Scarlett was the kind who had led herself out of harder situations than this before. She seemed like she could deal with anything life could throw in her way. She also seemed to know horses. The bite and the rodeo had been on his shoulders—if he hadn't distracted her, the bite wouldn't have happened.

He walked over to the family. Thomas's eyes were puffy from crying. "Mr. Miles, can we please keep going? I don't want to go back. Daddy says we have to go back."

"It is up to you guys what you wish to do. The ladies are headed to the ranch, but I'm willing to continue our ride as planned just for you, bud. Let's ask Dad." He looked up from Thomas to Aiden. He didn't want to appear as though he was seeking absolution or pity, but as his nerves rose into his throat, he found that he sought both. So much rode on Aiden's decision. Cameron and Jamie would be furious if he failed to help the boy and if this incident hurt their growing business.

"Daddy, *please*," Thomas pleaded.

"Things should go smoother," Miles promised with a smile. "I have a stop at a private lake planned. I packed some rods to fish. You guys will love it when we get some trout in our hands."

Aiden had been mollified. "Okay. Let's go." He looked at Miles with a scowl. "No more accidents, hear me? If another thing goes wrong, not only will we not be paying, but your new ranch will be getting a horrible review and you'll be hearing from my attorney."

"Mr. Sullivan, we've worked together in the past, and I'd hate for one little mishap to tarnish this new opportunity for Thomas to heal. Jamie's team of counselors are some of the best, and the horses are well...*horses*." Miles nodded, but his stomach lurched. He was playing with fire. "That being said, I always do my best to make sure everyone stays safe."

Promising safety was like promising love. A person could have the best intentions, but only time could reveal if the fates would play wicked or wild.

IT HADN'T TAKEN Scarlett and Kelcie long to get down off the mountain at Scarlett's preferred trotting speed. Kelcie hadn't seemed to mind the jostling, though Scarlett had kept asking if she needed to slow down—no doubt, Kelcie had wanted to get down the mountain and off the horse far more than Scarlett.

She should never have come back to the ranch. From the moment she had bought the airline ticket online, Scarlett had known this trip would be a disaster. Her brothers and sister hadn't seen her in years, and thanks to their narcissistic father and his golden-child system of parenting—wherein only one of them could ever be loved at a time and the rest were found lacking—it was unlikely she would have been met with open arms. That was, *if* she had told them she was coming. As it was, she was glad she had kept her family and their staff in the dark about her arrival. As it stood, she could simply slip out just as quickly as she had crept onto the ranch.

The only problem was, she didn't know where else to go. Butch was still out there and looking for her. This was the last place he would think of looking for her—he knew how much she hated this place and how much she had hated her father.

Then again, he also knew her father had been killed. Yet, there was nothing here that would have drawn her back. They had talked about it a few months before everything had blown up in the headlines of the small town of West Glacier.

Butch had loved to make fun of her melodrama of a life back in "Hicksville," as he called it. He wasn't wrong in some ways—it was a little backwoods—but at the same time it was its antiquated ways and old-world manners which imbued it with its certain charm. When she had driven to the ranch from the airport, when she'd gotten off the high-way and onto the smaller roads, people still did the two-finger wave as they passed. At the gas station, where she had stopped for a terrible burnt cup of cheap coffee and to freshen up, the cashier had recognized her as being from out of town and had started a full ten-minute conversation about California.

It was a well-known fact native Montanans didn't like Californians, and there were bumper stickers on many cars that read No Vacancy with the Montana state outline. But when people spoke face-to-face, it was rare that folks were anything other than cordial and welcoming. In fact, in the case of the gas station attendant, Jose, they were almost a little too welcoming. They hadn't seemed to pick up on her body language cues that she had wanted to leave and *really* didn't want to make small talk about "home."

If she had told Jose the truth, that she was one of the

long-lost Trapper daughters, the secret would have spread like wildfire through the prairie and her family would have known she was back before her tires touched the ranch's dirt access road.

Things could work to her benefit like that here, too. If she wanted to know gossip about someone, all she had to do was ask the right person and she could find out just about anything she wanted to know. Hair salons, bars and churches were the best places to go for the full gamut of dirt. Nothing ever stayed a secret in a place like this for long, unless a person was the only one to know.

She glanced over at Kelcie. Her assistant knew her secrets, but Scarlett wasn't worried. It wasn't as if Kelcie was from here or talking to anyone in this small town. She knew the rules of her position and she had signed the nondisclosure agreement when she took her job. It all came with the territory of working in Hollywood and film. There were more secrets and skeletons in the business than there were buried under the city of Savannah.

As they arrived back at the ranch, there was another hand standing outside the barn, a man she didn't recognize. He had dark black hair and looked like he was in his midtwenties. He wasn't bad looking, but nothing compared to Miles.

It was good she was leaving the ranch. She had no business being around a man like Miles. He was far too good-looking and the man most likely to next break her heart.

A man who spent his days breaking horses and pleasing guests, well…he would probably know exactly how to run her heart directly into the dirt in the corral near her family's barn.

The cowboy walked over and took hold of the reins of Kelcie's horse. "What are you guys doing back? Where's Miles?" he asked, his voice raspy. He smelled strongly of leather conditioner and hay.

"He stayed up on the trail with the other guests," Scarlett said, speaking over Kelcie, but sending her a smile to try and make up for her rudeness. "My friend had a bit of a bronc situation with her mare here, and we are going to need to run to Logan and get a few X-rays."

"Oh," the man said, glancing to the handkerchief sling and then instinctively down at her leg and stirrups as though he knew only too well what kind of injuries occurred when a horse went wild. "I'm sorry to hear you had problems on the mountain. I would have come up and helped you back had I known you needed anything." He held out his hand. "By the way, I'm Jackson Miller."

"Are you Miles's brother?" Kelcie asked, sounding just a touch too drooly.

"Why, yes, ma'am, I am." He gave her an over-the-top tip of his white cowboy hat.

The action almost made Scarlett laugh at its touch of unctuousness, but Kelcie let out a schoolgirl giggle.

Scarlett wanted to smack her gently to pull her back into reality and away from whatever fantasy she was having about the admittedly handsome cowboy right now. Then again, if she did, she would be some kind of hypocrite when she had been doing the same up on the mountain about the man's brother.

What was it about this family that brought on the swoon factor? Maybe they were the ones who should have been in Hollywood.

For a moment, she envisioned walking onto the red carpet for her next premiere with Miles on her arm. He was wearing a black suit, black shirt, bolo tie and a white hat like his brother's. Every woman in the entire state of California, not to mention the rest of the world, would stop in their tracks. She would be the envy of them all.

And yet, he was nothing but trouble.

"We need to go," she said, pulling herself back to reality.

Kelcie shot her a look, as though she had momentarily forgotten her pain—that was until Scarlett silently noted her arm and ankle. Kelcie sighed and her body sank deep into the saddle. The mare under her dropped into her haunches as her rider moved, following her lead.

"I don't know what happened on the hill," Jackson said, "but your horse seems to like you. You will need to come back when you are done at Logan and visit her." He sent Kelcie a spicy smile as he wrapped the reins around the hitching post and then helped her down out of her saddle.

Kelcie limped on her ankle, her face contorted with pain, but she tried to control it as he helped her over to the wooden and cast-iron bench on the other side of the sliding doors of the barn. She had her arm over his neck and was leaning into his body, and as Scarlett watched a strange wave of jealousy washed over her. On the other hand, she was happy for her friend. It had been a long time since Kelcie had dated anyone. In fact, she couldn't remember anyone serious in her life for the last few years. Lately, it had only been one-night stands or situationships with other people on sets.

It seemed like everything Kelcie did was in line with their lifestyle.

They both sacrificed a lot for this job. If Kelcie wanted to go heart-eyed for this cowboy, she would have to be supportive. Her only fear was that she would get hurt, but if she did, Scarlett would be there to help pick up the pieces. It was the least she could do.

As Kelcie and Jackson talked about what had happened on the mountain, Scarlett climbed down off Seagrass and looped her reins around the post. She didn't fail to notice that Jackson had completely forgotten there was another guest to take care of, but instead of being upset she found it sublimely cute, albeit with a side of the green monster.

If only they hadn't had issues on the mountain, she could have lived out her fantasy of being a cowgirl high in the backcountry with a handsome cowboy she barely knew and may never see again. Oh, where could things have gone.

She ran her hand down Seagrass's neck and cooed her thanks to the beautiful mare as she loosened up the girl's saddle. She moved to Kelcie's horse and followed suit.

Jackson was busy taking off Kelcie's boot, and from the look on his face, her ankle was going to need attention. He turned to her. "I know you said you would take your friend here to the hospital, but I wouldn't mind running her in for you. I know the roads inside and out and I can get there quickly. How 'bout I take her? Or, we can all go together?"

She wasn't about to go and rain on Kelcie's parade, and she didn't want to tell the man she probably knew the roads just as well as he did, so she simply shook her head. As much as she didn't want to stand around and wait on the ranch for her friend to return, she wasn't about to block her friend from spending a few hours with the man who would undoubtedly be the focal point of her upcoming fantasies—and potential reality.

The lucky woman.

Kelcie, who must have picked up on her conundrum, turned and put her hand on Jackson's chest. "Is there a guest-house or somewhere that we can rent for the night? Somewhere that Scarlett can put her things down and get some rest while she waits for us? We hadn't gotten a hotel around here yet, and I'm sure she could use some downtime."

Oh, how she loved her friend. Especially when she understood and appreciated her need to hide.

"I would say you could have my place, but I have a

crummy apartment, and you wouldn't want to stay there—it's not up to your standards, I'm sure." Jackson sent them an apologetic glance. "However, they have guest cabins here, and I can get you set up in one of them."

"That would be great," Kelcie said, limping behind Jackson as he moved toward the small shed-style building that acted as the guest services area.

"There's a really nice cabin, the Saint Ignatius. It's right down by the river and it has a porch where you can sit on the swing and watch the river go by. It's awesome, I just need to make sure it's available. It's normally only for our VIP guests, so it'd be perfect for you. To be honest, I'm surprised you don't already have it booked." Jackson opened the door and walked inside the office building. He clicked away on the computer. "It looks like it's open, and I can give you a free night tonight because of what happened on the mountain, and a great rate if you guys want to stay longer."

"We're not staying for free," Scarlett said, taking out her phone and pulling up her digital wallet. Nothing in this life was free, and she didn't want to owe her family anything if they found out who she really was. "Charge us the going rate. I want to support the ranch."

"I'll talk to Miles when he comes out, but you won't be charged until the end of your stay. Do you know when you'd like to check out?" Jackson took her phone.

"I need to get back to work soon," she said, which wasn't entirely a lie, though she didn't have any concrete plans. "Let's say a week?"

"Done." He clicked on a few buttons, and she tapped her card.

As he handed back her phone, she motioned toward the horses, which were still tied up outside the barn. "If it's okay, I'd like to take care of them so you guys can get going. Is that okay?"

Kelcie shot her an appreciative smile.

Jackson chewed at the corner of his lip as if he was concerned about getting in trouble for shirking his duties if someone came out and saw a guest, alone, putting away the tack and brushing down the horses. "I don't know."

"Just go. No one has to know. And if they find out, I'm sure they'd understand the extenuating circumstances." Scarlett sent him a wilting smile.

Kelcie touched his arm and nodded in agreement. "Let's go, please."

It was the straw that broke the camel's back.

From the pale color of Kelcie's face as Jackson helped her into his pickup, Scarlett was glad he didn't resist her request to head out. Yet, as the sound of the truck and the crunch of its tires on the gravel road faded into the distance and was replaced with the quiet sounds of the ranch, a sense of fear and loneliness swept through her. For the first time since she'd arrived in Montana, she wasn't sure exactly what it was or why, but she felt truly vulnerable.

Chapter Six

Miles was exhausted as he made it back to the ranch, dropped off the Sullivans at their guest cabin, and rode back the mile or so to the barn. He spotted the starlet's white rented Mercedes-Benz in the parking area, and a lightning bolt of excitement buzzed through him. She hadn't hit the road—or maybe she had, and she had just abandoned her rental car there with the intention of having one of the ranch staff members return the car to the airport.

It wouldn't have been the first time an entitled guest had made an unusual request.

What was wrong with him? First he was glad to see her car and then he called her entitled.

He just couldn't decide how he really felt about the woman. There was something about Scarlett that had immediately rubbed him the wrong way, but there was also something so ethereally beautiful about her soul that he wanted to pull her into his arms and kiss her until he could understand every part of her being.

He thirsted for her in ways only a man who was dying of thirst on a desolate island could fully understand.

He was pathetic.

He'd only just met her.

There was no such thing as love at first sight. Lust, for

sure, but love—no stinking way. Insta-love was for mushy, gushy date-night movies. Reality sucked. Love in real life was broken promises after years of dating and engagement, breakups and shattered hearts. For him, it was finding out he had been cheated on by way of an unlocked phone screen and one unforgettable naked man's picture.

If only he could burn that image from his mind.

He could have even believed his ex, Chloe, when she had tried to tell him the picture was unsolicited, but when he'd asked to see the rest of their communications and she had blanched, everything ended. He'd walked out of their apartment and never looked back.

Yeah, forget love. Forget lust. Forget women.

Then again, maybe Scarlett was different. She wasn't from here. Maybe in Hollywood they had come full circle and returned to the land of mutual respect and upheld promises.

All the women he'd ever been with had wanted him as their protector, and he'd happily taken the role, but losing Chloe had shaken his ability to feel up to the task in a romantic relationship. It wasn't that he was incapable of protecting them, it was just that in doing so, he risked losing himself and his heart. And now he had a sinking feeling Scarlett was looking at him in the same way.

Yet again, she had ridden away on the mountain after making a point of telling him they could make it out on their own—and thanks to the heavy prints in the dirt leading toward the barn, and the flurry of texts he'd received from Jackson about him running Kelcie to the hospital, it was safe to say Scarlett had been right.

As he pulled his horse to a halt and got off, hitching her to the post, Scarlett came prancing out of the barn. Her long hair was pulled up into the sexiest messy bun he'd ever seen in his real life. She looked like the starlet she was, and tonight she was playing the role of cowgirl.

He wanted to dislike her for it, and yet there was that damned draw to pull her into his arms. He focused on the freshly stitched brown leather cowboy boots on her feet, with the J toe. They had to be pinching the hell out of her toes and hurting the balls of her feet thanks to the long day of riding and their newness.

Maybe there was something to being broken by women—at least he had learned to protect himself thanks to his pain. If nothing else, the past hurt could help from encountering future agony. *If a guy was smart.*

"How's Kelcie doing?" he asked. "Jackson told me he ran her to the hospital to get checked out. Have you heard how it went?"

"Hello to you, too." She pushed a strand of hair out of her face. "I haven't heard a word from either of them since they left." She stopped beside him and waited for the horse to acknowledge her before she ran her hand down her neck.

"Sorry, didn't mean to be rude." He patted the horse. "You're good with animals."

She shrugged. "Apparently not good enough to stop Kelcie from getting hurt," she said, regret flecking her voice. "I can't believe I let Seagrass get away with that. You had even warned me." She let out a long huff.

He didn't want to tell her that it was more his fault. "Things happen on the trail. I'm just hoping Kelcie will be okay and that—"

"I don't *cause problems* for you." She didn't even blink as she finished his thought, as though litigiousness was so prevalent in her world that it was an everyday conversation piece.

"No," he argued, halfheartedly.

She stopped him with the raise of a finger. "It's fine. I already told you, I don't plan on pursuing any lawsuits, and I know Kelcie feels the same. She isn't one to make waves. If anything, I think she was glad to be with your brother." She sent him a coquettish smile that chipped away at the ice he'd tried to use to enshroud his heart.

"He's a good man. Smarter than he looks." He chuckled as he remembered his brother's party the night he had graduated from the University of Montana. "He has a degree he will likely never use in mathematics."

"He's a mathematician and he works as a ranch hand? How does that happen?"

He arched a brow as he picked up the judgment in her tone. "Can't smart people work on ranches?"

She opened her mouth, looking horrified, as she must have realized how she had sounded. "I'm sorry, I didn't mean it like that. Not at all. I'm just surprised he isn't working for a tech company or something." Her cheeks were flushed with embarrassment, and it made her look impossibly sexier.

"He could. He had job offers in other parts of the country, but he didn't want to leave Montana. After everyone went back to the office, his former job did, too and he wasn't willing to give up the West."

She looked at the snowcapped mountains that seemed to rest just at the edge of their fingertips in the sky. "That's something I can understand. Your home is beautiful. Leaving Montana is for the stupid." She smiled, but there was something in the way she looked back at him that made him wonder what he was missing. "Do you like your boss?"

"Mr. Trapper?"

"Isn't it Cameron?" she asked.

He nodded. "He and his new wife are great. Good to work

for. He's always out doing something on the ranch, and he puts in as long, if not longer, hours than the rest of us."

Her phone rang, and a darkness cast over her features.

"Everything okay?"

She nodded, but she couldn't look him in the eyes as she silenced her phone and dropped it into her purse.

"You must have a ton going on in your life. You get a lot of calls. You working on a show or something?"

She gave a dry laugh. "Busy, yes. I have an upcoming project for a streaming service, but I'm looking for new roles. I'm trying to get myself into the right chairs, but I'm constantly finding them pulled out from under me."

"Nothing quite like landing square on your ass to reset your life's compass." As he spoke, she turned, and he couldn't tell whether or not he had plucked the right thread. "Is that what brought you here? Work troubles?"

"Something like that." Her phone buzzed from her purse, and she pulled it back out.

He tried to see who was calling, but as he stepped around her, all he saw was the black screen.

She turned back to him, appraising his closeness with a disapproving scowl. Instinctively, she placed her cell phone over her heart and away from his prying gaze. "Would you text Jackson? Kelcie isn't responding. I'm getting concerned. She's always on her phone."

He nodded as he pulled out his device and sent his older brother a message. It went unread, and, trying to call, it went straight to voicemail. Jackson wasn't great at the phone, but given the circumstances, there were only a few explanations as to why the two weren't answering.

For now, he had to hope it was that they were just busy with a doctor or nurses and held up from answering. The only other explanation was if they were doing something that Jackson had no business getting involved in when it came to a ranch guest.

Scarlett cleared her throat and pulled his attention to her and the fact that if he was judging Jackson for going after the hot Hollywood girl, he was the pot calling the kettle black.

He lifted his phone in surrender. "I'm sure they will get back to us as soon as they can. They know we are waiting." He had to do something that would keep this woman at arm's length long enough for him to get his head clear, but not so far as to run into problems with Cameron. "When did you fly in? Have you had a chance to look around the area much?"

He felt stupid making small talk, but there was something in the way she looked at him that made him feel like he was back in high school, and he had no idea what step to take next. He hadn't dated since things had ended with Chloe, and his ineptitude was creeping up in his bones. It had been five years since he'd gone on his last first date.

It wasn't that he hadn't noticed women. There was one particularly good-looking thirtysomething who worked at the family-owned six-aisle grocery store a few miles from the ranch. For a man who didn't have to cook much, he was hitting the market far more often than most would have considered necessary. However, after a long day in which he'd only spoken to horses, sometimes it was nice to see a pretty woman who always met him with a warm welcome.

There wasn't anything there with her, once they went beyond pleasantries, but when loneliness crept in, he hadn't needed more. Truth be told, he wasn't even sure he would have been, or was, ready for anything beyond hello. Based on the way he was acting around Scarlett, he would be ready to date sometime around the next millennia.

"We just flew in and got the rental car." There was a

strain in her tone that edged on reluctance, but he wasn't sure why or what she would have been hesitant to tell him.

Maybe he was just picking up on her concern for her friend. He couldn't begrudge her there.

Her phone pinged, and she took it out of her pocket.

"Kelcie?" he asked.

She shook her head as she let out an audible groan.

"Do you want me to answer it?"

She didn't seem to hear him as she looked at her phone. Some of the color bled from her face. Her hands began to shake.

He reached down and put his hand upon hers, drawing her attention back to him. "What's going on? Really."

She pulled her hand away from him, making sure to hide her phone's screen as she moved. "It doesn't matter."

Her phone buzzed again. She tilted her head back in exasperation, but instead of ignoring the annoyance, she turned around and pressed onto the screen. Her fake fingernails clicked hard on the screen as she typed away, and he could hear the fury in her harshness.

He had no idea what was going on, but the intensity of her rage pulsed off her and filled his soul.

This kind of reaction from a woman, especially one who didn't want to talk about it, could only mean one thing—she and her boyfriend were having a fight.

Chapter Seven

The messages on Scarlett's phone were breathtakingly simple, and heart-stoppingly short:

You think you are clever.

Thirty seconds later, she was hit with the next blow.

You can't get away from me.

Butch was baiting her. She had fallen for this trap and answered, afraid that he was telling the truth and forcing her to act, so many times in the past year it made her nauseous at the thought. He wanted her to answer. He was just bluffing. He had no idea where she was or what she was doing.

If she answered now, he would know he had gotten to her. This cat-and-mouse game would be intensified, and she would be pulled back into a text string that she didn't want to endure. No doubt if she did fall for it, he would end up telling her how much he loved her and then telling her how much she *loved him*, when in reality there was nothing about her former agent that she found attractive.

When he had first discovered her and pulled her up from

the no-names to the silver screen, she had been so young, excited and naive that she had been his perfect victim— tailor-made to fall for his quick wit, his lies, his promises of grandeur and the false sense of security that came with being his "number one."

It hadn't started as anything—it was just a friendship, banter between colleagues. Looking back, what a fool she had been, but when an actor was young and hungry, the agent working for the talent was never supposed to be the one in the power position. They were to be a team, making money together, succeeding and moving her career in an upward direction.

If friendships transpired, so be it, but they weren't a regular occurrence and certainly not normal. It was more of a realtor-seller relationship. Civility, decorum, aplomb and grace were common—yet, when he had started texting her late into the evening and well into the night, she had thought he was just being a great agent. She hadn't seen it for what it really was.

She had been a fool.

Yet, when did flirting turn dangerous?

She had thought two adults could laugh and flirt without fear of stepping into the forbidden. Money, business and her continued growth as an actress were far more important than sex—he had to see that, too. Sex was easy, but they both needed each other to make a go of the dog-eat-dog world of Hollywood.

She had been wrong.

Her friend was someone she could trust. They'd been talking for a long time, and he'd never crossed the line. Usually, they discussed nothing beyond topics in line with their business, but then he'd go a little too far—telling her how beautiful she was, what a great actress she was and would continue to grow to be if she stayed close to him, and how if she just trusted him they would be a power couple.

Looking back, the trap she had fallen victim to had been so easy to see.

She had bought it all hook, line and sinker. She had been a sucker for his charms. Desperation had primed her for his grooming.

What she would give to go back in time.

That night when he'd followed her home, he had first tried to kiss her. She could remember it as if it was yesterday. She had been telling him about the producer who had gotten a little too handsy at dinner and how uncomfortable he had made her. In response, Butch had been telling her how sorry he was and how she hadn't deserved that kind of treatment.

Stories of slick-handed producers in the business were common, and she hadn't walked into the business completely unaware, but she'd never realized she had been standing in the fire and merely watching it cast off embers.

He'd come up behind her, asking to touch her. It had been strange, but he had touched an arm, laughing and grazing, the simple touches that were almost mindless. Then, he started to massage her shoulders. At the time, and slightly drunk, she'd yielded. Her brothers had massaged her shoulders, men could touch women without it being something more.

Oh, to have been twenty again.

She couldn't even blame the man—not completely. He'd asked to touch, she just hadn't understood what he had meant, and how the massage would turn to a hand over her shirt and against the soft cup of her bra.

She had pulled away. She had said no.

In that moment, he'd stopped. He backed away, moving

to the couch near her and falling back. His eyes welled with tears, and he began to cry.

The emotion was so strange to her, a cowgirl in the big city, that she hadn't been able to comprehend the guy's reaction. She had said no—what was there to cry about? He had been the one to invade her space, to press the boundaries—and she had made him honor her wishes. If anyone should have been upset, it should have been her.

Eventually, he apologized and told her how sorry he was. Once again, she'd fallen for his game. Yes, she'd screwed up. She was the one who had allowed him back in her suite.

He had been in her room before. Yet nothing had ever happened.

She must have been sending off signals. It had to have been her fault. It always took two people. Maybe she hadn't made her line with him clear enough. Or, maybe, had she not spoken about her disinterest at all? Had she taken it for granted that the silent lines of business would keep his feelings in check?

It hadn't been that she didn't like him. No, she had. That was what had made it even more confusing. They were so close. It made sense that he had gotten the wrong signal.

Yet, when he'd finished apologizing and composing himself, she'd asked him to go back to his hotel. That was when things went from bad to worse. He'd barricaded the door. Refusing. He'd threatened her, her career, her life.

Her hands started to shake. Her phone and the messages were still glaring at her.

The phone rang.

She hit Ignore.

"Scarlett?" Miles said, pulling her back to where she stood and the reality outside of the black contraption in her hands, which acted as handcuffs and blinders instead of the amenity it had been supposed to be.

"Sorry."

"You don't need to apologize," he replied, frowning. "What are you fighting with him about?"

She jerked her head up and met his gaze. "What? How did you know?"

"No one reacts like that to a normal business call." He gave her a sweet, considerate look. "I know we've only met, but you can talk to me about this stuff. I have some experience when it comes to dating and breakups."

Oh. He had it all wrong, but she could understand how he could have made the assumption.

"I don't have a boyfriend. That's not it."

The tightness in his features seemed to dissipate ever so slightly. "Then who is it you're fighting with? Family?"

"No, not family." She jerked, and she instinctively glanced toward the ranch house. Thinking about family infighting, the last thing she needed to do was be spotted by one of her siblings. "If you don't mind, I'd like to freshen up. Jackson set me up in a cabin, but he didn't tell me which one or where it was located. If you'd point me in the right direction, I'd appreciate it."

His dark look returned, but he nodded. "You got it."

She hated the tone in his voice. It was so dry and crisp—like she had stepped on autumn leaves and everything they worked so hard to grow was now turning to dust beneath her feet.

In an attempt to make the look in his eyes disappear, she added, "And, as much as I don't want to be a pain, I could use some food." She sent him her best winning smile. "Your sandwich was great up on the mountain, and I'm starving."

He returned her smile with a guarded one of his own. "Glad you think so, Ms. Leafletter. I'll make sure you get something else to your liking."

Her chest ached at the sound of her formal name. She didn't like this game. But she had already been testing fate by standing out here and waiting for him as long as she had. If her brother or sister saw her out here, they would have all kinds of questions for her that she wasn't ready to answer.

That was, if they didn't just kick her off the ranch. The last time she had seen any of them was the day she had left this damned place. She had told them where they could all go, and how she never wanted to see any one of them again. At the time, she thought she'd meant those words, but now she had come to realize that the one person she had always really hated was her father.

Oh, daddy issues rearing their lovely heads. Again.

It was no wonder she had gotten herself into this situation. If only she had been stronger. If only she hadn't tried to paddle in a pool where she should have been wearing a life jacket—or better yet, not even have jumped.

He walked her to her Mercedes-Benz. "Why don't we take your fancy little car here. I can just walk to the bunkhouse from there. It's not far."

"It was the only rental the place had left. I would have preferred something more suited to the dirt road, but c'est la vie." She put her hand up in resignation.

She took the keys from her jacket pocket and tossed them his way. He caught them in the air with a flourish of his hand and a triumphant smile that quickly disappeared as he looked at her and seemed to remember the tension that rested between them.

He walked to the passenger's door and opened it for her. Waiting for her to buckle, he closed the door, but not before she saw his gaze drift down to her breasts. She celebrated her small victory. He wanted her, even if he didn't want to admit it, and even if neither of them could act on their mutual desires.

At least he didn't know that she wanted him as much, if not more, than he appeared to want her.

She watched him walk around the front of the car, his jeans tight on his ass as he moved. For a moment, she caught herself wondering what kind of surprise he kept hidden beneath. If the rest of him was as great as she could already see, she would be in trouble if she ever got the chance to be with him.

The car dipped slightly as he got in. He smiled as he started the engine, and he looked around the auto, assessing it like it was a new horse he was looking to purchase.

"You approve?" she asked.

He gave a dip of the chin. "I like my truck, but this is a nice rig. Gotta say, though, you're right. It wouldn't do well around the ranch in the wintertime. The roads can get a little dicey. In fact, even now, with the back roads of the ranch being muddy from the spring rains, it may be better if we hit the main highway and come around the back instead of trying to get you in the usual way."

She thought about how many times, when she had been a kid, they had pulled her truck out of the knee-deep mud in the far pasture when she had been tasked with feeding the cows. Those were days she would be only too happy to never repeat. Apparently, some things on the ranch hadn't changed, even if they had been updating the place. "Do whatever you think is best. I'm just the passenger."

He sent her a questioning glance. "You hardly seem like the kind of woman who just goes along with the plan."

She cocked her head, trying to decide whether she should be offended or not. "What do you mean by that?"

He pulled her car out of the spot, and they made their

way toward the highway. "Don't get me wrong or anything, but from the moment we left the ranch this morning, you've had your own way of doing things and you always make sure to put in your two cents."

Yep, she was offended. "I guess you must not be used to women who are assertive." She could hear how she sounded, but she didn't care. If he wanted to say triggering things, he could deal with the bullet.

He let out a long exhale. "Don't be upset. Please. I was really trying to pay you a compliment. I like how you're not afraid to speak your mind."

She nodded but had the distinct feeling that was the last thing he'd intended. "I come by it naturally." She looked back at the ranch house as it faded into the distance. "My dad wasn't one to mince words, either."

There was the sound of sirens in the distance. As they neared the highway, there was smoke billowing up in front of them. It was hard to tell where exactly the smoke was coming from, the road or from the ranch behind it.

She twisted her hands together as she tried not to think the worst. Kelcie and Jackson still hadn't answered. What if the smoke was coming from an accident? What if something had gone wrong?

Miles's face darkened and he sped up. Neither spoke. He pulled out his phone and checked for messages, as though he'd had the same thought.

"I'm sure it's fine." She reached over and put her hand on his arm as he dropped his phone into his lap.

He was hot under her touch, and there was the gritty feeling of dried sweat on his skin. He put his hand on hers and gave it a friendly pat. "Yeah." His smile was forced, and as she dropped her hand from him, she couldn't help wondering if her touching him had been a terrible mistake.

She'd been trying to make them both feel better, and less on edge. Instead, the acrid smoke permeated the air in the car, and it mixed with the tension she felt and made a sickening feeling rise within her. She couldn't explain why, but something was wrong.

Perhaps it was in the way he'd only patted her hand, or maybe it was Kelcie being gone, or the unknown billowing before them.

They turned the corner leading directly to the highway. There, at the end of the driveway, was the black Jeep Grand Cherokee, with a rental car sticker in the window. It was on its roof, and one of its tires was gone, only shreds of rubber and metal bands still on the wheel.

On the ground around the upside-down car was a pool of glistening liquids, black and brown, mixing and swirling and reflecting the late afternoon sun.

There was a set of footprints where someone had gotten out of the passenger side of the car and walked through the oil. The prints were smeared, and there was a mark on the road, near the black marks left by skidding tires. In the median, there was a pair of women's boots sticking out above the edge of the concaved and grassy surface.

"No…" Miles whispered.

"Do you know whose car this is? It isn't Jackson's, is it?" she asked, panicked as they slowed to a stop. "That's not their car. It can't be."

He came to a full stop. There was a gray Hyundai pulled over to the side of the road, and a man was on the phone. He looked panic-stricken as he motioned wildly with his hands as he spoke.

The world stopped around her as panic moved through her. Kelcie may be pinned inside, hurting or worse.

She reached down to grab at the door handle to jump out of the car. She had to help them. She had to help her friend.

"That's not Jackson's car." Miles's voice sounded like it was coming through a tin can on a string.

She looked over to him. His face was emotionless. "Whose car is it?"

"It's the Sullivans' rental. I saw it parked outside their cabin when I dropped them off. They must have been coming over here for something. Do you see the little boy? Where's Thomas?"

The horror of what she was seeing spread out in front of her hit her with the pressure of a hurricane. She couldn't stay in the car. She had to act. She had a little boy's life to save.

Chapter Eight

Miles moved to the driver's side of the Jeep as he listened to the sirens that were moving steadily closer. When he approached the smashed-out window, he carefully picked his way through the shattered pieces of glass, which littered the ground like crushed ice.

There was blood on the roof of the car, and as Aiden came into view, he could see the man's eyes were closed and his head was cocked at a strange angle. Blood was dripping down his hairline and falling onto the black fabric ceiling of the car. He pressed his fingers to Aiden's neck, searching for a pulse. It was slow and nearly imperceptible.

If the ambulance didn't arrive soon, he doubted the man would survive.

He'd sent Scarlett to check on the people in the Hyundai in hopes to keep her away from any of the horrors he feared he would find inside this Jeep. She had argued but not put up as much of a fight as he had expected—she must have been as afraid of the possible carnage that came with this horrible of an accident.

Kneeling down, he checked the Jeep's back seat. Thomas was strapped into his red and blue Spiderman booster seat, and he was crying. As the little boy spotted him, his quiet sobs turned loud. "Miles! Help me." His face was red and puffy, and tears poured from his eyes and moved down his temples and into his hair.

"I got you, buddy. You're okay," he said, trying to sound calm and even as to not further scare the boy. "You are being really brave, Thomas. Do you know that?"

He didn't want to move the little boy, but he had to get him out of the car. Help was on the way, but with the way the boy's face was so red, he worried that if he didn't the boy would pass out.

Thomas hiccupped as he nodded. "Is Daddy okay?" he asked.

Miles glanced at the back window to keep the boy from knowing the fragility of his father's condition by looking at his face. The glass had blown out in the back, as well.

"Your dad's going to be okay and so will you, buddy." He did a visual assessment of the boy, as he had been trained at the ranch for emergencies. Glass chips were embedded in the boy's cheek. Thankfully, Thomas didn't seem to notice, and the shards looked to be only superficially lodged. They weren't even bleeding. "How's your neck feeling? Does it hurt at all?"

The little boy shook his head. "My shoulder hurts," he said, touching the seat belt that was across his chest and where he had likely taken most of the impact from the crash.

"Can you breathe okay?" he asked, pulling the knife he always carried out of his pocket and flipping it open. "Do you hurt anywhere else besides your shoulder?"

Thomas sucked in a big breath between hiccups but was stopped by a new spasm. However, he nodded. "I'm okay."

"Good, you're a good boy," he said, forcing a smile to help the boy feel more comfortable. "I'm going to cut your seat belt, okay?"

The boy nodded.

"You might slip down to the roof of the car. After you do, I need you to lay real still and I'll pull you out. Do you understand?"

"Yes, Mr. Miles." He sounded so tiny and frail that it tore at Miles's heart.

No kid should have ever been in an accident like this, but thankfully at least he was alive. He couldn't bear to think about what he would have felt if he had found Thomas in the same state as his father.

He lifted the knife for the boy to see. "Isn't this a cool knife?" he asked, trying to shift the boy's focus away from the pain he was likely about to feel when he released the restraint.

The boy stared at it as Miles reached toward him and pulled the strap just loose enough to slip the blade beneath. It sliced through the strap like it was warm butter. He held the strap tight as he dropped the knife on the ground and out of the way.

"Okay, buddy, I'm going to start letting you down. You ready?" he asked.

Thomas's eyes were wide with fear. It made Miles wonder how badly the boy was really hurt. Right now, the little dude was probably in such a state of shock that if he had sustained any injuries, he may not have been able to completely acknowledge them yet.

He'd have to be careful with the boy's neck. The last thing he wanted was to make the situation worse, or to further injure the child.

"I want you to keep your head and neck as still as you can, okay?"

The boy's eyes grew impossibly wider. "Why?"

"I think pretending is so fun," he lied. "I bet you do, too. So, I want you to pretend that you are like a big tree. Strong and straight."

Thomas's body stiffened against his hand where he held the belt tight.

"Good boy. You're doing such a good job." He smiled. "All right, here we go. You're like a big pine tree." He started to move the belt, loosening its hold on the boy, and he started to slip out of the Spiderman booster seat.

The boy smelled of urine and sweat, and he reached out and took hold of Miles as he got free of the seat completely. Miles slipped his arm under the boy and let go of the strap, holding the boy in place. "Here we go, my big pine tree." He reached in and took hold of the boy's legs. "Don't move your back." He eased him out of the car and maneuvered his tiny frame through the broken window, carefully avoiding the shards of glass that littered the edges.

Thomas moved into his chest, burying his face in his shirt. He could feel the hot wetness of his tears against his skin. "You're okay, buddy, you're okay," he cooed, trying to make the boy feel safe.

He looked back at Aiden, who was still unconscious in the front seat. The sirens were growing nearer. They'd be here within a few moments. As much as he wanted to help the older man, he held the boy tight. Thomas was the one awake and aware—he needed Miles more.

"The ambulance will be here in a second." Scarlett came running over. She looked as though she wanted to take Thomas into her arms but stopped herself. "The guy over there wants to know how Thomas is doing."

"He's good but going to need to see a doctor," he said, but he showed the man Thomas and glanced to the glass in the boy's cheek. "He is so strong and brave."

"Is Aiden okay?" She looked toward the Jeep.

Miles pulled Thomas in slightly tighter to his chest as if the action could guard the boy from the truth. "Aiden…"

He paused, glancing down at the boy in his arms. He was already hurt enough—he didn't need to hear that his father was possibly dead. "I'm not quite sure." Making sure Thomas couldn't see, he gave her a slow shake of the head as he pursed his lips.

He glanced over at the Hyundai and the driver, who was still on the phone with 911. "Did he see what happened?"

"He said the Jeep was already on its roof when he got here, but it was still spinning." Scarlett nibbled at her lip. "He wasn't sure, but he thought he passed a truck with a dented-up grille on the front leaving the scene. Like I said, though, he wasn't sure."

"Thomas," he said, "do you know what happened?"

He looked up at him, tears streaming down his face. One of the pieces of glass had wedged loose and blood was starting to seep from the wound on his cheek.

"Is Daddy dead?" he asked, his voice quaking with fear and the seemingly infinite sadness of youth.

Miles's chest tightened and he didn't know what to say, so he said nothing. Instead he pointed in the direction of the red and blue lights that were permeating the gray dusk. "Look, here comes your ride. Are you ready?" he asked, but he didn't wait for Thomas to answer. "They're going to take you to the hospital. Doctors and nurses are going to check you out. I'll tell them all how brave you've been, but I want you to keep being super brave."

Thomas nodded.

The ambulance careened toward them, pulling to a stop. A woman jumped out of the passenger door and rushed toward him, carrying a large black bag full of medical supplies. "Hi, guys," she said, trying to sound calm, but her gaze kept moving to the car on the ground. "My name is Becky and I'm here to help you. How are you doing?"

"Hi, Becky. I'm Miles, that's Scarlett, and this is the bravest kid I know, Thomas." Miles lifted him gently so the EMT could do a quick visual assessment. "I hope you don't mind. He was scared and upside down, so I pulled him from the vehicle."

"That's okay, Miles," she said, giving Thomas a wide smile. "I'm so glad to make a friend with such a cool kid! Will you be my friend, Thomas?"

He gave her a tiny nod.

"I bet that was super scary, but we're here to help. Can you be a big kid and keep being so brave while Miles carries you to the ambulance over there?" She pointed toward the vehicle. "There, I'll have him put you on a nice, comfy bed so we can check on your heart and your lungs to make sure they are all right, okay?"

Thomas looked up at him, questioningly.

"It's all right, bud. They just need to take you and your dad to the hospital. I'll get there as soon as you are taken care of and settled in."

The driver of the ambulance jumped out and opened the back doors of the ambulance. He grabbed his black bag, and the two EMS workers gave each other a knowing look. Miles had seen that look before. That was the look of resolve that came when people knew what they were about to encounter was going to leave behind a mark on the soul.

Chapter Nine

The world of one little boy was never going to be the same.

The evening air was pressing down, carrying darkness with it as Scarlett sat on the edge of the road next to Miles and watched as the wrecker arrived. Its yellow lights were streaking across the road and they cast an eerie shadow on Miles's face. She hated those lights, this place, the smell of death in the air and the horrific reality surrounding her.

Aiden was barely clinging to life, and from what she'd heard the first team of EMS workers say before they'd left, it sounded as though it was unlikely he would wake up. If he did, there was talk of severe traumatic brain injuries, but she didn't know how the workers would have known based on what they had seen.

Miles had been silent as they had watched the ambulance leave. He'd offered to go along but was turned away when Thomas had lost consciousness. She could still hear the wailing of the sirens as the ambulance had sped off toward Kalispell.

Hopefully Thomas would be all right and the EMS workers were wrong about his father. It wasn't fair that this little boy had to go through this kind of trauma so early in his life, especially so soon after he had lost his mom. No one deserved the hand life was dealing him, but least of all such an innocent boy.

As the police officer investigating the incident talked to the man who had been on the phone with 911, Scarlett overheard him saying something about another car, but she couldn't quite make out his words thanks to the ringing dissociation in her ears.

If they had been just a little bit quicker leaving the ranch, it could have been her clinging to life instead of Aiden. Or, it could have been Miles they raced to the hospital.

She looked over at him. His eyes were dark, and he looked somehow older than he had when she had met him that morning.

For a single day, it was one hell of a throwaway.

This one was definitely going to leave a mark.

The driver of the tow truck was taking notes beside the investigator, and he kept glancing over at them as if trying to get a read on how deeply they were involved with the accident and if they had something to hide. If only the things she was hiding were that two-dimensional—her secrets went far deeper and into a much darker past.

They had made their initial statements to the investigator, but he'd told them to wait for him to conclude his questioning in case he had any follow-ups. Right now, all she could think about was how sideways everything had gone. She'd come back to Montana to avoid death, and now the man she'd been riding the trail with only hours earlier clung to life.

Fate had a way of destroying even the most beautiful moments by reminding a person what evils lurked in the shadows—and she knew only too well how death watched and waited.

Miles reached over and put his hand on top of hers. As he

did, she soaked in the warmth of his touch, but the weight of him pressed her hand into the gravel and glass on the side of the road. It dug into her skin, making pain spike up into her wrist and arm. She didn't pull away or even move. Sometimes pain had a way of pulling a person back to the present, and as badly as she didn't want to be there, she had things in her life that still needed to be seen to.

"Have you heard from Jackson?" she asked, looking at his fingers as he started to caress her hand and dig the detritus farther into her skin.

He shook his head. "Kelcie?"

"No." She motioned toward the detective. "Did he tell you anything about the truck? Did they look into the lead?"

He nodded. "I couldn't make out everything. But they are thinking it was some kind of hit-and-run."

She sighed. "Look at the Jeep... I'd say there's a damned good chance." She pointed toward the passenger side of the rig, where there was a concave mark as if the vehicle had taken an impact. There was black paint on the door from the collision.

"I hope they find the bastard responsible." Miles rubbed at a droplet of dried blood on his forearm.

"Do you think the deputy would be upset if we just left?" she asked.

Miles leaned back. "He knows the ranch. His boss is Cameron's wife, Emily. I have a feeling if he has a problem, he will know where to find us. If you want to go, I'll cover for you. You just go get in the car and I'll be right behind you."

She sighed, not really wanting to feel his touch disappear—it was the only thing in this moment that felt *warm*. His comfort was welcome, but she wasn't sure whether to trust the man who had literally ridden into her life on a beautiful horse.

Technically, she was the one who had come to him, but she wasn't about to argue with herself about the one thing that brought her comfort.

"I think we should run to the hospital. It's tearing at me that Thomas has to face this alone." She looked in the direction the ambulance had disappeared. "Plus, maybe we can still catch Kelcie and Jackson. I can only think they are still there and that's why they haven't been getting in touch."

Even as she spoke, she could hear the feebleness in her words. The days of cell phones not working in hospitals were long passed. Kelcie knew how to get in touch with her. There had to be something wrong with her friend, but she couldn't handle the thought of one more thing going wrong.

THE HOSPITAL WAS busier than Miles would have expected when they pulled into the parking lot. The ambulance, the one he assumed had picked up Thomas and Aiden, was parked in the loop outside the emergency entrance, its engine running and its headlights shooting off into the distance and bouncing off the windows of the administrative offices across the street.

Miles hated hospitals. They reminded him far too much of all the things in his past and all the things he never wanted to think about in the future. In his world, hospitals only meant one thing—death.

In this case, in the life of the boy they had come to see, he had to hope this would be the one time death would wait. It had already come for the boy's mother—it could hold for Aiden.

Scarlett had been eerily quiet on their drive to the hospital, seemingly at odds with what they had experienced. If he had to guess, she had probably been wondering exactly why she and her assistant had come to Montana. It had seemed to be one heck of a cluster since the moment they had stepped foot on the ranch.

She had promised that they wouldn't cause issues for him or his employers, but he would understand if she changed her mind. In fact, he wouldn't be surprised if, as soon as she got a line on her assistant, she caught the next flight back to California. It would tell him exactly how close they were if she waited for Kelcie to get out of the hospital before she set to the air.

She'd been fighting with someone earlier. She'd said it wasn't her boyfriend, but dollars to donuts, that was the person and the reason she had run away to his neck of the world in search of reprieve. No matter how bad the scuffle, it couldn't have been bad enough to keep her from going back with things being as big a dumpster fire as they were.

"Do a loop through the parking lot. See if you can spot Jackson's pickup." She didn't ask and it should have rubbed him the wrong way, but he appreciated her taking control. In fact, he had been thinking the same thing.

They did a slow crawl through the lanes, but nowhere in the lot was his brother's beat-up Ford, the one he'd gotten after mowing lawns and doing maintenance at the local golf course for four summers during high school. Jackson had worked his butt off for that pickup, and with its one blue door on the gray rig, it was distinctive.

She was scanning the parking lot, her head on a swivel, and it reminded him of Emily, who worked for the local sheriff's department. She had the same way of constantly scanning wherever they were, as if she was always on high alert and expecting trouble.

Given the day they'd had, Scarlett's reaction wasn't a surprise, but it also wasn't a mannerism that was picked up by one crappy day.

"Did you ever play a cop?" he asked, trying to make a bit more sense of her.

She shook her head, but she had a thin smile as she thought. "No, I'm always cast as the thick-skinned businesswoman. Why?"

"No reason," he said, returning her smile. "You'd be good at playing one. I could see you being a badass detective or something. You'd definitely be the kind who wouldn't take any guff."

"That's why they put me in as the witchy woman." She laughed, but it carried a tone of a residual sting. "The last character I played was at least redeemable. Her name was Julie Crawflight—cosmonaut attorney and power-hungry social climber who was hell-bent on taking out her enemies. She was jumped after prosecuting a man who'd been arrested for killing his clan's leader. He was found guilty, but he was affiliated with the rival species, the Ragnons."

"Sci-fi and brawls, sounds like my kind of show. If there were naked chicks… I'm all over it." He laughed, but his mind went straight to her and how much he would give to see her without a stitch of clothing.

He felt his body stir with the thought.

"Oh, don't get ahead of yourself. It was just one season and hasn't aired yet. I'm supposed to start filming again in a few months, but that depends on—" She paused, looking away from him before seeming to collect her thoughts and planting a smile on her face that wasn't quite real. "It depends on a variety of things. This business is complicated."

"Did you get a copy of the show yet?" he asked.

She laughed. "Not yet, but I get to go to the screening soon."

"I'd like to see it. Maybe if you are taking auditions for a date, you'd let me give it a shot."

"It's not worth the minute to audition, trust me. Showings are so stressful." She sighed. "Truthfully, becoming an actress might be the worst thing that could have happened to me."

"I thought you said it was what gave you hope, empowered you?"

"And that, that right there is why it was the worst thing to happen. If I'd have just failed as an actress, I could have been justified in giving up and I'd have been forced to do something else. As it is, I keep pushing. I'm close to hitting it big, I can feel it, but then it seems like no matter how much success I attain, I'm still not getting to the levels I hoped for as a child. The best gift and the worst curse can be just that—hope."

"You're a dark horse, Scarlett."

"You have no idea." She pointed at a Ford pickup that looked similar to Jackson's. "Is that his?"

He shook his head. "They aren't here." He pulled into a spot by the doors leading into the entrance of the emergency room.

She made a strange sound as she sucked on her teeth. "I can't imagine where they are. I'm worried about them. Is this kind of thing, disappearing, normal for your brother?"

He shook his head before getting out of the car and walking around and opening her door for her. Jackson was many things, but unreliable wasn't one of them. If he gave his brother a task, it got done—no questions asked. He didn't want to tell her that he was more than concerned, but there was no denying that he was terrified about what could have happened to the duo.

They made their way into the emergency room in silence. The woman behind the desk was tapping away on the keyboard, and she didn't even look up as they approached the glass partition that kept them safely at arm's length.

After a couple of minutes of standing there in awkward silence and waiting for the woman as she sipped at her coffee, Scarlett said, "Excuse me?"

The woman finally looked up and seemed annoyed with their presence. "Can I help you?"

"We are here to see Thomas Sullivan. He came in via ambulance in the last hour."

The woman looked from Scarlett to him and to her computer. "Are you his parents or guardians?"

Miles shook his head. "Unfortunately not. They were involved in the accident as well. I'm not sure, but I believe the boy's father is already here."

The secretary nodded. "I'm sorry, if you aren't family we aren't allowed to have you back here."

"Can you tell us if any of the boy's other family is here? I'd hate to think Thomas is alone."

"His father is here and currently in critical condition. Thomas is considered stable. There're no other family members here. And that's all the information I can share with you at this time. If you'd like, when they are available and have been moved up to the floors, I can let them know you stopped by."

It made his hackles rise that he was being turned away from a child in need, but he'd known they were rolling the dice on getting through the doors to get by his side. "We are also hoping to check the status of her sister—Kelcie Sherry." He motioned toward Scarlett as the smooth lie melted off his tongue like butter.

"She was in a horse-riding accident this morning. Did she get moved up to the floor?" she asked, mimicking the woman's language.

The woman tapped away on the keyboard, but she sounded put out that they would have asked her for another second of her precious time. "How did you spell that last name?"

Scarlett spelled it out for her, but as she did the woman's scowl deepened.

"There doesn't appear to have been anyone here by that name. In fact, she's not even in our systems."

"What does that mean?" Scarlett asked.

The woman, whose name badge read Mary, finally looked up at them and met his gaze before looking toward Scarlett. "It means that she hasn't been seen here or any of the clinics associated with our hospital—that's any of the small walk-ins in the area. Are you sure she didn't go to Missoula to be seen?" If eye rolling could be heard in a tone of voice, it was in that exact moment even though the woman was keeping a professional stoicism on her tired features.

Scarlett looked toward Miles, her eyes wide with fear. He hated that look, but it echoed his deep unease.

"You know," the woman continued, "for this woman being your sister, I would think you would at least know what hospital she'd gone to. Some sister you must be. *Tsk.*" She gave her an appraising up-down glance. "I bet you're from California. Maybe it's best you just leave."

Scarlett lunged toward the counter and her mouth opened like she was ready to take a bite out of the woman, but Miles put his hand on her back and gave her a small shake of the head. This wasn't a fight they needed to have. The rude woman could wait. Right now, he couldn't explain it, but he had the feeling that his brother and Kelcie were in deep trouble, and if they didn't get more information—it would be them who would be the next to disappear.

Chapter Ten

It took Scarlett ten minutes to cool off and stop seeing red while they stood in the parking lot outside the emergency room. She couldn't believe the receptionist would have had the audacity to say a single thing about her level of care and consideration with Kelcie—regardless of the fact she really wasn't Scarlett's sister. The woman had been asking for a fight.

She was lucky she was behind a pane of glass, or Mary would have been picking bits of lip out of her teeth. It was personnel like her that gave hospital staffers bad names and reputations. Unfortunately, it seemed like in the last decade it was more common than not that Scarlett dealt with the Marys of the world rather than anyone else.

The crickets were chirping in the grass around the outside of the building, mixing with the sounds of cars passing on the road outside of Logan Health Medical Center. Scarlett hated the sounds of crickets. To some they were calming, even the harbingers of summer, but to her they were reminders of lonely nights and feelings of inadequacy. More, they were the sounds of agonizing loneliness. And for good or bad, they were the sounds of a sleeping ranch—without the bawling cattle.

Come to think of it, the sound of Mary's voice reminded

her of the latter. Maybe this entire state was one in the same as the ranch.

"I don't know about you, but I don't like the idea of Thomas being in there without someone he knows helping to get him settled in his room for the night. He must be so scared." She looked up at the mirrored windows of the second and third floors of the hospital. "I can't even begin to imagine what he is thinking. He came here to get over the loss of his mother and now this… The poor kid."

Miles put his arm around her, and there was such strength in his embrace that it reminded her that in this battle, she wasn't fighting alone. Thomas had both of them standing in his corner, and no matter what was to come, they would do whatever it took to help.

"Let's go find him." He gave her a searching look as he pushed down a flyaway hair.

She couldn't help the faint smile that took over her lips at the sweetness of his touch. "Unless you become a relative, I'm not sure how we are going to get in." She motioned toward her watch. "And now, it's after visiting hours."

He sent her a mischievous grin. "You know…you didn't seem to have a problem calling Kelcie your sister in there. Your acting could be just the key we need to get us into any door we need."

"Yeah, but my acting job is also the reason we were thrown out on our asses. She hated me and, for all we know, she lied about Kelcie and probably set security on us."

"You didn't like her, and she most definitely didn't end up liking you, but I didn't get the impression that she was lying. She wasn't screwing with us about Kelcie—she wanted us out of her hair. Sending us to her room would have been the quickest way to get rid of us."

The woman was a jerk, but she had at least given them

enough information to be reasonably sure Kelcie had never stepped foot in the hospital. Which left them with *nothing*. Which was perhaps why she was so angry. There were so many things happening, and all she wanted were answers but all she found were questions.

"We should have told her we were related to Thomas. That was stupid of me."

"No, you were worried about Kelcie, and you assumed the woman would be kind." He gave her a gentle squeeze before moving away. "Besides, you know there's more than one way to open a beer."

She cocked her head. "What in the hell is that supposed to mean?"

"It means that there's more than one way into this hospital and to Thomas." The mischievous grin returned. It made him look so handsome that her heart nearly stopped. "Your great acting skills are going to have to come back into play."

She shrugged. "I don't know about *great*, but…"

"Now isn't the time to be humble." He took her by the hand, and he pulled her in the direction of the main doors of the hospital that were a few hundred yards down the sidewalk from where they stood. "Just follow my lead."

An unexpected giggle rose from her, and its sound was so out of place that for a moment he paused and looked at her until she waved for him to keep moving forward. She didn't want to explain to him that it wasn't that she didn't take what they were doing seriously, it was just that any time she had to get into character, the first thing she had to do was get the nerves out—and in this case, it meant forgetting how handsome he was and how warm his hand was when it was wrapped around hers.

He laced their fingers together tighter as they walked around the side of the hospital and made their way into the front doors. There sat a college-aged young woman who had been tasked with working the night shift.

"Hi," he said, striding up to the front desk with a concerned look on his face that she forced herself to mirror.

The woman behind the desk looked up. At seeing them, her smile disappeared and turned to an expression of concern. "Good evening. How can I help you?"

"My name is Jim Sullivan and this is my wife. Our nephew was brought in here after a car accident tonight. Is there any possibility we can get his room number?"

"Of course," the young woman said, tapping on her keyboard. "What is your nephew's name?"

"Thomas," Scarlett added, her voice worn and tired. It felt wrong to be a fake family given everything the boy had been through, but if Thomas's mom was watching she hoped she knew that they were doing this to help comfort the little boy and be there in his time of need.

No child should have had to go through something like this alone. The thought had broken her heart since the moment she had seen Thomas whisked away in the ambulance.

Sure, there were nurses and hospital staff there to help attend to Thomas's needs, but when the thoughts of the accident crept into his mind, he needed someone there to hold his hand and be there emotionally.

As though his mother's spirit was there, Scarlett felt warmth on her forearm like someone had laid a hand upon her in reassurance. She didn't know why, but the strange sensation brought her a level of peace she hadn't realized she needed.

The front desk secretary looked up from her computer. "Your nephew has just been given a room in peds. It looks like he will be in room 316, but they are just moving him up from the Emergency Room. You're welcome to head that way. The elevators are just down the hall, or you can take the stairs, just there," she said, motioning toward the door just down the hall from they stood.

"Thank you, ma'am," Miles said, dipping his chin in appreciation.

Scarlett leaned into his arm, letting him support her as a mother would have given the weight of the situation they would have been facing if this really had been their son. He wrapped his arm around her and led her toward the elevators. They waited in silence until the doors slid open with a *ding*.

They stepped inside and hit the button for the third floor, and as the door closed, she eased out of his embrace. "Good job handling that," she said, smoothing her hair where it had been pressed against his chest. "I wasn't sure it was going to work, but I'm glad you got it done. I'm sure Thomas is going to be glad to see a familiar face."

"She was going to let us in, or I was going to have to go back to Ms. Mary and ask if she had ever seen a six-foot man come over a five-foot counter. There was no way I was going to leave Thomas."

She laughed, and the hollow sound bounced around the empty elevator like a loose basketball on an abandoned court.

Without thinking, she leaned into him again, and he put his arm back around her. Miles bent down, and she felt him kiss the top of her head. The feeling and the connection were so natural that she didn't question it. Instead she sank into the solace of the sensation of him.

The doors opened far too quickly, and he let go of her as they stepped out into a small pediatrics unit. It smelled of antiseptics, industrial cleaners and bland food, and the unit appeared to be made up of just two short hallways of rooms.

Two nurses and a tech were making their way out to a far room and toward the stairs, talking animatedly. She caught them saying something about a car accident, but the door slammed as they made their way into the stairwell before she could make out anything else.

There was no one sitting at the main desk, and so they slipped past and made their way toward the room, and she peeked inside. Thomas was sitting in his hospital bed, looking wide-eyed around the room. He seemed stunned.

There was a nurse sitting beside him in a taupe vinyl chair, tapping away on a tablet, as she must have been asking him questions. Scarlett wasn't sure whether to interrupt, but when the nurse noticed her, she stood up and smiled. "Good evening. You must be Thomas's family."

Scarlett smiled, and before she could respond the nurse walked toward them.

"Thomas is just getting settled, but you are welcome to check on him. I can come back later to finish up my paperwork. If you have any questions or concerns about him, you're welcome to come chat with me when you are done talking." She moved past them, giving Miles a onceover and an approving nod before disappearing out in the hall.

The boy looked over at them and smiled widely. "Hi!" he said, sounding excited, but his voice was tired and worn as though he hadn't stopped talking since he had left them on the roadside.

"How're you feeling, kiddo?" Miles asked, as they made their way to the side of the bed.

Thomas shrugged. "My arm hurts," he said, lifting up a fresh cast on his right arm. It was bright blue, and it smelled like glue. "You have to sign it for me."

"You got it, buddy." Miles patted his leg.

"Did you see Daddy?"

Miles sent her a sideways look. "We didn't, but I'm sure you'll get to see your daddy soon, bud." He carefully stepped around the issue.

"Do you remember what happened?" Scarlett asked, wondering how much Thomas recalled seeing and whether or not the boy had an idea of what had truly taken place.

Thomas picked at his bottom lip. "I don't know. There was a big truck. Then there was a big *boom*. Everything went dark. I remember you guys on the road. I was coming here in the big 'bulance."

She smiled at the way he said the word in true five-year-old fashion.

"Did the big truck hit your car?" Miles asked.

Thomas nodded. "Santa was driving."

"Santa?" Scarlett asked.

He nodded again, still picking his lip. "He had gray hair and a big beard. He didn't have any elves with him, though."

Her stomach tightened. Butch had often been teased about his resemblance to the man in red. "What color was his truck?"

"Black."

"Did you tell the police about the truck, Thomas?" Miles asked.

Thomas nodded. "They saw my new cast, too." He smiled. "The policeman said he would sign it, too."

"I bet it's going to be covered in no time," Scarlett said, grinning.

There was a knock on the doorframe. "Excuse me." The nurse they had interrupted when they arrived was standing there, looking in on them. "I just received a call. Can you please step into the hallway so we can speak alone for a moment?" She had a look of grave concern on her face as she looked at them.

Miles turned to Thomas. "We will come back to see you, buddy." He walked over to the whiteboard on the wall and picked up the marker and wrote down his name and phone number. "If you need anything, you can have the nurses call this number. Okay?"

Thomas nodded. "Can you sign my cast before you go?" He pointed at the marker in his hand.

Miles clicked the lid back on the dry-erase marker before putting it back on the board. "Unfortunately, that one won't work, but I'll bring the right kind when I come back. Okay?"

Thomas looked crestfallen. "Okay."

"I promise we will. Right now, you need to get some sleep. It's well past your bedtime, lovey," Scarlett said, pushing back the boy's hair and moving it from his face. She leaned down and gave him a soft kiss to his forehead. "We'll be back to see you in no time. Again, if you need anything, we are here. And I know your daddy will be here to check on you as soon as he can."

The nurse cleared her throat.

Miles made his way out and Scarlett followed, giving Thomas one more quick wave before closing the door behind them. There was a large man dressed in black standing there, SECURITY emblazoned in yellow over the pocket on his jacket.

"David, our security guard over there, called," she said motioning toward the man. "It appears that they saw you trying to get through the Emergency Room entrance before falsifying information to gain access at the front desk." She sounded angry, but her voice and her face didn't match. "Since Thomas appears to know you, I told David we'll not be filing trespassing charges, however in the future I recommend that you do not try to gain access to minors through deception."

"How is his father doing?" Miles asked. "In all honesty, I'm a friend of the family. We were with them today on the mountain."

The nurse's expression softened, but only slightly. "Aiden is awake, but he is going into surgery tonight. He broke his back in several places and has a fractured pelvis. He's likely going to have to stay in the hospital for some time."

"Does he remember anything about the accident, or the man who was behind the wheel of the other vehicle?"

The nurse shrugged. "That's something you'd have to talk to him directly about. *Tomorrow.*" She waved over to the security guard. "David, do you mind escorting them out?"

The security guard scowled as he stomped toward them.

"If anything happens in the night, we put our number on the board," Scarlett said, motioning toward the room. "We just want to know Thomas is safe."

Chapter Eleven

Safety was an illusion. Locks, cameras, seat belts…they all served good purposes, but they didn't stop people from getting hurt or bad people from doing bad things. Miles knew only too well how horrible people could be, especially when it came to getting what they wanted.

As they pulled onto the back road of the ranch and made their way toward the guesthouses, he couldn't help but wonder if they had skirted the line between good and bad in their attempt to gain access to Thomas. Even if their intentions were pure, their methods *were* a little questionable.

He recalled the expression of shock and fear on Scarlett's face when Thomas had told them about the man who had struck them. He wanted to ask her about it but was probably making something out of nothing. She wasn't from here, and it wasn't like she knew anyone in the area.

She had been strangely quiet ever since they had started back toward the ranch, though it was more than possible she was just as tired as him. It had been one hell of a long day.

They hadn't eaten in hours, and as he pulled up to the guest cabin his stomach gave a loud grumble.

She unbuckled her seat belt then turned to him. "Would you mind walking me in?"

The way she asked surprised him. It didn't sound like an

invitation for sex—if anything it carried an air of fear. "I'd be more than happy. I know you're worried about Kelcie. If you want, I'll stay with you until we get a line on them. They have to be popping up anytime now."

"That's what you've been saying…" She gave an exasperated sigh as she opened the door of the Mercedes-Benz and stepped out.

She slammed the door shut behind her, not waiting for him to help her out.

This woman confused the heck out of him. One moment she wanted to be treated like a princess and protected, and the next she seemed to be pushing him away and resolved to take on the world alone. He wished she had come with instructions, or at the very least, that she would tell him exactly what she expected of him. If it was only a person to be by her side, it would be torture having to breathe in her sweet floral scent and know that he would never have a chance to kiss her soft pink lips, but at least he would understand the boundary lines.

As it stood now, all he wanted to do was take her inside and push her against the wall and kiss her until she couldn't speak and all she could do was moan for more.

His body stirred at the thought of the feeling of her soft lips on his.

She tapped on the passenger side window and pulled him from his fantasy. "Are you coming in?"

"Yep," he said, clearing his throat and forcing himself back to the reality that she was barely more than a stranger, a guest of the ranch, and utterly untouchable thanks to her celebrity status.

He followed her into the house, trying not to stare at the wide white stitching on the back pockets of her jeans. The round arc of her ass pressed hard against the fabric, making his mind drift back to the thoughts of pressing her against the wall.

She turned around as she got to the door, and she pointed toward the keypad. "Do you know the code?"

He walked up beside her, trying not to notice the way the breeze picked up the remnants of her flowery perfume, the hospital and horses on her skin. He pressed the numbers as she watched, and the door clicked open. He waved her forward and put his hand on her lower back as she stepped forward. She stopped for a split second, and she drew in a gasping breath as she tensed under his touch.

He dropped his hand.

He didn't understand her reaction. What had happened between the hospital and now? She had eased into him in the elevator, even initiated the touch, but now…his touch was unwelcome?

It had been a mistake to touch her.

Clearly, she must have come to her senses and realized she was so far out of his league that it was like he was playing T-ball, and she was in the major leagues. If only he hadn't let his daydreams get away with him, or if he hadn't gotten caught up in watching those jeans move over the perfect round curves of her body.

He stepped into the house behind her and closed the door.

At least he had shot his shot.

And hey, she hadn't slapped him or shut the door in his face.

Maybe there was some sliver of hope that there was a possibility for more between them.

Slipping off his boots, he made his way toward the kitchen in the large cabin. The place was huge, and it reminded him of what most people who came to Montana expected. It had an upstairs loft with two bedrooms and a bathroom, and a large bedroom, a kitchen and a living room on the main floor. Downstairs was a game room in a walk-out basement that led to a patio complete with an eight-person hot tub, which he often thought about sneaking over to use.

He'd never actually stayed in the cabin, but on occasions when the housekeepers needed help, he'd lend a hand in keeping the place. Once, earlier in the season, they'd had a family of six stay here and they had left one hell of a mess— even breaking one of the hickory dining chairs, which had cost more than five hundred dollars to replace. Until then, he wouldn't even have thought one of those monstrous chairs would have been possible to break without a jackhammer and a chisel, but three five-year-old triplets and a seven-year-old had managed to get it done.

That was to say nothing about the eggs that had been smeared all over the wall to the point that they'd been forced to repaint one area in the kitchen.

They had rapidly been added to the persona-non-grata list that started and ended with them.

Though he shouldn't have, as there was nothing particularly funny about what the family had done, he chuckled at the thought. Perhaps it was just the audacity and the lack of accountability and self-awareness that some people had when they stayed at places; it was as if they felt if they paid, they had the right to do whatever they wanted.

"You nervous?" Scarlett asked, dropping her coat and purse onto the edge of the chair in the living room.

"No. Just thinking," he said. "I hope you like the cabin. It's my favorite on the property. Honestly, I think it's even better than the main house. It's newer."

"I know. When was it built?" she asked.

He wasn't sure how she knew. It must have been on the

website or something. She had already admitted she had done her research on the place. "It was just a year ago, or so. Before I came on. They've been renting it out as part of the new guest ranch endeavor. So far, it's been doing well. You have to come check out the view."

He moved to hold out his hand for her to take, but just as quickly dropped it, thinking about her earlier reaction. He didn't need her to kick him out of the house for real this time. He'd already pushed his luck further than he should have, especially considering that he was here simply to be a part of her guest experience and nothing more.

Though, admittedly, their guest experience was to have ended that morning. She was getting preferential treatment, but his bosses would have it no other way if they were to find out about everything that had happened.

He led the way to the stairs, and she followed him out to the back patio. There, babbling not ten feet away and down a set of steps, was the Flathead River. It was crystal blue in the lights cast by the house. The water moved slowly in this section of the river, but in the spring, it crept up the levee that had been built until it spilled over the opposite bank.

"The river comes out of Glacier National Park, so it's heavy with glacial till, or loam. It's basically the dirt that comes from the glaciers as they melt, and it erodes into the waters and runs out. There are certain areas in the park where the water actually looks milky white during certain times of the year thanks to the runoff. It's beautiful. You'll have to go with me to see it sometime."

He'd not intentionally offered her the invitation, but apparently, he couldn't help himself.

She gave him a sidelong glance. "Yeah, maybe I'd do that sometime. I've always wanted to visit Glacier during the runoff. I bet the flowers are amazing."

"The runoff up there doesn't happen until around early June. Actually, they normally don't even have the roads completely open until late that month sometimes. You'd really have to stick around for the full summer if you wanted to appreciate all the park had to offer."

She smiled at him. "You know, one could say I'm here already." She stepped closer to him, and he caught the familiar scent of her. "That being said, I did miss the *spring* flowers."

He wasn't positive, but it felt like she was flirting with him. She must have been bored or something. There was no way she wanted him in the way he wanted her. She could do so much better than a guide working for a ranch. And it was just a few minutes ago that she had moved away from his touch. Seriously, she was so confusing.

She stepped closer to him and put her hand gently on his sternum. "Do you want a beer?"

He stared at her fingers and where they crumpled the soft flannel of his shirt and pressed into the hair at the center of his chest beneath. "Let's go grab a couple. We keep this cabin stocked for guests." His breath hitched in his throat. "There should be some steaks, too. I'll cook." His words came out staggered and airy as he spoke, but he tried to sound as cool, calm and collected as possible even though his heart was racing beneath her touch.

"I already told you that I wouldn't sue you for the accident today. You know you don't have to try to butter me up by making me dinner to keep me on your good side." She smiled, but her eyes were tired.

"Well, until we find my brother and your friend, I figure I must keep buttering you up. I may need to keep you deep in my pocket if Jackson decided to kidnap her, or something." He smirked as he tried to ignore the concern in his gut.

There was only so much they could do, and right now, for another twelve hours, they weren't considered missing persons, and they couldn't be reported to the police. Mary popped into his mind, and he groaned.

"Is that what my touch does to you?" Scarlett said, and she moved to pull her hand back, but he stopped her by pressing his hand over hers on his chest.

"No. That groan wasn't about you." He smiled. "I was just thinking about something else."

"If I'm touching you and you're thinking about something else, I'm not quite having the effect on you that I was hoping to have." She gave him a half grin that suggested she was fishing for a compliment.

"Oh, you're having more of an effect than you should be, trust me." He gave her hand a slight squeeze. "I'm just trying my damnedest to keep it professional. I have already been screwing things up right and left with you. I don't want to make things a thousand times worse by disappointing you, too."

"You think you'd disappoint me?"

He threw his head back in a laugh before catching her gaze. "A woman like you? I think I could keep you on your toes in bed, but what would you want with a cowboy? Our worlds are like comparing a longhorn to a lariat."

"I haven't heard that one before. Am I the longhorn or the lariat?" She laughed. "I'd prefer you didn't liken me to a cow."

He blushed. "Don't be twisting my words now, and don't change the subject. However, I would say you're the rope. You certainly have a way of tying me up in knots."

She stepped closer to him and moved up on her toes. His lips met hers. The kiss blindsided him in the most beautiful and seductive way, and in a way he'd never experienced before.

He'd been right about the knots.

She fingered the buttons on his shirt, loosening them and letting his shirt fall open. She pulled it loose of his jeans. Before she could move lower, he pulled her close, hard against his body. His hand moved up in her hair, and his thumb moved against the soft skin of her face. He owned her with his mouth, kissing her in a way that spoke of how badly he wanted all of her.

She tasted like cinnamon and desire, a heady mix that made him hungry for more.

She moaned into his mouth, and he swallowed the sound like it was an appetizer for his soul.

He pulled at her shirt, loosening it from the back of her pants. She stepped back slightly, not enough to break their kiss, but just enough to be able to get to his silver belt buckle. She flipped it open and slid the leather strap loose, making his body instantly react. He ached for her.

He glanced at the hot tub that sat under the stars. There was a mink blanket folded and placed atop one of the Adirondack chairs. The last thing he wanted to do was break their kiss, but he brushed her cheek as he gently moved and touched his forehead to hers, looking her in the eyes. "Wait here a second."

He rushed to the blanket, but as he moved to grab it, he froze. Splattered across the surface of the hair was a dried blood-like substance. On the concrete, near the hot tub and around the chair was more dried blood. The chair had been scraped over the concrete, leaving behind splinters of wood, and droplets of blood had been spilled atop, plastering the splinters to the ground.

Something had happened here. Something bad. He looked for feathers or fur, in hopes what he had just found was nothing more than remnants of nature being its brutal self.

"What is it?" Scarlett asked.

"I'm not sure. Don't move, though." He put up his hand. "And don't touch anything for a minute."

She walked over to him. "Oh, my God. What happened? Is that from you?" She grabbed his arm and looked at it like she expected him to be cut, though the blood was already dry.

"That's not from me." He shook his head. "You and Kelcie hadn't been here yet, right?"

"No. Jackson just checked us into the cabin. He didn't even tell me where it was, he forgot in his hurry. That's why I had to wait for you."

That didn't mean that Kelcie and Jackson weren't there.

"Was Kelcie bleeding after the accident on the mountain? Do you think this could be from her?" He wasn't sure if he wanted the blood to be hers or just some stranger's. Either way, whatever they had walked into wasn't good.

"She wasn't actively bleeding, and certainly not enough to have left a trail like this if that's what you're getting at." She started to follow the trail. It led around the hot tub and up the hill to the main level of the house. She disappeared around the side of the cabin. "Come here. Look."

He followed, careful not to step in any of the droplets. As he came around the corner, he found bits of glittering glass strewn across the concrete outside the side door. The glass was shattered inward, where it appeared as though someone had punched in one of the glass panels of the door to get at the lock on the inside to let themselves in.

"We need to call the police," Miles said, slipping his phone out of his back pocket. "I'm sure they're going to be just thrilled to speak to me again today." He let out a long sigh.

He also needed to make the call he'd been putting off

all day—to his boss, Jamie, who would undoubtedly need to chat with her husband, Pierce, and her brother Cameron about everything that had happened. His ass would be on the line and so would Jackson's. Everything he'd been working for would fall apart.

There would be no more hiding anything that had occurred, and all would be lost.

If anything, he feared he would be in even more of a pickle for not coming out and telling them about the kerfuffle that'd happened earlier in the day.

Before he could dial, Scarlett put her hand on his arm and stopped him. "Hold on, before you call. Let's take a look around. Maybe this was Kelcie and Jackson, and they didn't know the combination to the front door or something. I don't want to get anyone in trouble unnecessarily, if we don't have to."

There was a strange inflection in her voice, almost as if she was trying to hide something, but he feared calling the police and unleashing the events that loomed over his head. If he started asking questions about her tone, he might start pulling at strings he wasn't ready to pull.

"We won't touch anything," she said, pointing at the door. "Let's just go back the way we came. See if Kelcie was here. Maybe this isn't even from them, but if it is, for all we know, maybe they are in one of the bedrooms." She gave a forced chuckle. "If they are, you are the one who has to knock on the door."

"Deal," he said, hoping against all hopes that it was the case and the blood that was splattered on the ground wasn't an indication of something more ominous.

They made their way back around toward the hot tub as he buttoned his shirt back up and tucked it into his jeans, carefully pulling himself together. If they were inside and getting together, the last thing he wanted to do was look like they had been on the cusp of doing the same thing.

Jackson would never let him live it down. On the other hand, given how this day had gone and the fears he had been carrying about the two disappearing, he would prefer it to the alternative of them simply being missing.

In fact, when he did find them, Jackson would be getting a piece of his mind. His brother knew better than to just go MIA—he had to have known he was losing his cool about him.

As they made their way through the back door it occurred to him that it hadn't been locked. And it was odd that the blood had been around the back. Why, if the person punched in the glass of the side door, would they have walked around back?

The order of events was strange.

Had the person accidentally broken the glass and panicked? Had they not really been trying to go for the lock?

And why hadn't Jackson or Kelcie answered their phones or returned their texts? It wasn't as if the phones didn't work down here. He had just looked at his phone to call 911 and he'd had service.

Even if his brother was getting some action, he would have had a second to let him know he was okay. They had a system. Or at least Miles thought they did. And if they didn't, he was damned sure that Scarlett said she and her assistant did.

In the kitchen, there was an open beer sitting beside the sink. It was half empty, and the bent cap had been flipped haphazardly onto the floor. He moved to pick it up but changed his mind and left it lying where it had been carelessly tossed.

The door of the fridge was ajar, and he pressed it closed,

surprised that the damned thing hadn't started beeping. Did that mean it hadn't been open that long? Or had it been left open so long that the beeping simply stopped?

The two lovers must have been in one heck of a hurry.

Yet, there had only been one opened beer.

"Jackson?" he called, walking toward the master bedroom. "You in here?"

There was no answer.

His heart pounded in his chest. He wasn't sure what exactly he feared the most.

"Kelcie?" Scarlett called from beside him. She slipped her hand in his.

Her hand was damp with sweat.

He found comfort in the fact that she must have been feeling as concerned as he was.

They moved down the hallway together, following the faint trail of blood. It was silent inside the main bedroom. The door was closed, and he rapped his knuckles on the wood, the sound echoing through the house.

He pushed open the door. The bed was in bloody disarray. Beside the side of the bed was the red shirt Kelcie had been wearing that morning. By the end of the bed was Jackson's blue plaid shirt.

Next to the door, and at the tip of Miles's sock, was a single brass shell casing.

Chapter Twelve

Deputy Trapper stood inside the cabin's living room tapping her pen against her chin as she took the report. She was wearing a pair of black UGG slippers and black-and-gray-plaid pajama pants, and her hair was pulled into a messy bun. She looked annoyed that she had been pulled from her bed at the main house to come out to the guesthouse.

"You know, bad news doesn't get better with time." She picked up her phone and typed away. "I let my husband know about what happened here tonight. As for my department, I want to keep a lid on this—at least from the public—as long as possible. That means we have to get this figured out in the next day or two."

Scarlett chewed at her lip, grateful her brother wasn't the one to show up at the cabin and out her, as she had expected. Now, it felt as if it was only a matter of time until the truth came out about who she truly was, and why she had come. Like her sister-in-law said, bad news didn't get better, yet she wasn't sure how she would deal with the fallout.

Her brother didn't even like her.

There was no proof that what had happened in the cabin tonight had anything to do with her, but the man Thomas had described sounded only too much like her former agent, and if he was slinking around, he would do anything to get at her.

For all anyone knew, maybe Kelcie hadn't even been there. They had been in a hurry to get to the hospital when they had gotten off the trail. It was strange that they would have come back to the guest cabin before leaving. There were a number of things that just didn't make sense.

To top things off, if her brother found out that she had possibly brought trouble to his doorstep, any chance of their having a relationship was out the window.

If he kicked her off the ranch…she would have nowhere to run.

Maybe that was what needed to happen—maybe she needed to face Butch once and for all. If she was going to do that, she needed a gun. Or a man who was handy with the steel.

No.

She just had to wait for him to lose interest.

Not for the first time, she wished she could go to the courts and get a restraining order against him. She'd talked to an attorney about it, but the woman had told her the truth—restraining orders were only pieces of paper. And while the paper said he couldn't be near her or harass her, it did little for her when he followed her around the country and barraged her with social media garbage and spoofing phone calls. The man was a troll, and like most professional and smart criminals, he knew just enough about the limits of the law to keep from getting caught and charged with a crime.

Which was why it would have surprised her if he'd had anything to do with the bloody scene at their cabin. Since he'd been hunting her, he hadn't been so bold. He loved to hide behind his screens and occasionally pop his head up when she was standing in hotels or doing public events—he knew when she least wanted to be rattled and that was always when he struck. Yet, it was possible he'd been the one to hit the boy and his father.

If he was so angry, and if he had gotten the drop on her best friend and Jackson, why hadn't he just killed them here and waited for her to show up so he could finish her off once and for all?

It didn't add up.

Maybe this was all in her head and she was just aligning things that really didn't match up. There were plenty of older men that a five-year-old would describe as Santa. What other reference did they have?

She had never been a mother, she had no idea what a kid was capable of coming up with, but at that age, she doubted it was much more than that.

What was she thinking, being afraid of something and someone because of what a child had told her? Maybe this scene had nothing to do with the accident, maybe Kelcie and Jackson had gotten in a fight, maybe one of them had gotten hurt after they'd gotten locked out of the house while taking a dip in the hot tub.

From the state of the bedroom, they had started to take things there—or they had completed things there, she didn't want to know.

Maybe Mary was right, and they really had just gone the two hours south to the bigger hospital in Missoula, but if it was just for a sprained ankle or stitches…

"Ma'am, what did you say your name was?" Deputy Trapper asked, pulling her from her circular and nonsensical thoughts.

"Scarlett Leafletter. I'm just a guest here."

"Scarlett…" She nodded, but she frowned as she gave

her an appraising once-over. "Pretty name. I know I've seen you somewhere."

She felt the heat rise in her cheeks, but she looked away in an attempt to hide the thoughts of this woman running across pictures of her as a child and possibly making the connection. It didn't seem likely, but she couldn't help herself from going to the worst possible outcome.

"Yeah, I've been working in film for a few years." She brushed back her hair and rearranged it into a new messy bun.

"I'm sure that's what it is." Emily smiled. "I'm sorry about your assistant. Like I said, I will be making some calls tonight, and I'll do everything in my power to find out what has taken place. For now, I recommend you guys move to the Chief Charlo cabin, Miles. If I need any further information or statements from you guys, I'll get ahold of you in the morning. You've put in a long one. Go get some rest."

She would have been slightly put out by the abruptness of the deputy's dismissal, but Emily was right, she was exhausted. It was probably evident on her face. Her eyes always tended to get dark bags underneath that the makeup artists commented on during shoots. She had always done her best to hide them with makeup, but no makeup was heavy enough to mask what had happened to them today.

It DIDN'T TAKE long for Miles to get Scarlett and her gear loaded up into the Mercedes-Benz and to make their way to the cabin just a few hundred yards down the road. It was slightly smaller than the other cabin, lacking an upstairs, but with the smaller size he actually felt more at ease.

After having cleared the cabin, and fearing making the same mistake twice, he escorted Scarlett inside.

She looked road worn, but still as beautiful as the first

time he had laid eyes on her. He wanted to pull her into his arms and tell her how sorry he was about everything that had happened since she entered his life, but he found himself wondering if taking things to that level again was even more dangerous.

If he'd been paying more attention to details earlier, then maybe they could have had more of a chance of making a difference in his brother's disappearance. As it was now, all he knew was there was blood all over the damned place and even more questions than they had faced the rest of the day.

Nothing seemed to be going right.

To make matters worse, now his bosses knew about all his screwups and, without a single doubt, he'd be getting a phone call for a meeting in the near future. They'd be horrible business owners if they didn't just outright fire him for bringing chaos to their door.

Regardless of the circumstances, this day had gone all kinds of sideways, and he was the one standing at the epicenter.

Scarlett sat down on the leather Pendleton couch by the fireplace and let her hair out of her messy bun, letting it flow down and over her shoulders. She was so pretty, even when she wasn't trying.

He couldn't even begin to imagine how many men would give everything they had to stand in the same room as her, let alone kiss her as he had.

He still didn't understand why or how he had gotten so lucky—all he could come away with was that she was scared, lonely or tired. Heck, maybe it was just the search for vacation sex. People did it all the time—go to a place and meet someone who was no more than a ship passing them in the night. Or, in this case, a cowboy sharing the sheets for a romp around the arena.

He took a step toward the couch, thinking about how much he wanted to put his arm around her, but he didn't want to be there just for a good time. He didn't have a lot, but he had more to offer to someone than just his body.

Not that he wouldn't do it under different circumstances.

With so much on the line, and facing so much emotional turmoil, it seemed like taking her to bed tonight was wrong in every conceivable way…except when it came to the lust he felt. He wanted to rip her clothes off and make love to her right in the middle of the cabin's floor and in front of the fireplace—the day be damned.

When lust was leading the way, the only place a person was going to end up was at the corner of heartbroken and confused. For now, he'd take just getting some answers and keeping his job. All he had was being a cowboy—that was why she wanted him—and if he lost that there would be nothing left to him.

He made his way to the kitchen and made two ham and cheese sandwiches before opening a bottle of white wine. He poured them each a glass and made his way back out to the living room, but as he walked into the large room, he found her balled into the fetal position on the couch and fast asleep.

Her dark hair was splayed over the pillow in an angelic halo, and there was a loop of hair that had haphazardly fallen over her forehead. He desperately wanted to walk over to her and sweep the wayward hair from her skin but stopped himself. She was peaceful and perfect just the way she lay.

He was glad she had found a moment of respite, and it was far from him to want to steal a moment of this time from her. She needed a break.

The world around them was in flames, and for this brief moment in time, he could simply be here for her and be her greatest protector.

Chapter Thirteen

The morning came earlier than Scarlett would have liked. When she woke up, she had no idea where she was, but she was covered in a fuzzy blanket and found a down pillow under her head. Miles was sitting in the leather chair perched up awkwardly on his elbow, sleeping.

She watched him slumber, taking in the peacefulness of his features. His stubble had come in over the night, and she thought about how it would feel caressing against the skin of her face. Last night's kiss had been so special. And such a mistake.

It had been a moment of weakness to allow him that deep into her life. Yes, flirting was fun and tiptoeing along the line of impropriety was a thrill, but that was all she had wanted to do. To take it further was to risk making things immeasurably more complicated and would undoubtedly leave her feeling guilty the moment she left the ranch.

And that was what she had to do—leave.

As soon as she found Kelcie, they would have to search for another place. She'd been wrong in coming here and bringing her drama to the people she had once called family but were now nothing more than strangers.

She needed to concentrate on what needed to be done. And she wanted to talk to Thomas again. Maybe there was something they had missed, something he had seen that he had forgotten to tell her about.

Taking out her phone, she clicked it back on, and after a few moments, she was flooded with texts, emails and missed calls. Her voicemail was full.

She opened her messages, desperately hoping at least one of the dozens of messages was from Kelcie. Instead, most were from a barrage of different numbers, all from the same source: Butch.

Looking at the time stamps, the manic messaging had started around the time she had turned off her phone last night. As time wore on and the numbers changed, the messages grew shorter and angrier.

The first had read:

I hope I have your attention. If you would just talk to me, we could sort this out. You know you love me just as much as I love you.

Then it escalated into:

Answer me. If you don't, you'll never work again. I'll end you and your career.

And the most recent was simply skull emojis.

Among the messages were some in which he lost his temper, calling her every name in the book and telling her what she had done wrong as an actress and as a person. The following messages, a half hour later or so, would be messages of apology.

Emotionally, the man was all over the map.

Part of her actually felt bad for him. If she had only stayed in Montana, if she hadn't tried to break the mold, and if she had just played by the rules set forth by her father, she would have never found herself in this position or made this man spiral the drain.

Logically, though, and she'd heard it from Kelcie any number of times, stalking and a man's poor judgment was not her responsibility or fault. She was the victim.

Yet, she hated that word, *victim*.

It implied that she was powerless, that she was the damsel in distress who couldn't save herself.

She sighed. Then again, she ran here for a reason. She *was* the damsel, and she hadn't been able to free herself of this man's abusive grip. It sickened her that she was so weak.

She had even given in to him kissing her once, hoping that it would be so bad and lackluster that any desire he felt for her would be extinguished.

That had blown up in her face and became the day when everything had escalated.

She thought about the day she had first spent real time with him. She had been kind, talking about their families, and he had told her about his abusive, alcoholic father. His mother had put up with the abuse and fallen in line with his father's abusive behavior in hopes that if she just did what he asked things would get better. She didn't want to destroy their family, and she didn't want to take him and his brother away from their father.

In those days, he had told her, his mother feared the economic fallout of becoming a single mother. His abusive father had made it no secret that he would make life as hard as possible for her if she ever chose to leave him. She was a prisoner to her children, to her husband and to the circumstances of her life.

It was that story that had brought her closer to her own

personal demon. She had fallen for his sob story, one that had deeply paralleled her own.

Until recently, Scarlett hadn't truly understood why her mother had stayed with her father. Now, having endured the abuse that came with toxic relationships, she held an entirely new opinion. If she could go back in time, she'd have done anything to help her mother escape.

Miles stirred slightly in his chair, exhaling hard as though he was escaping some stressor in his dream. This simple action made a new wave of guilt flow over her. Even this man's dreams terrorized him. And she had a feeling it was because of her.

There was only one option.

She quietly got up from the couch and made her way to the back of the house, where she stood in front of the river and watched it pull against the banks. The world was always changing, just like the river, and no matter how hard she fought to escape the erosion that came with life, it would constantly tear away at her. If she was going to make a difference, she had to build her own walls. She couldn't wait for other people to save her.

She was strong. She could handle this. Perhaps, she could even stop any further harm from happening if she just took a stand.

Making sure the door was closed behind her, she made the call she was dreading the most.

He answered before it even rang.

"I had a feeling I would hear from you today. It's about freaking time. What else did I need to do to get your effing attention?" Butch asked, his voice sounding coarse and harsh, like he had spent all night talking in a smoke-filled bar.

She wouldn't have been surprised if she was right. It

would help to make heads or tails of the text messages he had been sending throughout the night—he had gotten progressively drunker.

"Why is that, Butch?" she asked.

"If I've told you once, I've told you a million times. If you'd only listened, we wouldn't have any of these problems. But you refuse to take me seriously and you refuse to change. Why does it always have to be me who comes your way? Don't you care about me?"

She hated the way he rambled, spewing a myriad of thoughts and questions before she had a chance to even address one. He did it on purpose to control the conversations and to be able to tell her how stupid she was and how much she didn't listen.

"I'm listening now, Butch. What do you want?" she asked, trying to keep her thoughts under control when all she wanted to do was yell at him and tell him to leave her alone.

"I want you. I've wanted you from the first moment I laid eyes on you." He sounded beaten and battered by her, and it had a strange effect on her heart.

She hated him—how could he make her feel anything but just that?

She hated the way he made her feel.

She hated everything about him.

Yet, she owed him so much. She owed him for making her career. If she could just make him act right, they could have even continued working together and maybe she could have continued her upward trajectory in the business.

She turned to look inside, making sure that Miles was still asleep in the chair. His head was tilted back, and his eyes were closed. She turned back to the water, unable to think about him.

The cost would be too high if she kept playing Butch's game. Not only would it be her soul, but now it would also be anything she hoped to find—even if it was only a kiss—with Miles.

She wouldn't let this jerk stop her from living her life for another moment. And, if he had anything to do with what had occurred in the last twenty-four hours, she would seriously think about ways to end his.

"Butch, I don't want you. I've never wanted you. I've told you."

He laughed, the sound as dark as she knew his soul to be. "We both know that's not true. I felt it in the way you kissed me. I know you love me when I look into your eyes."

"Butch, you haven't seen me in three weeks. Not since New York. The last time you saw me, I can promise you what you saw in my eyes was as far from love as a human can possibly get."

"Why do you always have to play so hard to get with me? It drives me wild." The way he spoke the last word made her skin crawl.

Everything about this man made her want to take a shower.

"Where are you right now?" she asked, hoping he wouldn't play some stupid game like he always loved to do with her by either not answering or by trying to frighten her with his nearness.

"You know where I'm at."

So, it was one of those days where she was to let the games begin.

"I'm hoping that is Santa Barbara." She tried to sound cool, calm and collected, but her palms were beginning to sweat with nerves.

"Is that where you are?" he asked, sounding like the weasel he was.

"That wasn't the question. Just answer me. I want to know."

He laughed, the sound making her stomach ache. "See, you do care about me. I knew it. You even want to know my whereabouts."

"Stop. Just tell me the truth."

"You want the truth?" The mirth in his voice was replaced with the sharp edge of rage. "I'm tired of your games."

Her games? She made a squeaking noise as she nearly choked trying to hold back her outburst.

"All you ever do is make me chase you," he continued. "It's getting tiresome, and I'm not chasing you anymore. If you want to get Kelcie and her little boy toy back, you're now going to have to come to me. If you want your friend back—I want you and five hundred thousand dollars. Cash."

The phone line went dead.

Chapter Fourteen

Miles had no idea how he'd actually slept. It had to have been pure exhaustion that had sent him into a near coma while he had been watching over Scarlett. When he woke up, however, he had absolutely failed at his job of being guardian.

Scarlett's blanket and pillow, the ones he had gently placed on her while she was sleeping last night, were neatly folded and stacked on the edge of the couch. She must have been up for hours, as he could smell the strong coffee permeating from the kitchen. As he stretched, he could hear her moving around in the other room and the sound of a metal utensil clanging against a bowl.

There was the sizzle of bacon, and the scent wafted out to him after a few minutes.

He stood up and stretched before checking his phone for messages.

Of course, there was one from Cameron and three from Emily, both wanting to meet up with him later today, but he sent Emily a quick text asking if they had gotten any new information on the whereabouts of his brother and Kelcie.

He waited, but the message remained unread, and so he checked his emails and then finally put away his phone and made his way to the kitchen. Everything could hold until he had more answers from the police.

With all the tech and eyes in the sky that law enforcement had, he held out hope that he would at least have an idea if the ranch truck that Jackson had been driving was still in the area. If nothing else, it would be a place to start.

He made his way into the kitchen, where Scarlett was wearing a black apron with colorful peppers printed on the fabric over a pair of jeans and a white T-shirt. Her hair was pulled back into a long, beautiful ponytail that cascaded down her back, and for a minute his mind wandered to thoughts about pulling it while he was behind her in a moment of carnal pleasure.

He checked himself.

Last night he was as close as he wanted to come to carnal pleasure with her. He couldn't make that mistake again. Not with his job and his future riding on the line. However, that didn't mean he couldn't enjoy being around her while they tried to figure things out.

Even if he wanted to make her a part of his life, it wasn't like such a thing was even remotely possible. She was a traveler by nature. There was no way she would be happy just staying here on the ranch and settled down with a ranch hand. She could do so much better than him.

She had to have known it, too.

She turned around, but instead of greeting him with a smile, she looked upset. Her eyes were puffy and red, as if she had spent most of the morning crying. It made his entire core clench to see her like this.

"What's wrong?" he asked, not even bothering with false pleasantries.

"I… I don't even know what to say," she started, but she looked down at the spatula in her hand. There were bits of eggs on the plastic edge, and she turned back to where she had been working on the stove.

He didn't know if it was what had transpired between them or the events of yesterday, and he wasn't sure he wanted to press too much out of the fear she would start crying. She was the most incredible woman, and if she started to cry, he would have to pull her into his arms. If he pulled her into his arms, he would have to kiss her. And if he kissed her, well…he wasn't sure he would be able to stop.

She couldn't cry. His heart couldn't bear it.

"Take your time," he said. He bridged the gap between them and moved to put his hand on her lower back but stopped himself at the last moment and instead gently took the spatula from her hand. "Here, you let me do this. You sit down."

She didn't fight him. Instead she simply nodded and moved out of his way. She grabbed two cups out of the cupboard and poured them each a cup of coffee, then sat down at the island in the center of the open kitchen.

He moved the eggs around the pan out of the need to move rather than any pressing cooking requirements as he waited in awkward silence for her to talk. Finally, after sipping on her coffee for what seemed like an hour, she ran her hand over her face and sighed. "There's no good way for me to talk about this," she started. "But I think I may know who has Kelcie and Jackson. He took them because of me, and he's holding them for ransom. I haven't told Emily yet, but we need to. Have you spoken to her?" All her thoughts bubbled over and spilled out into the room like boiling water.

He could already feel the burn.

He turned off the stove and grabbed the bacon out of the oven, taking a moment to get himself in order so he could be careful in his approach of this. He didn't want to come off like a jerk, but a part of him wanted to come at her about why she hadn't mentioned that it was possible she had played a role in their disappearances before now. Emily could have been working on that line all night. Instead, she told him *now*?

He tried to temper his anger. He didn't have all the facts. He couldn't make a judgment just yet, but if Scarlett had been lying to him and in doing so had put his brother in further danger…he couldn't forgive her.

"So, wait… You know the guy behind this *for sure*?"

She nodded, but she wouldn't meet his gaze.

He handed her a plate with eggs and bacon. Then he pulled a fork from the drawer and slid it over to her before getting his own. "Why would his taking them be your fault?"

She sighed, and there were tears welled in her eyes, but she took a deep breath. "His name is Butch Hafner. He is my former agent."

He was confused. "Why would your agent want to take anyone? Is he hard up for money or something? What am I missing?"

"He has been stalking me. I was trying to get away from him for a while, get a break from the chaos, and I came here. I think he must have found us, but I have no idea how. As for the money, he is just greedy. He knows how hard I've worked for it. It's just insult to injury. He wants to make sure I have nothing left."

The anger he was feeling shifted and became the fury that came with the prickling of fear. "How long has he been stalking you?"

"It's been unhealthy between us for a long time. I fired him six months ago as my agent, after he pinned me in a car and tried to assault me." She paused and cleared her throat as she struggled to keep her tears in check.

"You know…" He paused, seeing red. "Montana is one of those places where things go to disappear. We have a strong belief in taking care of our own problems. Especially when the problems are jackasses like him."

She smiled, but it didn't quite hit her eyes. "That's what I was hoping for when I came here. I just wanted him to stop, but now I want some vigilante justice."

"I can promise you, Scarlett, I'll let him buck."

Her eyes widened at his expression, and this time the smile worked up into her gaze. "If you do, you're not doing it alone. I'm not leaving your side."

It was strange how quickly she could turn him around. "That's good, because you better know I wasn't going to do this thing any other way." He took her hand and picked it up and gave it quick kiss to her knuckles. "I'm your cowboy vigilante."

She plucked a piece of egg off her plate, and she motioned for him to open his mouth. He took the bite, smiling as she fed him. "If you're going to go out there and take care of things, you're going to need your strength."

Her come-on caught him off guard, and he stopped chewing and stepped back. Looking away, he picked up his cup of coffee and took a long sip. She was out of his league. He couldn't fall into a situationship with this woman, no matter how badly every inch of him wanted to fall into her.

He sat his half-drank cup next to the sink and straightened his hair. His stubble had come in over the night, but there wasn't a thing he could do about it without running up to the bunkhouse. Maybe that wouldn't be a bad idea. It would give him a little time to gain perspective when it came to her; however, there was no leaving her side now.

If this stalker was bearing down on them, then he couldn't risk leaving her alone for even a moment. A desperate and angry man was more dangerous than a raging bull. At least with the bull, a person could see them coming.

He sent a quick text to Emily to let her know they needed to talk, but it didn't appear as though she had even read the last one he'd sent about checking on things. She must have been sleeping, having likely been working on the scene all night.

"Let's run over to the Saint Ignatius cabin and see if the cops still have it blocked off. If they do, maybe we can talk to the officer in charge of holding the scene. I can't seem to get ahold of Emily."

She looked slightly confused, but the expression was abruptly replaced with one of apathy. "Yeah."

He was glad she wasn't pressing for some deeper conversation about emotions or expectations. He didn't want to deal with anything like that right now. He didn't know what he wanted other than to keep his job and to find his brother...and he did want love, but that wasn't a risk he could even start to take.

She took a few bites of her breakfast. "Let me eat a little more, brush my teeth, and I'll meet you at the car."

He nodded. "Take as long as you need, babe." As soon as the moniker slipped from his lips the heat rushed to his face. He hadn't meant to call her that. He'd done so well in stopping the advance of flirtation between them and then he'd gone and done something stupid like that. Why couldn't his head and his heart get in line and get it together?

Her mouth turned into a cute little O shape, and then there was a sparkle in her eyes he couldn't have missed if he tried.

Not waiting for her to speak, or to complicate things, he turned on his heel and marched determinedly out of the kitchen and away from the woman who made him more confused than a bullfrog in a ballet class.

He grabbed the keys and pressed the fob to automatically start the vehicle and put the keys back down on the table by the door. He opened the door, expecting to see the early rays of the sun just starting to peek over the crests of the mountains on the other side of the valley. Instead, he was inundated by the red and blue lights and police vehicles that surrounded the white Mercedes-Benz.

"Excuse me? Can I help you?" he asked, calling to the cop that was standing directly in front of him.

The man turned and gave him a quick up and down scan, like he was looking to see if he was carrying any concealed weapons.

What in the hell was going on?

Why were they suddenly the ones being looked at like this?

Or, rather, why was *he*?

Just when he thought he was hopping from one confusing situation, he found himself landing in an even larger one. He would take the ballet class over this any day.

"Mr. Miller, do you know where we could find your friend Scarlett Leafletter?" the officer asked, his voice even and calm, not giving him any clues as to why he would be asking after Scarlett.

If they had found Kelcie and were here to deliver a death notice, he would have to be there to pick up the pieces. If the cops were there for that purpose, though, what about his brother? And he couldn't imagine they'd have their lights on if they were there for such a sensitive duty.

He had a few bucks lying around. If they arrested her, he was pretty sure he could afford to bail her out. Then again, why would they arrest her?

Did they think she had something to do with the disappearances?

She *had* been all alone on the ranch and puttering around outside the barn, according to her. That presumably could have given her plenty of time to make it down to the cabin and hurt or kill the two and make it back to the barn before he had arrived back with the Sullivan family.

As far as the police were concerned, he wouldn't tell them a damned thing if it meant implicating her. He knew she didn't have anything to do with what was going on—she was the victim. She was the one being stalked and extorted.

By a man he'd never seen.

A man he hadn't even known existed until ten minutes ago.

Had she seen what the police were doing out here and then played him?

No. She wouldn't have done that to him. She wasn't some horrible creature.

He thought about the way her lips had felt against his. No monster could kiss him like she had or make him feel as he had felt when he had been holding her against his chest.

She was innocent.

"Sir?" the officer asked. The patch on his chest read Ramone.

"May I ask what this is in reference to?" he asked, trying not to sound unhelpful or like he was hiding anything—he didn't want him to get the wrong impression—he just wasn't about to leap blindly into the fire.

"Is this her rental car?" Ramone asked, not answering.

"It is."

"Did she spend the night here with you, Mr. Miles?"

He tried to keep his face placid and unreadable—the man didn't need to connect dots that hadn't and didn't need to be connected. "She did. And yes, she is inside. We were actually just on our way to the Saint Ignatius cabin to find Deputy Trapper."

The man's eyebrows shot up. "Oh? What did you need her for? Is there something you would like to tell me instead?"

He had a sinking feeling he was walking into a trap. "I just… I'd like to speak to her. Do you know where or when I can find her?"

"I'll let her know. For now, do you mind if we step inside?" The officer pointed toward the cabin.

The three other officers that were standing around the Mercedes-Benz were pretending not to be watching, as two of them tapped on their phones and the other was peering into the driver's side window with a flashlight.

"Sure, but what are you guys looking for in the car?" he asked.

"Let's go inside, and I'll tell you all about it."

He wasn't sure whether or not he should call an attorney, or at least his boss at the ranch, but if Emily was aware of what was going on he was sure she was at least letting her husband know. If they wanted him to have an attorney, they would find him one. That was, if they thought it was in the best interest of the ranch. As it was, he had the sinking sensation that his ass was hanging out in the wind.

Miles led him to the door and paused. If he let him go inside it was giving him a chance to snoop, but he had nothing to hide. He opened the door. "Let's sit down in the living room. I'll grab Scarlett and let her know you're here."

And see if she had known what had been going on outside before he'd awakened.

If she had…

The man nodded and strode past him, making his way inside. He walked into the living room and stood beside the couch, peering around the room until his gaze landed on Scarlett's suitcase, purse, and the coat she had been wearing yesterday morning when Miles had first seen her on the ranch.

"I'll be right back," Miles said.

"Take your time." The man walked over to Scarlett's bag and took a pen out of his chest pocket, using it to lift the straps of her purse and opening it slightly.

He rushed into the kitchen. "Scarlett?"

She was sitting at the island, picking at her breakfast, and she turned as he came storming inside. "What?" She looked at him and cocked her head and dropped her fork on the edge of her plate. "What happened?"

"Cops are surrounding your car and now there's one in the other room. Is there anything you haven't told me that I need to know? You have to tell me if I'm going to help." He moved close in hopes that anything they said couldn't be overheard from the other room.

"Why? Why would the police be looking into us?"

He shrugged and leaned over next to her on the counter. "Did you have anything to do with Kelcie and Jackson going missing? Anything at all?"

Her face fell, and she looked hurt. "Seriously?"

That wasn't exactly an answer, but if she didn't want to come out and just tell him, that was on her. From her expression, he felt like she was being earnest and hadn't done a thing wrong, but Scarlett was an actress. If she had done something, who was to say that she wouldn't have reacted the same way?

And yet even thinking this way about her, he felt like a jerk.

Why couldn't anything about this woman be simple?

"I hope you're telling me the truth." He pushed up and

tilted his head toward the other room. "He's looking at your purse right now. I don't think we should leave him waiting."

She scowled as she stood up and swept past him as if he had upset her. Her reaction did nothing to assuage his uncertainty or make him feel like less of an ass. He ran both hands over his face as he sighed. Just when he thought about getting wrapped up with a woman, of course everything would hit the fan. He'd forgotten how complicated life had a way of becoming anytime feelings started to get involved.

He was amazingly attracted to her, and wanted her, but if this was the chaos that she would bring to his life, he was going to have to take a moment to further reflect. If they did decide to ever take things to the bedroom, if he had the chance, he was going to have to gird his loins for a lifetime.

In the living room, the officer was seated next to her coat on the chair, and as he walked out the man smiled and slipped his pen back into his chest pocket. "Ms. Leafletter, Mr. Miller, I'm here to ask you both a few questions. This morning, we received an anonymous tip that there is a connection between you, Ms. Leafletter, and the disappearance of your assistant and a Jackson Miller. Do you know why we would have received such a tip?"

The color drained from Scarlett's face, and she shook her head. She drifted down to the couch like she was a feather. "I promise you, I didn't. I wouldn't. Kelcie's my best friend."

"Do you know who made the *anonymous* tip?" Miles countered. "I'm sure you have to have a clue if you think it was worth digging into."

The officer didn't acknowledge him. "Do you have any reason, Ms. Leafletter, that you and your best friend would be at odds with one another?"

She shook her head. "She and I get along really well. We have our rub points like any other friendship—we are together every day. We travel together. I'd never want to hurt her or see her put in danger."

The officer looked at him. "From the time you spent with these two women, would you say that she is telling the truth?"

Miles nodded. "Absolutely. They seemed to be very close and supportive of one another." So close, in fact, that he was the one who had felt like an outsider in their little club when he'd approached.

The officer stood up and took out his phone. "Had you been in the cabin at any point before you arrived with Miles last night?"

She looked over at him with a scared expression. "No, I didn't even know how to get here, and I didn't have the code to get in if I had."

"Hmm," Officer Ramone said. "Do you know how your wallet would have gotten under the master bedroom's bed?" He pressed on the screen on his phone and pulled up a picture of a blood-covered beige Louis Vuitton clutch. "This is your wallet, isn't it?"

Tears welled in her eyes as she took the man's phone to look more closely at the photos, but he didn't know how she could have seen anything clearly with as bad as her hands were shaking.

"That's my clutch. I… I didn't even know it was missing." A tear streamed down her face, and as she struggled, Miles wanted to pull her away from the officer and tell her everything was going to be okay and that this was all just a big misunderstanding. "I wasn't in the cabin… I promise. And after they left to take Kelcie to the hospital, I swear I haven't seen either of them since. I swear."

Officer Ramone took the phone from her and put it back in his pocket. "I had a feeling you would say that." He turned to Miles. "Due to Emily Trapper's closeness to this case, we have removed her from the investigation. I will be your point of contact in this investigation."

Miles should have known. Emily had always been so good about answering whenever he had needed her about something on the ranch. He was only surprised that she hadn't told him the news about her being taken off the investigation herself.

"That's actually great news. We were hoping to talk to her about a potential lead," Miles said, trying to take some of the pressure off Scarlett. Her hands were in her lap, palms up, and she was staring vacantly into space. "Scarlett has been the victim of stalking. We think the man who was after her in California has found her here, and he may be the one behind the problems."

"Scarlett, do you have a picture of this man?" Officer Ramone asked.

"I don't." Scarlett shook her head. "There is probably one on his website, though I don't know how up-to-date it is."

"What is the man's name?"

"Butch Hafner. He is my former agent out of Santa Barbara. He has been calling me almost nonstop for the last six months. I changed my phone number. He follows me to events and threatens me."

"Have you reported this man and his behavior to the police in California?"

She looked at the office. "I was afraid that if I did, it would only make things worse. I was just hoping he would go away."

"Ma'am, do you have any evidence that he has been harassing you?" Officer Ramone asked.

She took out her phone and pulled up her call log. She handed it to the cop. "You can see how much he has called me. All the random numbers are spoofs by him. He knows I won't answer if he calls."

Officer Ramone stared at the phone. "Ma'am, you said you don't talk to him?"

She nodded.

"It looks as though you were talking to him this very morning. How do you explain that, if you are trying to avoid him? Wouldn't you have blocked his number?" He gave her a suspicious and cynical look.

"I forgot I talked to him!" Tears streaked down her face in rivulets, but Miles wasn't sure if they were out of stress, fear or frustration. "I called him because of everything that happened yesterday. I wanted to know if he was in Montana and if he had followed me. I was afraid he had something to do with Kelcie and Jackson. He told me that I was the only one who could get them back."

"Hold on," Officer Ramone said, holding up his finger. "Do you know if he is actually in the state?"

She opened and closed her mouth. "He didn't tell me."

The officer sighed. "Do you have a recording of this phone call? The one you *forgot* you made to a man who you said was stalking you?"

"It wasn't a long call, and I… I didn't record it. I just freaked out and needed to know. Thomas said the man who hit him looked kind of like Butch and…" Her words came out in a jumbled rush, but Officer Ramone stopped her with a wave of his finger.

"You can see where I'm having problems with your story, Ms. Leafletter? Most women, who have problems like that which you claim, call and report the activities out of fear. In California, I'm assuming its laws are similar to ours in Montana, but if you feel as though you are being intimidated by someone, it is enough to get a restraining order. I'm just struggling to understand why you didn't file for one if what you're telling me is true."

"I'm not lying. I swear. Look into him. If you can track or trace these numbers, you'll see it's him every time. You can have my phone, I don't care. Take it," she said, desperately trying to hand it over to the officer.

"Ms. Leafletter, as much as I want to believe what you are telling me, and about this man, you've given me no tangible evidence, no legal history of a crime, and if anything, the only clear evidence that you have supplied is of *you* contacting *him*."

She made a strange, strangled sound.

The officer put a reassuring hand on her shoulder. "We do take harassment and stalking very seriously. If you think you can provide evidence of him making you feel intimidated in any way, I recommend you going down to the crime victim advocate's office and having them help you file a motion for a temporary restraining order until you can stand in front of a judge."

"Thank you, Officer Ramone," Miles said, trying to protect Scarlett in any way he could. "Is there anything else we can do for you?"

"Ms. Leafletter, is there anything else you want to tell me, before I search your vehicle? Is there anything that you are hiding from me that I need to know?" Officer Ramone asked.

She shook her head.

"Okay." The officer dropped his hand from Scarlett's arm and gave Miles an appraising look. "I recommend that you both stay in West Glacier and don't leave the state in the next couple of days. I'm sure that we will be back with further questions about your brother and friend. As it stands, there's enough evidence on the scene to connect you, Ms.

Leafletter, to their disappearances and possible murders. I won't arrest you today, however if we find anything further that implicates you, I'll be back with handcuffs."

Chapter Fifteen

Scarlett was beyond furious. Officer Ramone and his team of investigators were still outside, milling around her rental car. She could only assume they were waiting for a search warrant in order to gain entry to her vehicle.

The officer had been in such a big hurry to threaten her and tell her all the ways she had been delinquent in not adequately dealing with Butch that he'd not simply asked her if they could search. If he had, she wouldn't have stopped him, and yet she found a tiny glimmer of joy in the fact that they had to stand out there in the sun and wait.

They could sweat.

It was what he wanted her to do—unjustifiably.

Officer Ramone was wrong if he thought she had anything to hide. She looked out the front window of the cabin, her arms crossed over her chest as she tried to control her anger. She just couldn't believe the man could be so apathetic—it was like he had never been in a situation like hers and simply couldn't understand. That was probably exactly what it was. He just had no frame of personal reference. Or maybe he was used to dealing with false accusations or situations that were fueled by drugs and alcohol, and they had made him jaded.

As upset as she was, there was still a tendril of thought

that the officer might have been justified in his assessment of her ability to prove malfeasance or criminal intent. She'd been stupid and lacking in judgment for not taking action against Butch and his threats and attempt to extort her sooner. It was just that she had been afraid of amplifying the problems. Maybe this all was in her head, though, and the calls were nothing more than election officials or something. Maybe they *were* just robocalls. Maybe she was making something out of nothing.

How had Butch driven her to the edge of madness?

No, she wasn't going to allow herself to be gaslighted by law enforcement or by her own self, and certainly not by Butch. Before she arrived, he had been harassing her and stalking her, and she wasn't just making it up. If she had the chance to talk to him again, she would make sure this time to record the conversation. She wouldn't make the same mistake twice.

Yet his threat had already been delivered. She had to go to him to get her friends back. And if the police didn't want to believe her, and they thought that she was falsifying her testimony or whatever, she would do it on her own.

The catch-22 was rage inducing. To nab this predator, she would once again have to allow him to be close to her, and in doing so, she would have to put her friends and herself at risk.

That was all on the condition that Butch was telling the truth and had kidnapped her friend. Knowing him, he really could have been anywhere in the world and was just playing mind games with her, anything to keep reminding her that he was the one in control and that no matter where she went, she was never outside of his reach.

She only wished she could make the officer understand and help.

Ugh. Well, he had helped *somewhat.* He'd told her she could go to the advocates. But without any tangible proof of Butch's harassment and stalking, the word of a little boy who said he thinks he saw Santa wasn't going to cut it.

She really was on her own.

"Are you okay?" Miles asked, walking up from behind her and putting his hand on her lower back.

The simple action made her jump, and she threw back her hand, hitting Miles and making him jolt. "Sorry," she said, trying to calm herself after his jump scare.

"You're okay. We're going through a lot right now. You've every right to be jumpy. However," he said, lifting a mug of freshly made coffee that was now dripping down his arm, "I'm going to have to dry myself off." He lifted the mug for her to take.

She took the cup. "You're not burnt, are you? Oh, my goodness, I didn't hear you coming."

"Don't worry," he said, giving her a kind smile. "If anything, I'm impressed with your martial art skills. Nobody is going to get the drop on you."

Her thoughts went instantly to Butch and his stupid round face with his white beard and his graying hair. How many times had he gotten the drop on her at events, only to stand in corners and leer at her until he could try and get her alone?

Her hands started to shake, and the coffee sloshed against the cup.

Miles reached up and cupped her hands and the mug with his own. "Maybe caffeine wasn't such a good idea."

"That's not it." She couldn't meet his gaze, and instead she tilted her head back and let out a long, calming exhale. She didn't have to be scared right now. There was no boogeyman here to get her, it was only her thoughts. "I'm fine. Really."

"You can try and tell whomever you want that, but I'm not an idiot." He took the cup from her hands and sat it down on the stone-covered table by the front window. "Why didn't you tell me about the phone call?"

Her stomach dropped. "I thought I did. I told you I knew he had Kelcie and Jackson—that was because of the call."

He was watching her in a way that made her feel like she was being questioned by Officer Ramone once again, and she hated it.

"Or, at least I'm pretty sure Butch took them." She ran her hand over her face. It smelled of coffee. "I mean, it's possible he was just playing me when I talked to him. Maybe he could tell I was upset or something, but he told me right before the line went dead, 'If you want to get Kelcie and her little boy toy back, you're now going to have to come to me.'" She tried to mimic Butch's weak, mid-register voice. "He told me I would have to pay him five hundred thousand dollars. Which is almost the exact amount I have saved in my liquid accounts. It's like he knows. It was so weird that I'll never forget it."

"Why would he ask for money? Is he struggling financially?"

"No," she said, shaking her head. "He is a trust-fund kid. He can go anywhere in the world at any time. His father created the artificial heart valve and sits on the board for the AMA. He's fine."

"So, explain the ransom."

"He… When…" She paused, picking at her fingernail. "When I left home, I walked away with nothing. He told me that every penny I ever made was because of him. Apparently, he wants it all back."

"I'm so sorry." He took her hand in his and turned away to look out the window at the police. "Are they going to find anything in the car that we are going to need to worry about or explain?"

"No. I promise. And I promise, I'm telling you the truth about Butch…and about everything. I wouldn't lie to you." She hated how desperate she felt to be believed and validated by him, but she needed him in her corner so badly.

"I believe you, I do." He kissed the back of her hand and nodded.

They watched as Officer Ramone came sauntering back up the path and to the front door. They waited for him to knock before Miles let go of her hand and went to answer. He opened it up, and the officer had a dour expression on his face. "How's it going out there?"

Officer Ramone looked from him over to Scarlett, and the way he studied her made her want to shrivel up into a tiny ball on the floor. "We have yet to receive our search warrant from Judge Donovan. However, while I was waiting for his response, I pulled up a little bit of information about you, Ms. Leafletter."

Her blood drained from her face and down out of her chest, and she glanced to the floor to see if it had really, truly leached from her body.

"Does your friend here know your true identity? Does anyone?" Officer Ramone sent Miles a quizzical glance.

Miles looked shaken, and he stepped back from her as if she had just struck him.

"I'm sorry, Miles. It's not a big deal…" she started, but even as she spoke, she knew how damaging the next revelation would be to the man who she had, just moments before, promised complete honesty. Her promise hadn't even lasted five minutes.

"What isn't? *Who are you?*" Miles spat the words like they were bile on his tongue.

She wanted to tell him that she was the woman he had met, the woman who was devoted to her friend and would stop at nothing to make sure she was safe. And she wanted to tell him that she was everything he was looking for, but all she could think about was who she really was—flaws and all.

"I'm Teri Trapper. I'm Cameron's sister. He doesn't know I'm here, and he doesn't know my pseudonym. I came here to hide from Butch. Everything else I've told you about myself is true. I swear."

"You mean just like you swore you were telling me the truth before?" Miles's anger rippled through his voice. He turned and walked to the door but looked back over his shoulder at her as he opened it. "You know, from the moment I met you I felt something. I thought it was…" He paused, making her wonder what he was going to say, but instead his scowl deepened and his eyes darkened. "I just didn't know what I was really feeling should have been suspicion."

He strode out the door and slammed it behind himself.

Whatever they had going on, it was irrevocably and unquestionably over.

Chapter Sixteen

The police wouldn't let Miles anywhere near Scarlett's car. Or wait, was it Teri's?

Given how many times she had lied to him in just their short amount of time together, he had a feeling that if he stuck around, the police would next tell him that there were a hundred kilos of cocaine in her trunk, and she was a drug runner from Mexico.

Nothing about this lying woman would surprise him anymore.

He was glad he hadn't taken things further last night. For once, he had dodged a bullet.

One of the officers, Deputy Burns, sidled over to him, his right thumb stuffed under the top of his utility belt. "How's it going?"

He wasn't sure what to make of the man's informal greeting, especially considering how it had been going with Ramone. "I've had better days. You guys find anything?"

The man shrugged. "This your girlfriend's rig, sir?"

"No, she is just a guest who's staying at the ranch. And I'm Miles Miller. I'm only a guide hired to keep her...*entertained.*" After last night's kiss and the revelations this morning, it felt strange devaluing Scarlett to the level of another visitor on the ranch. She was so much more and had brought so much drama into his life that she had quickly embedded herself into the frontrunner position in his life. Who was keeping whom on their toes was up for debate.

Burns sighed. "I completely understand. Lots of dudes have been coming up here lately to play cowboy and cowgirl. You must get some doozies."

He hadn't had that many paying guests at the West Glacier Ranch, but when he'd worked as a hand at the Joy Luck Ranch in Somers, he had seen more than his fair share of poor behavior and rudeness. That being said, at least half of the people he'd worked with were kind and generous, many even becoming friends who had returned to the Joy Luck year after year just to see him again.

His least favorite guest of all time had been a moderately wealthy civil engineer with family money who had gotten upset when Miles had not been at their beck and call during the night to light their path while they'd been on an overnight horseback ride up into the Swan Range. He had been up all night with the flu and hadn't been able to get out of his sleeping bag, let alone hold a flashlight for someone else to pee.

The man had even gone so far as to call after he got back and complain about the lack of safety concerns and how lazy Miles had been on the trip.

It had been that complaint that had nearly gotten him fired. His former boss, Drake Rex, hadn't believed him about the stomach flu and paid him his weekly wages and ordered him off the ranch. Chloe had gone to Drake to talk. He'd gotten his job back, and that was the gateway to Chloe and Drake's relationship—and the real end of theirs.

After all he had done for the place and the guests he'd brought in and made happy, Miles had been incredibly hurt. Sick was sick whether a person was on the mountain or in the comfort of their own bed. He couldn't pick the time, and he certainly hadn't been in a position to do anything more than he had. It hadn't been his fault he had gotten sick on the trail.

Come to think about it, Drake Rex may have been the biggest source of problems in his professional life. He always had something or someone he was complaining about. And no matter how hard his employees worked, it seemed as though it was never quite enough. In one weekend, Miles had brought in forty thousand dollars in revenue thanks to a repeat client. Instead of congratulating him and thanking him for his great work in keeping clients and guests happy, Drake informed him that he would need to do it again.

His indifference was one of the reasons Miles had been only too happy to take his last check and leave. It also hadn't hurt that he was leaving his ex-girlfriend on the ranch to take over his place as head guide. Miles kind of found a wicked sense of joy in the idea of her having to fill his shoes and play nice when it was often nothing more than a thankless job.

"Miles, is your brother Jackson Miller?" Burns asked, pulling him from his thoughts.

Miles nodded. "Yeah, did you hear from him?"

The officer shook his head. "Actually, I was wondering about where your brother was staying. Did he live out here on the ranch with you or did he have another place he's been renting? The information we have on him in our system has him still living at your parents' home. However, when we went to check his residence, no one there had heard of him, and it appeared as though that house changed hands."

Miles sighed. "Yeah, my parents passed away shortly after a car accident a few years ago. My siblings and I had to sell it to take care of their medical bills and care. Jackson had been staying at my old apartment—he took over my lease. If you want, I have keys and I'd be happy to take you over there."

He doubted they would find anything about his brother, at least nothing that he hadn't already known—that Jackson could be a bit of a slob, he didn't own a vacuum, and he liked to drink Miller Lite. He had no doubt that the garbage can at the end of the kitchen counter was probably spilling over with empty cans.

Burns cast a glance over at the other officer standing by the car. "I'm going to take a run over to Jackson's apartment, see if we can dig anything up there about his possible whereabouts. If you guys need me, just call. Shouldn't be too long."

The other officer sent them a finger wave in acknowledgment.

"We can jump in my car," Officer Burns said, pointing in the direction of the squad car parked in the back of the line of three. It was a compact sedan, and it was still running, as though he assumed he would be leaving at any moment.

"We?" Miles asked, surprised that the officer would want him along for anything.

"Yeah, I'm going to need your key and your permission to enter the premises—that is, if your name is still on the rental agreement."

He was angry and hurt at Scarlett's lies, but at the same time, he didn't want to leave her on the ranch alone. She needed someone in her corner. However, she had Officer Ramone. But Miles had promised her he wouldn't leave her alone.

That had been before she had promised him she was telling him the truth.

His anger started to seep up from the edges of his being once again.

"Let's go." He turned and gave the cabin one last look before walking over to the man's patrol car and stepping inside.

The ache in his gut grew larger as Burns stepped inside and they drove off.

He watched the ranch disappear in the side mirror as they made their way to the highway and toward his old apartment. He regretted leaving her, but he couldn't help but wonder if he hadn't gone, if he would have regretted staying.

SCARLETT STARED OUT the front window, watching as Miles got into the cop car and drove away. "Where are they taking him?" she asked Officer Ramone.

He tapped his finger on his belt as he leaned forward and peered out the window to see what she was talking about. "I couldn't tell you."

She wasn't sure which way he meant the words, but she knew regardless of inflection, the answer she would receive from the tight-lipped officer would be the same. "Are they going to bring him back?"

A new fear twisted through her—that of being truly alone.

He'd promised her he would stay, but she had screwed everything up. If only none of this had happened.

Yet, what else had she expected? She had come here knowing about Butch and his problems, then she had kept her truth from the one man who had wanted to help her. She could hardly blame him for getting in the cop car and driving away.

She wished she could go back in time and redo everything.

She wouldn't have come here.

She wouldn't have put Kelcie and Jackson in harm's way.

Hell, if she could have gone back in time, she wasn't sure she would have ever left this ranch in the first place.

Nothing had gone right in her life since she had thought she had escaped.

She closed her eyes and sighed as she considered what a naive child she had been when she went running off to Hollywood. Her story was like thousands of other women's—coerced and used, then disregarded and minimized and made to feel so small that they quit on their dreams, or worse, were killed.

She couldn't let Butch win. If he did, and she gave up on her dreams and on the woman she wanted to be, then she might as well just hand over her soul. She'd always think about what would have been if she'd fought the man harder.

Yet, how was she going to fight a shadow? Especially if she was nothing more than his puppet.

"You know, you can just look through my car. I don't care and I have nothing to hide."

At least, nothing *anymore.*

Officer Ramone looked at her with surprise. "Are you sure? It is within your legal rights to wait until we have obtained our search warrant. And so you know, you are welcome to retain an attorney at any time."

"Am I under arrest?" she asked.

"Not yet, but you not disclosing your true identity to me has done nothing for your credibility. And, from the look on your boyfriend's face, I'm going to say it did nothing for your budding relationship, either."

She huffed but tried to cover the sound with a cough. "There's no relationship. We are just friends."

"You do know that I've been in control of many investigations in my time as a law enforcement officer. I've made a living out of telling when people are lying to me. And trust me when I say I have had a lot of people lie to me, and most are far better at it than you—actress, or not."

She didn't know how to respond. Instead, she grabbed the fob off the table by the door and handed it over to the officer. "Here. Have at it."

He took the keys and gave her an appreciative dip of the chin. "Why don't you go ahead and walk out here with me?" He opened the door and waited for her to step outside before closing it behind them.

She followed in his footsteps as he walked toward the Mercedes-Benz.

"Do you mind if I look in the trunk?"

"Go right ahead." She waved in the direction of the car.

He hit the button on the fob and the trunk latch popped open and the lid started to rise. Inside the trunk, lying on a bloodied white mink blanket were two pairs of steel handcuffs. Each pair was slathered in sticky, drying blood.

She fell to her knees. "Oh, my God."

Her breath caught in her throat, and she slumped forward as hot rivulets of tears streamed down her face. A faint wind kicked up, carrying the scent of iron-rich blood in her direction, and it made her stomach turn sour.

Officer Ramone stepped closer to her and unclicked the metal cuffs from a leather case on his belt. "Scarlett Leafletter, would you please lay down and put your hands behind your back? I'm placing you under arrest."

Chapter Seventeen

After banging on the cheap wooden front door of his old apartment, Miles unlocked it, and the yeasty smell of a stagnant hot room wafted toward him and Officer Burns as he opened the place up. The studio apartment in the basement of the landlord's house was as he expected it—filled to the brim with empty beer cans and there were heaps of clothing in piles around the main room.

It would have never looked like this when he lived there, but aside from the clutter, thankfully his brother didn't seem to have let it get too deeply into disrepair to threaten his sublet agreement.

"You can do whatever you need. I gotta say, though, it doesn't look like he has been around."

Burns stepped around him and made his way into the apartment. "Where is the mailbox for this place?"

Miles pointed out toward the road. "It's the black box by the road."

The officer nodded. "I'm going to request to get a warrant to locate your brother's last cell phone ping, but that can take some time when we are working through cell phone companies."

"I appreciate that," he said. "My brother and I are pretty

close. He has always been a good apple, and I just can't see why anyone would want to hurt him."

Burns walked toward the kitchen table that sat in the middle of the open kitchen. He stared at the stack of papers that were sitting on the surface. He had his thumbs stuffed under his Kevlar vest as though he was trying to intentionally keep from touching anything.

"Did either of you know Kelcie or Scarlett before they came to the ranch?"

"No." He thought about Scarlett and who she really was. "Scarlett said she had looked into the ranch before she came. Based on who she really is and what she said, you should really ask if she knew me before she arrived, not the other way around."

Burns looked up from the stack of papers. "Interesting. It sounds like you don't care for her very much, that you don't think she is worthy of your trust. Is that true?"

When the man put it like that it had a way of stinging.

He wasn't sure what he truly thought or felt when it came to Scarlett, but there was one thing he knew—she was more than met the eye. As for malicious intent and guilt, he wasn't sure.

"I think that she's really afraid."

"Do you think that she could have had anything to do with her friend's disappearance? Was there any sort of friction between the two that you noticed?" the officer asked.

"Far from it. They seemed like they were really close, and I can't say that I got any impression that there were issues between them. They seemed like sisters." Miles closed the door to the apartment behind him.

Officer Burns moved out of the kitchen toward the small bathroom and peered inside. "Hmm."

Officer Burns made Miles deeply uncomfortable, but he

wasn't sure if it was because of the situation or if it was because they were standing in his former apartment, the one he had shared with his ex-girlfriend Chloe from the Joy Luck Ranch. Jackson had taken over the lease, but he hadn't spent much time in this place. In fact, he had intentionally avoided it thanks to the memories cast by the location.

Burns walked down the hallway to the single bedroom and opened the door. He motioned for Miles to come over. Inside the room was a dresser with open drawers and socks and underwear scattered over the edges. The closet was open, and empty hangers littered the floor. The bed was pristine, with blue sheets and a matching quilt. Each of the pillows was placed carefully at the head of the bed. It ran in strange juxtaposition to the chaos of the bedroom.

"Is this how your brother always lives?" Officer Burns asked.

"My brother can be a bit of a slob, but did you see his bed? It's made."

"I noticed the same thing. Did your brother have a duffel bag or suitcase that you know about?"

"Do you think that my brother planned to abduct Kelcie or something?" Miles tried not to sound affronted. However, the idea sounded so out of left field to him that he wasn't quite sure what to make of it. "That doesn't make any sense."

The officer walked over to the closet and peered inside. "There don't appear to be any clothes in here, or a suitcase." He turned back to face Miles. "And as for people making sense, that's like thinking you can assume what people will do. People never cease to surprise me."

He appreciated that the man didn't seem to be putting him on trial, but it was so strange standing in the bedroom talking to a police officer, the same bedroom where he had spent many nights with Chloe.

He hated thinking about her and how she had cheated on him, possibly exactly where they were currently standing. "I have found that it's the people we think we can trust the most that always disappoint. And often, it's the people that we least expect who come through in the end."

"It sounds like you've been through the wringer."

"I'm sure you've had your fair share of relationships, too."

The officer huffed. "I don't know that I'd call them relationships or opportunities to watch train wrecks up close and personal." He gave his slight laugh. "I'll leave it with cops don't have a reputation for failed relationships for no reason."

"I think that's one thing that we cowboys have in common with you." He laughed. "Is there anything else you were hoping to find here? Do we still need to keep looking, or are you ready to head back to the ranch?"

"I know you don't think that your brother had anything to do with Kelcie's disappearance, but I have to say I think it's odd that his clothing and personal items have been rifled through, and his suitcase is missing. Even his toothbrush was gone from the bathroom. It looks like he was planning an extended stay somewhere, or with someone. He didn't have a girlfriend that you know of, did he?"

"No. My brother was kind of a lone wolf type. I think he likes several women right now and isn't ready to be tied down to one of them."

"I envy him that. He needs to get it all out of his system. It makes life a lot easier when you get a little older. For me, I think I've figured out what I want in life. Or at least I thought I had, right up until my current divorce."

"I'm sorry to hear about it. Those can be tough."

"Did you ever go through one?" Burns asked.

He shook his head. "I was just living with a woman, and

she managed to break my heart by cheating on me with my boss from my former job. Now she has my job and she's working arm in arm, or hopping into bed, with my former supervisor. It's one of the reasons I had to go to work for the West Glacier Ranch."

"You're lucky you found out who she was before you made a real mistake."

He wanted to argue that falling in love with her had been the real mistake, but he didn't push the issue with the man who was clearly jaded.

"Do you know the names of the women your brother was dating? Or, if any of them are the jealous type?" Officer Burns asked.

"No. My brother and I don't really have that kind of friendship. Even if we did, he is the kind who keeps things close to his chest."

Burns smiled. "You gotta love brothers." He looked back at the table one more time as he stopped at the front door. His cell phone vibrated and started to play Five Finger Death Punch. He pulled it from his pocket and put up his hand, motioning for Miles to stay put as he stepped outside.

Miles could hear him speaking. There was something about an arrest. He promised whomever he was on the phone with that he'd be there in twenty. If nothing else, at least they were done poking through his brother's apartment. It felt awkward and wrong, and he could honestly say he never wanted to step foot back in the place.

He walked over to the table and took a peek at the papers Burns had been so interested in. The paper on the top was a credit card bill. He moved the envelope covering the amount due. He had to read the number twice. A lump grew in his stomach. His brother owed more than thirty thousand dollars, and the compounding interest was swamping him.

Why hadn't Jackson told him? He would have helped him out.

That number was more than half of what his brother made annually. No wonder he had been so desperately interested in coming to work for him at the ranch.

As soon as he found him, they would need to talk. That was *if* he found Jackson and his brother was still alive.

His brother had made some mistakes in life, and he liked to party and gamble, but Miles hadn't thought getting himself in this deep of water was one of them. It made him wonder what other kinds of issues his brother was having.

His mind whirled with possibilities. If his brother was that far in debt, he had to have been desperate to get out. If he was desperate enough, would he have or *could* he have kidnapped Kelcie? Perhaps he was just biding his time until he made his demands known.

Scarlett wasn't poor, and as it so happened, she didn't come from a poor family. She would have been a perfect mark to use for a huge payout in a kidnapping. Miles wasn't a criminal, but if he wanted to get Scarlett to do what he wanted, he could have gone after her best friend.

While Jackson had his faults, he'd never been arrested for a crime, and he'd never had run-ins with law enforcement. In high school, he had done well but had liked to skip class any chance he got to spend the days hiking around the mountain, and hunting or fishing. He was just a good ole Montana boy.

His parents would have rolled over in their graves if they knew what he was wondering about his brother. They had raised them to have integrity and honor, but they had also taught them not to live outside their means.

Jackson wasn't a suspect in Kelcie's disappearance. No. Scarlett had already told him that her stalker had basically admitted to taking them. They just needed to dig deeper into the creep.

Officer Burns opened the door and waved for him to come outside as he hung up his phone. There was a strange expression on his face. "We need to hit the road. Let's go."

He followed the officer up the stairs and out to his squad car. As he got in and buckled up, Burns opened his computer that was mounted between them and started to type.

"I don't know if you heard," Officer Burns started, not even bothering to look up from his computer, "but your client, Ms. Leafletter, was arrested. She is on the way to jail, where she will await arraignment."

He jerked. "What? What was she arrested for?"

"Officer Ramone believes there is enough information to charge her with murder." Officer Burns shrugged. "I have no idea what went on after we left the ranch, but if you're her friend, you should make some calls to lawyers. She is going to be facing some major obstacles."

"She didn't *kill* anyone." He balled his hands into tight fists, readying himself for a fight to protect the woman he had come to secretly love.

Chapter Eighteen

She felt absolutely sick. In her entire life, Scarlett had never imagined that she would find herself waiting in the jail near the Flathead County Courthouse after being cuffed, stuffed, booked and waiting for arraignment. If they offered bail, she would need to make a call. To whom, she wasn't sure. Kelcie would have been her go-to, but now…

There were five other women in the jail cell with her. One was lying on the only concrete slab and was asleep or doing a great job of pretending. A blonde sat in the far corner, her knees tucked into her chest, and she was mumbling incoherently. Two were sitting together and whispering, and the last stood at the front of the cell, holding the bars and watching whatever was going on outside their unit.

In her wildest nightmares, she couldn't have come up with a situation like this.

She wanted to cry, to scream to the universe that she was being unjustly treated, but given how the world had been bearing down on her since she'd gotten here, to speak out would only lead to more problems.

When she stood in front of the judge, she would plead not guilty, but she would need a good attorney. Hopefully, the judge would see things from her perspective and have leniency. She had been framed for a crime she had most definitely not committed, and just because there was evidence of something heinous, Officer Ramone had made a mistake.

The brunette woman who was standing at the front of the cell turned. "Someone is comin'. Who ya'll think they gonna see next?"

Scarlett stood up from her place against the wall and smoothed the jeans she had bought online from the ranch supply store before she'd come to Montana. No matter how much she dressed the part, she would never be able to fit into this rough place where justice was an illusion. Apparently, she wasn't the only one faking an appearance.

The jailer walked up to the bars. "Ms. Falconer, you need to step back from the bars," he ordered the brunette.

The woman let go of the steel bars and stepped back with a tip of the head.

"Ms. Leafletter, would you please approach the cell door?"

Her stomach lurched and cold sweat broke out on the base of her neck at the sound of her name being called. The judge must have been working fast.

Her feet felt as though they were encased in concrete as she made her way to the door.

"Turn around and put your hands behind your back," the man ordered.

She did as she was told, but her hands were trembling. He slapped the cold steel handcuffs around her wrists. They seemed heavier than the ones Officer Ramone had put on her at the ranch, but it could have just been in her head.

The jailer led her out of the holding area and to the stairwell. "Officer Ramone wants to see you in his office."

"Do you know why?"

He shook his head. They didn't share another word until she was standing outside Officer Ramone's office and the man tapped on the heavy oak door. "I have Ms. Leafletter here to see you."

"Come on in."

The man opened the door and waved her inside. He gave her a scowl as she passed by, and the look made her feel as though she was the biggest criminal on earth, and he was the one passing judgment.

So much for being innocent until proven guilty.

"Thank you, Taylor. You can go," Ramone said.

The man tipped his head and closed the door as he made his way out.

"Did you change your mind about me? Decide that I'm not actually one who would go around murdering my friends?" she asked, suddenly angry. She didn't know what hit her, if it was her anxiety or the nerve of him having put her in this position, but she couldn't help the sensation of rage that was bubbling up from her core.

"Actually, I did want to talk to you a little bit. Why don't you take a seat, and then I will take off those cuffs?"

She frowned. This man had been a pain in her ass since the moment she had met him and now he was offering to chat and make her comfortable. She couldn't trust him. However, she sat down as he asked and turned so he could unlock the cuffs behind her back.

"Have you heard how Thomas and his father are doing?" she asked.

He stood up and walked over. "Thomas is still in the hospital. They're trying to get in touch with a family member who can take him. It sounds like he doesn't have any other family. I don't know how that is going to work out. As for Aiden, he's still in critical condition. They have placed him in a medically induced coma."

Thomas had been so scared, and she could only imagine what he was feeling now that his father was standing at the brink of death.

She could hear the metal key move into the lock and the snap as he opened the cuffs and removed them from her wrists. "There, that has to feel better. Doesn't it?"

"Much." She turned to face his desk and rubbed at the place on her wrist where the steel had chafed her skin. There was a set of marks where the cuffs had started to cut in because the jailer had pressed them too tight.

"So," Ramone said, walking around his desk as he dropped the open cuffs onto it like some sick reminder of the damage he could inflict. "I have been looking into your former agent, Butch Hafner. How well do you know this man?"

A sense of relief flooded her. This was the last thing she had expected from the man who had arrested her. "He was my film agent for two years. We spent some time together when I was filming. He liked to drop in and take me out to lunch and things. He always called me his 'Big Fish.'"

"I bet that felt pretty amazing, being an up-and-coming actress who was being fawned over by her agent, didn't it?"

She didn't like his tone, but she tried to ignore it. "Yes. It's always nice to be appreciated."

Something she doubted he felt very often.

"Uh-huh. Did he ever tell you much about his background?"

She thought back for a moment. So much of what he had said to her had been in one ear and out the other, as she had taken it mostly for small talk—at least, at first. "I remember him saying he was from the New England area originally, and his father was abusive. Oh, and he graduated from Harvard. Beyond that, I'd really have to think. Why?"

"I've been doing some digging."

"You mean like you did on me?" she spouted, more than aware that her best bet would have been to be quiet, but she simply couldn't help herself.

"You're the one with bloody cuffs in your trunk. Do you really think you should be talking to me that way? I would be more than happy to drop you back in your jail cell."

She sighed. "I know. Sorry. I can't help it…" She ran her hand over the back of her neck. "Just tell me one thing."

"What?"

"Do you really think I had something to do with my best friend's blood getting in my trunk?"

"Well, for starters, we don't know whose blood that was, or if those cuffs were on your friend and Jackson at any time. Until the tests come back, County Attorney Yates doesn't actually think we have enough to formally charge you."

"Wait… So you're letting me go?" She couldn't hold back the relief and excitement in her voice.

"Officially, I can hold you up to forty-eight hours to question you in your possible role in this crime. If you don't want to go back down to the cell for the remaining forty or so, I would appreciate it if you could drop the attitude and work with me in getting as much information together as possible to help your friend—who is hopefully still alive. Capisce?"

"Fire away. You know all my secrets now. I've got nothing else to hide." She opened her hands like she was opening a book.

"Great. Now, did you know that Butch Hafner was also known by another name?"

"No. I'm surprised that he never mentioned it to me, but it's not uncommon for people in our line of work to assume pseudonyms for privacy and safety."

"I can understand the desire, especially nowadays. However, this guy's legal name is now Butch Hafner. Before he was known as Butch Harrington."

"Why would he change his name?"

Ramone smiled. "That's what really made me start digging into him. I had the same question. I went down the rabbit hole, and it appears as though this guy was a felon."

A cold chill ran down her spine. "And as for Harvard, there is no record of him ever attending or graduating from the Ivy League school. However, he did grow up in Boston and he lived near the college, but in a different part of the city."

"Everything I thought I knew about this man was a lie." Her voice was flat at the realization of how much she had been lied to and manipulated by Butch.

She hated him.

Actually, hate wasn't even the tip of the iceberg of loathing she felt at the mere thought of him. She had never wanted to kill someone, but for a brief moment she could understand how a person could be pushed to the extreme.

"You would be surprised by how often I hear people say that."

She wasn't surprised. There were sheep and wolves in the world, and she knew both kinds. If only she hadn't been the one to show her woolly throat to the predator.

"What felony was he convicted of?" she asked, a thick numbness settled over all the feelings that had been sifting through her until all she could feel was the cold steel arms of the chair pressed against the bottom of her forearms.

She pressed her fingers into the edge of the chair until her knuckles cracked and she could feel the bones under the pads of her fingers press against the metal until it hurt.

"He got himself wrapped up in an undercover sting. Apparently, he was involved in human trafficking and the abuse of underage girls."

She stared at Ramone. His eyes were dark brown and there were heavy, fatty bags under his eyes. His left eye twitched slightly as they looked at one another.

"He was convicted four years ago. Two years later, he legally changed his name and filed to have his record expunged."

"Was it?"

"If it had been, I wouldn't be reading about it in our database."

At least the court system and one judge had seen him for who and what Butch really was—a criminal.

"Do you finally believe me about him being a stalker?"

Ramone tapped his fingers on the desk. "I think that a zebra can't change his stripes. That being said, I think that if you want to handle this and him correctly, we need to get some evidence that we present to a judge."

She reached over to Ramone and took his hand in an awkward grip. "Thank you, Officer Ramone. Thank you for finally understanding."

"Is there anything else you can tell me about Butch—if you do think he was the one responsible for these disappearances—that could help us pin him down? Do you know where he is?"

She shook her head as she let go of Ramone's hand and leaned back in the stiff chair. "I have no idea, but if I know him even a little, I know he will reach out to me. He never wants to lose control."

He reached into his desk and pulled out a business card. He took out a pen and wrote something down on the back and slid the card over to her. "Here is my private cell phone number. If you see him, you need to call or text me as quickly as possible."

She took the card and slipped it in her back pocket.

"For now, you can go. Collect your personal items from the front desk. They will help you get a car or ride if you need one." Officer Ramone tried to smile, but his lips quaked with the unaccustomed movement. "And hey, I hope you know that everything I do is to keep my community safe. My arrest of you was nothing personal. I hope I don't have to ever do it again."

She stood up and brushed her hands over her hips. "It's my hope you never have to, either." She extended her hand. "If anything, I hope the next time I see you, you'll be telling me that you have Kelcie and Jackson and they're alive."

Chapter Nineteen

After collecting her personal items, Scarlett made her way down the white corridor leading out of the jailhouse. The place was quiet this late in the afternoon. Most people had gone home for the night, and as she walked her boots clicked on the tile and echoed through the open space. The sound made her nervous, though she couldn't explain why. Of all the places in the county, standing in the jail, where there were a myriad of cameras pointing at every possible corner, she reminded herself she was safe.

She of all people knew what an illusion safety really was. Safety couldn't even be found in the moments one spent alone in the comfort of their own home. The chaos of memories and the pain left in their wake had a way of creeping in, taking over and pulling off even the thickest scabs.

Her phone was running out of battery, but she had just enough charge to order a car. She was surprised Kalispell had an Uber service—some things about her former home state had changed for the better. Then again, its lack of amenities, tech and people were the reasons people left the cities and wanted to move to a place where it was gray and cold seven months of the year, and there was only about a three-week period when the weather was not too hot, cold or too smoky.

The place carried the scent of fear, stress and unwashed bodies. As it melded with the nervousness she felt, her pulse quickened, and a wave of sickness rose within her. The jail gave her the creeps.

The cold brass handles on the door were in sharp contrast to the heat of the summer evening as she stepped outside. The courthouse sat in the center of the city, the beige brick and stone building taking up the middle of a roundabout at the edge of downtown. It was ostentatious in its placement, as though the builder had chosen the spot so that the monument would stand as a constant reminder that the law would always be at the core of the town.

Unfortunately, thanks to its location, she had to stand outside the courthouse and watch as the constant stream of traffic passed by. Most people didn't seem to notice her as she watched the traffic, but some would rubberneck and stare at her like they were trying to figure out if she was a criminal or a courthouse employee.

She couldn't stand the looks of contempt.

Perhaps this was why the original city planner had placed the city center as they had—the public could focus on every possible criminal, and in doing so, they could act as judge, jury and executioner.

There was a grassy park across the street, the edges lined with maple and horse chestnut trees. In her summers as a kid, when her mother and father had come to the city for supplies, she and her siblings would make a game of picking up the spiny chestnuts and throwing them at one another. She still had a scar where one had stuck in her ribs like an angry porcupine and then got infected.

It was a silly memory, but it made her smile to think about one of the few fun memories she had with her brothers and sister. Most of the time they were fighting or spread out over the ranch, each taking care of the chores and tasks her father had used to keep them occupied.

A white pickup stopped for her as she waited at the sidewalk to cross the street toward the park. She barely looked as she gave the driver a quick wave of thanks and hustled across the road. When her feet touched the green lush grass she slowed, strolling beneath the lush canopies of the trees overhead. She picked up a horse chestnut and played with the spines with her thumbnail, as she thought about Cameron, the loss of Ben, Jamie and Wade.

When she got back to the ranch, she would have to see them. It was more than likely they'd already heard about her being back. Officer Ramone hadn't mentioned saying anything to Emily Trapper about her true identity, but between professional courtesy and her arrest record on the ranch, she was sure Emily had come to know her true identity.

Cameron had been far more kind than her other brothers, but he was still going to come at her with both barrels. She didn't know how much Ramone would have told Emily about what she had revealed to him, but she hated the thought of having to meet her brother and possibly her sister, Jamie, for the first time since coming back to Montana and confessing the drama that had followed her to their doorsteps.

If he told her to get out, she didn't know where she would go. She couldn't leave until she found Kelcie and Jackson. She had a man hunting her down, and the one man she wanted in her life had cast her out. If only she could call Miles and tell him how sorry she was for not having told him everything.

Their kiss haunted her.

He probably thought she was just using him and that she was nothing more than a two-bit actress who would manipulate anyone in her life in order to benefit herself. If he did, he probably wondered how she had caused the problems with Butch and what kind of relationship they had that would have caused him to feel so protective.

She stopped walking and put her hand on the coarse bark of a maple tree as emotions threatened to overtake her, though she didn't know why. Maybe it was that she had been through so much in such a short amount of time, or perhaps it was the thoughts of Butch and the loss of Miles, but she couldn't stop the tears from welling in her eyes and blurring her vision. They spilled over, and she let them stream down her cheeks as she leaned against the tree for support.

She hated being this emotional, but it felt cathartic to let all the fears and anxiety she had been feeling for so long fill her tears and pour down her face in hot rivulets. A sob rippled from her throat as she thought of Kelcie and what she could have possibly been facing—*if* she was still alive.

If she was dead, it was Scarlett's fault.

Her tears fell faster.

"Scarlett?" A man's hand grabbed her shoulder, and she jumped and turned.

Standing behind her was the overweight and graying Butch Hafner. He looked shorter and heavier than the last time she had seen him in New York. His hair was slightly mussed, like he had been running his fingers haphazardly through it while he had waited for her. His lips had sticky white saliva pooled in the corners, and the full effect of him made a chill run down her spine.

"What in the hell are you doing here?" she asked, her voice scratchy and weaker than she wanted.

She couldn't believe he had found her—and while she was crying, no less.

This is what came from allowing herself to feel. She had been so stupid.

"I've been waiting for you." He smiled, his teeth showing, and the effect reminded her of a growl. "That was nice of you to come alone." He took her by the arm and shoved her toward the road next to the park where a white truck with a grille guard was parked and running.

She jerked out of his grip. "Where is Kelcie?"

His smile turned to one of malice and hate. "If you were a better friend maybe she wouldn't have gone missing on your watch."

"You mean a *friend* like you?" she challenged, angrily wiping the tears off her cheeks with the back of her hand.

"I'm the greatest ally you've ever had. I *made* you who you are. You know I did and you know you owe me. You should be goddamned grateful."

He wasn't wrong. His ruthlessness in business had gotten her bumped to the front of casting lines, and his ability to feel nothing while negotiating had gotten her the best money, but that didn't mean she *owed him* anything. She wanted to tell him exactly that, but she needed to play it smart. She couldn't upset him any more. If she played along with him, he would bend. It was the only thing that had ever worked when dealing with him.

"I'll be grateful when you tell me where my friends are," she countered.

He laughed. "I bet you would. As soon as we get back home, I'll let them go."

"Home?" she asked, taken aback.

"Yes. *Our* home. I've been getting things ready ever since you said you wanted me."

She stopped. "When did I say I wanted you?" She knew she shouldn't have asked, that she should have just gone along with whatever it was he was saying, but she couldn't bear it.

"Don't you remember? It was when we were at dinner in Belarus. We were eating the fig and goat cheese pizza along the river. You told me you were glad to have me by your side, that you were happy, and you wanted me to work with you forever."

She didn't remember the conversation, but she did remember the wine they had been drinking. "I *did* want you to work with me…" *That was, until you had crossed the line*, she thought, proud of herself that she hadn't let it slip past her resolve.

"That's not all you want. I've always seen the way you look at me." He took her hand in his and pressed his cold fish lips against the back of her hand.

The feel of his skin was repulsive, but she did her best not to pull away. Instead, she moved inconspicuously for her phone. If only she had put Ramone's number directly in her phone, maybe she could have called him without Butch noticing.

"How do I look at you?" she asked, moving her pawn.

Butch took her hand again, stopping her from reaching for her phone. "You looked at me like you wanted to be the most powerful couple in Hollywood."

She hated him and the way his damp hand felt against hers. He disgusted her in the way his lip twitched when he smiled and how there was a thin sheen of sweat on the sides of his nose and over his brow. It reminded her of a man wanting sex, and her stomach turned.

He would never have her, no matter how *powerful* he thought they would be.

Her hand tightened around the horse chestnut she was still holding. The sea urchin-like spines poked into her hand like tiny needles, but the pain was reinvigorating and pulled her back from the disgust she felt from his touch.

"I'll do whatever you want if you just let Kelcie and Jackson go."

He glanced away and tilted his head back with exasperation. "Is that all you can think about right now? You haven't seen me in weeks, and you're only worried about *them*? Just get in my truck with me. We can talk all about your little friends in there." He motioned toward his running pickup.

"Are they okay? Unhurt?" she pressed.

"Don't worry about them." He turned his face away from her, making it impossible to read him.

There was something strange about his reaction to talking about Jackson and Kelcie, and it scared her. "You didn't hurt them, did you?"

"I'm not a monster, Scarlett."

She begged to differ. Normal people didn't track a person down across state lines and were so bold as to stalk them outside of a county courthouse filled with law enforcement.

He didn't care who saw him, like he thought he was smarter than anyone and above anyone's laws. The worst part is that she felt as powerless as he felt powerful.

She loosened her grip on the horse chestnut, and she glanced down at the spiky ball in her hand. There was only one way to take her power back. "Butch?" She said his name like it was a secret.

He shifted, and his brows rose with surprise and his eyes darkened with lust. "Yes, baby?"

"I hope you go to hell." She pulled her hand loose of his and swung wide, striking him hard in the side of the ribs.

"What in the—"

With the spiked chestnut in her palm, she slammed it squarely into his left cheek and eye.

He howled with pain as he grabbed at his eye. He swung his fist at her, wildly, connecting with her jaw, but she barely noticed.

The chestnut was lodged in his skin just under his eye.

He stepped back with pain, his body curling forward. She pulled her hands into tight fists and bore down, striking him in the back, hard. The sound was hollow. He put his hand up as he cried out, gasping like he was searching for breath. But she didn't care.

She hated him.

She grabbed his shoulder as he took hold of her hips. Before he could stop her, she kicked her knee in his face with the sound of cracking bone. He let go, the place where he'd gripped hot with pain.

She turned and ran. His truck was running.

Not thinking, she ran to it, pulling at the door handle. It was open. Keys were in the ignition.

"You stupid cow!" Butch called from behind her, but she didn't turn to see if he was following.

All she could do was run away. She had to get away from this man. If he got his hands on her, she would never get away again.

"I will kill you!" Butch screamed.

She climbed inside the truck and locked the doors. Butch was stumbling toward her as she put the truck into Drive and skipped the tires as she slammed down the gas pedal.

As the truck tore off down the road, she heard a strange, dark sound. Looking in the mirror, she saw her contorted face. Inexplicably, she found that the mirthful sound was of her furious laugh.

Chapter Twenty

Officer Burns dropped Miles back at his truck outside the barn. The evening sun was bearing down, and he had chores to do. No matter what was happening in his personal life, he still had horses to feed. The animals depended on him, and unlike people, they were predictable.

He couldn't wrap his mind around the state of Jackson's apartment. If Burns was right and his brother had packed up in a hurry, that could only mean one thing—he had been behind Kelcie's disappearance. *If* that was the case, then the entire scope of their problems shifted. If he had taken her, the next question had to be whether or not Kelcie was going with him against her will.

He loved his brother, and though Jackson loved to drink and get a little Western on a Saturday night at The Mint Bar, Miles didn't think his brother was capable or motivated to commit such a crime.

Then again, he hadn't thought Scarlett was lying to him, either.

Maybe his ability to read people was the issue, and the people around him were far more nefarious than he had ever realized.

He walked into the barn and over to a stack of what was left from last winter's hay. It smelled of sweetgrass, alfalfa and dust. It was one of his favorite scents, reminding him of all the best parts of his life—sunshine, riding and the value of hard work.

It made him wonder what Scarlett's signature scent would have been—probably champagne and caviar. He stopped himself. He had been so wrong about her.

She was a Trapper. No matter how deeply she inserted herself in the world of actors and actresses, he had seen a spark of the real her when she had been riding. There was a cowgirl in her still.

The duality of her soul was one of the things he loved most about her. It was what had called to him before he'd even really given her any thought beyond that of her being a beautiful guest.

Yet, if she was such an actress, was it possible that she was trying to use this talk of a stalker and kidnapping of her assistant to get notoriety? People were always looking for insta-fame. He'd heard about it time and time again at the ranch. In fact, their marketing team at the Joy Luck had always talked about wanting to go viral. It was something they strove for but had never attained while he'd been working at that ranch.

He hated social media and the inanity of the beast. It was so fake and just a mask for the ugliness of life. People could put anything out there without fear of repercussions or reprisals. And, depending on how it was used, it could make a career, or end a life.

Scarlett had concealed her truth from him, and she had hidden painful parts of her past, but in hindsight he could understand why, and he could hardly blame her.

He plopped down onto a bale of hay and pulled out his phone. Looking up her social media accounts, he found no mention of anything that was going on at the ranch or in her personal life. The only thing she had posted in the last week was something about the show's upcoming episode.

It brought him a sense of relief.

Out of curiosity, he looked up the Joy Luck Ranch on Instagram. On their story were a series of pictures from last night's car accident on the ranch. They had used the hashtags #WestGlacierRanch, #DisasterRanch and #Wreck-AtTheRanch.

He couldn't believe it. What would possess the owners of the Joy Luck to post something so thoughtless? A man's life hung in the balance and a little boy could easily be left without a family, and these jerks were using it as a smear campaign against the ranch he worked for.

He had always known Drake Rex was a monster, but he hadn't known he would stoop this low.

Taking a quick screen shot, he sent a text of the image to Emily and Cameron, along with a simple question mark. They could make of it as they would, but they needed to be made aware of the smear campaign that was happening about the ranch.

If this was in direct response to his coming to work for the Trappers, he would have a bone to pick with Drake. The next time he saw the guy—they would have words.

Thinking about the accident and the Sullivans, Miles called up to the pediatrics floor at the hospital. A secretary answered the phone call on the second ring. "Pediatrics, this is Summer. How can I help you?"

"Hi, Summer, my name is Miles. I'm calling to check in on Thomas Sullivan. I was there with him last night. How is he doing today?" He was careful how he worded his question as to not raise any red flags or have the woman resist giving him information.

"He is doing well today. He'll be staying another night

while he is on IV antibiotics, but I would think he will be able to go home in the next day or two."

"By chance, do you know how Aiden is doing?" He knew he was pushing his luck, but he also knew how word spread in and around hospital staffers when families were involved in accidents like this.

"I'm sorry to tell you, but it sounds as though Aiden recently passed unexpectedly."

His heart broke for the kid.

"We attempted to contact his grandparents and other family members but have not been successful, thus far. If you could come in and help us with some paperwork, we would appreciate it. We currently need either a sworn statement or to get him assigned with a temporary guardianship if there are any decisions to be made."

"I'll be in as soon as I can," he said, though he had no idea how he would swing things in order to help the boy. "If things change, or he needs me in the meantime, please let me know."

"Will do, sir."

He hung up the phone, feeling more lost than he had before. Just when he thought he couldn't get more confused, something like this fell in his lap. There was no way he could take on the role of caring for a child—he barely had a job or a place to live. He wasn't stable enough to even consider caring for Thomas. He either had to find this boy's family or figure something out to help him—or hope the hospital could do something to help.

There was the sound of a truck racing down the drive, and it skidded to a stop outside the barn. Jamie must have been coming over to check on the horses or coming to ride her horse, Mac. Thankfully, there weren't supposed to be any more guests on the schedule until next weekend for the equine therapy program.

He stood up and shoved his phone in his pocket as he walked toward the front of the barn. "How's it going, Jamie?" he asked, before he stepped through the doors.

Instead of Jamie, he watched as a disheveled Scarlett stepped out of a white pickup with a dented grille guard on the front, one he didn't recognize, and slammed the truck door and stood there, lost. She looked frantic, and there was dried blood on her right hand. "Are you okay? What happened?" he asked.

She stared at him for a long moment, almost as though she didn't recognize him or couldn't make sense of where she was standing or what she was doing.

"Scarlett." He spoke her name softly. She didn't move. "Babe, it's okay." He eased toward her, walking slowly like she was a scared mare, and he was afraid she would bolt or start kicking.

He had no idea what had happened, but it had to have been traumatic, and it both frightened and infuriated him that he hadn't been there at her side.

She followed him with her eyes, but she said nothing as he drew nearer. He took the truck keys from her hand. "Whose pickup is this?" he asked, looking at the paper tag on the keys. It had PriceLess Rental Car Company printed on the ticket, along with a number.

Her gaze moved to the keys in his hands. "Oh." She sounded surprised and she stepped back, bumping into the truck. "I... I didn't mean to. I was just trying to get away. I'm going to be in so much trouble. Don't call the police."

"Slow down," he said. "Just start by telling me what happened." He put the keys in his pocket.

"I was coming out of the jail... Butch was waiting for me. He jumped me. I fought." She lifted her hands and turned her palms up.

There, on her right hand, were a series of bloodied pin-pricks as though she had held a porcupine. "I hit him with a nut." She gave a strangled, victorious laugh.

"With what?" He couldn't have heard her correctly. "Did you kill him?"

She shook her head as she lowered her hands. "He's going to come for me. *Us.*"

He took out his phone and texted Emily, telling her about the attack outside the jail.

Her response was almost immediate:

I forwarded this to Ramone. Go to the CVA's office. Meet u there to help file a report.

"Do you know where he would have gone?" he asked.

She shook her head.

"Did he say anything about Jackson? Kelcie?"

Her eyes met his, and it was as though she was staring into the depths of his soul. "There was something about the way he talked about them. He was so…*vague*. It was unlike him."

"What do you mean?"

"I don't know… I can't be sure, but I don't know if he took them."

He understood what she said, but he couldn't make heads or tails of what she meant. If Butch hadn't taken his brother, they were back to the possibility that his brother was behind taking Kelcie—or someone else had taken them both. Yet, it didn't make sense.

Jackson didn't have any motivation for kidnapping Kelcie and then going absolutely silent.

His thoughts turned to the Joy Luck social media post

about the accident. Would Drake have done something to his brother and Kelcie?

As ridiculous as Drake was, reveling in the tragedies of others and using it for personal gain, Miles couldn't imagine that he would orchestrate a kidnapping or potential murder. To do something like that was downright sociopathic.

They still had no idea where his brother and Kelcie were—and the more time that went by, the less likely they were to get them back.

"They want us to go to the crime victim advocate's office, and there we can file a police report about Butch's attack and also start the process of getting you a restraining order."

"They don't work." She shook her head, and her voice was weak, but he could tell by her tone that she was resigned to the idea.

"They may not, but I do. And come hell or high water, you aren't leaving my side again until we have this mess sorted out."

"Butch will stop at nothing to get to me. You don't understand."

He reached over to her and took her hands in his. She was trembling with fear. "I don't think *he* knows who he is dealing with, now. I will stop at nothing to make sure you are safe." He felt a sense of hypocrisy rise within him as he had promised her before that he would let nothing happen to her—and then he'd allowed Butch access. "And I'm sorry."

She tilted her head as she looked into his eyes. "What do you have to be sorry for?"

There were so many things, a litany. "I promised I wouldn't let him get to you. I should have been waiting for you at the jail. I should have been there when you needed me."

"You didn't know Ramone was going to cut me loose."

She laced her fingers between his. "And I'm sorry for keeping my truth from you. I shouldn't have come here."

"This is where you were born and raised. Why do you think you shouldn't have come here?"

She dropped her gaze. "I told my father I'd never come back."

"That was your father. And from what I heard, your father was no peach." He paused. "But, if that's true, why *did* you come back?"

She sighed. "I told Butch how much I hated my dad, and we had talked about some of my memories as a kid. I thought that this would be the last place he would think of looking for me. He knows I wouldn't have wanted to come here—at least while my father was alive."

"Did he know your father passed?"

She shrugged. "He must have found out. And I have no idea how he tracked me here. I was careful to keep everything under wraps."

"Interesting." He had already hated the guy, but the thought of how deeply he had infiltrated her life made him hate him even more. If he saw him, he wasn't sure he would be able to refrain from becoming a monster.

Chapter Twenty-One

She must have looked like a disaster after meeting with the crime victim's advocate. The woman had been sweet and soft-spoken, asking Scarlett more questions than she wanted to answer, but getting every detail about Butch's attack outside the jail and even making sure to take pictures of the puncture wounds to her hands and sending them on to Emily.

Together, they made a quick call to Officer Ramone. He had been kind on the phone, gracious even, and there had been what almost sounded like relief in his voice when he'd heard she was in the office making a report.

As she made her way out of the small office, she found Miles sitting with Emily, and they were leaning toward each other and chatting quietly, looking conspiratorial. Seeing her, Emily stood up and sent her a caring smile. "Hi, Scarlett. Or should I say, sister?" she said, extending a welcoming hand.

She stopped mid-stride, her stomach instantly in knots. "I'm so sorry. I never meant to hurt anyone. I just—"

Emily stopped her with a raise of the hand. "You don't need to explain. I know all about your father, and I understand why you would have chosen to do what you've done in keeping your coming here a secret. As for you thinking I didn't recognize you… That's where you're wrong. I knew who you were from first time we saw each other." Emily gave a small laugh.

"What?" A profound sense of surprise and relief washed over her. "Why didn't you say anything?"

"Discretion is the better part of valor. If you wanted to be recognized and come in as family, you would have made it known." Emily smiled. "You're hardly the first person I've been around who wanted to keep things quiet." She pointed at the badge pinned to her chest.

"I appreciate your keeping things private. I was worried." She paused. "Did you tell my brother I'm here?"

Emily shook her head. "Miles and I've been talking about everything while you were in the office. I will contact your brother when I get home, if you're okay with it. In the meantime, we just need to make sure you are safe and protected. You don't need to worry about doing what you had to do. In the new generation of Trappers, we forgive, and we trust."

Of all the ways she thought it would go, this was the last.

"You really don't think Cameron is going to be upset? He hates me. I don't know if he told you, but the last time I saw him, we had a huge blowout."

Emily frowned. "What? If there was, he never mentioned it. If anything, your brother's super proud of you. He has been following your career and is always telling people about his famous sister."

She was embarrassed. After she had left in such a chaotic way, and with such bitterness in her heart, she would have never considered that her brother still cared about her, much less followed her career.

"I yelled at him when I left. There's no way he's not angry with me."

Emily put her hand on her shoulder, giving it a light and

reassuring squeeze. "Who hasn't lost it on their brother at one point or another? I, personally, have raised my voice at your brother several times." She laughed. "You'd be surprised at the forgiveness that your brother is capable of. He's nothing like your father."

"I think my brother Ben was the most like him."

Emily nodded. "I'm sorry about his death, by the way. I'm sure it was hard on you, losing them both."

She tipped her head in acknowledgment. "I was surprised. I didn't think Ben was in so deep."

"It just goes to show you that you never really know who someone is. When a person is desperate, they will do almost anything to get what they want," Emily said, with a pinched expression as though she had seen that exact experience play out a million times.

Miles didn't seem able to meet her gaze, and Scarlett desperately wanted to talk to him and to keep apologizing for everything that had gone wrong between them from the moment she had set foot on the ranch. Yet, even if she did, she had the sinking sensation that he would still want nothing to do with her. She was nothing but trouble, and now she was also trouble with a capital *T*—as in Trapper.

Finally, he looked up as they neared the pickup. "You know, I've been thinking," he said, stopping. He leaned against the hood of the ranch truck. "When Butch came after you at the jail, did you get a good look at his hands and arms?"

She thought back. He'd been wearing a short-sleeve shirt. A button-up. Blue. Kind of preppy and out of style. Jeans that looked like something he'd bought at a high-end boutique on Rodeo Drive, but were really for men twenty years younger than he pretended to be.

"I don't know." She could only think about how it had

both hurt and freed her to shove the impromptu weapon into his face. "Why?"

He tapped his fingers on the hood, making a hollow sound that echoed down the alley behind the indistinct white building that held the CVA's office. "I'm just thinking about the blood we found at the cabin. If he was the one who broke in—and if that's where he took them—then he would have some kind of cut on his arm. Right?"

"You're right," Emily said, pointing to him. "We did collect a few fingerprints on scene." Her fingers tapped on her phone, and she didn't even look up. "I'm going to have my team at the lab run them against Butch's and see if anything matches there."

"What if they don't?" Scarlett asked.

Emily looked up. "Why do you ask that? Do you really think that someone else could have been behind the break-in and kidnapping?"

She didn't know what had made her ask. Maybe it was fear. "I just… I don't know. I guess I just can't imagine Butch breaking a window. He's kind of a wimp."

"A wimp who tried to kidnap you outside of a county courthouse," Emily countered.

"Touché."

"I want you to text him." Emily lifted her phone. "Ask him for proof of life of both Jackson and Kelcie."

"Don't you think he would wonder what was up if I asked for that?"

Miles tipped his head as though in agreement.

"Call it whatever you want when you talk to him. Just say you want to know what he's asking for to get them back. And before you agree to anything, say you need proof they are safe." Emily went back to her phone. "I'm going to call in reinforcements."

"You're assuming he doesn't sniff us out."

Emily tipped her head in acknowledgment. "He may, but I'm thinking he has his hands full in trying to get a new rig. You took his truck. How is he getting around? I'm going to get my guys to watch the local taxi and car services. If we watch, he may lead us directly to our missing persons."

That was, if they got lucky. So far, luck had never had a presence in Scarlett's life.

"Text him," Emily said, motioning toward Scarlett's phone.

Scarlett's hands were shaking as she clicked on the screen. She typed:

I want my friends back, but first I need proof they are okay.

Not waiting, she sent another quick message.

Send me a pic.

The message was marked Read. Then a series of dots showed up on her screen, letting her know that Butch was typing. They stopped, then started again as though he was thinking about what he was typing, deleting and typing something out instead.

Did you think you could hurt me and get away with it?

Her breath caught in her throat.

Kelcie will pay for what you did to me.

He wouldn't hurt Kelcie. Not if he really wanted to be with her. If he hurt her best friend, there was no way she could ever forgive him. He had to have known that. She sent a message.

Don't you dare! Don't lay a finger on her. If you want me
to play your game, you have to play by my rules.

The message was marked Read, but he didn't respond.

She waited, hoping he would send a picture. Nothing
came. No three dots. No indication he was typing. He was
angry—and more, now he was truly dangerous as he was
more unpredictable than ever.

You're kidding yourself, Scarlett. You play by mine.

Emily stepped beside her, reading the texts from over her
shoulder. She sucked in a breath and reached for the phone,
motioning for her to hand it over.

Scarlett hesitated, unsure whether or not to trust the
woman, but she had no other options. Her sister-in-law was
the greatest weapon she had in this war. Her fingers moved
fast as she typed.

Show me Kelcie and Jackson. Now.

A minute later a picture arrived.

They said a picture was worth a thousand words. This picture was so much more, but less, and in a singular word—
sickening.

Kelcie's face was black and blue, her left eye was a purple so dark it bordered on black, and it was swollen shut.
On her eyebrow was a large cut where she must have taken
some kind of blunt object to the face.

There was another cut like it on her cheek on the other
side of her face, below her eye, and blood seeped from the
cut and had dried in a long brown crusted river. Her hair
was still in the same ponytail Scarlett had seen her wearing

but it was pulled into patches that had come loose and now lay limp against her neck. Below the hairs on her neck were scratch marks and well-defined red and purple fingermarks as though Butch had tried to strangle her at some point.

She was tied to a chair, and behind her, there was the back of what she assumed was Jackson's head. His hair was dark and matted with dried blood. His head was drooped down like he was sleeping or had lost consciousness.

Show me Jackson's face.

Emily texted, obviously as concerned about the man as Scarlett.

A moment later, a picture came through. His eyes were closed and there was dried blood at the corner of his lip and under his nose, none was fresh. Jackson's head was tilted sideways and back, his mouth slightly open as if he was snoring—or dead.

Emily tapped away on the phone.

Where do you want me to meet you? When?

There were the dots. Then more dots. Then nothing.

They waited for five minutes. They were the longest minutes of her life—each felt like an hour of sitting on a fire ant hill, each ticking second a stinging bite to her soul.

Still there was no answer.

Emily sighed. She sent pictures of the texts to her phone and then handed Scarlett back her cell phone. "I let Ramone know what is happening. He recommended that we move you to a safe location until we have this situation under control. Would you be willing to go into hiding?"

"What does that mean?" She looked at Miles. She wouldn't leave him.

"We have agreements with some of the local hotels. We will get you a room where you can stay as long as you need." Emily smiled as she seemed to pick up on the way Scarlett silently pleaded with Miles for help. "And Miles is welcome to remain with you, should you wish."

For the first time since she had stepped foot in Montana, Scarlett finally felt the knot in her gut loosen. She was no longer fighting alone—she had law enforcement and Miles at her side. She needed to pay attention, but thankfully they didn't think she was crazy, and now Butch was no longer just a shadow lurking at the corner of her nightmares.

Chapter Twenty-Two

Miles was only too happy to see Emily get back into her rig outside of the Hilton Garden Inn in Kalispell after she had followed them there and set them up in an adjoining room suite. Though no one had said anything, the door between his room and Scarlett's wasn't going to be closed—not as long as he had a damned thing to say about it. He'd made her a promise and he was standing by it. He wasn't leaving her alone again, not when there was a stalker on the loose.

Scarlett stood at his side in front of the lobby doors of the hotel. The awning was overhead, blocking the moon but casting long, dark shadows across their faces thanks to the fluorescent lights installed overhead.

The hotel was nice by Montana standards, with its slate and river rock aesthetic, but he doubted that it compared to anything that Scarlett was used to—that was at least now that she had escaped this world and become established in her new California persona. Rustic was a far cry from the marble and gold encrusted world of the rich and famous.

Then again, she had come back. This is where she had run to when she needed help. There was power and unquestionably something unchained in this Western world. This was the place in America where people came to free their hearts and untether their souls—even if that meant unburdening themselves of their enemies in the process, no matter what that process entailed.

If this unburdening included Butch's death, Miles had to admit he would be only too happy to pull the trigger if the man put Scarlett's life at risk. Miles would stop at nothing to keep her safe.

Almost as if the deputy could read the thoughts on his face, she scowled. "I don't want you to do anything stupid while you two are here. Do you hear me? You are here as a representative not only of the ranch, but of my family, as well. Okay, Miles?"

She seemed to have forgotten that it was his brother sitting next to Kelcie in the picture Butch had sent, as well. Scarlett wasn't the only one hurting and afraid, but he wasn't about to point it out. Silence was his best play.

He answered with a simple nod.

She looked at Scarlett. "I set up your phone to forward anything from Butch directly to my team. Anything you send to him will also be mirrored to our systems."

"Are you monitoring everything on my phone?"

"If I have your consent, I'd like to."

Scarlett opened her purse to pull out her phone and stared inside for a long moment before reaching in and grabbing it. "Here."

"Oh," Emily said, waving her off, "we don't actually need it. We can do everything remotely. We have the ability to access. I just needed your okay."

He would have been lying if the invasion into her privacy didn't make him just the tiniest bit uncomfortable. It wasn't that he didn't know everything on every digital device was like a giant open source of information to anyone who was the slightest bit technically savvy, but he was just so far from adept at that side of life that he'd liked to stick his head in the sand.

For some reason, it made his thoughts move back to the trail cameras when he'd taken Scarlett, Kelcie and the Sullivans on the mountain. It was almost laughable to think how annoyed he'd been to have them looking into their activities, when anyone in the world could have been doing basically anything they wanted to be doing on the tiny devices that each one of them had along with them in their pockets and purses.

Privacy and anonymity were truly nothing more than an illusion in the modern world.

Scarlett dropped her phone back into her purse. "I know this is a horrible question, given everything that is going on, but my wallet..."

Emily's eyes darkened and she tapped on her chin. "Oh, yes... I bet you are missing that. Do you know how your wallet would have come to be found under the master bedroom's bed? I know you told Ramone that you hadn't been in the cabin and that you didn't realize it was missing, but do you know the last time you had seen it?"

Scarlett shrugged. "I told Ramone that the last time I know for sure was when I had it hanging in the barn while we were getting the horses ready to go. I remember it hitting against my perfume bottle. Oh, wait..." She gasped and opened her purse wide. "I just now realized, my perfume bottle is missing, too. It's a bottle of YSL. I always carry it with me."

He couldn't see where her missing a bottle of perfume would have a bearing on what was happening, but it was a strange thing to have been gone from her things.

"And did you see anyone you didn't know while you were getting ready to go?" Emily asked.

She shook her head. "It was just us. Kelcie, Miles and me."

"No Butch?"

"I didn't see him, but that doesn't mean he wasn't somewhere."

That was the thing about stalking, a person could have been in any corner. If the stalker was good, a person wouldn't even have a clue they were being watched.

He sent Emily a look. "Maybe it's time we talk about putting some cameras up around the ranch."

She answered with a stiff nod. "Don't think that hasn't already crossed my mind." She tapped her fingers on the steering wheel. "Go get in your rooms. If you need anything, charge it to the room or keep receipts. We will cover your expenses, but keep it between the mustard and the mayonnaise." She gave him a sly smile.

"You got it, boss." He chuckled.

"I'll sit out here for a bit and make sure that no one comes or goes that shouldn't. I also have talked to the hotel staff. They know no one is to go to or from your room that is not associated with law enforcement or the hotel staff. If you need anything, call."

"Thank you for everything, Emily," Scarlett said. Her voice sounded scratchy and heavy with emotions. It was so thick, he reached over to her and pulled her hand into his.

"I've got this under control for now." He put his entwined hands on Scarlett's lower back and turned her toward the door. He gave Emily a slight two-fingered wave as they made their way into the hotel and out of sight.

It shouldn't have brought him any relief to leave his boss, but perhaps it was because he was once again alone with Scarlett that he felt a sense of peace. He'd wanted this moment for a while now. He needed to know she was really okay. He needed her to know she was safe and cared for as long as she was with him, even if nothing ever happened between them. Not that he wouldn't have wanted something to happen... He certainly would.

They made their way to the top floor and down to the end of the hall where their suite waited. Considering the Flathead County Sheriff's Office had put them up, he was impressed. He would have expected something at the hourly rate motel at the edge of town, not at the best place in town and in the nicest room. Emily must have really been trying to make good with her newly minted sister-in-law.

He couldn't blame her—he was trying to make up for a few things himself.

Scarlett waited for him to scan the room key to let her in, and he followed her inside, not missing his opportunity to check out her perfectly fitted jeans and the view they created from behind. His hand twitched as he thought about how badly every part of him wanted to reach out and touch her round behind.

This woman drove him to the brink of glorious madness, but at the same time she was all the most beautiful parts of life. She was adventure, chaos, passion, emotions and a hunger for life all wrapped up into the most stunning woman he'd ever seen. He could imagine no more perfect woman on the planet—especially for him.

There was only a handful of issues that held him back. All of them were massive on their own, but none of them were completely insurmountable.

He closed the door behind them, then made his way through both suites, clearing them. Nothing had been disturbed since Emily had gotten them the rooms and done a quick walkthrough. They were safe—or, at least, as safe as they could be with a stalker trying to get to the woman he loved.

Wait. Did he *love* her?

He stopped moving, pretending to stand at the edge of the curtain and stare out the window, which looked out onto the city center.

Her footfalls sounded as she moved on the hardwood floor toward him. She put her hand on him, making heat rise from the place where her fingers grazed against his skin. "Is everything okay?"

He nodded, afraid that if he actually spoke his voice would crack and everything he was thinking and feeling would come spilling out like some wave of unchecked flotsam.

She didn't need his chaos to add to the upheaval happening in her personal life. If she wanted him, she could make that choice, but he couldn't be the one to make a move.

"I appreciate you being here." She moved beside him and under his arm, pushing her body against him and making his heart race. "You kept your word to me. After everything that has happened, you don't know how much that means to me. I know I didn't earn your loyalty, and I most certainly don't deserve it, but I'll do everything to show you that you were right in placing it with me."

"I don't know why you're being so hard on yourself, Scarlett," he said, making sure not to let go of her as he turned ever so slowly to face her. "You did what you had to do to keep yourself and your friend safe."

She looked down. "But I failed."

"You didn't fail. You did what you could. You got here. You came to a place you knew people would help you."

"But I didn't know for sure."

He lifted her chin gently with his finger. "Look at me. I'm up here."

There were hints of tears in her eyes. "You did know. You

knew exactly what kind of people you would find here at the ranch now that your father is gone. You can fight and bicker, but your family will always support you, and so will the people that they have invited into their lives, like me."

"You say that now, but there was no way I was to know that. I haven't even seen Cameron yet. Plus, the last time I saw them, I had them all lumped up together as my father's flying monkeys. I didn't think there was much of a chance that I would come back here to open arms. Emily's reception of me was a huge surprise—one I'm exceptionally grateful for." She looked at him like she was weaving herself into him. "And I'm so thankful for you."

He leaned in and found her lips waiting for him. The world around them disappeared into a flurry of moving hands and clothing being pulled and unbuttoned and unzipped. She threw his hat onto the counter of the kitchenette, and she stopped for only a brief second as she looked at his belt buckle.

"That's beautiful. Yours?" she asked, pulling it open.

He shook his head. "Grandfather's."

"Nice." She kissed him again as he moved out of his pants, and she followed suit.

They moved toward the bed, his hands tracing over the lines of her expensive-looking black lace bra and panty set. It didn't escape him what kind of woman she was, and how lucky he was, that he had found a woman who could live through a day straight from the pits of darkness and still look like she had fallen from the beauty of the stars.

He lifted her into his arms, working her hard nipple through the thin fabric of her bra with his mouth as she wrapped her legs around his waist. She gasped as she ran her fingers through his hair and pulled tight. The edge of pain made him nip, running his teeth against her hardness.

She pulled his head up and devoured his kiss. He moved her against the wall beside the bed, pressing her back against the cold sheetrock as he let his hand move down to her breast. He cupped her flesh, feeling the full roundness of her in his palm. Every part of her was perfect for him, with all of its dimples and tiger stripes from its formation and growth.

He ran his tongue along the line of a fine, faded and silvered stretch mark on the top of her breast, and she moaned. He basked in the salty flavor of her vanilla-scented skin.

"Miles, I want you. Now," she begged, her breath filling his mouth, and he breathed her in.

The sensation of taking her into him like that was so sensual and sexy that it made him grow impossibly harder.

Sex had always been important to him—in that way he was different than a lot of other dudes he knew. It was about emotion. He had to connect with a woman, and really connect, not just on superficial nonsense, to want to take things here.

Now that they were crossing this bridge, and she was in his arms, the last thing he wanted to do was not make it last. He needed to slow his roll.

He leaned back and looked into her eyes, studying her in the thin light cast from the moon peeking through the window. "Do you know how exceptionally beautiful you are?"

She smiled, and there was a sparkle in her eyes as she met his gaze. "And do you know how handsome you are?" She tilted her head ever so slightly as she tightened the grip of her thighs around his waist. "You are one of the main reasons I came here. I saw you…and I knew."

He kissed the mark on her breast softly, letting his exhalation caress the wetness he'd left on her skin before casting his gaze back up upon her. "What did you know?"

"I knew…" There was a moment of hesitation, and she

tried to cover it up with a sweet kiss to his lips before she released her legs from him and slipped down.

Part of him wanted her to say that she loved him, too. Yet, he was afraid that if she did, this would all be too real and even more dangerous than it already had become. She was going to break his heart, that was a known, but to have this one night with her was worth all the heartbreak in the world. She was his Aphrodite.

He longed for the words to fall from her lips, but he feared them just as much.

"I knew," she finally continued, in what felt like hours later, "that I would be *safe* with you."

Safe was a hell of a long way from love. In fact, it lived on the opposite ends of the universe.

Both words carried such weight that he wasn't sure which he feared more—and yet, in his heart for a fleeting moment, he realized that in a just and right world, safety could only be brought through the bounty of love.

She sat down on the bed and pushed his boxers down to the floor in one swift motion. A small squeak escaped her lips as she stared at his wanting body. He wasn't sure what to make of her noise until she looked up at him, took hold of him and sent him a wide smile.

"I knew I was lucky, but I had no idea exactly how lucky I was going to get tonight." She laughed, moving her hand down his length.

"Oh…" He moaned. "I'm the lucky one." He pushed her down onto the bed and moved between her naked thighs. He found her wetness and let his tip press ever so slightly against it, teasing her with what was to come. "Tonight, we're going to let 'er buck, baby."

She wrapped her legs around him and lifted her body as he drove inside of her, making her gasp. "Oh, my… Miles."

She said his name like each letter was its own syllable, and he moved his body with the sounds.

He would give anything to make the sounds she was making and the sensations she was making him feel last forever.

Scarlett's body pressed against him, her breasts damp with sweat and her hard nipples pressing against his chest.

He flipped her over in one swift motion, not letting his body slip from her. Her eyes were wide with excitement and thrill as she laughed and moved to sitting atop him.

The motion of her hips came naturally, flowing and ebbing, rounding and striking like waves cascading and crashing with the tides of ecstasy.

Her body quickened and the round circling of her hips became more focused and driving. The expression on her face changed to one of beautiful concentration as she held her breath, and the wave he'd been hoping to help her catch took her away.

She collapsed onto his chest for a moment, her heart hammering against his, but she smiled at him with the glazed expression of a satisfied woman who was far, far from sated.

He was going to be in for one hell of a ride.

Chapter Twenty-Three

Last night had been the best night of her life. Hands down. It was complex and deep, soft and compassionate. Yet, there was a brevity and lightness to it that Scarlett's heart had desperately needed.

There were so many things she appreciated in Miles, and as much as she wanted to tell him that she loved him last night, she was glad she hadn't taken that leap.

If he had been paying attention, though, her body would have already told him everything. She had given him everything she'd ever wanted to give to a man and feelings within her that she had not even known she was able to give.

She looked up at his sleeping face. He looked so at peace. The thought of ever leaving this place, this room, his arms, made her body ache.

There had been men in her life before, but she had never felt as she did in this moment. It was as if he held the power to make every horrible thing, every memory and every fear simply disappear. He was the one thing she had always been searching for, and now that she had finally found him, the last thing she wanted to do was go back to the nightmares of their shared reality.

She snuggled deeper into the nook of his arm and laid her head down on his chest and watched as it rose and fell with the comfort of sleep. He was tanner than she would have expected, and he had visible muscles even when he was sleeping. She was used to men who worked out—the men on set were usually the kinds who counted each individual gram of protein and took every supplement known to mankind, but they didn't have bodies that compared.

Miles's body was the kind that came from real hard work and long days spent taking care of the needs of the ranch and its guests. She could only guess how many bales of hay he moved in a day and how many saddles he put on and took off.

The thought of him manhandling the leather saddles made her have a flashback of her running her fingernails down the perfect curves of the muscles of his back last night. He had smelled so good, and the way he moved when he worked to pleasure her… She would give anything to feel him between her thighs every day for the rest of her life.

If only she could be so lucky.

He was a rugged ranch man, and she was a city girl.

What kind of future could their love have?

Right now, that was the last thing she wanted to waste time or energy thinking about. Instead, she lazily ran her fingertip down the chiseled line at the center of his abs. He was so damned hot.

He shifted under her touch, and she smiled, thinking about what they could do if she woke him up with just the right amount of grazing fingertips.

Miles opened his eyes, squinting as he gazed down at her. "You are playing with fire, princess." His voice was sexy and rough from the ravages of a night spent in the throes of ecstasy and the exhausted sleep that followed.

"Oh? Am I? I thought I was provoking a stallion, cowboy." She giggled.

"Whatever you want to call it, but if you aren't careful, you're going to be riding me until you can't walk." He sent her a devilish grin.

"I hope that's a promise." As it was, staying in bed with him was the only place she really wanted to be.

For all intents and purposes, they were in protective custody until further notice, which meant until they heard otherwise—what had he said to her last night? She could *let 'er buck.*

She moved her hand lower, but just as she did, there was a hard knock on the hotel room door.

Miles jumped from the bed and hurried out of her bedroom and to his own as if their shared bed had been electrified. His sudden departure unexpectedly hurt, but she didn't quite know why—perhaps it was because it carried an air of possible embarrassment of his being seen with her in such a compromising position, or maybe it was that he seemed so well practiced at running.

The knocking sounded again.

"Who is it?" she called.

There was only a muffled sound from the hallway. Whoever had knocked probably couldn't hear her any better than she could hear them.

Grabbing her clothes, she pulled them on. She wiggled her jeans up her leg, hopping as she slipped them the last bit of the way up and pulled closed the zipper. Her hair had to have been a mess, and she gave it a quick brush with her fingers and then pulled it back into a messy bun as she stepped to the door.

Clicking open the bar lock, she flipped open the cylinder and then opened the door. She expected to find Emily standing there in her black uniform, her standard resting cop face in place, but instead there was a woman in blue jeans, a brown button-down shirt and a straw cowboy hat that was dirty around the crown from sweat and dust. The cowgirl was about her age, maybe a bit younger, but her skin carried extra years thanks to sun and wind.

The woman weighed and measured her messy bun, disheveled clothes and sockless feet and found her wanting. She moved to push past her.

"Can I help you?" Scarlett asked, standing her ground.

The woman gave her a look that could have nearly been deadly. "I know who you are and exactly what the hell you have been up to, you harlot. Get out of my way."

The woman's fiery outburst made Scarlett laugh, the sound coming unexpectedly and from deep in her core. Given all the things that had happened in the last week to her, this woman's pitiful show of strength was the least of her concerns. "I'm doing no such thing—and as much as you seem to know who I am, I can't say I know a thing about you. So, unless you want me to call the police, you better turn your country ass around and head out from whatever rathole you climbed out of." Scarlett pointed toward the hall.

The woman's scowl deepened, and her hands balled tightly. Scarlett saw the punch coming a second before the woman's fist even started to arc wildly through the air. Reaching up, she grabbed the woman's arm with her left hand, and the cowgirl yelped with shock and anger. The woman punched with her left, connecting weakly with Scarlett's ribs.

"What in the hell?" Scarlett cried, letting go of the woman's arm and pushing her away and into the metal doorjamb with a loud *thump.*

"What's going on?" Miles called from behind her.

She turned as Miles stepped out of the door connecting their suites. He was slipping his white T-shirt on over his head, and he stopped mid-stride. The woman behind her grabbed a fistful of her hair and yanked, hard, sending her reeling backward.

Scarlett spun on her heel, her right fist instinctively flying and connecting with the woman's gut. The woman let out a grunting wheeze but didn't let go of her hair. Scarlett swung again, full on facing her this time as she lunged toward the woman. Her fist connected with the woman's cheek so hard it made pain run down her hand and into her arm.

The woman's hand relaxed, and Scarlett pulled herself loose of the woman's grasp and stepped back into Miles's arms. "Chloe? What in the hell?" He moved Scarlett behind him, giving her a quick once-over as if making sure there was no blood drawn. "Are you all right, babe?"

Scarlett smiled wildly. "That cowgirl picked a fight with the wrong Trapper."

"Don't think you're tough just because you got the drop on me. I was playing nice," Chloe called, leaning around Miles like she was looking for another round.

"Come at me," Scarlett jabbed. "We both know the only thing you are good at is picking the wrong man." She laughed, well aware she was kicking the hornet's nest, but she wasn't afraid of any potential sting.

Chloe lunged, but Miles stopped her with one hand. "Don't you dare." He stepped into her, moving her farther out of the room and now fully into the hallway. "Why are you here, Chloe?" He peered around, but it appeared as though she was alone.

"Drake sent me."

"Your new boy toy?" Miles's voice was darker than Scarlett had ever heard, and it tore at her heart.

"He is more of a man than you'll ever be," Chloe said with a near growl.

"If that was true, he wouldn't have sent you to do his job," Scarlett countered.

"You need to go." Miles moved to close the door in her face, but Chloe moved her foot into the doorjamb and stopped him.

"If you think I wanted to be here, you're stupid. This was our attempt at an olive branch so maybe you'd lay off stealing any more business. If you want to be a jerk, so be it—we can play dirty. We just thought you'd want to know we heard about what was happening and we have a line on your brother."

Miles pushed the door wide open.

Scarlett couldn't have been more surprised if the woman had sprouted wings and started to fly around the room like a sparrow.

"Don't trust her, Miles." Scarlett searched his face to see if he was tempted to actually believe the woman.

His expression softened and Scarlett panicked. She moved to touch him.

"Don't listen to your new piece of ass, Miles. If you had answered your phone, I wouldn't have just shown up like this, but you've been ignoring me. If anything, my being here is a sign you *can* trust me."

Scarlett sent Miles a questioning glance, and he sighed in acknowledgment. She couldn't be mad that he'd failed to mention anything about his ex-girlfriend reaching out.

"How did you get past the cops and the hotel security? They are supposed to be watching the rooms," Scarlett asked, a new fear rising within her at how easily this strange woman had been able to get access after Emily had promised them anonymity and safety.

"My cousin Amber works here. She knew I was trying to get in touch with Miles. She helped me get in and bypass people. Don't be mad at her. She knew this was important." Chloe gave Miles a pleading look. "You remember her. You liked her."

Miles nodded. "Okay, Chloe. But why exactly did you come here? You can't say you care about me or my family."

"You and I both know you and I were never going to work out as a couple. I went about it all wrong, and I shouldn't have acted the way I did, but I loved someone else. Life happens. That doesn't mean I hate you or your brother. I don't want to see him get hurt."

Scarlett hated the woman, there was no question about those feelings, however she wasn't sure whether or not the woman was telling Miles the truth. If anything, she almost felt like an interloper in a life that predated her, and it made her hate the woman even more.

Then again, she had to give her a modicum of respect for trying to bridge the gap between right and wrong by keeping her former lover's brother safe.

That didn't mean they would ever be friends.

"Well, I appreciate your reaching out. I do." Miles ran his hand over the back of his neck in discomfort. "I'm surprised you'd want to help, but…"

"I've never hated you, Miles."

"And I've…" he started, but there was hesitation in his attempt to return the sentiment.

"It's okay. I deserved it. I didn't treat you right. And I sure as hell shouldn't have called and threatened you. I was just pissed when I saw y'all on our trail cameras." Chloe sighed. "I'm sorry."

"I appreciate the apologies," Miles said.

Scarlett turned and walked into her room. The cowgirl could have her minute—she'd paid her black-eye toll. It would never be enough, in her humble opinion, but if the woman hadn't fumbled the handsome Miles, then Scarlett wouldn't have landed him—so really, she was the true winner in every way.

Scarlett pulled her bed together. It was a little petty, but she couldn't help but leave it somewhat imperfect as a hint of what had transpired last night. Miles had come out on top in life, and they were the winners.

Chloe cleared her throat. "That's what brought me here… The cameras. I called the police department, but they gave me the runaround when I told them who I was. I think they took me about as seriously as Scarlett there," she said, motioning toward her. "Can't say I blame any of them, but I'd like to think you know me better than that. I'm not a total piece of garbage."

She still couldn't come to terms with trusting the woman, no matter how much she tried to convince Miles to the contrary.

"Where did you see Butch taking Jackson and Kelcie?" Miles asked.

"Who's Butch?" Chloe asked, frowning. "I just saw Jackson on the cameras with Kelcie. She was hiking with him on the south trails—not far from where you guys went up. She had her arm wrapped up in a sling? Black bandana. Walked with a limp."

"Wait. What?" Scarlett asked, walking back and facing the woman. "What were they doing? Did you hear what they were talking about?"

It didn't make sense. Butch had them. He'd told her that he had them. He was in Kalispell. He was stalking her. He was holding them over their heads.

"I don't know. The cameras only take stills every thirty seconds or so. They're not videos. Not what we do." Chloe reached into her pocket and pulled out a folded note. "Here are the GPS coordinates of the last spot we saw them on the trail cams. We sent the cops the same. I hope this can be of some help. From here on out, we want you to shut down the guest services side of the West Glacier Ranch. You can keep the JMac Therapy going."

Miles took the piece of paper and, opening it, studied it for a long moment. "I can't make any kind of deals with you, but I'll talk to my bosses. Your help will go a long way in a healthy working relationship moving forward."

"If you need anything else from us, you know how to get in touch." Chloe stepped out of the room. "And good luck getting your brother and your friend back," she said, motioning toward Scarlett.

"Yeah, thanks," Scarlett said, half embarrassed and not quite sure how to feel. "Sorry about the fireworks."

Chloe nodded. "Me, too."

Miles closed the door and turned toward Scarlett. "If this is below where we rode in, I think I know exactly the trail where we can find them."

"Is there a house there or something? How did Butch send us a picture of them tied up? How did he get that kind of image?" Scarlett couldn't put the pieces together. It just didn't make sense.

Miles shook his head. "There's a house back there. It's small. Maybe they're in there. And for all we know, maybe he just didn't show up on the trail cameras. It's possible he was just out of the frame."

There was also the sickening possibility that she had been wrong all along, or that this disappearance had just gotten a whole lot more complicated.

Chapter Twenty-Four

Miles nudged Oreo forward, making sure that Seagrass, Mac and the rest of the string of horses and their riders were following behind him. Scarlett had been off ever since Chloe had shown up at their hotel room, but he could hardly blame her. No one was supposed to have been able to have access to them—and then bam, the one person he never thought he'd have to deal with showed up on their doorstep.

He had hated her over the last few months because of what she had done to him and how their relationship had ended, but it had taken some gumption for her to come to him with what she had found on their trail cameras. There was still some niggle of doubt that she was to be trusted. Chloe had rarely done anything that didn't serve her own selfish purposes first and foremost. Her reaching out was to attempt to gain leverage for Drake. Which was where Miles's greatest hang-up lay.

The coordinates she'd given him did line up with the old miner's cabin in the woods, though. It would have been a perfect location for someone to hide out or to post up with hostages. Which was the next major obstacle and question they faced—was this a kidnapping, or was this all some-how staged?

Who was really behind Jackson and Kelcie's disappearance? If Butch was involved, how and why?

There were very few who knew about the abandoned cabin. It was utilized by Forest Service workers, backcountry hikers and trail riders. It was comprised of nothing more than a couple of bunks and a small kitchen area. Outside there was a latrine, frost-freeze spigot and water trough for folks who stopped with horses.

For years, it had been known only to a handful of people and the local ranches when they ranged cattle in the high country. Between Jackson, Kelcie and Butch, only Jackson would have known that place had existed.

Which meant his brother could have played a role in this kidnapping and ransom attempt.

Emily was at the back of the string with officers Ramone and Burns. They were talking quietly amongst themselves, but from snippets of their conversation he had been able to pick up since they had left the barn, they had been just as confused by the events that had transpired as he was.

When he'd told them about the coordinates of the possible location of Jackson and Kelcie, he'd made sure to leave out the part about Chloe stopping by their hotel room to hand them off. Instead, he'd left it vague in an attempt to keep her from getting in trouble. If she had been doing them a favor, then he didn't want to cause her problems—but if she was lying, he would be the first one to throw her under the bus.

Scarlett rode up beside him. "Do you think that they are going to be there when we arrive?"

The concern that they would already be somewhere else had crossed his mind. "I don't know, but we need to start somewhere. Chloe didn't say she had pictures of them coming out, so we have to hope that they only went in."

"If they never came out…" She sent him a pained expression.

"Kelcie's still alive. She's going to be okay. If Butch wants you and his money, the last thing he would do is kill her." *Jackson, on the other hand…*

He swallowed back the bile rising in his throat. His brother would be okay. Sure, the only pictures they'd gotten of him since he'd been held for ransom were of him completely incapacitated, but that didn't mean he was dead.

Scarlett slipped her hand into his as they made their way along the trail, as though she could sense his fears. They were in this together.

"Scarlett?" He spoke her name like it was a question.

"Yes?" she asked, clenching his hand as she smiled at him.

"No matter what happens out here today, you are safe with me. I hope you know that."

"I know," she said, but there was a strain in her voice, and she let go of his hand and nudged her horse forward.

He wanted to tell her that he loved her and he would take a bullet for her—literally or figuratively. But from that tone, he wasn't sure she would believe him, and it definitely wasn't the time or the place. He didn't need to make things more confusing for either of them.

Ahead the trail zigzagged and dropped down. It would level out and from there they would drop into the small valley where there was the cabin, a log corral and a hayshed. Normally, he would take the horses right in and tie them up or corral them and give them some water, and this group of animals knew the drill.

They started to head down the trail, unbidden. Seagrass was in the lead, and it made his thoughts turn to Thomas and the last time they had been riding together. The memory made him smile, but it also made him realize exactly how much had transpired in such a short amount of time. It was no wonder his emotions were so raw and he felt as he did toward Scarlett. They had gone through a lifetime's worth of drama in a blink of an eye, and their bond was something that would never be broken—at least, if he had anything to say about it.

He gave a low whistle to Scarlett, and she turned to look at him. He motioned for her to stop and pointed toward a thicket of trees. He moved Oreo off the trail and led the way toward where he'd shown her. The officers behind them followed.

As he got down, he tied up and helped the others. Emily and Scarlett were good on their own, but the other two were soup sandwiches as they got off. Ramone walked stiffly toward him, half hunched like he hadn't been in a saddle in twenty years.

Ramone cleared his throat. "So, I want you and Scarlett to stay with the horses here. We don't need things going sideways and you getting hurt. You hear me?"

There wasn't a chance in hell that he was going to let Scarlett walk into the lion's den. The man hadn't needed to tell him.

"I'm not just some damsel in distress that needs babysitting," Scarlett countered.

He should have seen that one coming.

"That's not what I'm saying," Officer Ramone said. "Not even close."

Emily walked over and put her hand on Scarlett's arm. "Sister, I know how tough you are. You're a Trapper. We just can't put you in any more danger than necessary. As it is, we are pushing the boundaries by having you up here on the trail with us."

"I told you there was no way I was staying behind," Scarlett said. She kept her tone low as though she didn't want to pick a fight but wanted to make it clear that she wasn't going to be kept in a corner. "And I do understand that my being here is a liability for your department, but like I told you before we left—Butch wants me. I'm your most powerful bargaining chip."

Emily nodded. "Which is why we need you safe. We are just going to go down to the cabin and see if there is even any credibility to the tip. If our vics are there, great. And if Butch is there and we need you, you will be the first to know. I promise. Just be patient with us. Okay?"

Miles took mental notes. Emily was good at talking down what could have been a potential problem. It made him feel better that she, Burns and Ramone were the ones going into that cabin. If there was any chance of a verbal resolution, Emily seemed like the best one to make that happen.

Scarlett sighed. "We will be here when and if you need us," she said, walking over to him and taking hold of his hand.

Emily sent him a toothy grin. "Thank you."

"Please, just come back with Kelcie and my brother."

Scarlett nodded. "I need to know she's okay."

Burns walked up beside Emily and whispered something into her ear. Her smile and the softness she'd had for them disappeared. "Guys we will do all we can. For now, the rest of our teams are about in place that are coming up from the other side. It's time. Promise me…don't go anywhere. Okay?"

They both nodded. "We will be here with the horses." Miles crossed his heart with his finger.

The officers huddled up and did a quick equipment check, and he could hear them going over some of their strategies about moving in on the cabin and clearing the building when they arrived, but he couldn't hear everything they were saying. Part of him wished that he could tag along and be a part of bringing down Butch. He would have given his figurative left foot for the chance after all the things that Scarlett had told him about the man.

As it was, though, this was an operation that, more than anything, would rely on their getting lucky and getting to him at the right place and at the right time. In all reality Butch could have been anywhere, and they were just searching for a needle in a haystack.

The thought made him shudder.

If they could just get their hands on Jackson and Kelcie, that would be enough. At least, for now.

The cops disappeared into the timber, moving silently as they hiked toward the cabin and following the directions he had given them. Seagrass nickered as though she could sense the tension in the air.

He walked over to the horse, Scarlett's hand still in his, and ran his free hand down the horse's neck. "She's nervous," he said.

"The last time I was this anxious," Scarlett whispered, "I was working as an extra on this show about dogs for some educational programming station. It was a stupid job, really, something just to make some rent money and pad the portfolio."

"What did you do as an extra on a dog show?" he asked, chuckling lightly and more out of nerves than at the thought.

"I was supposed to walk the dogs out so they could be introduced by the professionals and discussed." She ran her hand down Seagrass's haunch. "It was such a silly thing, but it ended up being probably one of my most enjoyable roles to date. All I did was play with puppies all day long. And it empowered me in a way that made me want to stay in Hollywood for a really long time. And it's moments like those that led to this." She motioned around the woods.

Miles smiled. "I know you mean that like a bad thing, but not everything about this trip has been a complete bust. I mean…" He leaned in and gave her a kiss to her forehead. "I did get to meet you."

She caught his gaze. "That's the only thing about my life which is keeping me going right now—you. You have no idea how happy you make me."

His heart thrashed inside his chest. "And you made me realize that some people are worth fighting for—and trusting."

He moved a hair out of her face as he leaned in and kissed her lips. He took her into his arms. She tasted of sweat and dust, and he could imagine no headier mix—it epitomized his perfect love.

"I wish we had met under different circumstances. I hope you know, I would have asked you to stay with me, forever," he whispered into her hair. "But I know you have a life out there that doesn't involve me, and I'm crazy for thinking that last night meant anything."

"Don't talk like that," she said, pulling back and looking up into his eyes. "Last night meant something special to me, too. I don't just spend the night with anyone. I—"

"That's not what I meant," he said, not letting her continue.

She pulled loose from his arms and turned her back to him. "Just give me a minute, Miles." She motioned for him to stay put. "I won't go far. I just need to think." She pointed vaguely north.

He nodded, afraid to say anything out of the fear that if he did, she would tell him that he was right and that her life outside of their blink in time together was what mattered.

What he should have been thinking about was Jackson and Kelcie, but with them being put on the shelf, the only thing he could think about was Scarlett, and those thoughts were killing him.

Scarlett looked over her shoulder at him as she moved into the brush. He could have sworn there were tears on her cheeks, but he couldn't bear the possibility of him being right, and he looked away. The horses moved around him. Oreo sent him a white-eyed look and pawed at the ground with her front hoof nervously.

"I know, Oreo, I don't like it, either." He refused to look in Scarlett's direction.

He needed to get used to her leaving.

No. He couldn't do it. He couldn't stand idly by while she decided what she thought about him and what had gone on between them. He had to say his piece.

He charged off into the woods after her. His footfalls sounded loud and heavy as he hurried through the timber, weaving and bobbing as he followed her tracks. It only took a minute before he found her with her back turned to him, and the sight of her made his racing pulse calm.

"Scarlett?" he asked.

She turned and motioned for him to be quiet. Her face was an ashen white and her eyes were round with shock and fear. She wiggled her finger to come closer and to get low.

The momentary calm was replaced by a new sense of fear. He moved to her side. "What is it?" he whispered.

"Look," she said, pointing out to a creek bed where a beaver had built a dam and a small pond had formed.

Splashing around and laughing in the pond, bare-assed naked, was Kelcie, her arm tied up with his bandana, with a gray-haired and paunch-bellied man.

Jackson was nowhere to be seen.

SCARLETT DIDN'T KNOW what overtook her, but she finally knew what it meant to see red.

Kelcie moved into Butch's arms and threw her uninjured arm around his neck and planted a kiss on his pudgy fish lips. If she hadn't seen it with her own eyes, she would have never believed such a thing had really taken place. Kelcie had known everything that Butch had done, how he had harassed her and called her incessantly.

She had even been the one to help her navigate the chaos he had tried to create in her career with producers.

Now this?

She let out a tiny squeak of pain and panic as she thought about just how long Kelcie could have been with Butch and all the reasons why they would have ended up together.

She couldn't face it, she just couldn't.

Scarlett bent down and picked up a rock the size of her fist.

"What are you doing?" Miles asked.

"I'm going to kill him."

"No, Scarlett." Miles took her free hand and held on with all his might. "You can't become a criminal because of hate. I know the anger and rage you have to be feeling right now."

"My best friend… She went behind my back. She set this up. She had to have told him." The words came flooding out as she realized what must have happened. "We have to find Jackson."

She stared at him, but where the anger and rage had filled her there was a new sense of nothingness and merely the dissociation that came in moments of such complex emotions that the body took over.

It was in this moment that she truly understood how people who had never been driven to murder could kill.

"You just take out your phone. Remember, the police are watching it. Take a video. We will beat these jerks in court."

That wasn't enough, not for the sting of betrayal and anger she felt in her heart. Yet, her hands shook as she took out her phone and took the video of the two lovers playing and caressing each other. After a minute or so of recording, long enough to make bile rise in her throat, she sent off the video to Ramone, Burns and Emily and then sat her phone on the ground as it kept recording. It was strange, but it felt far heavier than the rock in her other hand. She couldn't watch any more.

Miles let go of her. He pulled the rock from her fingers. "Baby, you don't need this."

There was a strangled cry from the pond and the sound of splashing. "What in the hell are you two doing here?" Butch cried.

She turned to see Butch rushing to the edge and pulling a revolver from under his pile of clothes. He fumbled with the small silver gun.

Miles had a feral smile on his lips as he whispered to her, "Did I ever tell you that my favorite movie was *Braveheart*? Watch this." He pulled back his arm and hurled the rock.

It struck Butch right between the eyes as if the man had a bull's-eye painted on his face. The impact made a dull *thump* sound like that of a ripe watermelon. The pale bloated carp of a man dropped the gun in his hand and slipped down and under the water.

Kelcie looked at him, confused. "Butch? Baby? Are you okay?" She tried to pull at him and lift him from the water, but she struggled with his mass. "Butch. You can't die! Miles, what did you do?"

Though she wanted to watch Kelcie struggle and panic as

Butch succumbed to the water in some poetic and cinematically perfect justice, her love for Miles surfaced.

"That was one hell of a throw." She smiled. "Remind me not to piss you off from a distance." She gave a slight laugh.

He smirked. "It's not the first time that skillset has come through for me, but usually it's helpful with hardheaded cattle and its squarely on the rump."

"Same difference." She tilted her head toward her enemies. "I don't want more problems." If Butch drowned, they had more than enough evidence that Miles had acted in self-defense, but she didn't want to make Miles have to be drawn into a lengthy possible homicide investigation for her.

As much as she hated the idea, she had to keep Butch and Kelcie alive. They had to face the judge for the things they had done.

"Stay behind me," Miles said.

Scarlett nodded. She didn't know if she would be able to control her mouth.

The moment Miles and Scarlett came out of the thicket of brush and into the open, Kelcie started to wail and scream. She rushed from the water, pointing back at Butch. "You have to help me! He…he took me!" she cried as she looked toward the gun as though she considered reaching for it and taking a shot.

Miles rushed to the gun and picked it up, dumping the rounds on the ground and stuffing the pistol into the back of his waistband.

Kelcie's clothes were on the ground beside the creek, and Scarlett grabbed her bloody shirt and threw it at her in disgust. "Cover yourself."

Miles moved past her, not even sparing her a wayward glance as he went to Butch and took his arm and yanked him from the water. He pulled him up onto the silty bank and dropped him haphazardly, facedown but able to breathe in the dirt.

Kelcie blubbered and sobbed as she tried to speak, but her words came out in unintelligible gibberish of the hysterical guilty. She put on the shirt, covering her nakedness, but only barely.

"Pull yourself together," Scarlett ordered. "Where's Jackson?"

Kelcie put her hand up in submission. Her hands were shaking. She dropped to her knees in the mud beside Butch. "Jackson…" She hiccupped and pointed in the direction of the cabin where Emily and her team were investigating. "He's going to be okay. Butch said the drugs will wear off."

She sent Miles a look of guarded relief.

"When did you tell Butch we were here?"

Kelcie dropped her gaze to the ground. "As soon as we booked the trip."

"Why did you tell him? What was in it for you?" She looked at the pale, unconscious man. "Do you love him?" The thought made her nauseous.

Kelcie shook her head. "He told me he'd sell my screenplays. I saw what he did for your career." She started to cry again. "You know your career is coming to an end. What was I going to do?"

Scarlett balled her hands into tight fists as Miles stepped beside her and held her arms to her sides as though he could see how much she wanted to strike. "Not screw over your best friend."

Miles pulled her back. "Let's just restrain Butch and wait for the police. We have what we need. Don't make it worse."

She was so angry, she was the one shaking now. "I hate her. Do you know how much I did for her? We traveled around the world on my dime. She knew all my secrets."

She paused. "Wait… Did you guys have something to do with Aiden and Thomas getting hurt?"

Kelcie didn't answer.

"Tell me!" Scarlett ordered.

"Butch thought the rental was yours." She shook her head. "They weren't supposed to be there."

"Kelcie, your selfishness cost a man his life, a boy his father, and now it will cost you your freedom. I won't even mention our friendship. I hope you both get what you deserve in prison."

Chapter Twenty-Five

"When you broke into the cabin on the West Glacier Cattle Ranch, were you hoping to find our witness, Ms. Leafletter?" the prosecuting attorney for the state asked Butch.

His puffy, pale face was covered in a layer of sweat, and a bead rolled down his temple and slipped to his chin. He dabbed it away with the back of his sausage-fingered hand. Everything about the man made Scarlett want to stand up and scream, but she was never again going to run away from the swine.

Kelcie was in an orange jumpsuit on the television screen, waiting but unable to hear or see what was happening in the courtroom until she was asked to take the stand.

"I didn't want to kill Scarlett. I just wanted to talk to her. She wouldn't take my calls."

"Objection!" his defense attorney countered.

Scarlett hated the courtroom games, and she barely listened as the defense attorney spoke to the judge. She couldn't understand why anyone would want to become a criminal defense attorney—or what kind of person would stand beside someone like Butch, a man who had knowingly and maliciously attacked with the intent to kill. It was unforgiveable.

Thankfully, before court had even started, and while the

detectives had been questioning them about the stolen wallet and how Butch had broken into the cabin, it hadn't taken much for the two to turn on each other. Butch had pointed the finger at Kelcie for her complicity while Kelcie had told them about their plans—every detail, down to his desire for the ransom money to wipe out her savings and remind her of what he'd done for her financially, and then his wish to kill her in the end. Or, as Kelcie had put it, "If she refused to love him, then she didn't get to love anyone else—not after all he'd done for her."

Later, in front of the detectives, Kelcie had also admitted that they had planned on using the media frenzy created by Scarlett's death as a launching pad for her career. Everyone would want to talk to the dead actress's agent, and "*Bing, boom, bang*, she would be in," or so she had said.

Scarlett was no Julius Caesar, but she had her own Brutus.

According to the prosecutor, the trial was more of a formality, and at the end of the day, he would offer them both plea deals. If they took them, which they would most likely do, Butch would serve a minimum of fifteen years in a state prison without the chance for parole for his role in Aiden's death and her attempted murder.

Kelcie would serve a minimum of five years for her role as his accomplice.

When the judge called for a recess, she made her way from the courthouse, and Miles caught her outside. "How are you doing?" he asked.

He was wearing a dark suit, but it was such a juxtaposition from the man on the mountain she had met a few months ago that she had to stare for a long moment to make sense of exactly the man whom she was seeing. She couldn't help but smile. "I'm doing okay."

"Thomas called while you were on the stand. He says he can't wait for you to come home tonight," he said. "We're making elk spaghetti tonight. Jackson is sitting with him for now, until I get back."

After Aiden's death, Miles had taken over custody of Thomas, acting as his legal guardian. She'd been staying the occasional night with the duo while they had been awaiting trial.

"That sounds amazing," she said. Her phone vibrated in her pocket, and she took it out to take a peek at the message. It was an email from the agent she had reached out to in reference to the new season of *Rogue Crafter*. She wasn't sure if she was excited or reticent about opening the email that lay at her fingertips. Her future waited and could all change with this one tap.

The producer wanted to negotiate terms but was on the fence about bringing her back. It was a game, one only a good agent could help her navigate. If this agent didn't agree to work with her, her career would be over.

Part of her wanted to stay in Montana, to live in the world she had been holing up in, and where she had grown up. She had run away from the place because of her father, because of abuse and neglect, but she had faced her ghosts— the same ones that had followed her to every corner of the planet and back here. The one thing she had learned was that it didn't matter where she ran, or what role she played—the happiest she had been was at peace with Thomas and Miles.

This trial would pass, and she could go back to the life she had before, but she would be alone.

The thought made her feel incredibly lonely, and the pain was sharp.

"Everything okay?" Miles asked, pointing at the phone in her hands.

"It's the agent." She looked into his eyes. He knew how much was riding on this email—her future, their future, Thomas's future. "I'm glad it came while we were standing together, but I'm not sure I'm ready to open it."

He smiled, but the action didn't quite reach his eyes. "No matter what you choose, I support your decision. I just want you to be happy."

"Miles, I'm happy with *you*." She leaned in and kissed him, the action gentle and sweet. "I love you."

He cupped her face in his warm hands and looked into her eyes. "And I love you, more than you will ever know. If you want to be together, I'll give up cowboying and I'll follow you around this planet."

"You can't do that to Thomas."

His expression faltered. "A boy can travel."

"Some is okay, but he also needs stability, and the ranch would provide that. My family would give him an incredible home. If I stayed."

"You want to stay?" he asked, sounding surprised.

"For you, and us, yes." She reached up and took his hand with her free hand.

"Would you want to be my wife?" he asked. It sounded like a question that had come out of the blue, nothing rehearsed, but something he had given great thought.

"In a heartbeat. Yes."

Though she had no idea what their future would bring, and she didn't care, their lips met and there was no on-screen kiss that could have compared, not even that of *Casablanca.*

He pressed his forehead against hers, half breathless. "Open the email."

She fumbled with her phone. "But what if—"

"It doesn't matter. We will figure it out," he said, cutting her off. "And I'm sorry I don't have a ring. I'll let you pick out anything you want as soon as we can."

She smiled as she opened up her phone. She didn't even care about the ring. It was the furthest thing from her mind. Opening up the email, she read it aloud:

Dear Ms. Leafletter,
I'm excited to offer my representation for your up-coming series. I'm also excited to let you know I've been in talks with the producer, Mr. Anciaux, and he would be interested in filming on your family's ranch in Montana. Please give me a call to discuss. I have attached a contract. Please let me know if you have any questions.
Sincerely,
Adam Goldblum

She squealed with excitement as she dropped her phone and launched herself into Miles's arms.

For the first time in her life, she had it all, but most importantly, she had found the things she had been searching for the longest—security, family and love.

* * * * *

COMING SOON!

We really hope you enjoyed reading this book.
If you're looking for more romance
be sure to head to the shops when
new books are available on

Thursday 26th February

MILLS & BOON

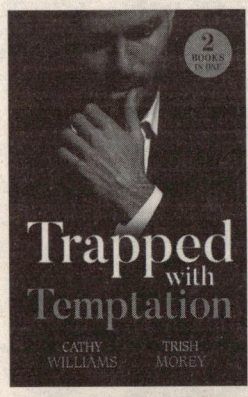